SHIFTED RULE

THE WOLVES OF FOREST GROVE: BOOK 3

ELENA LAWSON

Copyright © 2020 Elena Lawson
All rights reserved. No part of this publication may be reproduced, stored in a retrieval system, or transmitted in any form or by any means without the prior written permission of the author except for the use of brief quotations in a book review.
This is a work of fiction. Characters, incidents and dialogs are products of the author's
imagination and are not to be construed as real. Any resemblance to actual events is strictly coincidental.

1

"Put your body into it," Clay said, studying my form as I squared off to take another swing at his heavy bag.

"I *am* putting my body into it," I hissed in reply, throwing my shoulder into my next hit. The heavy bag swung and the chains holding it in place rattled.

Clay stepped up behind me. "That isn't bad," he said. "But you're still not putting your whole body into it. There's more force you can tap into if you move your whole torso."

His hands settled onto my hips, squaring me off again at the bag. Sweat beaded along my brow and the tops of my breasts. With his hands on me, my body grew hotter. When his fingers brushed over the bare skin where my tank top rode up, I wanted to scream. Not even the cool autumn breeze blowing into the shop was enough to douse the flames.

He moved one hand to tap the side of my right thigh. "Dig your heel in and push off with your legs. Then turn your whole body into it."

Clay guided me into the next swing, showing me how my body should move in slow motion.

"See?"

"Yeah," I gritted out, swallowing and shaking off the tremors caused by his touch. My inner wolf whined audibly in my mind, trying to clamber to the surface so she could reach out and touch him. Since I was too afraid to.

I wasn't sure I could stop if I did.

I continued throwing hits, switching sides every so often. Clay watched with his arms crossed over his thick chest. His sea-glass eyes never leaving me. Every so often, he adjusted my stance, gently nudged my legs back into place.

This was a *tame* self-defense session with Clay. Usually, he had me run for an hour before we even started. Then he would have me spar with him until my muscles were shaking. It was why I preferred it when Jared taught me, but I knew—despite how much I ached after a session with Clay—that he would push me to learn more. To learn faster.

Where Jared was patient and took more time to explain the *why* behind everything, Clay just shoved me to the edge of my limits. And every day, those limits grew further and further away.

If I were being honest, I preferred to be pushed.

When the initial shock wore off after the Four Corners, I couldn't stop moving. Silence and stillness turned to buzzing, unstoppable energy. If I stopped, I would have to think. To remember.

Charity managed to get Quinn to an Alchemist in time to save his life. She was paying for that kindness now. Ryland was none too pleased that she'd left without asking his permission. That she *saved a human boy* without so much as a word from her alpha.

Lucky for Quinn, he couldn't remember a thing about that night.

I wished Layla and Vivian had been as lucky. They were cursed to remember every awful, blood-soaked moment. After we brought them back to the cabin that night, got them bandaged up, the guys and I did our best to explain things. I'm not sure what they actually digested. They'd been in shock. Angry. Hurt. Terrified.

I explained as best as I could what might happen to them on the next full moon, even though they were the hardest words I'd ever had to speak. I explained how they couldn't tell a soul and that if they did, I may not be able to protect them.

They nodded and sniffled and waited until I was finished. That was when Vivian asked if they could leave. She tucked Layla under her arm and accepted a ride home from Jared. The sound of the screen door banging shut behind them felt like a slap in the face. One I deserved.

They hardly talked to me now. Or each other, really.

We sat together at lunch like we always did, but now the easy laughter is gone. Quinn tried his best to lighten the mood. He always had his arm around Layla. The poor guy didn't understand that there was nothing he could do. I think Layla resented a little that he was the only one blessed with the ability to forget it all.

I'd have left them alone, but Jared insisted we keep an eye on them.

The best part was that after Layla and Viv left around eleven, the night wasn't even over for me. I began to feel the effects of the moon-triggered shift coming on just ten minutes after they left.

I got to learn where the other locked door in the cabin's basement went. A cell. Or I guess they called it a *moon room*. Clay had to be the one to chain me up. Jared couldn't stomach it.

Clay was the one who stayed with me through every aching moment. He listened to me scream in agony as the moon-triggered shift stole all my self-control. Snapped each of my bones. It was *nothing* like a voluntary shift. It was torture.

And when the shift was finished and I was left on all fours, sweating and whining through canine lips, there was only the barest trace of my consciousness remaining. I knew what was happening, but I couldn't control myself. Couldn't control my urges. I nearly tore my arm from its socket that night trying to get free.

The moon released me after a mere twenty-minutes, but it felt like hours.

And apparently, I should have been grateful for that. Jared told me most wolves couldn't change back so fast after a moon-triggered shift. Most remained feral in their wolf forms until dawn. At least, that was how it was in the beginning for changed wolves. Or how it should have been, but I guess I had to be an anomaly in all things. In this, at least, I *was* grateful. Twenty minutes was plenty.

"Okay," Clay said, putting his arm between me and the heavy bag. I glared at him.

"You're not here right now, Allie. Your form is all over the place. What's up?"

I gave his arm a little shove and went back to work on the bag. "I'm fine."

I got in three good hits before Clay moved his whole enormous self in front of the bag. I ground my teeth. "No. You're not."

He jutted his chin in the direction of the worn sofa across the shop. "Take a breather."

"I don't want to take a breather."

I wanted to keep hitting shit.

Between my early morning bow practice, my early afternoon run, late-afternoon self-defense, and late-nights spent helping Clay in the shop with his bike repairs, I'd been doing pretty good keeping busy.

It was only when Jared or Clay forced me to stop that things got shitty again. The emotions kept at bay by busy hands and a focused mind came slowly creeping back in. They whispered things.

Like how I am death incarnate.

How everyone I love gets hurt.

Like how every good thing in my life must be paid for by at least two bad things.

And then the most agonizing thought: It's all my fault.

My fault.

My fault.

I shook my head and sighed heavily. "I just need a drink, then we can go again."

"No, Allie. That's enough for the day."

"The hell it is," I retorted, feeling my inner wolf rear her head and my upper lip curl.

Clay just raised a brow and re-crossed his arms. Amused.

The bastard.

He looked me up and down, a frown drawing down the corners of his lips. "You need food," he decided.

It was no secret that I was getting a little on the thin side. With no appetite to speak of and the inability to stop moving, it was bound to happen.

"Come on, we'll make some dinner before Jared gets back from the Quarry."

I groaned, letting my head fall back in frustration as I shoved my wolf back down with a promise to let her out for a good long shift later tonight. I'd been shifting daily now for almost five days. Turned out Clay and Jared were right, the more I shifted, the more cooperative she was willing to be.

And I needed her to cooperate. Now that Ryland wasn't as busy with getting the new pack members into line, he wanted to see me. Tomorrow. Well, not just to see me, really.

How had Clay put it? Oh, right. *He will want to assert his dominance.* I.e. he was going to want to use the pack bond and his rule to control me.

If Clay were right, he'd want to make an example out of me. Bend me to his will. Though Clay had assured me that his interest will fade in time. He made Clay run that gauntlet once, too. Now, Ry pretty much leaves him alone.

I could only pray that his power trip would be over quickly.

"Come on," Clay urged. "I'll get you some ice for those."

He pointed at my hands. Even through the wrappings it was clear how swollen my knuckles were. I had no doubt that if I removed them, they would be an angry red. There really wasn't much point in using ice, though. My body would heal by the time dinner was ready. If not quicker.

It healed the mangled bite in my ankle from the wolf I'd killed at the Four Corners in less than twenty-four hours. A few bruises were nothing.

"Fine," I said, setting to unwrapping my hands, discarding the tensor strips onto the chair pressed against the wall. "But I'm cooking."

Clay rubbed a wide hand over his face but said

nothing. He knew better than to argue with me these days. He wouldn't win. I wasn't afraid of his grumpy ass anymore.

I followed Clay from the shop, falling into stride next to him. I didn't miss how he was working his jaw. Or how hidden within the pockets of his jeans, his hands were balled into fists.

"Are you, *uh...*" Clay said, and I could tell he was working through how to say something, as he'd taken to doing more and more lately instead of spewing the first words to come to his mind. "Ready for tonight?"

I dug my fingernails into my palms and licked my cracked lips. A sarcastic laugh bloomed on my lips.

"Are you?" I scoffed.

He inhaled deeply and then shrugged.

That's what I thought.

I still didn't know whose idea it was, but I could guess.

The guys wanted to *have a chat* tonight.

About *us.*

As if there weren't a million other more pressing things to fucking worry about.

"We don't have to—"

"No," I interrupted him. "We should."

As much as I didn't want to have this conversation, it needed to be had. Might as well get it over with. I had a pretty good idea where this chat would lead us, and I didn't like it. Not one bit. Though it was probably for the best.

Clay and Jared had been tense with each other since Clay kissed me and then went and confessed to Jared before I could be the one to do it.

Their friendship was more important than whatever this thing was between us. Sacred or not, the mate bond only complicated things. When they told me they'd decided to both keep their distance, to remain only as friends, I'd agree that that was for the best. And I assumed to be able to do that, they would need to ask me to move out. It was too hard to ignore those urges living under the same roof. I'd tell them that was for the best, too.

No matter that it was the last thing in the world that I wanted.

Certainly not what my wolf wanted, either, but I could go back to ignoring it, right? I could pretend like every time Clay touched me, I didn't quake inside. I could act like it wasn't the hardest thing in the world not to allow my gaze to fall to Jared's lips when he spoke to me. That it wasn't impossible not to imagine what it would be like to kiss him, too.

Those were things I could totally do.

"Coffee?" Clay asked, holding open the door for me to walk inside the cabin.

At that, I smirked. "Do you even have to ask?"

A grin that didn't reach his eyes pulled at one side of his mouth as he flicked on the Bluetooth speaker and set to pulling out coffee and what looked like the ingredients to make pasta to go with our nightly steaks.

It had become something of a habit since I came out of my shock coma and Ryland sent Jared away to work at the Quarry—Clay and I cooking together while we listened to music instead of talking. Sometimes, when he forgot I was listening, he would even sing a few lines. His voice deep and yet soft as butter.

"I'm going to wash up really quick and then I'll chop, 'kay?"

Clay nodded, scooping several heaping tablespoons of ground coffee into the filter.

Past him, out the window by the little table pressed against the wall, my wolf sensed Jared approaching. Sure enough, within a few seconds, I caught glimpses of his lithe white wolf snaking through the trees.

"Jared's home," I told Clay, and then rushed the rest of the way upstairs, eager to put off *the talk* for as long as I could.

2

Jared didn't seem any more ready for it than I was.

After Clay and I finished with dinner and Jared with showering and getting changed out of his rock-dust coated coveralls, we ate in absolute silence.

The kind of silence that's heavy and suffocating, like there were storm clouds gathering in the air between the three of us. I cleared my throat as I rose to rinse my plate. "So," I said, trying not to let the cocooned butterflies in my belly burst free. "How're things at the quarry?"

"Good," he replied tersely. "Fine."

Oh god, this is painful.

I glanced at him as he finished his last morsel of rare meat, taking in the long line of his neck and those absurdly sexy cheekbones. How his gold-threaded dirty-blonde hair was getting so long that it brushed against them now.

How those green-flecked amber eyes had a tendency to cut through me even when I had my guard up.

"Fuck this," Clay barked, and his chair scraped back against the tile as he rose and stomped out of the kitchen.

Jared and I shared a look before Clay returned with his whiskey decanter and slammed it down in the center of the small table. He nudged past me to snatch three short glasses from the cupboard and then banged those down next to it.

He poured generously into each of them and then shoved one to Jared and moved to pull my chair back out from the table. He stood there, holding the back of it with a white-knuckled grip.

Our eyes locked, and his nostrils flared.

"Sit," he ordered when I didn't move on my own.

Jared sighed.

Swallowing past the hard lump in my throat, I set my plate down next to the sink and did as I was told, glad someone had the balls to start ripping this Band-Aid off.

"Thank fuck," I whispered under my breath as I sat down and saw Jared's face twitch with a smirk. Clay shoved my chair back into the table with me in it, and I had to catch myself so I wouldn't be clotheslined by the wooden edge.

"Here," Clay said, sliding another of the whiskey-filled glasses to me. I caught it before it could tip from the ledge and quirked a brow at him.

If it were possible, he seemed more on edge than I was.

Clay downed his in one long swallow and then knocked his glass back down onto the table and filled it a second time.

Jared and I followed suit.

"So, here's the thing," Clay said after finishing half of his second pour. He paused, a furrow in his brow. "The thing is..." he tried again then sputtered to a stop.

He looked to Jared for help, and for a second, it looked like Jared was going to give it to him, parting his lips to explain. But then he shut them again, going pale.

I groaned and leaned back in my chair. Was I really going to have to be the one to do this?

More silence.

...here goes...

"You want me to move out," I stated. "And you want to go back to how it was before I turned. Go back to just being friends. That's it, right? You don't have to make it so ominous—"

"What?" Jared demanded, sitting up straighter in his chair, his eyes narrowed in confusion. "Allie, no. No, that's not—"

"You idiot," Clay muttered to himself, cutting off Jared, and I wasn't sure if he was calling me an idiot or himself. "Did you really think this was about *kicking you out?*"

I choked on a response, suddenly uncertain what to do with my hands. Where to look. "Well, I mean…yeah. What else could it have been about?"

They'd said they wanted to talk about us, hadn't they?

Clay and Jared shared a look. Jared's Adam's apple bobbed in his throat and the color returned to his cheeks rapidly, staining them, and the tops of his ears, a shade of pink.

"Clay and I have been talking," he began, squirming slightly in his seat as though it were suddenly the most uncomfortable thing in the world.

Meanwhile, Clay just sat in his chair, stoic still and brooding, his lips slightly pursed.

"About?" I prodded.

Jared took a quick swallow of his whiskey, and his eyes flitted in my direction before landing back onto the table. "About who you should date."

I felt my brows lower, and my wolf began a low growl deep in my belly.

"I suppose you thought it was up to the two of you?" I demanded, my skin bristling. "That I didn't have a say in it at all?"

This was the hard part of being half wolf. Before, I could bottle up my feelings and lock them away. Pretend they didn't exist. Now…not so much.

If someone made me angry, I was *angry.*

"Well?" I prodded when neither replied, both of them sitting there with their eyes trained on knots in the wood grain.

"No." Clay finally joined the discussion, his voice rumbling so deep that I could feel the reverberation of it in my chair. "We want to give you an option that wasn't on the table before. If you'd chill out for a second and hear it."

He cut his brilliant blue eyes to me, and something in them gave me pause. The coolness of them doused the growing flames, and I crossed my arms over my chest with a sudden chill.

I didn't like the vibes they were giving off. The whole emotion-sharing thing was hard enough on a day to day, but this was something else. The nervous energy was making my wolf want to run for the hills. Hell, I may just let her if they didn't hurry up and get this over with.

"Okay, I'm listening."

Jared leaned forward and crooked his head at me. I hated how even as annoyed with them both as I was right now, I couldn't help the near-irresistible desire to reach out and touch him. "Do you remember what Hazel said that night she came for dinner?"

"About how you wouldn't ever mate to anyone else for as long as I'm living?" I asked through gritted teeth. How could I forget?

Clay shook his head. "No, not that part…"

"The part about getting used to the idea of sharing," Jared finished for him.

"I'm not following."

Jared sighed, and I could tell he was getting ready to blurt out the rest. "After what happened between you and Clay," he said with great effort, and I flinched at the reminder. "He and I had a talk. We'd planned to loop you in on it right after you joined the pack but then..." he trailed off.

Then all hell broke loose, and my friends were casualties in the fight.

"Anyway," Jared picked back up where he left off, "we knew it wasn't a good time."

"And you think *now* is a better time?" I prodded, thinking of all the other things we should be talking about but weren't.

Jared didn't seem sure what to say to that, a pained expression crossing his face.

Clay poured more whiskey into my cup and leveled his stare on me. "Look, Allie, if it's even half as hard for you as it is for us to keep your distance, then this conversation needs to happen."

I groaned.

"So, what? Are we really talking about what I think we're talking about here?"

Had they somehow actually agreed to *sharing*?

...to have been a fly on the wall for that painful conversation...

"Yes," Jared said. "We decided that if you're willing to give…three-way dating…a try, then so are we."

"I don't think that means what you think it means," Clay said gruffly, his voice dripping sarcasm.

Jared waved him off. "Whatever, she knows what I mean." Then he turned back to me. "We'll have to be super open about it. Super honest. There will probably have to be rules. It's probably going to be weird for a while—"

I couldn't help a snort at that. "Ya think?"

Jared retreated back into himself a little at that, and the weight of guilt settled in my belly. I was not taking this how they'd hoped, I realized, and tried to school my face. "I'm sorry," I whispered. "This is all just a little out of left field, you know? I thought you were kicking me out. This is…this is not what I was expecting."

"Our options are kind of limited," Clay interjected, swirling his glass.

Jared nodded, but I couldn't help but notice that even now, he was having trouble looking at his friend. "We both have feelings for you Allie. We both did even before you were bitten and turned," he said with a swallow.

My mind raced at that. I looked between Jared and Clay. There was truth in Jared's bright eyes, and even though Clay wasn't looking at me, I could see how his jaw was tightening. He wasn't denying it.

I couldn't believe it.

All this time…

"And we think that maybe you have feelings for both of us...right?" Jared continued, his face pinched while he awaited my response.

My throat was suddenly desert dry, and I had to gulp down some more whiskey to wet it, feeling a hot flush crawl up my neck that I knew had nothing to do with the drink.

"I do," I finally managed, heart fluttering in my ribcage like a trapped bird trying to get free.

They both seemed to relax visibly at that. Shoulders lowering and lined foreheads smoothing. I was glad they both seemed so at ease with it. I was still feeling dirty and like I was somehow doing something wrong even though I constantly tried to tell myself that it wasn't my fault. It wasn't like I asked to be mated to two shifters.

And if Jared and Clay wanted to do this, how could I say no? How could I snub their only chance to both be with their intended mate when I knew they would never have another as long as I was living.

Even I had to admit: the idea of dating literally anyone else was absolutely repulsive. I couldn't even imagine it. I had to assume they felt the same.

"So, will you try it or not? Clay demanded. "Will you date both of us?"

"I..." I stammered, taking in both of my mates. My wolf swelled beneath my breast, dying to launch herself up my throat and do zoomies at the mere thought. I could almost hear her in the back of my mind.

Please, she begged.

But she didn't need to.

"If you're sure you want to do this," I told them, gathering up the courage I needed to say the words. "Then…I guess I'm in."

"We should probably decide what the rules will—"

"I think that's enough for one night." Clay interrupted Jared and stood to go trade his whiskey glass for a mug of coffee. He poured a second one and brought it to me. "I have something for you," he said. "But I need you to sober up real quick."

I glared at him. "What is it?"

Sobering up wouldn't be an issue. Ever since I'd turned, my body burned off alcohol at break-neck speeds. Which was really too bad because some nights I'd have liked nothing more than to get stone-cold drunk and sleep through the night.

I took the proffered coffee mug, and Clay grinned at me. One of his rare smiles that stretched wide enough to show teeth.

It was infectious. I found myself blushing again and hating that they could both make me so comfortable and *uncomfortable* at the same time.

"Clay," I growled.

Jared was smiling and I knew whatever it was, he was in on it, too. "Jared?" I tried, knowing that of the two he would be the more pliable.

But the traitor shook his head. "This one was all Clay, Allie girl. I'm not saying a word."

Clay stomped to the door, sipping his coffee. "Hurry up and drink that then meet me around back," he said and then let the screen door bang shut behind him.

Jared stood once Clay was gone and cleared both his plate and Clay's from the table. "I actually have to get back to the Quarry," he said solemnly. "But I promise I'll be back in time to take you to your meeting with Ryland tomorrow."

"You have to go?" I couldn't help sounding disappointed, but that only seemed to make him pleased that I didn't want him to leave. I stood to stop him from trying to wash the dishes. I would do them later, he had enough to worry about lately. "You just got back."

"I know," he said and came to wrap me in a quick embrace, filling all my senses with the heady scents of birch and sandalwood and that trademark *Jared* smell that was his and his alone. He brushed his lips lightly over my cheek, eliciting a shiver from my spine. He seemed to like that, too.

"Back before you know it," he said with a cheeky grin and then slid from the cabin, gone as quickly as he'd arrived. Leaving me with a flutter in my belly and a tickling heat licking up the back of my neck.

3

Grumbling to myself, I took my time draining my coffee in the kitchen alone, needing a moment to process everything that'd just happened.

I was going to be dating two guys.

Two extremely hot, infuriating, and completely different guys who also happened to be best friends.

I shook my head as I set my empty mug into the sink. This was going to be a complete and utter disaster…and yet, beneath all the layers of unease, there was something else: hope. I wasn't naïve enough to think that it was all going to work out, but there was a calmness in my bones now. A sort of peace that had my wolf rumbling contentedly within.

Hope was a dangerous thing, though.

I had hope when my father was sick.

I had hope when Clay and Jared took me under their wing.

It was hope I felt when I escaped from Devin at that awful cave in the mountainside.

And there was hope the day I walked into the bloodbath at the Four Corners—hoping that I could bow and that would be the end of it.

Having hope had never helped me. Better not to hope for anything at all.

Smoothing my rumpled t-shirt and pulling my unruly turquoise hair up into a messy bun, I strode from the cabin and around back to Clay's shop.

When I entered, a leaden weight in my gut, he was standing there in the middle of the shop. In the spot where we'd both had our hands deep in the cavity of an old Harley the night before.

The Harley wasn't there anymore, though. A yellow Yamaha 250 stood next to Clay instead, gleaming as though she'd just been polished to within an inch of her life.

It took me a second, but I recognized it. Clay and I had worked on that bike for a client barely a week before. "We finished with that one days ago," I said, confused. "Did something break again already?"

An uncertain smile twisted at the edges of his lips. "No," he replied. "She's ready to be returned to her owner."

I scrunched my nose. "You...want me to help deliver her?"

He shook his head, a rare laugh blooming on his lips as he kicked the stand away and rolled the Yamaha forward. Understanding widened my eyes as he handed her to me. "No need," he said in a low rumble. "Her owner is already here."

I floundered for words, wanting to cry and punch him and hug him all at the same time.

I can't ride it. I don't ride anymore. Vivid images of riding with my dad bombarded my thoughts and my eyes stung with hot, angry tears.

Picking up on my emotions, Clay settled his wide, warm hands over my shaking ones on the handlebars. "Hey," he said, waiting until I met his gaze. "It's yours, but only if you want it. If you don't, we can sell her. I got her cheap, *real cheap*—practically free. And you did most of the work fixing her up. We can sell her and split the—"

"Shut up," I said, my voice watery.

Clay's lips pressed into a hard line as I warred with myself over what to do.

My grip tightened on the handlebars and Clay removed his hands from mine, taking a step back while lines formed in his forehead once more.

"Look, if I overste—"

"Shut. Up."

One deep breath. Two. Three.

Craning my neck to one side so he couldn't see, I brushed the back of one hand over my damp eyes and gritted my teeth before speaking. "Thank you," I finally managed around the ball in my throat.

"You want to hit me, don't you?" he asked in a joking tone. "Because if you do, we can spar, and you can take your best shot. I won't even stop you."

"No," I said with a laugh, a sudden surge of adrenaline spiking my blood. No, not just adrenaline… excitement. I smoothed my palm over her nimble body and the supple leather of her freshly polished seat. "Let's ride."

Fire sparked in Clay's eyes.

"For real?" he asked, barely able to conceal his own surprise.

I grinned at him. "Yeah," I said through the bubble of a laugh. "Yeah, for real. I want to ride."

I was even more surprised to find that it was the truth. I *did* want to ride. I hadn't wanted to ride since…

No, I wasn't going to think about that right now. I was going to give this beast a proper breaking-in. "I can't believe you had her all this time and didn't say anything."

Clay went and brought his own bike out from the back of the shop, rolling toward me. I knew he owned a big Sportster Forty-Eight. An absolute beast of a Harley. Midnight black with shocks of vivid, shimmering blue and shining silver chrome. But this wasn't that.

This was a flat black ATK Intimidator. One of the fastest and biggest bikes in the world.

Of course, he would have a dirt bike *and* a Harley.

I shook my head.

"One day," I said, matching his pace as we rolled both bikes out into the cool autumn night. "You're going to let me ride that thing."

He scoffed. "As if. You'd eat dirt for sure. Not a chance I'd let you ride The Direwolf."

"The *what?*"

"You heard me," he said.

"You named your bike *The Direwolf?*"

"Yeah," he said with a taunt in his tone as we neared the entrance to a narrow trail I'd never noticed at the edge of their property. "And yours is called The Runt."

"Fuck that," I growled, hopping onto the bike's back and starting her engine. She flared to life with a rumbling purr that I felt all the way down to my bones. That adrenaline I was feeling earlier was nothing in the face of this. As I revved her engine, I felt my body tremble with the insatiable need to feel her move beneath me. I was ravenous for it. Didn't realize how much I missed it.

"I'll show you how fast this runt can move."

I took off at breakneck speed, lifting my body as she bumped onto the trail and her back end fishtailed as I got the feel for her size and power. A smile snaked across my lips, and despite all the awful, terrible things that kept me up at night, when I put her into second and then third gear, laughter bubbled up from deep within me.

The whine and rumble of Clay's bike on my tail spurred me faster. My canine vision making the trail clear as if it were early afternoon instead of evening. The cold snap of wind over my body coaxed all my hairs to standing and lit all my nerve endings ablaze. I whooped as I went around a corner and found a small inclined patch of dirt.

I jumped it, reveling in the split second when me and the bike left the ground. The impact of landing coiled up through my arms, my back tire skidding as I bumped around a corner, staying firmly ahead of Clay.

"Allie!" I heard him call over the roar of the wind rushing in my ears, over the sound of my own heartbeat like a drum in my ears.

"Allie, slow down!"

A spark of defiance zipped down my spine.

What? He didn't think I knew what I was doing?

Besides, my new wolf-toughened body could handle a wipeout. I smiled at that, empowered by it. A reckless desire to see how far I could push myself stole through my mind, and heedless of Clay's warning, I kept on, going faster, taking turns sharper. Tuning him out.

There was nothing except me and the bike and chewed earth beneath its tires. There was no Clay. No Jared. No pack alpha.

No best friends who barely spoke to me anymore.

No pain.

No fear.

Just wind blowing my hair back and making my eyes water.

Just this bike. This trail. My pulse.

"Allie!" Clay's bellow cut through my walls only an instant before I saw the turn in the trail. This one was sharper. Too sharp. And I was already on top of it.

I kicked her down a gear and twisted the handlebars, trying to drift her rear end enough to make it around the bend. Heart in my throat, I threw my whole body into the maneuver, the sharp edge of panic twisting her blade in my gut.

Almost.

Almost...

The bike kicked out just a little too much to the right, and I fell to the left, taking her with me. We skidded through sharp rocks and gritty earth, her hot as hell exhaust pipe searing into my inner thigh.

"Fuck!" I cursed through clenched teeth, shoving the bike off me once we stopped sliding over the ground.

Clay's bike ground to halt and he let it fall to the ground. I only heard his heavy footfalls before my bike was torn out of my grasp and discarded three feet away as though it were a toy.

His hand came around my thigh where a singed hole was burned into the denim of my jeans, revealing bright red flesh beneath. My left arm was chewed from elbow to shoulder, too. I could feel it, but I didn't move, not wanting him to see.

"Are you hurt anywhere else?" Clay asked in a voice so cold and so threatening that I flinched.

"No," I said breathlessly as I batted his hand away. My thigh was already beginning to heal. The itch of the skin renewing itself made me grit my teeth.

He took me by my right arm, wrapping his hand around his upper forearm to lift me to standing. "What the fuck were you thinking?" he demanded, his blue eyes glowing with the presence of his wolf.

I felt my own wolf rush to the surface in response.

Where I was pissed the hell off, she was preoccupied with the fact that we could smell his leather and engine grease scent, and that his warm callused fingers still brushed over the sensitive skin at our elbow's crease.

I pulled my arm away and took a step back, willing my wolf to be on my side with this.

"Riding," I snapped. "I was riding."

He shook his head and a muscle in his temple twitched. "That wasn't riding, Allie. That was fucking reckless and stupid. You don't know these trails."

I poked him in his big fat chest. "You don't know how I ride," I countered. "I know what I'm doing."

"Do you?" he challenged, stepping in closer. "Because it sure as hell didn't look like it. It looked like you were trying to get yourself hurt."

The truth in his words stung, and I recoiled from them as though they were a physical blow, teeth grinding.

"Don't—"

"No, *you* don't," he interrupted in a growl. "You could have been seriously hurt."

"So what! I would heal."

He stepped in, sealing the gap between us until I could feel the brush of his chest against mine. He leaned his head down to meet my fire-filled gaze with a burning one of his own. I didn't back down.

Didn't back away.

His breath tickled my lips and it took everything inside of me not to give my wolf what she wanted. She pawed and scratched, whined and mewled. She wanted to devour him. I wanted to let her.

Something flipped hard in my belly, and I gasped, hating how I could both *hate* him and *want* him at the same time.

His eyes flicked to my lips and a bolt of white-hot energy shot through me like lightning. I leaned in, ready to surrender.

That's when he pulled back, leaving me unsteady on my feet as his face turned to stone. "I won't watch you do this to yourself," he said in a hard whisper.

Something like acid pooled in my gut and suddenly it was impossible to look him in the eye. My fists squeezed and I bit back a scathing remark.

Clay lifted my bike easily, wrapping his hand around the middle of the handlebars before he went and lifted his own bike back to standing, holding that one up in much the same way. "You can walk back," he said over his shoulder without any remorse. "Then you and I are going to have a little chat."

There were so many things I wanted to say. To shout. To scream as he faded around the bend and all I was left with was an ebbing rage and shaking fists while I listened to the sound of the tires slowly rolling over earth as he walked both bikes back toward the cabin and left me in the dark.

If he thought I was going to fucking follow him like some sad puppy, tail tucked between my legs, the bastard had another think coming.

Right there amid the trees, with pine scented wind stinging my fury-warmed skin, I stripped down until I was naked. Bared to the leaf-dappled moonlight beneath the tree canopy.

Shifting was still painful, but over the last week, it'd become more bearable each time. I was already getting faster at it. Relinquishing the reins to my wolf and letting her overtake me made the transition so smooth I only had to endure a few seconds of agony before I felt my paws pushing into the dirt and the air taking on a crystalline quality.

The sound of the forest magnified in my canine ears. The skitter of a squirrel fleeing up a tree. The buzz and chirp of insects. The sound the wind made when it whistled through needles and branches. And very distantly, Clay, at the trailhead now. I could hear him sigh as the bike's tires rolled to a stop.

He was waiting for me.

He may have been pissed off, but he wouldn't leave me out here all alone.

He could keep waiting.

My wolf strained to go to him, but I asserted my own dominance over her, something else I'd been practicing.

Jared, I spoke in our shared mind.

I had no interest in going back to the cabin with Clay right now. I didn't want to hear what he had to say.

Let's go to the quarry.

Sufficiently satisfied with the alternative, we began to move. Slowly at first, gaining speed until Clay had no hope of catching us. We doubled back twice and ran splashing through creek water part of the way, careful not to mark any trees with our scent.

It was another trick Jared had taught me—how to cover my tracks if I was ever out alone. How to give myself a head start. I was glad my wolf seemed happy to cooperate so long as I allowed her to run in the direction of at least *one* of my mates.

I'd been to the local quarry only once when I was a little girl. Dad had taken me on an errand to buy some flagstone for the curving stone pathway out behind our back deck. But I remembered where it was well enough by the road. Getting there via the forest proved a more challenging route, but my wolf seemed like she already knew exactly where she was going, and I had to wonder if she could somehow sense Jared's location.

It was about twenty minutes later when the last dregs of my anger wore off and I began to regret taking off on Clay. I couldn't say I was ready to admit he had a point, but there was a small bud of guilt poking its head up through my belly and into my ribcage. Soon, it would bloom and grow heavy with seed.

Ugh.

Didn't he understand?

Didn't he get how fucking hard I was trying to hold it all together?

My wolf let out a little yip, and I refocused to find bright lights filtering through the tree branches ahead. The beep and groan of machinery hauling stone and the shouting of men.

We found it.

No point in turning back now. I could ask Jared to send Clay a text telling him where I was. It was the best form of apology I could give. I was still too frustrated to give him any more than that.

Tomorrow at school I was going to have to face Layla and Viv again.

Tomorrow night after work I was going to have to face Ryland. Submit myself to his command.

And by the end of the week, when the full moon reared its ugly head, my friends' fates would be decided and there was nothing at all I could do but wait for the ax to fall.

My painful reminder of what awaited us forced a long howl from my wolf's lips. Our chest ached with it, and when we were finished, a bone-weary exhaustion set in and we lay against the cool earth, resting our chin against our paws.

We didn't have to wait long. Jared found us not more than a couple minutes later. The moment we caught his scent on the wind and began to feel his nearness through the mate bond, a rush of exhilaration brought us back to life.

His silhouette appeared amid the trees, tall and lean. The bright lights of the quarry set his dirty blond hair ablaze, so it looked like a halo rested atop his head.

I gave a little yip of excitement and then my wolf, sated from her long run and the presence of her mate, yielded the reins, putting them back in my hands.

"Allie?" Jared called as he neared, squinting to see me in the dimness. "What are you doing out here?"

I realized, a little belatedly, that I didn't exactly think this through. I bowed my lupine head, examining my fur coated limbs and swishing tails. I hadn't brought any clothes.

Jared kneeled in the leaf-strewn dirt; he reached a hand to me, pushing it into my fur. His eyes blazed vibrant deep amber—that small green fleck like the spark of fire in a rushing verdant river. Unable to help myself, I pushed my head against his touch, letting the pull and give of the mate bond bring a calm clarity to my mind.

He smirked and a dimple formed in his left cheek. I licked it.

He barked a laugh and reeled back.

Mortified, I lowered my head. I hadn't meant to...

God, did I really just lick Jared?

"Here," he said and stood, rubbing the back of his hand over the wolf slobber on his cheek before he tugged off his long sleeve gray t-shirt. It was a study in self-control not to drool at the sight of his naked torso. That body belonged to a man. Defined abs and thick biceps. A whisper of light-colored hair disappearing below the belt of his jeans.

Mine, my wolf growled in the furthest reaches of my mind.

I agreed.

"It should be long enough to cover...everything," he prompted, holding it out to me with one arm and turning his head the opposite way to allow me to shift back without him watching. Always the gentleman.

Shifting back had gotten easier since I started letting my wolf out daily, too. Before it was like coming up for breath after suffocating under water. With my insides aching like they were deprived of oxygen and every muscle was on lock.

Now it was just like opening a door and stepping through it. The pain was always less than making the transition *to* wolf.

Still though, I shuddered as I took the t-shirt from Jared's fingers and pulled it over my head. He was right, the hem of the thing came nearly to my mid-thigh. But without panties or a bra, I still felt way too exposed.

"Good?" Jared asked.

I nodded, then realized with a flush that he wasn't looking at me. That he wanted *verbal* confirmation I wasn't naked anymore. "Yeah," I stammered. "Thanks."

He spun with eyes half-closed and his bottom lip caught between his teeth. When his gaze met mine, the tiniest of smiles pulled at my lips.

Jared reached up a hand to scratch the back of his neck and looked me up and down.

"Did you come alone?" he asked, peering into the darkened forest at my back as though expecting company.

I nodded. "Yeah," I told him, pursing my lips. "I know you guys still don't like me going out on my own, but—"

He held a hand up, a knot forming in his brow. "You don't have to explain yourself to me, Allie. I want you safe, but what you do is your business. I'm not here to control you."

I sighed. How could he and Clay be so similar in so many ways, but so very different in others. "Thanks," I muttered. "I just…needed to get away."

He raised a brow at that. "Should I be worried?"

I grimaced. "No, but maybe you should text Clay and let him know I'm here with you. Safe. I kind of took off on him."

Jared stifled a laugh and gave a little nod, as though he wasn't the least bit surprised.

"I take it riding didn't go so well?"

"Understatement of the century," I joked.

"Well, come on," he said and extended his hand to me. "My cell's in the office, and I just made hot chocolate. Stay for a while?"

My belly did a little flip and I took his hand, super conscious that if I bent over even in the slightest, the whole quarry was going to see my lady bits.

"Don't worry," Jared said, squeezing my hand as he led me toward the lights in the distance. "The office is at the edge of the quarry. And it's got a back door."

4

Jared busied himself cleaning out an extra mug once he drew the blinds closed at the front of the portable office.

The space was larger than I pictured it to be. With a long desk spaced a few feet ahead of the back wall and a plush leather chair sandwiched between it and the wall. In front of that there were two chairs, for visitors or clients, I assumed. And on the other side of the long space was a makeshift kitchenette, complete with microwave, plug in kettle, and enough ramen noodle cups and hot cocoa packets to last someone at least a year.

Next to the kitchenette was a deep-burgundy sofa. A pillow wadded up on one end and a threadbare taupe blanket folded over the top.

Jared gestured to the sofa once he was finished adding a small handful of marshmallows to the top of two steaming mugs. I couldn't remember the last time I had cocoa, and I salivated at the smell when he pressed the mug into my hand.

With the conversation from dinner still fresh in my mind and Jared right here in front of me, I couldn't seem to think of anything else and easy conversation eluded me.

So, we were dating now.

Me and Jared.

Me and Clay.

Weird didn't even begin to cover it.

Jared sat and thumbed out a quick text to Clay like I'd asked him.

I opened my mouth to attempt to string together some form of a sentence that didn't giveaway how the twelve inches of space between us was driving me mad, but Jared beat me to it. "How are Layla and Viv?"

Talk about a fucking buzzkill.

Sensing my change in demeanor, his brows lowered. "Sorry."

I shook my head. "No, it's okay. You haven't been at school for a while, so I guess you wouldn't know."

I took a deep breath. "I think they're taking it okay. I'm not really sure to be honest."

His eyes narrowed.

"They aren't exactly talking to me."

He licked his lips, seeming to consider something, as though if he could just think hard enough, he could find a solution to all my problems.

"It'll be over soon," he said. "They might not even shift, and then when they don't, Ry will have them compelled to forget any of this ever happened."

I sighed.

Ah. The mysterious Mr. Grey. The vampire I met briefly in Ryland's house the night of the bonfire. Apparently, they had the ability to *compel,* which from what I understood was just a lax way of saying that they had the ability to fuck with your mind.

The guy already gave me the creeps the first time we met, now he's firmly in *hell-no* territory for ever wanting him near me or any of my friends.

It was what Ryland had planned for me the night I took off only to be captured and turned by Devin. He wasn't going to kill me at all.

Fancy that.

If I'd stayed, I wouldn't have remembered Jared or Clay becoming wolves. Maybe, if Ryland wanted to be extra cautious, I wouldn't even remember that Jared was the one who saved me in the woods. I wouldn't know them. I may not be a shifter right now.

The former are the reasons why I could never wish I'd stayed.

Looking into Jared's kind stare now only reinforces it: I was *meant* to meet them. I knew it as surely as I knew the sun would rise tomorrow morning.

I was *meant* to love them.

I dropped my head. "I know."

"Have you told them?"

"That if they don't shift, they'll be forced to forget it all ever happened? No. Not yet. I think if I tell them vampires are also real right now, they might implode."

Jared nodded his agreement. "What about Quinn? Has he remembered anything?"

I sipped my hot cocoa, letting my body meld to the worn sofa cushions. This was still painful territory he was poking at, but it was less difficult to talk about. Quinn was the lucky one of the three. He already didn't remember anything from that night. "Nothing at all. He still thinks we're all going to a bush party on the full moon. He has no idea it's a shifter camp."

We'd figure out how to handle that when the time came. Layla was adamant that he not be told anything about what happened. Not until he had to know.

I assumed the waiting to learn their fate was eating at them both. I didn't have that.

I turned mere minutes after I was bitten.

I couldn't even imagine what they must have been going through…

My chest ached, and I set my cocoa down on the rickety side table, stomach suddenly a bit sour.

"That's probably for the best."

"We can trust him, right?" I blurted, needing it to be confirmed at least one more time. "Ryland. We can trust that if they don't turn, he'll let them walk out of there."

Jared's lips pressed into a thin line, and he reached across me to set his mug down, too.

For a second, he seemed to be chewing on a response, then he looked up at me from beneath his caramel colored lashes, gaze flitting to me briefly before falling back down to rest on the sofa cushion between us.

He shifted in his seat and threw a hand through his tousled hair to get it out of his eyes. "When you were little," he started, and I'm confused at where he's going with this. "Do you…"

He paused. Swallowed.

"Do you remember hunting with your dad? You would have been maybe seven or eight."

He waited, and my heart began to pound in my chest. My skin tingled all the way down to my toes.

It couldn't have been…

"You came upon two skinned wolves in the woods."

My eyes welled and a hard ball formed in my throat.

No.

"Huddled against their corpses, there was a young wolf pup."

Beneath the streaks of dried crimson and clotted dirt in its fur, it was the purest white. It'd growled at us. Snarled and swiped. But it was starving. Malnourished. It looked like it had been there for days if not longer. It was all alone. To my eight-year-old self, it was just a little white puppy with sad amber eyes and no one to care for it. How Dad had tried to pull me away, warning me with threats that he'd need to take me to get a rabies shot if it bit me. But I'd fought him.

Dad wouldn't let me take him home.

But I wouldn't leave it with nothing.

Jared's jaw twitched as he continued, his hands in fists. "You…you came to me even though your Dad was trying to pull you away," he said with a little laugh of incredulity. "Just this tiny thing…but you had a fire in you even then."

Dangerously close to tears, I dug my fingernails into the palms of my hands, trying to regain control. It wasn't just my own emotions I had to contend with, Jared's sorrow pierced me straight through. Like an arrow of misery burrowing its high carbon steel into my still-beating heart.

"You gave me this little dish from your hiking pack and filled it to overflowing with all the water in your canteen," he said, and some of that sorrow eased. "Then, with your dad groaning at your back, you dumped an entire Ziplock bag of deer jerky onto the ground beside it."

The memory came back so clear it was startling. I remembered how the little wolf had looked at me curiously, edging closer to the jerky and water with an upper lip curled back, ready to attack if he needed to.

"Do you remember what you said to me?" Jared asked, finally lifting his head, amber eyes bright like warm, spiced cider.

I tried to chase the memory, but it was a faraway thing, flying just out of my grasp.

"You told me I was going to be okay," he said with a sad smile. "With this serious little face and tears in your eyes, like you were so sure it was true."

I missed that sense of optimism. It sure would have come in handy now.

At his reminder, the fleeting memory returned, and I remembered how Dad had shaken his head at me. He'd always thought it was strange that I talked to all the animals we came upon in the woods. Little did he or I know that there was one who could truly hear me.

"If it weren't for you…" Jared trailed off and then seemed to come back to himself, as though he'd shucked off the weight of the memory. Put it back behind him where it belonged.

"Anyway," he said. "My point is Uncle Ry picked up the pieces. After you…I gathered the strength to find my way back to the pack. He was there for me when I had no one else. He's an ass sometimes, I'll give you that."

He tipped his head to the side with a short laugh.

"But Ry is the only family I've got."

"No, he isn't," I said, moving myself closer to Jared on the sofa. I waited for him to fix those amber eyes back on me before continuing.

The bond between us pulsed. That tether between our two souls grew taut.

I knew, now more than I ever did before, how much this made sense.

My heart broke for that little white wolf in the woods that day. Dad had to deal with my wailing for the rest of the hunting trip. Something in those sad eyes had sliced into me, burrowed deep.

Even then, I think somehow, I knew...

That maybe there was a connection even then, as children, that could not be denied.

"Ry isn't your only family, Jare. You have Clay," I told him, searching his gaze.

He lifted a hand and brushed a length of hair back from my cheek. His fingertips brushed over my cheekbone and I shivered involuntarily, something tightening in my chest.

Jared looked like he was about to disagree, but I wasn't finished.

"And now you have me."

His hand stilled, and I glanced at his full lips, my wolf hedging back to the surface.

I don't know why I ever tried to fight it. It was pointless. This was always going to happen. We were on a collision course, destined for impact. Not a thing in the world could stop it.

"Allie..." My name was a sigh on his lips, and his warm palm pressed against my cheek. I closed my eyes and let out a small sigh of my own, skin bristling.

When I opened them again, Jared's wolf stared back

at me. The glow around his irises and the strain in his expression told me all I needed to know.

He was still holding back. Not allowing himself to take what he thought he couldn't have.

But hadn't I always belonged to him?

"Allie, I—" he began, but I cut him off.

"Just kiss me, you idiot."

Jared's hungry eyes widened for an instant before he let himself loose. The hand on my cheek snaked behind my neck, knotting in the small hairs there. I gasped, but the sound was swallowed by his lips.

Jared kissed me like a man starved. His hands gripped me hungrily, drawing me to him. His lips moved expertly against mine, provoking a shattered moan from my throat. I pressed my hands to his chest, looking for something to hold on to, afraid if I didn't find my grip, I'd fall.

My body came alive with sensation. Heat and tension and electricity swirled and crashed as Jared pulled me onto his lap and my legs fell to either side of his hips.

His hands gripped hard at my waist, holding me there as he swept in with his tongue, the kiss tasting of mint and chocolate. He sat up, wrapping his arms around my middle as he pressed into my chest, making my breasts harden beneath the thin t-shirt.

I was losing it. Losing my grip on reality. On control.

Each of his fevered kisses sent me speeding ever

closer to oblivion. My body, naked beneath Jared's shirt, hummed with latent desire, and I realized I didn't want him to stop.

Not ever.

This felt *right*.

My hands on his arms trailed lower, reaching between us. I felt his body still as my hands brushed over the top button of his jeans.

"Jared!" A gruff voice called from outside the office and two sobering *thuds* pounded against the front door.

The kiss broken, I scrambled from Jared's lap, skin flushed and knees trembling as I tried to get my footing.

"Shit," Jared cursed, rising and readjusting his jeans.

"Uh…" he said in a whisper, looking around as though for some means of escape.

The silver knob began to turn, and I spurred into action, rushing around the desk at the back of the office. I'd planned to tuck myself in the nook beneath, but it was already filled with stacks of old files. The door swung open, and I did the only thing I could think of and sat in the chair, pulling it as close to the desk as I was able. Close enough that I hoped the man wouldn't be able to see that I wasn't wearing any pants.

I brushed my hair away from my face and straightened my spine, willing my breathing to level out just as he entered.

Jared rushed to grab his mostly empty cocoa and

leaned casually against the wall where the kitchenette stood opposite me.

"Oh," the man said, taking in first Jared and then me behind the desk. "Didn't know you had company."

"Nah," he said, clearing his throat. "Allie just popped by to borrow my Jeep," he said and lifted the keys from his pocket to toss them to me.

I scrambled to catch them.

"Right," I agreed.

Greg didn't look convinced, but he also looked a hell of a lot like he didn't give a shit one way or the other what we were doing. His chapped hands and coveralls were coated in a thick layer of rock dust, and his eyes told of his exhaustion. He jutted his chin back in the direction of the loud quarry outside the still-open door. "Got a bit of a situation with the skid-steer. She's stuck real good."

Jared's demeanor changed, and he bent to gather a vest and hardhat from a box in the corner, tugging them on.

The look...definitely suited him.

I bit my lower lip, pressing my thighs together beneath the table to keep from making any sound.

"I'll come have a look," Jared told Greg, who turned and left without another word. Jared followed him to the door, pausing in the frame to toss me a wink over his shoulder. "Don't go anywhere," he said with a sly grin. "Back in no time."

I nodded, fully intent on waiting however long it took.

The door swept closed behind Jared, making the blinds rattle against the glass windowpane. Jarring the portable building enough that the mouse atop the desk moved, making the desktop screen come to life.

A web page covered the screen. I was about to look away when the headline of the page caught my eye.

How to use a bow.

A smile tugged at my lips, and I laughed quietly to myself. I wondered offhandedly if he was actually interested, or if he was taking an interest only because he knew how much I liked going out to shoot my bow every morning.

Hesitantly, I scrolled down the page, curious about what it said.

When I got to the end, I noticed the little mail icon flashing on the taskbar and hovered over it, shaking my head at myself when I realized I was about to open it.

What am I doing?

I moved my hand from the mouse but managed to accidentally click the button before I did. An email screen materialized, and I jolted, knowing I should've looked away, but unable to.

Ryland's email address. There was a posed photo of him in the upper right corner. If that weren't enough of a giveaway, there were several already opened emails that showed samples of their hidden content, most of which contained some form of Ry, Ryland, or Mr. Stone as an opening line.

A new email rested at the top, its bold font begging to be clicked on.

A weight settled in my belly and the tips of my fingers tingled as I hovered over it. My palms grew sweaty.

The top three emails were all from the same address. No name in the sender field. Just an *X*. The subject line on the second one down, one of the ones that was already opened read: *The list you asked for...*

The other two didn't have any subject at all.

Before I could think too much about it, I clicked the one about the list and scrolled down through the completely blank email to where there was a file available for download. It said simply: *List.*

Gritting my teeth, I clicked on it. The computer chirped loudly, and I sucked in a breath, staring at a little popup that told me this file was password protected. The empty text box taunted with the flashing black line, as though asking me what the hell I was doing.

Groaning, I exited the popup and clicked over to the next already opened email. That one was blank too, but also contained a file. This one was labeled simply: *Jared.*

An icy chill snaked down my spine at the sight of his name. I tried to tell myself that this was nothing. It could be this person was Ryland's accountant or something. Maybe they were sending out copies of paystubs or lists of expenses.

But then why did I feel like that couldn't have been farther from the truth?

Emboldened, I click on the last email—the one not yet open. This one, blank like the others has two files down near the bottom waiting to be opened. They are image files, but only black squares show where samples would normally be. They must have been password protected, too. Both are labeled with names. One is labeled *Dean*, and the other is labeled *Andreas.*

Footsteps coming back up to the portable door send my pulse skittering into overdrive. With sloppy fingers, I exit out of the email and right click it, marking it as unread and then quitting out of the window.

By the time Jared re-enters the cabin, hands covered in gray dust, I'm leaning back in the plush office chair, doing my absolute best to calm the fuck down before he notices anything is amiss.

"Hey," he said with a grin. "Sorry about that."

I shook my head, standing on leaden legs. "That's okay."

My blood felt near boiling, and I knew that if he looked at me too closely, he would see the evidence of what I'd just done all over my face. *God*, what was I doing?

Snooping on his uncle's—*my alpha's*—computer?

That was a surefire way to earn myself some scorn right off the hop.

I held out his keys to him. "Here."

He pushed them back. "I'd rather you take it," he said. "It'll be safer than running back to the cabin. If you don't mind?"

How could I say no when he was making that face? The one with the dimple and the sweet smile.

"I really shouldn't," I told him. "I'm supposed to only drive with a licensed driver in the passenger seat."

Jared pursed his lips, considering. "It's all backroads to the trailhead. And you're a fast learner. Already a better driver than I was a few weeks in."

Not wanting to draw this out, I pasted on a wilted grin of my own and curled the keys into my fist.

"It's parked at the edge of the quarry, in the employee lot. I'll walk you through the trees."

"No," I rushed to say. "I mean, that's okay. I'm sure I can find it. How many lifted white Jeeps can there be out there?"

The joke didn't take, and I was left feeling guilty and awkward and wondering if I remembered to exit out of Ryland's email or not. The screen was still lit up and it took all the self-control I had not to lean back and peek just to make sure.

Jared, thankfully, didn't seem to notice my discomfort.

He stuffed his hands deep into the pockets of his jeans and nodded.

"'Kay," I said in a breath. "See you tomorrow night?"

I went to turn, ready to make a break for it when he

caught me around the waist and spun me back to him. His hand found the back of my head and his other arm kept me from falling as he pressed his lips to mine.

For a brief second, the guilt weighing on my chest turned light as air and I forgot why I wanted to leave so badly.

Then the kiss ended, and it all came rushing back with the air that returned to my lungs.

"Sorry," Jared said, a whisper against my lips. "I couldn't let you leave without doing that one more time."

5

It was time to go.

The day went by in a blur of classes I couldn't focus on and a shift at the bookshop that felt like it was over in minutes instead of hours.

At least Layla and Viv actually spoke to me today. I mean, it wasn't much, a quick conversation about the plan for the full moon, and them asking if we should make plans for my birthday. I shut down the latter, telling them I'd rather not make a big thing out of it. And I did my best to explain everything they needed to know about the former, glazing over the ugly bits.

I knew I should tell them *all* of it, but I just... couldn't. Every time I tried it was like a knife drove deeper and deeper into my chest.

But we talked, and in my book, that was progress. Painful, slow progress, but still progress. The fact that they asked about my birthday—of all stupid things—

gave me hope that it was more the situation they were angry at than me.

It didn't erase any of my guilt, but it made it a bit easier to swallow.

I flicked off the lights and dug out the keys to lock up. Clay's burly shadow appeared outside the front window a second later, and I sighed inwardly. Last night when I got home, he was there, sitting on the porch with a beer. Looked like he was ready to wait all night if he had to.

When he saw me coming, in my wolf form again, he gave one tight nod, as though to say *good, you're back*. Then he lifted the two other empty bottles from the steps and disappeared into the cabin. When I entered, ass naked, a few minutes later, it was quiet, and his bedroom door was sealed shut.

I'd been thinking about how to explain what happened all day. I knew he was going to be here, that we were going to pack camp together and Jared would meet us there, but I still hadn't figured out what to say.

I tugged the door closed behind me as I stepped outside, the bells rattling at the top of the door as I turned the key in the lock and readjusted my backpack on my shoulder, stuffing the shop keys into the little gap in the double zipper at the top.

"Hey," he said, kicking off from a leaning stance on the wall.

"Before we go," I said, biting my lip, trying to sort

through my mess of thoughts. "I just wanted to apolo—"

"Don't," he interrupted, face reddening. "I shouldn't have just left. I should have...I don't know. Tried to make you feel better or some shit."

He took a shaky breath.

"I'm, *uh,* not very good at...at..."

I cocked my head at him, holding in a laugh at his obvious discomfort. "At...being a boyfriend?"

He cringed. "Yeah. I guess."

"Have you never had a girlfriend before?"

I had to ask. He had a reputation at Forest Grove High when he was a senior there. And with that *face* and those *muscles*, I couldn't imagine him not dating.

He shrugged, leveling his bright blue eyes on me with a coy stare. "Depends what you think counts as dating."

A furious blush found its way onto my cheeks, and I dropped my gaze before he could see. He may be inexperienced with the kind of dating I was used to. But I could say with confidence that I was *definitely* inexperienced in the sort of dating he was used to.

"Okay," I said, suddenly eager to end this conversation. "So, I'm not going to say sorry and you're not pissed at me anymore. I guess that means we're good."

Clay smirked. "Yeah, Allie. We're good."

Thank fuck for that. Or this would have been a really awkward drive.

Or not...

"Where's the Jeep?"

Clay tipped his head to the sidewalk and began to walk, giving me a little tug on my jacket sleeve as he passed so I would follow him.

"Thought we'd run," he said. "You haven't shifted yet today."

My stomach soured.

Right.

Under normal circumstances I'd be all right to miss a day, but we were going to pack camp. I was going to get my first orders from my alpha. It was easy to read between the lines of Clay's words.

I needed to shift before I faced him so I could keep myself under control.

Ryland wasn't feeling particularly patient lately from what I'd heard when Charity came to visit a few days ago. She got chewed out for helping Quinn and was stuck on security detail, policing the new pack members all week and reporting back to Ry.

"That's probably a good idea."

Clay and I veered off the main road and onto a side street. Another few blocks and it would dead-end in the trees and we could shift.

"Have you spoken to Jared today?" I hedged, wondering if he'd said anything to Clay about what happened between us last night. This whole *sharing* thing was going to take some getting used to. The only way it would work was for us to be honest with each other and to set those ground rules Jared mentioned.

We'd have to have another toe-curling chat to do that soon.

Clay bowed his head. "Yeah. I should've figured you'd go there."

He didn't say it with any ire, just a sort of resigned, careful tone, and I knew right away they'd talked about it. My belly flipped. That was a conversation I was super glad I wasn't there for.

"We kind of established a ground rule," he continued when I didn't comment.

My brows lowered. "What's that?'

"No fucking."

"What?" I choked, a bit shell-shocked at how casually he was just throwing that word out there in that context.

He cut his gaze to me, eyeing me sidelong as we walked. "No. Fucking."

I ground my teeth together, remembering how difficult it had been to stop. Both with Clay and with Jared. I wondered if it was because they were both over eighteen and I was still seventeen?

I mean, I'd be eighteen in just days from now, but neither of them knew that.

Or it could be that neither could stand the thought of the other being that intimate with me.

Then, there was also the possibility that neither of them *wanted* to.

That one hurt the most.

"Fine," I said, unable to keep the biting tone from

my words. "It's not like either of you asked me, but…" I trailed off, shrugging.

"Allie—"

"No, it's cool. I get it."

"I don't think you do."

"Can we just not talk about this right now?"

I walked off the streetlamp lit street and stepped into the brush, moving inward to where the shadows hung more heavily to provide us the cover we would need to shift unseen.

Clay grunted and followed me, kicking off his shoes when we stopped. I opened my backpack and put my own shoes inside. Followed by my jeans, sweater, and tank top.

Clay had his shirt and socks off and was just unbuttoning his jeans when he paused, his mouth slightly agape as I unclasped my bra.

Still heated with fury at him and Jared for making a decision like that without my even so much as being present for it, I was feeling a little brazen. Maybe a little vindictive.

The clasp came free, and the chill of the evening brushed over my breasts as I dropped the bra into my bag with the rest of my clothes. A muscle in his neck twitched.

"*Allie,*" he growled, a warning.

"What?" I asked, the word dripping sarcasm as I hooked my fingers into the top of my panties, suddenly grateful I didn't wear my hello kitty ones, but the simple black ones with the sporty waistband. "Your rules. Not mine."

His nostrils flared and a fraction of a second before I worked up the courage to drop my panties, he turned his head to the side, averting his glowing blue stare. His hands clenched so tightly I could see every curve of his knuckles beneath the strained white flesh.

Perhaps a little too pleased with myself, I bent and zipped my backpack and then shifted, only a small cry leaving my lips before my wolf took over and I was staring up at Clay from all fours.

Clay trained his haughty stare on me, his face red.

Glad my wolf seemed to be on the same page as me, we sat still, staring at him with a little crook to our neck. Ready for the show.

Realizing what I was doing, Clay grimaced. "Want to turn around?"

We stared.

His brows lowered, and he turned around, dropping his jeans and shifting in one fluid motion that only afforded the briefest glance at his muscled ass and thick thighs. It was enough.

I lifted the pack from the forest floor with my teeth and took off at a sprint, leaving Clay to fumble to pick up his shoes and follow.

Not cool, Allie, his words floated through my mind as I ran.

Which part? I asked, finding it difficult to be sorry in the slightest.

You know *which part.*

I smiled, buoyant as we ran side by side, taking the long way around the creek and against the mountainside. Both of us needing the extra miles to cool off before we got there.

PACK CAMP BUZZED with noise and energy as we approached. My wolf could sense all the new pack members. She caught every individual scent on the wind. Clay and I came to a halt close enough to see down into the camp if we really strained our eyes, but far enough away that we could get dressed again without anyone seeing.

Clay might've been used to getting naked in front of the other shifters—it seemed second nature to them—but I had a feeling it would be a while before I got used to it. I may have teased Clay in the woods, but there was no way I wanted to show my goods to an entire pack if I could help it.

I shifted back, falling to my knees as a wave of dizziness washed over me, the world tipping up for a second before it leveled out. I held on to the earth for dear life until the vertigo passed.

"Hey," Clay said brusquely, and I felt his human hands curl over my shoulders and shuddered at the contact. "What just happened? You good?"

I struggled to swallow past a dry lump in my throat

and caught my breath. Stars crowded at the edges of my vision.

"Yeah," I managed.

"Bullshit."

He turned me to him, careful to keep his gaze level with mine. I can't say I did the same. Even with the stars in my eyes, his...package...was hard to miss.

Clay's index finger lifted my chin, and his blue eyes bored into mine.

"When was the last time you ate?"

I blinked.

And as though it was crying out for aid, my stomach growled loudly. I cringed.

"Um. Breakfast."

If a piece of burnt toast on the way out the door counted.

Clay rolled his eyes and handed me my pack, dropping it into my lap. "Get some clothes on. I'll go find you something to eat."

He rose and pulled on his jeans, now with darkened spots of drool on one hip from where he carried them in his mouth and then got his shoes on. "I'll come back and get you."

Before I could get enough breath and clarity of mind to argue with him, he was gone.

I let my head fall back and cursed my own stupidity. I'd been so preoccupied worrying and stressing about Layla and Viv and about tonight's meeting that eating just completely slipped my mind.

Vaguely, I remember pushing around my macaroni salad at lunch while I explained what was going to happen to my friends in mere days. I'm not even sure I had a single bite.

And water? Fuck, had I even drunk any water at all today?

I groaned and pushed myself unsteadily to my feet. I might've been fine if I hadn't shifted and run thirty miles from town. My hands shook with twitching tremors as I pulled on my panties and jeans, followed by my bra and top. Even with my sweater on, I felt cold as I put one foot in front of the other toward the smell of campfire and the low hum of classic rock filtering through the trees.

Seth was the first familiar face I spotted as I stumbled down the decline and onto hard packed dirt. He squinted to make me out at the edge of the trees and a wide grin broke out over his face. "Hey!" he called, running over.

His grin faded when he got a better look at my face. "Shit, Allie, you're looking a bit shit. Nerves?"

I shook my head and immediately regretted it when a spike of pain drilled into my brain. *Ugh.* "Nah," I lied. "Forgot to eat."

"Forgot...to *eat*?" Seth asked as though I were speaking a foreign language.

I nudged his shoulder as we walked together toward where the highest concentration of pack members awaited, nearest to the main fire ring.

"I know," I said. "I'm an idiot."

"I mean, I wasn't going to say it but…"

I made a face of mock insult at him when we came upon the furthest ring of shifters and Seth dragged me over to a smaller group hanging out near the open tailgate of a sleek black truck. Away from the sniveling glares of Harrison, Forrest and the other members of Ryland's merry band of butt sniffers.

"Allie!" Charity called, waving me over to sit on the tailgate's ledge with her. I happily obliged, not sure my legs could hold out much longer. I tossed my pack into the back of the truck and hopped up, accepting a tight hug from Charity. "How are you? You look—"

"Like shit? I know. Seth already told me."

She laughed.

"What the hell, Allie?" Clay's growl silenced what remained of the conversations from the small group as he barged in, a steaming plate of barbeque ribs and corn on the cob in his hand.

Oops. Had he asked me to wait?

Clay cleared the gap between us and laid the plate down on my lap, grabbing a bottle of water from his back pocket to set down next to me. "Eat," he ordered. "Ry's just finishing up dealing with some pack bullshit and then he's going to want to talk to you."

"You mean make an example out of me?"

"This one's got claws," Seth commented with a little swipe of an imaginary paw in my direction.

I rolled my eyes at them. "What? It's true, isn't it? That's totally what's going on here."

Charity bumped my shoulder as I ravenously tore a massive bite out of the piping hot meat, wholly unable to stop myself as the scent of it wafted up into my nose. "He isn't so bad."

I raised a brow at her.

"What?" she said with wide, innocent eyes, and I was reminded of the first time I was ever here at camp. When I went to use the bathroom in Ry's house and ran into the vampire Grey. Ryland had been busy talking to Charity while Creepy McBloodsucker and I had a stare down in the hall.

She'd been blushing while he looked down at her, his forearm pressed into the wall over her head as he looked down into her eyes.

Oh my god.

Ew.

"He needs to show the pack who their alpha is to keep everyone in line. If he's lenient with some and not with others, no one would ever listen to him. There would be anarchy." Charity said as she stole a rib from my plate, and I resisted the urge to growl at her, both for sticking up for the fucker and for stealing my food.

"And he's just a fucking dickhead," Clay muttered.

At least my mate agreed with me.

"Who's a dickhead?" Jared asked, seemingly appearing from thin air around the back of Clay.

Clay jumped, cursing beneath his breath. "The fuck, man?"

Jared held his hands up in a placating gesture and gave a little shrug. "Sucks getting snuck up on, doesn't it?"

He tossed me a wink while Clay finished fuming and grumbling to himself, and Jared pressed through to lean next to where my legs dangled over the edge of the truck bed. "So, is my Jeep still in one piece?"

I smirked and worked to chew the massive chunk of meat in my mouth before I answered, praying my face wasn't completely covered in barbeque sauce.

"Are you doubting my skills?"

He smirked. "Never."

Jared reached in, brushing a thumb over the corner of my mouth and bringing it away covered in a smear of sticky sweet sauce. He popped it in his mouth and his brows went up. "Are there any more ribs?"

The small group quieted. Clay looked like he might throw up.

"If you guys are going to be all cutesy and gross, go find your own flatbed," Seth joked.

Clay grunted.

"I think it's adorable," Charity said wistfully. "I hope I don't have to wait too much longer to find my mate. I thought for sure when the packs merged I would but…"

Seth laughed. "Better hope you don't end up like

Ryland. Dude's almost fifty and he still hasn't found his."

"Who would want to mate with that?" I grumbled through another mouthful and Charity elbowed me.

"And how in the hell is that guy over fifty?" I continued once I was finished chewing. "He looks more like, I don't know, maybe thirty?"

The group shared a look, and I got the immediate sense that there was something I was missing. When their stares all turned to me, a heat blossomed in my belly and I cringed back. "What?" I demanded. "Do I have some shit on my face or something?"

Jared bit his lip and muttered to the others, "We, *uh*, we haven't exactly told her yet."

"Oh," both Charity and Seth said in unison.

"Tell me what?" I asked, dragging the back of my hand over my mouth and taking a long pull of lukewarm water from the bottle Clay gave me.

I looked to Jared for an explanation, but it was Clay who spoke, surprising me. "Look, Allie," he said and then seemed to consider how best to phrase what he planned to say next.

Jared's pallor had changed from its usual burnished tan to a sallow shade of green.

A pit yawned open in the bottom of my stomach.

I turned my attention to Clay.

"Spit it out already," I urged, setting the plate down next to me. At least I got a few bites in before my appetite vanished again.

Clay wiped a wide hand over the shadow of scruff on his jaw. "Ryland looks like he's still thirty because… shifters don't age the same way as humans."

"What do you mean we don't age the same?"

A ringing began in my ears. I'd wondered before…

I'd wondered why no one at pack camp looked much older than their late twenties. Why hadn't I asked this before?

"Holy shit," I choked out. "Are we…*are we immortal?*"

No. There was *no* way that was possible. I mean, I would know, wouldn't I? I would've been able to sense it or something? How could someone not *know* they are immortal?

Clay shook his head, and I took a breath. "Not exactly."

"It's the pack magic," Jared explained, and I turned back to him, liking how his soothing, matter-of-fact voice sounded to my ears right now over the sound of Clay's gruff, unapologetic one.

"Pack magic protects the pack camp from being found by other supernaturals. Sort of like the spell on the cabin that keeps people away and shields it from view, except with pack magic, it's naturally occurring."

He took a shaky breath.

"Pack magic *also* slows the aging process."

"*Slows?*"

Clay pursed his lips. "It stops it."

If my brows rose any higher, they'd get lost in my

hairline. "So, you're telling me that as long as I belong to a pack, I won't ever get old? I won't ever die?"

"Well, you can still die," Clay corrected me, though he didn't look pleased allowing those words to leave his lips. "Just not from old age."

"Is that why Grams is the only one who looks old? Because she doesn't have a pack?"

Clay nodded.

"A lot of shifters leave the pack after a hundred years or so, so that they can age out and pass naturally."

"But there are some who are hundreds of years old," Seth added with a swig of his beer. "The oldest on record was over *four hundred* when he died. I plan to break that record." He winked, polishing off his drink. "Anyone want a beer?"

Numbly, I nodded. "Got anything stronger?"

Seth chuckled. "I'll see what I can find," he said and then took off in the direction of the fire.

Across the blinding orange glow and the curl of dark smoke rising in the air, I could see Ryland exiting his house, the door banging closed behind him as he stared out over his pack. Silver scars in his right cheek glistened in the firelight. The mark from where Samson bit him had left his face puckered and ugly.

I couldn't help but feel a little triumphant seeing it.

"We're sorry we didn't tell you before," Jared said, stuffing his hands in his pockets. Neither of my mates had seemed to notice Ryland scanning the shifters crowded around the fire. "There just never seemed to be a good time, I guess."

"That's bullshit," Clay said, beating me to the exact words I was going to say. "We should have told her, man."

"Yeah," I said grouchily and hopped down from the truck. "You should have."

But right now, I didn't have room in my brain to think about my possible immortality, because Ryland had his burning orange gaze on me, and he was coming this way.

I wasn't about to wait here, cowering as he approached. My wolf sparked to life in my chest and I soothed her softly spoken internal thought.

He's our alpha, I reminded her. *We are just going to get our orders and then we're going to leave. Easy.*

Clay and Jared, realizing where I was staring—*who* I was staring at—fell into step on either side of me as I strode with as much forced confidence as I could to meet him only a few feet away from the fire.

"You made it," Ryland said, the words betraying a note of surprise.

Had he really thought I wouldn't come?

I didn't trust myself to answer without the words coming out dripping acid, so I simply nodded. My wolf was on high alert now, and I was sure Ryland could see her in my eyes. If he couldn't, my clenched fists were probably a dead giveaway as to how hard I needed to fight her.

Clay had been right; the shift and the run had been necessary. I couldn't imagine how much more difficult it would be to stand here and take orders if my wolf had been properly fed, and I hadn't allowed her some time in the light.

"I trust you're…more *adjusted* now?"

Fucking prick.

"She's doing great, Uncle Ry," Jared spoke for me.

Ryland grinned, and I couldn't help but notice how the music seemed louder now, clearer.

Because everyone had stopped talking.

Everyone was listening.

My spine tingled at the pressure of a hundred phantom eyes watching my every move. My skin bristled.

"Good," Ryland said, never taking his eyes from mine.

A bruising force pressed down on my shoulders, and I had to grit my teeth just to remain standing. A small gasp left my lips.

Jared and Clay turned to check that I was all right and all at once, the pressure lifted, and I glared at Ryland. He was pushing me.

Testing me.

Exerting his dominance in a way no one would notice if he were careful.

He's trying to make sure he still had control of me.

If I ground my teeth any harder, I'm pretty sure one would've snapped.

"There seem to be a few wolves who've...gone astray," Ryland said, steepling his fingers and pursing his lips as though considering something carefully. "I need some help reining them in. Your particular strengths could come in handy for that."

"You mean the shifters from Dave's pack?" Clay asked.

"Charity's group has already searched everywhere for them," Jared said, confused. "They could be halfway to the east coast by now."

"Should I let what's rightfully mine go so easily, nephew?"

Jared, cowed, shut his mouth.

My upper lip curled.

"You'll join the search," Ryland told me, and something in his gaze dared me to fight him on this.

He wanted me to, I realized.

A sick feeling spread like sludge in my gut. "When do I need—"

"Tomorrow. You'll meet Charity here at five."

Charity appeared a moment later, and I wondered if Ryland used his alpha pull to lure her in. "We usually get back around midnight,"

I shook my head. "I can't," I said. "I have work at the shop six days a week. I could maybe go down to five if I really have to—"

"Are you disobeying a direct order?"

The fire in Ryland's tone could not be mistaken.

"*Ry,*" Clay hissed.

"Something to say, Armstrong?" Ryland pressed, and I heard someone to our right whistle low and someone else chortle. "I'm in need of my pack. I'm in need of Allie's strong will to wrangle these deserters back to camp so I can deal with them."

A pause and Ryland turned his heated gaze back to me.

"Is this going to be a problem?"

"I can go," Jared offered. "If Charity needs—"

"I need you at the quarry," Ryland barked, and I saw Jared flinch as his uncle used his alpha status to bend him to his will.

"It's fine," I all but growled, realizing all at once that what happened here, right now, hinged on whether or not I would be obedient.

Clay and Jared would stand up for me, and they would get themselves in some deep shit doing it. I couldn't let them. I had enough on my shoulders as it was.

"I'll be here at five."

"What about the shop?" Jared asked, and I could see an uncharacteristic amount of anger in his gaze when I turned to look at him. He was furious.

It took some doing, but I managed to smooth the angered creases in my own forehead and force my shoulders to relax. "It's okay," I told him. "Her niece watches the shop sometimes when I'm sick. I'll call her. It'll be fine."

The last part was a lie.

My boss, Jacqueline, was a kind woman. She was caring and understanding, but she needed someone reliable. It was one of the reasons I even got the job to begin with. I'd volunteered there for three weeks for a school co-op project and had shown her just how reliable I could be. How hard-working.

I was never late.

I didn't leave until everything was finished.

She'd been thinking of extending her hours for a while, and she'd hired me.

Her exact words were, *I've never met a more mature student, and I've hosted a lot of co-ops from the high school. I need someone reliable to close up the shop in the evenings. The job is yours if you want it.*

Someone reliable.

Depending on how long Ryland decided to punish me. I wouldn't be that person she was looking for anymore.

My dreams of renting the apartment above the bookshop—of being self-sufficient when I turned eighteen—would be dashed.

All because of this motherfucker.

"It's settled then," Ryland said with a self-righteous grin. "I'll leave you to work out the details with Charity."

He turned away.

"Ry," Clay called, stopping him.

I cast a warning stare in Clay's direction, urging

him to let it go, but he wasn't looking at me. He was glaring at Ryland's back.

Every muscle in his bare arms taut as a bowstring, he waited with a vein sticking a good half an inch out of his temple until Ryland turned.

Ryland spun and raised a brow.

"*Clay*," I whispered harshly.

He seemed to consider something for a moment and then shook his head, sighing. "My sister has requested permission to visit this month. Will you allow it?"

Ryland's eyes flashed for the briefest moment. "Your sister?" he asked, brows narrowing.

"You've never met her," Clay grumbled. "She moved away with my mom before you came back and took over as alpha. She's with a small pack in Alaska now."

Ryland considered the request, a keen interest in his gaze. "I'll allow it," he said after a lengthy silence.

"I appreciate it," Clay managed through clenched teeth.

"But, Clayton," he added before Clay could leave. "You'll be responsible for her while she's here."

Clay nodded.

"Remember this kindness," Ryland called after a retreating Clay as though he'd just given him a wonderful gift. The kind that he expected to be thanked for. The kind that he expected to be repaid.

"Stay," Ryland said, turning to Jared. "The quarry

will survive without you for one night, nephew. Have a drink. Enjoy the bonfire."

Jared managed a nod, but the rage in his eyes was still unmistakable. I looped my arm through his and nudged Charity, pulling us away from our alpha. "Come on," I said, a sour taste coating my tongue. "Where's Seth? I don't know about you guys, but I'm going to need that drink."

6

"How much longer do you think he expects us to keep looking?" I asked Charity as she, Destiny, and I dressed away from the male members of the group so we could head back into camp for a quick bite before we all went home to bed.

Exhaustion clung to every inch of muscle and bone in my body. Over the last three days of nightly searches, we'd covered nearly a thousand miles of land. Not only did we not find the missing wolves, but there wasn't even a *trace* of them anywhere outside the borders of Ryland's territory.

Turned out those names on the password protected files on Ryland's computer were the names of the missing wolves. I had to admit, I was a little disappointed, but also a little relieved to know that. Ryland was obviously asking this 'X' person for help finding them. The images were likely last known locations or houses they were known to frequent or something like that.

"As long as it takes," Destiny replied as though it were obvious.

Charity rolled her eyes at the purple-haired girl with the perfect tits and sighed. "I don't think he'll make us look much longer. If we'd picked up a trail anywhere at all, then *maybe,* but they're just...gone. It's a waste of pack time and resources to keep looking. Especially when Ry would probably just wind up banishing them anyway."

"Pfft," Destiny chided. "Banish them?" she asked. "You really think he'd make us go to all this trouble if he just wanted to send them away himself?"

She asked this like it was the most obvious thing in the whole world.

"He's not going to banish if we find them, Charity. Don't act so naïve. He's going to want to make an example out of them. He'll execute them to send a message to the other new recruits that *no one* leaves the Forest Grove pack without his say so."

She's right, I realized. And I wasn't sure how I didn't realize it sooner.

If we found them, Ryland would want to make an example out of them like he was making an example out of me. Except he couldn't just kill me. Not now that I'd bent the knee.

Though I got the very distinct feeling that that is

exactly how he would prefer to handle me, even if Jared disagreed.

"I think you're wrong," Charity replied to Destiny, lifting her chin as she finished pulling on her shirt.

Destiny smirked. "You think you know him just because he let you into his bed, what? Once? He's still the alpha, Charity."

"Oh, fuck off, Destiny," Charity muttered.

Destiny shrugged and moved past Charity to head the rest of the way into camp.

I bumped Charity's shoulder as I passed, trying to get rid of the frown on her lips. I couldn't agree with her, in fact, I was with Destiny on this one, even if I found her to be an abrasive, doesn't-ever-sugar-coat-anything sort of person. "I'm starving," I told her. "Let's eat something before I pass out."

Between school and the nightly searches, I barely know how I managed to stay on my own two feet these days. Even Layla and Viv commented on my new zombie-chic look at school this morning, and that was saying something since we all seemed to share that look lately.

Purple half-moons beneath our eyes. Sallow cheeks and bent spines.

It got worse each day that brought us closer to the full moon. In less than forty-eight hours, it would be here. It felt like time had sped up and we were all being dragged along with it, hurtling toward it.

Clay was at the point where he was threatening to

do something about Ryland working me to the bone. I didn't know what that something was, but to avoid it, I'd been staying here with Charity for the last two nights.

Sleeping so close to where Ryland rested his head in the evenings brought me no comfort, but at least Clay and Jared didn't have to see me stumble into bed each night, half dead, and dirty from not having the energy to shower.

There were whispers at pack camp that Clay had been wanting to challenge Ryland for a while now. The only reason he wouldn't is because of Jared. How could he kill his best friend's uncle? And how would Jared feel if his uncle killed his best friend? It was a Catch-22. Ry took over uncontested from Clay's father after he passed because Clay had been unable to stomach doing anything but to sleep and drink for months. Now that Clay was a bit more stable, it was too late.

But for me...

I didn't want to find out what he would be willing to do.

He or Jared.

I'd seen the rage in Jared's eyes the night at the bonfire. If things kept going the way they were, I wondered if Jared would even try to stop Clay if he challenged Ryland openly.

I shook away the thought. It was barbaric. Savage to even think it.

But my wolf had no problem reminding me every

time we saw his scarred face and those creepy orange-tinted eyes: she wanted him dead. Even now, with this will exerted over us, she craved the feel of his windpipe in her jowls. The taste of his blood on her tongue. She still wanted to see him under her paws, obedient, submitted. Lifeless.

I shuddered.

"Hey," Charity said as we approached the fire ring, mostly embers now, a few stragglers huddled around it against the chill of the autumn night. "You okay?"

"Hmm?" I said, coming back up for air. "Oh. Yeah. Fine. Just tired."

"I feel that," Charity agreed and gave me a pat on the back. "I'll run and get us some food and then we can hit it. Want a drink?"

"Just water."

She nodded and then left. The guys, Seth and the mated couple, Trey and Todd came out from the tree line laughing, making their way through tents and cabins of sleeping wolves, probably waking them all up with their raucous laughter. As they passed by the cabin Forrest and Harrison shared, I grudgingly hoped they were loud enough to wake them.

They got back hours ago, having been given the better of the two available search shifts. *Fuckers.* I guess it paid to be a bootlicker in werewolf land.

Sure enough, a muffled shout of *shut the fuck up* filtered through a window as they passed, and they stifled the sound. I giggled.

The tents were a new addition. It was where the new pack members would sleep until more cabins could be built. There were already a few timber frames started around the perimeter. They should be finished before the first snow.

I dragged a few chairs toward the low embers in the pit, eager for some extra warmth. A lone chair was already there, filled with a guy I didn't yet know. He had reddish brown hair that glinted in the glow of the embers and brown eyes that looked near black.

"Hey," I said, trying to make awkward small talk while Seth and the others made their way over to us. "I don't think we've met. I'm—"

"I know who you are," he grumbled, and I noticed the half empty bottle of gin clutched loosely in his hand and the three empty beer bottles at his feet.

Okay then.

"And you are?" I asked, raising a brow.

"Sully."

"Which pack were you from?"

He took another swig of his gin and grimaced.

"Samson's," he said and then fell back into silence. This was the other problem with staying at pack camp.

I had my small cluster of friends and the rest saw me as something quite the opposite. Being here all the time, it was hard not to notice the way some of them stared. How they whispered. I could hardly blame them.

I was the reason their alphas were dead.

I was the reason their lives were uprooted and they were forced to move to Forest Grove.

But I didn't ask for any of this.

"Nice to meet you, too," I muttered to myself as the guys made it to the fire ring and took the seats I set out for them.

"Oh, don't be like that," Sully said, slurring the words a little. "I know it ain't your fault. Not really, anyway."

"Gee. Thanks."

"This guy bothering you?" Seth asked, flipping his mop of dark hair out of his face to stare unblinking at the drunk guy next to me.

I shook my head. "No, it's fine."

"Is it?" Sully asked. "Because I never asked to be part of that asshole's pack."

He jabbed a thumb toward Ryland's house only fifteen meters or so from where we were sitting. The windows were all dark, but that didn't mean Ryland was asleep. This guy should be careful what he said.

"Ry's not so bad once you get used to him," Seth said, and I could tell he was trying to put an end to this conversation.

"Tell that to Dean and Andreas."

"You don't know what you're talking about, friend."

"What?" I prodded, my interest piqued.

Sully pulled himself upright and pointed two fingers at Ryland's house with a sneer. "Bastard killed them."

"Okay," Seth said, rising. "Where's your tent, dude? I think it's time for you to hit the sack."

Sully laughed. A throaty, hollow sound that gave me chills.

He wiped at his watery eyes. "You really believe the bullshit yarn he's spinning?" Sully asked Seth. "That Dante's pack is to blame for them vanishing? That that *coward* has somehow grown the balls to stand up to anyone?"

Seth opened his mouth to rebut, but I interrupted him. "What is he talking about Seth?"

Seth pinched the bridge of his nose and sighed. "There are whispers that the other pack alpha that was at the Four Corner's that night is trying to pick off our numbers bit by bit."

I remembered the one alpha who ran away when the fighting broke out. The one who looked like he was in his forties. Short and stout. Both the wolves he'd come with had been collateral damage in the fight, and he'd left them to die. Some alpha he was.

"Is that what Ryland said?" I asked.

Seth gave a one-shoulder shrug. "I mean, it makes sense, doesn't it?"

No. I didn't say it, but I glanced at Sully, a question in my stare and the answer in his. I agreed with him. That coward wouldn't be picking off our numbers, but apparently Ryland had the whole pack believing it.

"Then why don't we take the fight to them if Ryland

is so sure?" I asked Seth in a whisper, eyeing the alpha's darkened cabin at his back. Being careful of my words.

Seth shrugged again. "No proof. Ry knows it's possible they've just run away, which is why we're looking for them."

"Right," Sully said with a sniffle, dragging the back of his hand over his running nose. "It has nothing to do with the fact that my boys had some dirt on your dirty alpha."

They were his friends then. A vise clamped around my heart. I wanted to ask him what sort of dirt that was, but I got the feeling he wasn't about to tell me even if I asked. Not in front of the others. Especially not now that Charity was approaching with a tray full of steaming dinner. It was common knowledge now that she had the hots for the alpha.

Sully may have thought he could get away with saying some shady shit in front of Seth and the boys, but if he had half a brain cell left in that skull, he would know saying that shit in front of her would not bode well for him.

I'd have to get him alone when he was *less* intoxicated if I planned to find out what it was he thought got his friends killed.

"I'm sorry," I told him instead of pressing further, eager to change the subject before Charity got back. "About your friends. Maybe we'll find them."

Sully shook his head and got unsteadily to his feet. He leaned to one side and nearly fell. Without thinking,

I jumped into action and caught him before he could trip backward into the firepit. His head kicked against mine, and he whispered breathily in my ear, his eyes aglow with reddish light. "We both know they ain't coming back."

Then he left, stumbling and nearly falling every few steps as he did, until he vanished from view.

"Allie?" Charity called, eyeing where the drunken shifter had vanished around a cabin at the edge of the camp. "You good?

"Yeah," I said, gulping down the feeling of dread as the lie slid from my tongue. "I'm good."

7

"Where's Quinn?" I asked Layla when she and Viv came to meet me out front of Viv's place. Jared hovered at my back, and Clay was already waiting for us all at pack camp.

Layla tucked a lock of black hair back behind her ear and shivered as she slung a messenger bag over her shoulder. "He should be here soon."

We were all going to camp together. The full moon would be high enough in the sky to trigger the shift within several hours. It was meant to be a clear, cold night, which apparently would make the shift cleaner. *Nothing worse than having your first shift on a cloudy night,* Jared had told me. It was easier to make the transition in full moonlight. A sky heavy with the burden of clouds slowed it to a crawl.

"Did you bring it?" Layla asked, unable to look me in the eye.

I dug the small bag from my pocket and handed it to her. "Are you sure you want to do it this way? We could explain—"

"No," she cut in. "This way will be easier. If he doesn't shift, then...he'll never have to know."

I nodded gravely and released the pill to her. Charity had gotten it for us from her alchemist friend who healed Quinn. It was an elixir of some kind. None of us had any idea what was inside, but if it did its job, it would knock Quinn out until morning. At least, it would keep him knocked out as long as he didn't shift. Nothing could be strong enough to make someone sleep through *that*.

I still hadn't brought myself to tell them about Grey, and what he planned to do to them if they didn't shift. I supposed, like Layla was trying to protect Quinn, I was also still trying to shield them from as much of it as I could. I had no idea if it was the right thing to do or not.

"What did you tell your parents?" I asked them.

"That we're going camping," Viv answered for them both. "They won't expect us back until Monday."

Which gave us four days. If they shifted, would it be enough time for them to get the control they would need to be around their families? I cringed. I didn't think so.

Especially not Layla with her seven younger brothers and sisters at home. There was no way she could be around them all with a testy wolf trying to jump out her throat, was there?

Fuck.

At least I would be there the entire time to help them if it came to that. I'd already left a voicemail for Jacqueline at the shop, explaining that I wouldn't be available until early next week at the soonest. Just another nail in the coffin for my job...

Jared, sensing my emotions, stepped into my side and wrapped an arm around me, rubbing my back. I melded into his touch, letting him push some of his strength and calm into me. I was going to need all I could get.

"There he is," Viv said after a few seconds of strained silence, and we watched Quinn pull his punch buggy up to the sidewalk and step out, bag slung casually over one shoulder while he yanked a big tent bag from his backseat.

"Hey!" he called, rushing over, bright with enthusiasm.

I saw what Layla meant now. How could she do anything to ruin that smile? She did her best when he was around during lunch hours at school to paste on a smile for his benefit, but the one she painted on now looked painfully forced.

She accepted his warm bear hug, digging her fingers into his shoulders. "Hey," she replied and dropped her head as he pulled away.

"So," Quinn said. "We're headed to some place off the map, that right?"

Jared nodded. "It's my uncle's camp," he explained and then seemed to think of something, adding, "He keeps wolves as pets. So, if you see any, don't freak out. They're mostly friendly, just keep your distance."

"No shit!" Quinn said, eyes bugging out of his face. "That is *dope*."

"If only," I muttered.

"What?" Quinn asked, turning a curious look in my direction. Then, as if seeing me for the first time, his eyes widen again. "Shit, Allie. You look terrible. Are you sick?"

I couldn't help rolling my eyes. *"I'm fine,"* I said through gritted teeth. Why was everyone so damned preoccupied with how I looked.

I look like shit. I get it.

"Whoa," Quinn said with a mock defensive stance, his hands raised. "I mean no offense. I just...I have some antacids in my bag if you need them. Just ask."

Rage dissipating, I sighed. "Let's go. Ryland's waiting."

"Who's Ryland?" Quinn asked, falling into step behind Jared and me to walk down the street to where we found an empty spot to park Jared's Jeep.

"He's pack—"

"My uncle," Jared cut in, giving me a pointed look.

Right. No shifter talk.

I supposed we just had to pray no one decided to up

and shift in the middle of the camp until Quinn was knocked out. Then we'd have no choice but to explain.

"Hop in," Jared said, taking both Layla and Viv's bags while I went to open the door for them. He and Quinn packed up the back while Layla and Vivian buckled themselves in with shaking fingers. I jumped in the front passenger seat, knowing I was too on edge to drive.

"Does it hurt?" Layla asked, keeping her voice hushed so Quinn couldn't overhear.

I winced.

"If we shift, does it hurt?"

I couldn't lie about that. I was sure she would already be able to see the answer written all over my face. Eyes burning, I nodded mutely, not trusting myself to say too much. "But not for very long."

It was true enough for me. My shift had only lasted seconds, but then, I'd only just been bitten and the moon was already shining. I had no idea what they were in for. I could have asked Charity, she was changed only a couple of years ago, but I didn't have the stomach to find out.

Now, I was regretting that decision. If I found her before we were all taken to the moon room, I would ask. Better to be prepared.

Vivian stared resolutely out the window, her gaze trained on the clear sky. On the iron bars partially blocking her view of the moon already visible perched high in the heavens.

I could already feel its pull. Not very strongly. Not yet. But from the moment I awoke this morning, there had been a noticeable shift in my wolf. She was restless. I wondered if they could feel anything *other* inside of them. Would they even know what it was? Would they notice?

From the way Vivian's jaw was set, her gaze unwavering and spine rigid as she stared at the moon, I thought maybe she could feel its pull, but I was terrified to ask her.

"All right," Jared said with forced cheer as he hopped into the driver's side of the Jeep and started the ignition.

I jammed the button for the sound system and Clay's playlist was picked up from my phone. "Start a Riot" by Banners began to play, and Jared slid his hand over the center console to twine his fingers with mine, squeezing. "You ready?" he asked me, and a sliver of ice lodged itself into my heart.

Clay asked me that just weeks ago in the cabin. Right before we left for the Four Corners. Before my whole world came crashing down around me for the second time.

My response was the same now as it was then, and I tasted the words like an omen of death on my tongue. "Ready as I'll ever be."

8

"How far in is it?" Quinn asked, brushing his dark hair away from his face as he stared dubiously at the tiny deer path snaking out from the inlet where we parked the Jeep on the side of a gravel road. It was as close as you could get to pack camp by car.

It would only take Jared and me about five minutes at a hard sprint in our wolf forms to get there from here, but at a human pace...

"It's about an hour hike," Jared said with an apologetic frown. "I'll carry the tent. Mine and Allie's things are already there."

"I call dibs on your bags," I said, trying to inject some cheer into my voice as I rushed around back to pull both Viv and Layla's bags out of the back of the Jeep.

"Allie, you don't have to—" Viv began, but I cut her

off with a shake of my head. Quinn was busy adjusting the steps on the tent bag to better suit Jared's tall, lanky frame, but I kept my voice down anyway.

I pulled on Layla's messenger bag first, and then shouldered Viv's backpack on after that. "I know I don't have to," I replied. "I want to. And honestly? I could probably carry both of you all the way to camp and barely break a sweat, so don't worry about it."

Viv raised a brow. "So, it's not all bad then, I guess. Super strength would be kind of cool."

It felt oddly like Viv was extending the proverbial olive branch, and I wanted to take it. They'd barely asked me any questions about what would happen if they *did* shift. They both seemed to only want to hold on to hope that they wouldn't. Now there wasn't enough time for me to explain all the...perks.

Thinking on it now, I realized there were a fair few.

Speed. Agility. Heightened senses. Strength. Incredible night vision. Fast healing. I could never get sick. I no longer felt like I had to power walk when I left the bookshop after dark in case there were any early evening drunks hanging around the local pub a few blocks down.

"No," I told Viv, feeling like my chest was being cleaved open and all the oxygen I'd been dying for, for *weeks* was rushing in. "It isn't all bad. Not even close."

A smile ghosted across Viv's lips for a second and it was enough to make this all just the tiniest bit less painful.

"What isn't all that bad?" Quinn asked, coming back over to the Jeep to haul his pack out from the back.

I cleared my throat. "The hike," I said. "It'll be over before you know it."

Quinn sidled up next to Layla, sliding his hand into hers as Jared shut the back of the Jeep and locked it up.

"Okay," Jared said, stuffing his keys into his pocket. "Allie and I will lead the way. Stay close. It's easy to get lost out here."

"Aye, aye," Quinn said with a little salute and fell into hushed conversation with Layla as they walked several meters behind us.

Viv rushed to catch up with me and Jared and leaned into my side to speak low so Quinn and Layla wouldn't overhear. "Can you guys tell me a bit more? You know, just in case."

Jared smirked.

I gave her a nod, peeking back to make sure Quinn and Layla were far enough away, but close enough that they wouldn't lose us. "I thought you'd never ask."

"I want it all," Vivian said, and I saw a flash of her usual fiery, take-no-shit-self coming through the dark shell she'd been keeping herself in for weeks. "The good and the bad."

I clenched my teeth. "Okay. All of it."

It took us a little under an hour to get to camp. We kept up a brisk pace as the sun began its rapid descent down the clear blue canvas of the sky. Vivian, still chewing on everything I'd told her, hardly noticed when the camp came into view. It wasn't until Charity, seeing us coming, shouted a greeting. Shouted it *extra* loud so that everyone would know there were mortals entering camp.

"Dude," Quinn said as he and Layla rushed to catch up, and I handed Layla and Viv back their bags. "This is fucking *epic*. Is it like a commune or something?"

Jared snorted. "Something like that."

Unconsciously, I took Jared's hand after he handed the tent back to Quinn and pointed out a spot at the southern edge of pack camp, away from where the new pack members had their tents. Closer to where Charity's cabin was. And the one Seth shared with a few other shifter bachelors. They more than likely wouldn't even get the chance to use the tent, but sending them to set it up would give us a few minutes to run and check on things and warn those who weren't already warned, not to go shifting in front of our mixed company.

"Charity!" Jared called. and she rushed over.

Quinn gave Charity a strange look, and I wondered if she seemed familiar to him. Layla and Viv seemed to recognize her straight away. Layla gave her a grateful, if a little droopy, smile. Viv stared warily.

"Would you mind helping them get set up over there while we go and check on a few things?"

She grinned. "Of course."

"Thanks," I said.

She winked.

"We'll meet you over there in a few and then give

you the tour," I explained before we let Charity walk my best friends to the outer rim of the camp. I watched them go, nervously eyeing the area around the spot where they stopped to make sure no one was lurking.

Jared gave my hand a little tug in the opposite direction. "They'll be fine," he said, leaning in to whisper against my cheek. He planted a soft kiss at my temple. "When we find Clay, we'll send him over there to keep an eye on them, too."

"Okay."

I let Jared tow me toward the fire ring and the company gathered there. Ryland was among them for once, lounging on one of the larger Adirondack chairs like a king on his throne. His eyes sparked with interest when he caught sight of us.

"Well," he said with enough enthusiasm to make my gut twist. What the fuck did he have to be excited about? "Where are they?"

Jared jutted his chin back the way we'd come. "They're setting up their tent on the Southern edge."

Ryland's brows furrowed, the one with the scar through it only lowering halfway. "Bring them over," he said with a wide grin and I caught the scent of whiskey on his breath. "We should give them a proper welcome."

I stiffened, my wolf pawing at the confines of my rib cage, eager to add another scar to the fractured mess of my alpha's face.

"We just wanted to check that everything was ready

before we brought them over," Jared told his uncle, a muscle in his jaw jumping as he clenched it.

Ryland cocked his head at his nephew. "Well, of course it is. Nothing but the finest accommodations for our potential new recruits."

I followed Ryland's gaze to the stone structure set next to and behind his house, several meters back, abutting the tree line. It was an ancient looking thing that blended in with the forest behind it. The gray stone was covered in moss. Trees and long grasses sprouted around it on all sides. I made Charity show it to me last night, needing to know what my friends were in for.

Unlike the cave where Devin kept me, or the small cellar moon room in Clay and Jared's basement, this was built specifically for its purpose. It housed enough space for up to eight wolves that needed chaining. A bare space with an icy floor and shackles spaced evenly as they ran along either side of the wall. With enough slack to be able to move a couple of feet once shifted, but not enough to reach any of the other wolves even if the space was filled.

Gratefully, there weren't any that needed the use of the room tonight save for us. The Forest Grove pack hadn't had a newly shifted wolf in nearly a year, and neither had the newly joined packs. As far as I knew, it would only be us, Jared and Clay—because they insisted —and Ryland inside the stone building. When the moon was high enough to trigger a shift, just before midnight in most cases, Ryland would turn a crank on the wall that would open three round holes in the ceiling, letting the moonlight inside to help quicken the transition.

The chains Clay had to clamp around my wrists and ankles at the cabin had been bad enough, pushing memories of Devin and the cave into the forefront of my mind. I had a feeling these chains would be far worse. And even more difficult to endure the sight of my best friends being chained along with me.

"Well, bring them over," Ryland pressed after a moment of tense silence between us. "I'd like to meet them—officially."

"There's one thing," I said, finding my voice. "I'm not sure if you know, but Quinn, the guy with them, he doesn't remember anything—"

Ryland waved off my concern before I could finish. "I've been made aware," he said with an annoyed roll of his ruddy orange eyes. "Don't worry. They're on orders not to shift until you're all safely tucked away in the moon chamber."

I nodded, unable to verbally thank him.

Jared tugged us away from Ryland as another shifter came up next to him, whispering something in his ear.

"Come on," Jared whispered to me. "Let's get a drink and then we'll go back and get them, okay?"

"Yeah. Sure," I replied numbly, letting him pull me

over to where Seth was sitting with Trey and Todd next to him on one side and Destiny on the other.

"...what an idiot." Destiny's haughty tone reached through my haze of chaotic thoughts and I perked up, curious who she was talking about. "I can't believe he just left. Like, did he really think Ryland wasn't going to go after him after we've been searching all this time for his buddies. Just watch. He'll probably lead us right to them in the search tonight."

Destiny paused as we came up, eyes widening as though she were surprised to see us. "Oh, hey," she said, the greeting mostly meant for Jared.

"Who are you talking about?" I asked, a sneaking feeling of dread clawing up my back. "Did someone else desert the pack."

"Tried to," Seth corrected me. "I'm sure we'll find him tonight. Too bad you won't be able to run with us. You probably got a good nose full of the fucker's scent at the fire the other night."

"Sully?" I asked, feeling the breath whoosh out of my lungs. "The guy with the red hair that was wasted?"

"Yeah, that one," Trey said with a pointed look. "The douche that almost fell in the fire. Would have too if you hadn't caught his ass."

I shook my head, incredulous. "When did he leave?"

Destiny shrugged. "We don't know. He was missing from his tent this morning. We thought maybe he might've just gone for a run, you know, blow off all that extra steam he's carrying around. But he still hasn't come back. Either that's a really long run, or he's gone."

"And no one has gone to look for him yet?" Jared asked, eyeing me curiously. I hadn't told him about Sully at the bonfire. We actually hadn't spoken much other than via text since the hot cocoa night at the quarry.

Destiny made a noncommittal sound and flipped her hair out of her face. "Ry's giving him until dark."

I couldn't believe it. Didn't.

Sully was angry and upset, but he wouldn't have left, would he? I mean, he did have some interesting theories about where his friends vanished to...maybe he thought it was best to get himself the hell out of Dodge before whatever he thought had happened to them happened to him, too.

For some reason though, I wasn't buying it.

"Does Ryland think Adam's pack is behind this one, too?" I asked, trying not to let it show in my tone how unlikely I thought that was.

"Could be," Todd said. "We won't know until we head out after him."

If there's a trail to find...

"Where are your friends?" Destiny asked, changing the subject. She glanced around Jared and me, as though she expected to see them appear out of thin air. "I haven't seen them yet."

"On the south side," Jared told her. "Pitching a tent."

"We should actually get back over there. I was going to send Clay over, but I haven't seen him yet."

Seth jabbed a thumb over his back. "Went that way a few minutes ago. Probably just taking a piss."

"Hey, mind if I come with you?" Destiny asked, directing the question at me. There was none of her usual bite to the question. No hot sarcasm or disdain.

"I guess," I said, studying her suddenly unsure expression. "Just...be nice."

She scoffed, her light grey eyes glinting with the last dregs of sunset. "I can be nice," she said as though offended, but we both knew it was a valid request. Destiny was one of those people who knew exactly what sort of person she was and wasn't afraid to own it.

I admired her that.

She reminded me a lot of Vivian in that way. And just like Vivian, I was sure Destiny would grow on me eventually. Once she got over whatever the hell it was about me she'd decided she didn't quite like.

"I'll believe that when I see it," I joked in return, breaking away from Jared to head back to where my friends were waiting.

9

Considering how fast the day seemed to pass from waking up to the end of the school day, to mowing down a quick dinner I didn't taste, and picking up Layla and Viv and bringing them here, it was strange how now it felt like time was moving through a thick pile of sludge.

My wolf had become antsy to a point where I knew if someone looked at me the wrong way, I may have growled at them. And I was just done with the waiting.

I needed to get this over with. My anxiety, which had been at a tolerable minimum for a while, was ramping back up to high gear. That awful fluttering behind my ribcage. Spots in my vision. An erratic pulse that skittered and spurted and felt like it may very well stop dead at any second. Oh yeah. It was coming if I didn't calm the fuck down. Soon I'd be shaking all over. Barfing my guts out. That would be a shitty way to have my third shift—in the middle of a full-blown panic attack.

"Allie," Clay growled against my ear. "Come here."

I shook my head, gripping my plastic cup of spirits tighter in my hands. If I weren't careful, I was going to wind up a full-blown alcoholic before I even turned eighteen.

Jared was chatting animatedly with Quinn while Layla looked into the bottom of her own cup, as though hoping it might hold a premonition of her future if she only looked hard enough into the amber liquid.

Vivian, on the other end of the spectrum, was smiling brightly as she and Destiny chatted on the other side of the fire. They both laughed, and Vivian blushed, casting her eyes away from Destiny. They landed briefly on me, and her smile grew tight until it vanished entirely. I frowned.

"Allie," Clay growled again, and I whirled on him, a snarl forming in the back of my throat.

"What?"

"Would you just come here. You're freaking out."

Breathing heavily, I heaved a sigh, forcing the edgy claws of my wolf to retract.

Clay patted his lap, and I cast him one last glare, but sat down, letting his radiating warmth soak into my thighs. I nearly moaned when he wrapped his arm around my waist, pulling me to him. Spice and engine grease filled my nose and his sense of numb calm washed over me like warm summer rain. It took barely a minute before the trembling in my fingertips stopped completely.

"There," he said, his fingers brushing the bare slit of skin at my waist, making me tremble for an entirely different reason. "Better?"

I grumbled to myself but gave him a nod. "Yeah."

"It'll be over soon," he said softly, and I let my gaze fall to his face. To those blue eyes. I let their steadiness calm me.

"Hey," Layla said, and I broke the stare, clearing my throat and pushing Clay's hand away from my waist to turn to her.

She wrung her hands in her long black sweater, sticking her fingers into the wide center pocket to draw something out. She held out the pill meant for Quinn to me and I snatched it quickly before anyone could see.

"What are you doing?"

She paled, her big doe eyes darting from me, to the ground, and back again. "I wanted to be the one to do it, but..." She paused, her throat thickening with tears. "I can't."

I lifted myself from Clay and pulled her hard against me, feeling her frailness beneath my arms as she shook. "I'll do it," I told her in a hush against her cheek. "It's okay. You don't have to."

"Thank you," she muttered into my shoulder and pulled away, sniffling as she tried to erase any evidence of her tears before Quinn could see. "Is there, like, a bathroom or something I can use. I should clean up before..."

She couldn't finish.

"Yeah," I told her, smacking Clay in the knee. "Clay will take you and I'll...I'll take care of Quinn, okay?"

Clay grumbled as he got to his feet, but didn't argue, dutifully taking Layla to Charity's cabin to use her composting toilet. Not even the lure of a real *flushing* toilet could convince me to use Ryland's bathroom ever again—much less allow my friends to go in there. I shivered, thumbing the smooth curve of the capsule beneath the plastic in my palm.

Fuck. I really didn't want to do this.

With my stomach roiling, I picked my way over to the keg and filled two red Solo cups with foamy beer. Then, checking to make sure Quin was good and distracted as he chatted with Seth and Kyle, I cracked open the capsule and let the fine powder fall atop the white foam. It took a minute to sink, and when it did, I swirled the plastic cup, making sure it was good and mixed.

We had to hope this would work fast. I'd been hoping Layla already had given it to him. It would be time soon. *Really* soon. I eyed the cup already in Quinn's hand and rolled my shoulders back, swallowing past the hard lump in my throat.

You can do this.

I went over to the small group of guys and stumbled

purposefully when I reached them, knocking my elbow into Quinn's wrist to send his drink sprawling to the dirt.

"Shit, Allie," he said with a laugh. "How wasted are you?"

Not even a little bit. "What? Me? Pfffft."

He laughed.

"Here," I said, passing him the cup from my left hand. "Have this one. I was grabbing it for you anyway."

Quinn narrowed his eyes at me for a second, and I just about shit myself, but then a creeping smile moved over his lips, and he took the cup. "Not trying to poison me, are you?"

I laughed, hoping he couldn't tell how I was on the verge of being ill.

"Don't worry," I said, trying to hide my discomfort. "It's the good kind."

I winked and held out my cup for a salute.

He rose to the bait, knocking his cup into mine and lifting it to his lips.

I took a long swallow of my beer, and Quinn followed suit, a furrow forming in his brow as he brought the cup away from his mouth. His eyes went wide. "What did you..." he began, but trailed off, a muscle in his cheek twitching.

"Shit!" Seth cursed as Quinn's eyes rolled back in his head and his body sagged to the ground. I tossed my beer in time to catch him before he could fall too hard, gritting my teeth.

"Fuck. You weren't kidding," Kyle said, his eyes wide with horror. "Why did you—"

"It's how Layla wanted it. He'll wake up if he shifts. If he doesn't…"

"…then he won't have to ever know that he was chained up in a moon room with a bunch of wolves," Seth finished for me.

I nodded.

"I mean. I get it, but that shit's savage," Kyle said, finishing off his drink and walking away.

I felt Seth watching me as I carried Quinn easily over to a camp chair and set him in it, making sure his head was tipped back so he could breathe unrestricted.

"That worked fast," Jared said, appearing behind me and just about earning himself a black eye.

"Whoa," he said as I whirled, my wolf about to crest the surface. "Didn't mean to freak you out."

I settled myself with a staggered breath and slumped into the camp chair next to my unconscious friend. A quick glance around the fire told me that in the last few seconds everyone had somehow found out exactly what I'd done. Suddenly, I was really glad Layla had asked me to do it for her.

I wouldn't have appreciated them looking at her how they were looking at me.

"I thought Layla was going to—"

"She couldn't do it," I snapped before I could get

myself back under control. Jared's jaw clenched, and he glanced up at the sky, taking in the ugly white face of the moon. Then he reached into his pocket and drew out his phone, the flare of the screen flashing over his face.

"I think it's time," he said, giving me one last look, studying the glow of my irises. "We should get you guys in there in case the shift is triggered early. It's been known to happen."

Judging by the tremble in my hands and the sudden ache in my muscles, I knew he was probably right.

"Clay went to take Layla to the bathroom," I told Jared. "Can you go bring them back? I'll grab Viv."

He nodded and leaned it to brush a kiss over my temple before he left. His eyes told me what he couldn't say, *everything will be all right.*

The lie made it easier to stand back up and do what I needed to.

"Viv," I said, butting into a conversation between her and Destiny. "It's time."

She visibly paled, her hand clenching around her plastic cup. "Already?'

I nodded.

Destiny reached over and curled a hand around Vivian's shoulder. "I'll go with you," she said.

"You don't have to,"

"I want to."

Viv finished her beer and tossed the plastic cup into a nearby metal bin, almost hitting Ryland as he reappeared from behind a cabin, buckling his belt. The alpha raised his eyes to the heavens and grinned, lowering them to meet both Viv's and mine with a challenging stare.

He swept an arm toward the stone moon chamber in the distance, peeking out behind the side of his house. "Shall we, ladies?"

10

The key turned in the lock on the old iron manacle, and I pulled against it, testing its strength. I looked up into Clay's blue eyes, and he set his warm hands atop my shoulders. "Just like last time," he said, never breaking eye contact. "You're safe here. No one is going to hurt you."

Mental images of the chains in the cave with Devin tried to crowd my thoughts, drag me down into the cloying pit of panic, but as long as I looked into Clay's eyes, I knew he was right. I was safe.

"It'll be over before you know it," Jared added from beside Clay, looking like he might be sick.

"I'm not worried about my shift," I said, my voice thick.

I cast a glance to where Destiny was finishing locking up Vivian across from me. Vivian kept her chin up. Her eyes hard and sharp as cut glass.

And to Layla, who was looking at her manacles in terror as silent tears streamed down her face.

My fault.

All of it was *my fault*.

Please don't shift.

Please don't let them shift.

And Quinn, lying still against the stone to my right. He snored quietly, his face a blank sheet of blissful ignorance. If he shifted, would he think it was some kind of nightmare?

He wouldn't be wrong. Except this nightmare wouldn't end by waking. It would go on and on for as long as he would live.

Please don't let them fucking shift.

I'd never been a religious person, but if there was ever a time for prayer, this was it. And I would pray to whatever god or gods would hear me.

Please.

"Hey," Clay barked, and I pulled my focus back to his face. "This is not your fault, okay. No matter what happens."

My throat burned.

"You hear me?"

"I hear you."

"We'll be right over there with Ry and Destiny," Jared added, pointing to the open archway of the entrance where Ryland waited with his hand poised on the old wooden crank handle that opened the panels in the ceiling.

The first gut twisting stab of the moon-triggered shift tore through my abdomen, and I struggled to stay on my feet, gaze darting between Layla, Viv, and Quinn to see if anything was happening to them.

They all seemed fine.

"Go," I ground out, the word exiting my lips with a feral, garbled hiss as my vocal cords began to shift.

"*Open it,*" Clay barked at Ryland and began removing his shirt. Jared did the same. Ryland was already stripped bare. Layla and Viv had asked if they should remove their clothes, too, when Ryland had entered buck-ass naked fifteen minutes ago.

He's shrugged and told them not if they didn't care to ruin everything they were wearing. Vivian had removed her jeans and converse shoes. Layla pulled her bra out through the sleeve of her sweater.

Priorities.

I was barefoot in my panties, with just a tank top clinging to my clammy skin. I wore the one with the mustard stain near the hem just for the occasion since I knew I was going to ruin it.

Clay and Jared finished stripping down to their boxers. Except I knew Clay didn't wear briefs normally. He must have dusted some off for the occasion. Pity. It might've been nice to have something to distract me as my insides began to boil and burn.

I clenched my teeth and let the weight of the moon shove me to my knees as the circular panels in the ceiling slid open.

"Allie?" Layla called tentatively, her bottom lip trembling. She was completely fine. Both she and Viv were still standing, watching me with mixed expressions of shock and dread.

"I'm okay," I managed through gritted teeth as I pressed both my fists to the cool stone beside my knees, feeling my spine warp. I bit back a scream, not wanting to frighten them even more. I would endure this shift without so much as a fucking grunt.

I couldn't help my body shaking. I couldn't help the sound of snapping and grinding bones, but I could stopper my voice at the very least.

Jared was the first to shift fully, with barely a hiss of pain as the moonlight cast its eerie white glow over all of us. Clay was next, with a low growl in his throat.

Then came Ryland. His body bending and breaking and sprouting fur so quickly that it seemed as though he went from man to wolf in the span of a single blink.

Destiny had shifted outside and loped in to take up a place next to Ryland, her thick tail wrapping coolly around her to brush her paws.

The four of them waited in their wolf forms, a wildness in their eyes that wasn't normally there. Even with their whole lives as practice, the moon-triggered shift still affected them with a spike of primal, animal instinct. They could just fight it better now. Control it.

One day, I would be able to, as well.

Clay and Jared waited for me to complete my shift.

Ryland's fiery orange stare affixed to my friends, as if willing them to follow.

Baring my teeth, I let go, allowing my wolf to finish what she started. I sent one last glance to Clay and Jared, gaze flicking briefly to Ryland, hoping they understood.

Because there was one other thing I was worried about tonight. Another horrible possibility to add to the list of others: that my wolf would challenge him. It was the first time we'd both been in close proximity in our wolf forms at the same time since the Four Corners. And the moon-triggered shift would give my wolf near full control.

Ryland's orange gaze moved to me as my shift completed, a small sound escaping my half-canine lips at the final stab of anguish.

My canine body shuddered, immediately moving to pull against the chains, to thrash in the manacles. My wolf snapped at Ryland, growling.

Enough.

The alpha's command punched into my chest and I whimpered, still thrashing, but unable to look him in the eye anymore as the weight of his will crushed down on my spine. Pressed hard on my windpipe.

Allie, it's all right, Jared's voice echoed in my skull, sounding foreign and distant. I could understand him, but I wasn't the one in control. Though the sound of his voice seemed to soothe my wolf enough to stop pulling too ferociously on the manacles. If she pulled and twisted much more, she was going to break our ankles.

Look, Clay's brusque voice brushed over my skull and my wolf followed his wolf's gaze to where Layla and Viv and Quinn were all still completely, *perfectly* human.

Even feral as she was with the urge to be free, my wolf settled, seeming to recognize them. To recognize that this was *good*. She whined happily, pulling on her chains with the urge to go to them.

They're okay.

They're not shifting.

The part that was still me wanted to shout in triumph. Though there was a small part, a part I promptly told to shut the fuck up, that ached with sadness. Because that part knew that this meant goodbye.

I would never put them in harm's way again. I would never risk this or something worse happening to them.

I just lost my best friends.

But at least they would get to live long, *normal* lives and—

Layla's shriek snapped like a bolt of lightning through the tepid air, piercing me straight through.

"La La!" Vivian screamed, trying to reach Layla as she crumpled to the stone floor, curling in on herself. Vivian's chains snapped tight, and she pulled on them. "Layla!"

But Layla was beyond hearing her. My wolf and I watched, mute, stupefied, and powerless as Layla's wrists snapped backward and she screamed. As her body contorted and she flipped onto her back, her eyes wide and glowing as she stared up at the spiteful moon.

Each of her screams sliced us so deeply, injured us so irrevocably, that I wondered if we'd ever recover.

That was when Vivian began panting and her back hunched, arms wrapped like bars around her stomach. She vomited onto the floor and staggered into the wall. Moonlight glinted on her elongated canines as she turned her bright eyes to the moon.

They're shifting, Ryland spoke in my mind, and I knew he was right. I knew it as my friends broke and reformed, their screams echoing all around me. I wanted to close my eyes. Plug my ears.

I didn't want to watch, but I did. I watched every pain-filled second. I took in every crunch of bone. Every tear. Every bloodcurdling pop of their joints. I didn't look away.

Wouldn't.

I did this.

Layla completed the shift first, scrambling to figure out how to stand on four legs instead of two. Her wolf lifted its black head to reveal a white starburst of fur over her forehead, spreading up behind her right ear. The white socks to match. When she felt my eyes on her, she snapped in my direction, then yelped when her manacles bit in, keeping her from lunging.

Vivian's agonized moan turned abruptly to a growl, and I turned my watery gaze to her, finding her wolf where she'd stood a moment before. She, too, snapped at me, her jowls frothing.

Her wolf was the color of wet sand, with rungs in the shape of a fish's gills around her shoulder blades that shone a pale gold in the moonlight. She snarled and yanked at her chains. Unlike Layla, she found her footing straight away and kicked out her legs and clamped her foamy mouth around the iron manacles, trying to get herself free.

Layla whined low in her throat, and I found her staring at Quinn where he lay, still virtually motionless against the wall. He'd have woken by now if he were going to shift, wouldn't he?

My chest ached as I watched Layla try to get nearer to him. Even in her wolf form, she seemed to know what it meant that she shifted and he didn't.

She'd just lost him forever.

With a quick jerk, Layla's wolf turned its burning eyes on me, her teeth bared and muscles shaking beneath her coat. She snapped in my direction, giving a forceful yank on her chains. The hatred in her gaze cut me deeply, scouring out my insides and burning down my throat.

Vivian, picking up on Layla's distress, abandoned chewing on her iron manacle. When her gaze fell upon me, she lifted her head and howled long and loud into the night before she began to pull on her own binds. Trying to lunge at me.

Their wolves wanted to hurt me, I realized.

They were trying to attack.

Layla's sharp claws scratched at the stone floor, leaving jagged white streaks where they managed to form divots in the rock. Vivian battered at her bonds, thrashing and pulling, yelping when the force of her lunges nearly snapped her bones around the manacles.

A cracking sound stole my attention from them for a second and I found a jagged line in the stone around where the chain of Vivian's manacles was bolted deep in the rock wall. Rock dust floated down from it. If she kept pulling, she would get free.

I viewed it all numbly. My friends, their clothes scattered like discarded rags on the ground. Snarling and growling and snapping...*at me*. Their binds beginning to loosen.

Quinn, unconscious and alone on the cold floor.

Jared and Clay, watching with bowed heads and sorrowful eyes.

Ryland sitting regally with a twinkle in his eye.

And Destiny...staring unblinking at Vivian, a whine in her throat.

I could feel my best friends' rage like a fire in my blood and I cowered away from it. It was too much. It hurt *too much*. My sides squeezed painfully, and I realized that awful keening sound was coming from my own lips. My canine eyes were watering, burning.

It's okay Allie, I heard Jared whisper soothingly in my mind.

They don't know what they're doing, Clay's voice joined his brother wolf's.

I shook my head over and over, wishing I could seal my eyes against what I was being forced to witness. To endure.

Their pain was my pain.

And I had a feeling they knew *exactly* what they were doing. This was all my fault. They should be angry. They should hate me.

They should have the right to tear me apart.

With each thought, I retreated further into myself. Deeper into that dark part of my mind where my wolf tucked me away when I gave her the reins. She already had control, but what little I may have been keeping for myself, I gave over. I couldn't do this.

I couldn't be here.

My wolf, fueled by pure animal instinct, gratefully filled all the gaps, helping to shove me back to my dark place. To the safe place where I could survive this storm.

The horrid sounds I'd been making faltered and then stopped. My body rose and instead of a cry of anguish, my chest vibrated with a furious growl.

Allie? Jared questioned, but we were beyond listening, even to our mate.

Letting my wolf take over and shoving myself in the backseat had been unconscious, but even now, from the darkest corner of my mind, I knew what she was doing.

I could feel it ballooning inside of us. That strength. That need to exert our dominance.

Wait, I whispered within, trying to stop my wolf.

But she wouldn't hear me.

Her intent, our instinctual intent, wouldn't allow our friends to harm us. We had things to do yet.

With our front paws pressed hard against unyielding stone, we lifted ourselves up, our shoulders back.

Bow, we snarled, fixing both newborn wolves with withering stares. In the recesses of my mind, I was shouting. Screaming. I didn't want to do this. Not to them. But I knew there was no other choice, so I screamed and shouted to no end. I'd tucked myself too far in and there was no stopping this from happening.

Layla was the first to buckle under the pressure of my stare, her eyes widening as her snarls gave way to tiny yelps.

Vivian was next, fighting it the whole way, steaming saliva dripping from her jowls as her head lowered. As her shoulders shook under the crushing weight of my will.

A primal, snapping growl left my lips, rebounding back to me in the echo of the chamber.

Bow!

Still shaking with the effort of fighting it, Vivian's body finally joined Layla's pressed flat against the stone. Their sounds of rage and pain muted, as though they too were muffled under the weight of my dominance.

But a new contender raced to fill the silence, and I turned my gaze in the direction of the frenzied snarl to find bright orange eyes locked on the bowing wolves.

He snapped at them, moving into a crouch with his hackles raised.

My insides twisted sharply as he lunged, putting himself in front of Vivian. He snapped at her face, and I went full dark.

Lights out.

Red.

Everything is red.

Something snapped.

A cry of hurt and there was something in my mouth like old earth and new pennies.

Pain blasted into my side and a sharp knock to my skull replaced the hazy red with shooting stars. Pops of color. My vision returned in spurts and flashes.

Ryland, Clay bellowed.

Don't fucking move.

The command was for more than just me, I realized, and even though I was lying on my side, still trying to clear the stars from my eyes, I found I still could. My paws twitched and I pulled myself back to all fours, keeping my right leg lifted. Something in it didn't feel right. Displaced.

That's when I noticed the manacles around my

ankles and wrists. The chains that'd been anchored in the wall lay broken at my feet. Still circling my limbs but attached to nothing. I peered up to inspect the spot where I'd been chained, finding four gouges in the rock where the chains had been rooted.

Destiny stood there now, her wolf breathing heavily as it locked eyes with Vivian. Vivian whined low in her throat, and I felt something shift in the air.

Destiny cleared the gap between them, nipping at Vivian's paws. Her tail began to swish over the stone, and she twisted playfully in her chains, nipping back at Destiny.

They...bonded a faraway voice whispered through my skull.

Then another stole the attention, and I was jarred back to the present.

You dare defy me?

The words were a twisted sneer in my thoughts, and I found Ryland standing over me, looking down into my eyes with such wild anger that it was a wonder he hadn't killed me already.

I'm sure that the wound I saw glistening with crimson in his shoulder is from my teeth. I can still taste him on my tongue.

You dare attack me?

His growl sent tremors racing over my skin, and I could feel his will—the will of my alpha—pressing down on me. I knew it was meant to make me bow. I *should* bow. But I couldn't.

He was going to hurt them.

My alpha didn't like to see them bow to anyone but him.

If I hadn't stopped him, would he have killed them?

Jared caught my eye with a little angered groan, and I twisted to see both him and Clay forced into low crouches and remembered they were compelled by their alpha not to move.

Their steady gazes begged me to follow suit.

Please, Clay's voice floated through my thoughts and something in that single word—in his broken plea—got through to me. I came roaring back to the surface, taking some control back from my wolf.

She wouldn't bow. But I could make her.

What other choice was there? Fight him here and now? Injured with stars still dancing through my eyes? Fight him and lose. Fight him and die.

Then what would happen to Layla and Vivian?

Who would protect them?

A low hiss skirted past our lips as I sunk into a crouch and lowered my head.

I should end you, Ryland's words rattled in my skull.

It was the moon-triggered shift, Jared's frenzied voice joined the conversation.

She wasn't in control, Clay offered. *She wasn't in control, and you know it.*

Except, that wasn't the problem, was it?

I defied my alpha. I *attacked* him. Was that not an outright challenge?

Should I even have been able to do that?

I didn't fucking think so.

But I was incredibly glad that I could. What would have become of Layla and Vivian if I hadn't done what I did?

I didn't regret it. I wasn't sorry.

But he needed to think I was.

They're right, I managed, pushing the thought toward Ryland, imploring him to hear me. *I should never have...I lost control.*

Ryland snapped at me and it took every last ounce of my self-control to keep my wolf from snapping right back at him. To keep her from tearing his ugly face clean off his skull.

Somewhere at my back, Layla whined softly. The happy sounds Vivian and Destiny were making a moment before vanished.

It wasn't hard to see why. Ryland had begun to pace. His muscled, lithe body flexed. His hackles up. His teeth bared.

Uncle Ry, please—

Shut up.

He growled at Jared, who to his credit, didn't so much as flinch.

Clay growled softly, his blue gaze never leaving me. His hard stare warned me not to react without the need for words. This would end badly if I did and we both knew it.

Jared may have been hopeful that his uncle would

be merciful. Would forgive. But Clay knew better.

So did I.

In a camp full of wolves who were all sworn to their alpha, if I made one more move against him, I'd never make it out of here alive. Hell, I may not already.

Ryland whirled on me in the blink of an eye. I barely had time to see him, much less react before his jaw clamped around my front leg. The bone snapped and pain unlike anything I'd ever felt screamed in every nerve ending in my body. Horrid, pitiful sounds scratched up my throat. The cadence of my voice changing as the shock of the pain jarred my wolf back enough that I was able to reemerge. The animal sounds turned to human gasps and sobs as I clutched my splintered limb to my chest.

Blood dribbled down my forearm where a knife-point of white bone protruded from my skin just below my elbow.

I gagged at the sight of it, my stomach turning and vision awash with watery stars again.

The cloying smells of pepper, firesmoke, and whiskey assaulted my senses as Ryland leaned in, naked and steaming in the cold. His human hand curled around my chin, gripping hard enough that I knew there would already be bruises beneath his fingertips.

"That was a *warning*," he spat. "You won't get another."

He shoved my head to the side, and I cried out as my body fell over, crushing my broken limb.

"*Get her out of my sight,*" Ryland hissed.

Human hands lifted me. A string of curses tumbled from familiar lips. Clay's voice whistled past my ears. "I'll fucking kill him."

"What was that?" Ryland demanded.

"I'm not leaving them," I managed through gritted teeth, blurting the words quickly before Clay could have a chance to repeat himself and get us all killed. "I won't leave my friends."

Ryland's eyes sparked back to an orange glow and his upper lip curled back. "What did you just say—"

"I'll stay," Destiny's voice rose above all other sounds and I craned my neck to see her standing next to a still canine Vivian, her right hand plunged into the thick fur on Viv's neck as my friend leaned into her human mate.

"What's going on?"

Charity, in a long t-shirt, appeared in the doorway, taking in the blood-soaked stones and my broken limb. The chains and manacles still attached to my wrists and ankles but no longer anchored to the wall.

The jagged bite mark still seeping blood in Ryland's shoulder.

"Charity can stay in your stead," Destiny offered, lifting her chin. She didn't trust Ryland right now, either, I realized. The way she was clutching my best friend to her told me she would die before she saw anything happen to her, too.

Ryland looked like he was about to disagree, staring

at Destiny and her new mate in disgust, but Charity spoke first.

"I will not move until you return," she told him, stepping the rest of the way inside and bowing her head to her alpha.

Mollified by her obedience, Ryland snapped, "See to it that you don't," and shifted back into his wolf form, casting one last scathing glare in my direction before loping out of the moon chamber and away into the night.

11

"We have to set it," Clay said in a hard monotone, his expression uncommonly drawn. Stiff as stone. "If we don't do it quickly, we'll have to rebreak it and set it again."

I grit my teeth, still clutching my bloodied and broken arm to my bare chest. I shook my head. "I-It's not a clean break," I managed, trying to sound strong and not like the pain was completely unbearable, because it was.

There really was no point in trying though. They were my mates and they were sharing the same airspace. I was willing to bet they could feel my pain as though it were their own.

I took stock again just in case I was wrong. I wasn't. After nine broken bones through my adolescent years, I could tell the difference. This pain was *definitely* not from a clean break.

"Are you sure?" Clay asked.

I nodded.

Jared was pacing back and forth, his chest rising and falling rapidly as he worked his jaw, a vein twitching in his forehead. "We'll take her to Stella. She'll be able to heal her faster and set the bone properly."

Jared spoke in a hiss, his eyes never landing on any one thing as he continued to move. I could feel his rage like a fire in my blood, trying to spark the gasoline still in my veins.

"By the time we get there, it'll already be half healed," Clay growled back at him.

"Stella will be able to numb the pain, too. Better than re-breaking it here."

"I won't leave them," I stated plainly. "I won't leave my friends."

Still in their wolf forms, both of them emitted pitchy whining sounds that were like nails on the chalkboard of my heart. I needed to be here when they shifted back. I couldn't leave.

"Besides, I seriously doubt Ry's going to let me go on a fucking field trip right n—"

"I should fucking challenge the bastard. I should do it right now while he's injured," Clay said and the lack of emotion in his tone scared me. This was beyond red-faced, spitting rage. He was pale with it. Sick. His blue eyes glowing and sharp like cut glass.

Murder.

There was murder in his eyes.

Scarier still was how Jared didn't say a word against Clay's intentions. He only continued to pace, his eyes darkening. Would he stop Clay if Clay made good on what he was saying right now?

"Calm down," Charity hissed at Clay, and I had to assume she either didn't see the murder in Clay's stare, or that she truly wasn't afraid of it.

I wasn't sure which.

"I know you're upset but—"

"*Charity*," Clay warned, and she shut up, grumbling something to herself under her breath.

"It isn't up to my uncle," Jared said, finally stopping the conversation. He crouched down to my eye level, and I struggled to keep my gaze on his face and not the coiled masterpiece of his body. His gaze darted to Clay. "Go. Take her to the healer. I'll stay with Layla and Viv. Nothing will happen to them while I'm here."

His eyes found mine again and he brushed a tear away from my cheek. "I promise."

I opened my mouth to protest, but Destiny spoke first. "I'll stay, too. Ry's pissed, but I don't think he'll do anything to hurt your friends."

"If he does?" I challenged her. She was one of Ryland's most loyal followers. Would she really stand up to him?

"*He won't*," Charity interjected, clearly not happy with where this conversation was going.

Destiny's gaze hardened, and she let it fall back to

Vivian, who lay panting in her arms. Completely ignoring Charity, she said fiercely, "I won't let him."

"Look," Charity piped up. "I told Ry I wouldn't leave until he returned. I said nothing about keeping any of you here for him. Jared's right, Allie. You should go to the healer. Your friends are going to be *fine*."

"I—"

A yelp came from my lips as Clay's thick arms curled around the back of my knees and barred across my back, lifting me to his warm, bare chest. He moved so smoothly that it barely jostled my broken arm, but even the slight movement sent stars blazing over my vision and set my stomach to roiling.

"Sorry, baby," he told me with a frown. "I'm taking you whether you like it or not."

I bit back a biting reply and instead, focused my gaze on Jared, needing him to understand what would happen if I came back to find *anything* had happened to them.

He met my gaze with a furious one of his own and gave one sharp nod of understanding without the need for words from either of us.

If Ryland hurt them, I was going to kill him.

He leaned in and pressed a hard kiss to my forehead. "I'm sorry," he whispered in a breath against my hair, his voice cracking.

"I won't be able to cover our tracks," Clay grumbled, his chest vibrating against my ribcage. "Everyone's probably finished their shift and back at the fire by now, but if they come looking—"

"I'll get Seth and the guys over here," Charity offered. "Tell them what's going on. They'll stall. We'll give you guys as much of a head start as we can. Just get back here quickly. It'll be better for everyone if you come back on your own versus if Ry sends someone to bring you in."

"Thank you," I told Charity, really meaning it. I knew how hard it was for her to go against what she knew Ryland would want. "For everything."

She was always sticking her neck out for anyone who needed it. One of these times, I was afraid she wouldn't be able to avoid the ax.

Clay stepped back into his pants with Charity's help and didn't waste any time leaving. He grunted as Charity removed her t-shirt and draped it over me just before we left, rushing away a second later, taking us deep into the dark forest. I was grateful for the thin bit of fabric. It blocked enough of the frigid midnight air to keep my teeth from chattering.

Like me, Charity still wasn't completely used to the whole being naked all the time thing, but she was definitely more used to it than I was. Besides, she planned to stay in wolf form while they awaited Ryland's return. Better hearing, and the ability to communicate with Seth and the guys made that choice an easy one.

I just hoped we could get to wherever we were going and back again before Ryland returned.

"I can walk," I offered once we got clear of hearing distance from camp. It was my arm that was broken, not my leg, after all.

Clay's jaw twitched.

"Really, it's okay. You don't—"

"I do," he all but barked, a little bit of that fiery anger I knew him for showing through his stony mask. His arms tightened around me, holding me harder against him. "Just…just let me take care of you," he added, pressing his lips into a hard line.

I didn't bother arguing a second time. His nearness and warmth were nearly enough to put me to sleep, even with the scattered battleground of my thoughts and the agony stabbing up my arm with each of his steps. The adrenaline was wearing thin, and a heaviness was replacing it. A sort of numbness that made it hard to hold on to any one thought.

That made my body sag and my eyelids droop.

Clay began to hum softly sometime later when I was nearing the edge of sleep. The rumble in his chest and the deep, rich, baritone of his voice sent me over the edge.

"CLAYTON?" The voice roused me from a fitful sleep, and I peeled back heavy eyelids only to have my eyeballs seared by a blight blue light flitting back and forth. I groaned, shifting.

A stifled hiss passed through my lips when I jostled my arm.

It didn't feel right.

Not in horrid pain any longer, it just ached dully. At a glance, I found that the bone was still protruding from my flesh, but that it'd stopped bleeding. And inside, I knew that it had somehow fused improperly, or had at least begun to. It felt pulled the wrong way and tight, stretching the muscle and sinew in a way that it shouldn't be.

"Who is that?"

"Allie," Clay replied, and I twisted my neck to find the woman who spoke.

She was maybe in her early thirties, with a shock of silvery white hair that fell in a messy bob to her shoulders. Her petite face was pinched as she took us in, a frown tugging down on the corners of her thin lips.

The blue light that'd burned my eyes, stilled above us. It was…a glowing orb. Like a little blue sun hovering in midair.

"Help her," Clay demanded.

The woman rolled her eyes and gestured to the house at her back. It was a modern looking thing. Not at all what I would've expected from a witch—*er*—alchemist. All black with a boxy shape, it hid like a shadow amid the trees on what looked to be a large property, concealed with high hedges all around it to hide it from view of people passing by on the street.

Though I doubted they were a necessity. I assumed, like Clay's cabin, this home would be warded against curious onlookers, too.

"A simple *please* goes a long way, you know," she said over her shoulder as she made her way to the door. Clay followed, muttering something I couldn't make out to himself.

We passed through the doorway and into a foyer that smelled of patchouli and something vaguely reminiscent of jasmine, but with an undertone of some scent I couldn't place.

"It's a bad break," Clay explained to the woman as he kicked the door shut behind him. "Can you do something for the pain? It'll need to be reset."

"This way," was the woman's only reply as she waved us through the foyer and down a narrow hallway. The warmth inside made me shudder after however long we'd been out in the cold. My skin burned from it, telling me it must've been a lot longer than I thought.

How long had I been asleep?

We followed her through a doorway and down a flight of stairs where the temperature dropped again, and through a dark crowded storage space into a room.

It was unlike anything I'd ever seen before.

"*Lucidus*," the woman said and that blue light that'd

been hovering over us outside reappeared, lighting the space just long enough for her to set about lighting some candles and flicking on a lamp.

One wall was entirely made up of tiny drawers. Each labeled by means of words scratched directly into the old dark wood. Ingredients, I realized, recognizing a few of the names.

A raised bed sat at the middle of the space and looked to be a recycled hospital gurney. The faux leather covered cushion torn in several places, foam spilling out.

"Sit her down," the woman said, bustling over to a tiny pedestal sink against the far wall to wash her hands.

Clay gingerly slid me onto the lumpy hospital bed and rolled his shoulders back, cracking his neck.

"What are you doing?" he demanded.

"Stella?" he urged when she didn't reply right away.

"You want my help or not, boy?"

Clay clamped his jaw shut.

It's okay, I mouthed to him when his gaze fell back on me. *Relax*.

"Are you going to give her some—"

"*Yes*," she said, snatching a bowl from the sideboard next to the sink and taking it over to the wall of drawers to begin filling it with various herbs and little sprinkles of what looked like confetti. "I'll give her something for the pain. It'll cost you, though. Charity already owes me for my help with the boy. She's lucky I have a soft spot for mortals. That boy was as good as dead by the time she got him here."

"Thank you," I blurted, finally finding my voice. "Thank you for helping him. He...he was my friend."

"Hmm," she replied. "Did he shift then? The boy?"

My chest squeezed.

"No," Clay answered for me. "But the other two who were bitten did."

"Good," she said, pouring a red liquid into the pewter bowl and beginning to grind everything together with a mortar. "I mean, about the boy. I was hoping my saving him wasn't for nothing."

Okay then.

I was getting the sense this lady didn't particularly like our kind.

As if reading my mind, Clay crossed his arms over his chest and pursed his lips. "Don't take offense," he told me, his tone dripping with disdain. "Stella doesn't like anybody. It's not just us."

Stella smirked. "True enough," she said with a sigh. "I keep to myself, if you know what I mean."

I did.

Probably better than most people.

That's exactly what I was trying to do before Jared and Clay took me in and my life turned into a proverbial shitstorm. Keep to myself. Mind my own business.

That didn't exactly work out for me though, did it?

Looked like it wasn't working out for her either. Judging by the fact that she had two shifters in her witchy cellar asking for help at god only knew what time.

Stella spoke some words I couldn't understand over the mixture in the bowl and strained it into a chipped teacup. She passed it to me, her dark eyes leveling on mine. "Tastes like sour pond water, but it works. Bottoms up."

My nose wrinkled as the tangy earthen smell of it reached me. I could already feel my gag reflex saying a huge *hell no* to drinking it, but I had a feeling I'd regret that choice. Re-breaking a partially healed bone didn't sound pleasant.

Clay gave me a tight, encouraging nod, and I downed the elixir, eager to get this whole ordeal over with and get back to camp. Get back to Layla and Viv and Jared.

Two big swallows got most of it down before I choked, only barely managing to keep it down. It made my tongue feel numb almost instantly, and a warm flush crept over the back of my neck. My chest slicked with cool, clammy sweat.

The floor tipped up as a wave of vertigo took me, and I gripped the edge of the gurney with my one usable hand to keep from falling. Clay was there in an instant, a hand holding onto my shoulder. His steadiness made the strange sensation subside, and I was able to blink back to myself, finding the room had righted itself.

Stella regarded me with a perplexed expression for a moment before stepping in to examine my arm. "That's an ugly one," she said with a little grimace, then sighed, gesturing to Clay. "Hold her steady. The potion should be good and soaked in by now."

She settled her gaze back on me as she gingerly began to draw out from arm from where I had it clutched to my chest. The shirt that'd been laid over me like a shawl fell away and I pulled it back onto my lap, needing at least to have part of myself covered in front of this stranger.

"It'll hurt a bit to be sure, but nothing you can't handle—"

A cry tore from my lungs as she tried to straighten my arm. This was no tiny amount of tolerable pain. Stars danced through my vision, and I had to go back to gripping the table.

"Give her more," Clay hissed at Stella. "You obviously didn't give her enough."

Stella paused, relaxing her hold on my arm. She'd managed to move it a whole six inches from my breast, but no further. She stared curiously into my watering eyes. "I already gave you double the regular dose."

My stomach twisted, and I bent over, grimacing as a tight cramp formed deep in my belly.

"What did you give her?" Clay roared, coming

around the gurney to take me by the shoulders. He shook me, trying to get me to sit up. To look at him.

But the pain in my abdomen was only getting worse, and the acid taste of bile in the back of my throat was the only warning I had before I leaned past Clay and vomited onto the floor.

The reddish liquid poured back out of me, the only thing my body expelled.

"Allie? Allie!"

I retched, my sides splitting as my body worked to get the last of it out in dry heaves. Shaking.

Finally, catching my breath, I was able to lean against Clay and slide the back of my hand over my lips. "*Ugh*," I groaned into his bicep. "I'm okay."

"What the fuck, Stella?"

The woman backed away, staring at me as though I were some sort of foreign creature. Her hands were raised in front of her like a shield against Clay.

"I've never seen someone reject that potion," she said in a whisper, her disbelief clear. It was obvious she hadn't done anything to purposely sicken me, even though I could feel Clay's sense of betrayal pressing into me.

I brushed my fingers over his arm and pushed myself to sitting with more difficulty than I liked. "Chill, crankypants," I told Clay, feeling strangely delirious for a moment while I got my balance back.

Stella hedged nearer, pointing at my arm. "May I?"

"Fuck no."

I glared at Clay then gave Stella a nod.

"I won't touch her," Stella said as she carefully put herself closer to me—and closer to Clay. Stepping around the puddle of regurgitated elixir on the floor.

Sufficiently subdued by her promise, Clay clenched his jaw and let her hover her hands above my busted limb.

Stella shut her eyes and a strange symbol, like a circle with a line through its middle materialized in the air beneath her palms. Crafted of pure light, it shimmered in the air for a moment before drifting down like magical glitter to rain onto my arm.

It felt…warm. But that was it.

"Should that have…done something?"

Stella snapped her attention back to me and withdrew her hands as though burned. Her mouth fell open. Her naturally olive-toned skin turned a chalky white. "I can't help you."

"What?" Clay demanded.

I deflated. *Well, fuck.*

"*What do you mean you can't help her?*"

In a daze, Stella stepped back and dropped her gaze, staring at her hands as though there may have been something wrong with them.

"Are you all right?" I asked her, much to Clay's annoyance. His upper lips curled.

"Hmm?" she looked back up, blinked. "Oh. I'm fine. I just—I'm not sure what it means."

"What *what* means?" Clay asked, still seething.

She bit her lower lip, giving me a sorrowful smile. "You seem to be unaffected by alchemist magic."

"Unaffected?"

"Your body rejected the potion. My healing sigil barely breached the outer surface of your skin. I could attempt casting another over you to test the theory, but I don't think…" she trailed off.

"Strange," she added after another moment. "I've never seen anything like this before."

Clay stared at the grotesquerie of my arm and bared his teeth. His eyes sparked with the blue flame of his wolf. "The fuck does it mean?"

"Like I said before," Stella said with the practiced patience a teacher may use to explain something to a kindergartener. "I can't help her. I'm sorry you came all this way."

Clay ran a clawed hand through his hair and groaned. "What the hell am I supposed to do then? Hmm?"

"We'll just have to reset the bone without your witchy magic shit." I held my arm out as best I could. "Let's do it now."

I didn't want to wait to get back to camp and have Layla, Viv, and Jared be party to my pain. I'd do my best to hold it inside for Clay's benefit. But he was the strongest of us. He could take it.

Clay looked like he might be sick, but he didn't argue.

"You're certain?" Stella asked with a raised eyebrow.

I pointed to a wooden spoon beside the sink. "Pass me that."

It was nearer to Clay, but it was Stella who retrieved it for me, pressing it into my palm. Clay just stood there, sweat beading over his brow. "You can wait outside," I offered him, sliding the rounded wooden handle of the long spoon in between my teeth.

Clay shook his head.

"Hold her still then." She ordered Clay, springing into action. She gathered out strips of cloth from a cupboard and dug around in a bin until she came up with a thin plank of wood about two inches wide. "I may not be able to heal you, but I've set a good number of bones in my ninety years. I'll get it set right and splinted. It's the best I can do. It should heal quickly nevertheless."

Did she say *ninety* years?

Clay moved back into position behind me and pulled me back on the gurney until my back was pressed against his chest. The skin to skin contact sent a shiver through me. Then he wrapped his arm around me, placing it like a bar across my chest, using his own body to brace mine from being able to move.

With his other hand he held on to my free arm.

Stella's slender fingers curved around my wrist and just above the break in my forearm.

She looked at me with a question in her eyes. *Are you ready?*

"Just do it," I said around the mouthful of wood, biting down and looking away.

"One," she said, and I bit back a whimper.

"Two."

Clay kissed the top of my head and held me tighter.

"Three."

Fuck.

12

With the bone set and my arm splinted and in a sling, the pain subsided quickly. Well, quickly enough anyway. The feeling of bone and muscle knitting themselves back together was almost just as bad, though.

Not painful exactly. Just cringeworthy.

Stella lent Clay her niece's bike. Clay wanted to get us back as quickly as possible. Shifting wasn't an option, and running wouldn't allow for my arm to heal properly.

I couldn't remember the last time I sat, perched atop the slim handlebars of a peddle bike. Probably not since I was eleven or twelve. Vivian was the one peddling back then.

Now, it was Clay. His frame dwarfing the bike as he stood up on the pedals to push us up an incline in the road, barely breaking a sweat. The little white basket and frilly ribbons hanging from the front of the handlebars bobbed with each pump of his thighs. The streamers glinted with silver and hot pink, trailing to either side.

His expression was unreadable in the first traces of sunrise.

The chilly air made the tips of my ears burn and clouds of air puffed from my lips. The backroads were entirely clear of traffic at this hour of the morning. Our only company for the ride were the sounds of our own breathing, the beginning of birdsong rising from the trees, and the chirp and croak of insects and other small creatures waking to start a new day.

So peaceful.

I could almost pretend my world wasn't shattered and burning.

I realized where we were a few minutes later, recognizing the slim bus stop sign that Maggie used to drop me off at weeks ago. My lips parted and whirled to face Clay.

"What are you doing?" I demanded. "Why are you taking me to the cabin?"

My pulse spiked as I turned to glare at him, shuffling on the handlebars and jostling my arm. I winced.

"There's not enough room in the Jeep for all of us," he grumbled in reply, not meeting my gaze. "I'll go pick everyone up—"

"Bullshit."

Clay's face darkened, and I lowered my leg enough

that if he kept going, he was going to see me knocked to the ground. He grunted and slowed, cursing as he came to a stop.

"Allie," he warned, his eyes glowing a dangerous blue as he tightened his grip on the handles.

I hopped off, grinding my teeth as I held my arm tight to my chest. "*Clay*," I mocked, using the same dangerous tone.

"I'm going back with you," I told him. "You really think I'm just going to wait at the cabin? Sit there and twiddle my thumbs while you go back there?"

Was he insane?

A muscle in Clay's temple twitched, and in the glow of the early morning, I saw how his tan flesh paled.

Something tugged in my chest, and it took me a minute to realize what it was.

Fear.

Clay's fear.

Shared with me through the mate bond. My brows furrowed.

"I don't want you near Ryland right now," Clay began, enunciating each word as though he needed me to understand their full implication.

I tried not to let the bubbling rage in my gut come out my mouth. I wasn't sure I'd ever felt fear from Clay before. Not like this. I couldn't ignore that. But he needed to understand something…

"I don't want you near Ryland right now."

His brows lowered.

He knew exactly what I meant.

Groaning, Clay threw a fist through his hair. "Why do you always have to be so goddamned difficult?"

"Why do *you* get to make my decisions for me? Hmm?"

Exasperated, Clay let his head fall back and sighed.

"If you think—"

"I can control myself," Clay said, completely cutting me off. He leveled his blue eyes on me, fixing me with a pointed stare. "I can walk in there, and I can take his bullshit, and I can get your friends back to the cabin."

I opened my mouth to disagree, but he stopped me with a look, continuing. "I can do that as long as you aren't there."

I cocked my head at him, confused.

"If Ry tries to punish you more than he already has…if he," Clay swallowed. "If he hurts you again, I won't be able to stop myself, or my wolf, from trying to rip his throat out. Jared's uncle or not, Allie, if he moved against you again and I haven't been commanded into stillness…" Clay trailed off, shaking his head.

"I need you to stay at the cabin. It's the safest place right now. Everyone's at camp. They'll all be waiting for us to get back."

"And do you think Ryland's going to be happy when you return without me?"

"I don't give a flying fuck," Clay bit out. "And I

doubt Jared will, either. If he has a problem with it, he can take it up with us."

I ground my teeth. I didn't like this. Not one bit. Even though I understood why Clay couldn't have me return to camp, I still didn't like the idea of him going back there. Especially due to the fact that he'd be returning without me. Ryland was going to be furious about that. And Clay would be on the receiving end of that wrath.

"Maybe I should just go back and get them alone," I muttered, knowing that the words were going to fall on deaf ears. "Jared and I can—"

"Fuck no."

I sagged and a ball formed in my throat. My chest ached and as much as I tried to hold it back, my eyes burned as they welled with angry, pain-filled tears.

This wasn't supposed to happen.

The crushing weight of everything that'd happened pressed down on me. I'd been numb to it before. It had been easy to focus on the agony of my physical pain, but as that began to wane, the reality of everything was setting in.

Layla and Vivian…

Oh god.

"Allie?"

A sob broke free from my chest, and I clutched at it, gasping at the sensation of a knife twisting somewhere unreachable beneath the bones of my ribcage.

How could this all be happening?

How had I *allowed* this to happen?

The bike fell to the side, crashing into the gravel along the side of the road. Clay's arms circled me gently, being careful of the sling. He tucked my cheek against his chest and wrapped himself protectively around me. His comfort only made me sob harder, my whole body shaking.

I didn't bother trying to keep it in anymore. I didn't bother holding back. I screamed into his chest, clutching at him with hard nails. Needing to feel something solid. Something steady.

I screamed until it hurt to scream anymore. Until my voice was hoarse and my lungs felt like they might give out if I made another sound. All the while, Clay held me there against him, not speaking. Not moving. Just being there.

When my breathing began to even out, he moved just enough to kiss the top of my head. Pressing his warm lips against my temple. "I'm so sorry," he said, his voice a gruff whisper. His body was completely rigid beneath me. I'd been so consumed with my own emotion that I hadn't felt his seeping through until now.

Guilt. Anger. Pain. Fear. Loathing.

I shook my head, smearing tears over his bare chest as I pulled away, wiping my nose. Suddenly eager to be alone with my thoughts, I gulped hard and heaved a sigh.

"I'm sorry," I managed, the words coming out jagged and watery.

Clay's warm hands cupped my cheeks, prodding me to meet his gaze. "Don't you dare apologize," he said, his eyes hard and beginning to glow around the edges. "Not to me. Not ever."

My chest ached again, but this time for an entirely different reason. I pressed my cheek into his palm and gave a little nod.

"I should go," he whispered after a moment more. "Let me get you home and then I promise you, I'll get your friends to you."

I needed him to promise me something else, too. One more thing before I could watch him leave. "I need you to promise me that you'll be with them when they come."

His lips pressed into a firm line, and he dropped his hands.

"I couldn't take it if anything happened to you."

I needed everyone else I loved to be okay. I couldn't take any more of this. The edge of my breaking point was near. That dark place in the back of my mind where the ugly thoughts lived had grown. I'd fought for years to keep that place at bay. To keep it contained.

It was too close to the surface for comfort now. The fluttering in my chest told me that if I wasn't careful, I'd soon be consumed by it. Unable to think. Unable to breathe. The panic would take over until dark spots crowded my vision and I fell into that dark place. Plummeted into the abyss.

And if I fell, this time, I wasn't sure if I would be able to rise again.

"Promise me," I demanded. "Or I'm just going to follow you."

Clay nodded once. A slow, measured movement.

I stood on tip toe and pressed my lips to his. Even a kiss as brief as this sent a wave of ecstasy rolling over my flesh. I broke the kiss and whispered, "Thank you."

Clay shook his head. "Don't thank me yet," he replied. "Thank me when I get all of us back here."

I nodded.

"Come on," he said and lifted the bike from the gravel ditch at the side of the road. "Let me get you home."

13

*T*he waiting was horrible.

I began to regret giving in and letting Clay go back to camp without me about ten seconds after he left. What if he couldn't help himself? What if Ryland said something to him and he snapped? What if he didn't come home?

And then there were the other worries. Was Jared held responsible for allowing Clay and me to leave without permission? Did his uncle punish him in my stead?

What about Layla and Vivian? Were they all right? Would they ever speak to me again?

And Charity...

Sticking her neck out for me *again*.

Even though my limbs were heavy with exhaustion, my mind raced to cover every brutal, terrifying possibility. I splashed cool water over my face. Over my arms and down my chest to keep the cloying grasp of panic at bay. I took deep breaths and tried to force myself to stop pacing. But that only made it worse it seemed, so I let myself wear a path into the hardwood between the living room and kitchen while I waited.

It was two hours before I began to hear the sounds of people approaching the cabin. Dawn had emerged in earnest now. No longer just a whisper of pink and purple on the bellies of clouds, the sun was a fat muted orange blob hanging in the sky just above the trees.

My bare feet squished into the dew-covered leaves and glass as I raced across the gravel drive and delved into the trees, following the deer path that led from the cabin to where we parked the Jeep at the tip of the trailhead.

I heard Jared's voice before I saw them. I couldn't make out what he was saying, but it was enough to allow me the first full breath since Clay left me alone to wait.

Clearing the remaining distance with my heart in my throat, I stifled the immediate urge to sob again when I found Jared, Clay, Viv, Layla, and Destiny emerge from the shadows.

Where was Quinn?

Jared's gaze was the first to find me, and he visibly relaxed when our eyes met.

"Viv? Layla."

They looked up, startled until they saw who it was.

Vivian's short blonde hair was clotted with dirt.

Layla's already pale complexion was downright scary. But they were all right. They were alive and back in their human forms.

It took every ounce of self-restraint I had not to rush over to them. Layla's gaze passed over me as though barely registering my existence. Vivian glanced at me only briefly before dipping her head to whisper something to Destiny.

Clay brought up the rear, his jaw flexing when no one answered me. There was an apology in his gaze that made my stomach turn.

"Quinn?" I pressed, a sudden, gripping terror seizing me.

Oh fuck.

Had Ryland done something to him?

It was Vivian who answered. "He's okay. We dropped him back at home after..." her brows knitted together. "After the vampire dude did some weird shit to make him forget everything."

A small sound escaped Layla's lips, and she shouldered past me without another word, heading for the cabin.

Her silence cut me worse than she could've done with any words.

Vivian dropped her gaze.

"Can we...can we talk?" I hedged, wringing my hands in the hem of one of Clay's baggy t-shirts I threw on when we got back. "I wanted to—"

"No," Vivian said. "I just want to go to sleep."

"But—"

"I said *no* Allie." She sighed, lifting a hand to pinch the bridge of her nose. "Just...not right now. Okay?"

The finality in her words stung.

"Let's get you to bed," Destiny whispered, rubbing her arm and leading her past me to follow Layla.

"Take my room," I called after them. "It's the last one on the right."

"Mine, too," Jared added, coming to stand next to me. A hand pressed against my back in an attempt to comfort me. "It's across from Allie's. We'll take the couch."

Yeah, right. As if I was going to be able to fucking sleep.

Clay's slow footfalls approached until he was on my other side. He brushed his knuckles against mine. I glanced up at him gratefully. He brought them back just like he promised he would.

But...

Then why didn't I feel any better?

"They just need time," Jared told me in a low voice and there was something in his tone that I'd never heard there before. I craned my neck to look up at him, finding his expression hard and unreadable.

I was almost afraid to ask, but I needed to know. "Is everything okay? Did Ryland..." I trailed off, not really sure what I had planned to ask.

Did he punish you? Get Charity into trouble? Did something else happen while we were gone?

Jared blinked as though coming out of a trance and gave my waist a little squeeze. "No. Nothing like that. He actually passed out about an hour after you left."

I lifted a brow, finding that hard to imagine. After how pissed off Ryland was, how could he just go and pass out? I rationed that he had been drinking pretty heavily earlier in the night and that maybe the drinks had just caught up with him, but it seemed a bit suspicious.

"You look exhausted," Jared said, worry in his eyes. "Let's go try to get some sleep. We'll figure out what comes next in the morning."

I didn't point out that it was already morning, instead letting my body wilt under the force of my exhaustion. I still didn't think I'd be able to sleep any time soon, but resting my eyes didn't sound like a terrible idea. They burned from lack of sleep and the remnants of salt from my tears.

"You coming?" Jared asked Clay when he began to tow me toward the cabin.

I peered back to glance at Clay. He stood unmoving amid the gently swaying naked branches. "No," he said plainly. "Someone should keep watch."

Jared stiffened, but didn't attempt to argue the point.

I was reminded of something Clay had told me once before, when I learned that their cabin was hidden from view by some form of magic. Magic that apparently didn't work on me, just like the alchemist's healing spell hadn't. I asked him why he stayed with me. Wasn't I safe if wolves from other packs couldn't find the cabin?

Some enemies hide in plain sight, disguised as people you trust.

"I can stay up with you," I offered, knowing sleep wasn't an option for me, either.

Clay solemnly shook his head. "No. Jared's right, Allie. You need to rest."

I didn't have the energy to argue with him either, it seemed, because I found myself nodding and submitting to the gentle pull on my waist from Jared.

"Check her arm," Clay called after us before we could completely vanish from view. "Make sure it's healing properly before you pass out."

"I will."

The cabin was already silent when we entered. The only evidence that my friends were inside were their muddy shoes at the door and the faintest scent of Layla's jasmine perfume clinging to the air.

"You can take Clay's bed if you want," Jared offered as he pulled a woolen blanket and a pillow from an ottoman I hadn't known doubled as storage.

Tempting as it was to lie enveloped in Clay's scent and snuggle into his pillow, I didn't think I could take being alone yet. The panic was still there, swimming beneath the surface, ready to boil over if prodded. The only way I was going to be able to lie still and give my body the rest it would need to be able to face tomorrow—or today?—was if I had at least one of my mates close by.

One day, I wouldn't need their strength to support me. But for now, it was the only thing holding me together.

I swallowed hard and shoved strands of dirty hair from my face. "I think the couch is big enough for both of us."

Jared smirked, but it didn't reach his eyes. "I think you're right."

He finished unfolding the blanket and fluffed up the pillow at one end of the sofa and sat down, beckoning me to join him.

"Let me see your arm."

His fingers reached up to untie the knot at the back of my neck, releasing the sling. The pain was no more than a dull, pulsing ache now. That terrible feeling of bone knitting back together had subsided nearly an hour ago, but still, I winced when he folded the cloth back to inspect the damage.

His eyes darkened at the dried blood still marring my arm as he brushed his fingers over where the break had been. "Does this hurt?" he asked, his voice a dangerous whisper.

I stole the cloth back and did my best to knot it again with my one available hand. "It's fine," I replied. "Seriously. I think it's almost healed."

I didn't like the way he was looking at it. At me. His cheekbones flared and his hands curled into fists as he drew them back. "I don't know what to do," he said so quietly I barely heard him.

"What do you mean?"

His Adam's apple bobbed in his throat, and his clenched fists relaxed. "Nothing."

"Jar—"

"Let's get some sleep."

He lay back, scooching as close to the inside of the couch as he could. He opened his arms and the invitation was too welcoming to ignore. I fell into his arms, let him tuck me tightly into his side, and lifted my injured arm so it could lie safely against this chest.

I breathed in his scent, nearly moaning at the comfort it brought. Cedar and birch with an undercurrent of musk. Like my own personal forest. The safe kind. Where there were no monsters lurking in the shadows and no storms could destroy my shelter. I relaxed into him, and even though I hadn't thought it possible, within minutes, his steady breaths lulled me into a deep and dreamless sleep.

14

*T*he sound of Layla's laughter carried through the cabin like a song. I cringed against the bright light of day, trying to peel my heavy eyelids back from my still-burning eyes. I was on my back on the couch, a low fire in the hearth ten feet away warming my cheek.

Where was Jared?

I must've actually fallen asleep.

The sound came again, Layla's melodic laughter, followed by Vivian's throaty chuckle. Confused and wondering if I was in fact still asleep, I lifted my aching body from the soft cushions and stood on unsteady feet, dark spots dancing in my vision for a second until I got my footing.

My throat was scratchy dry, and my arm and shoulder felt stiff from being held still in the sling for god knows how long. I eyes the kitchen clock, lips parting when I saw that it was somehow already after two in the afternoon.

No fucking way.

I heard Clay's deep timbre outside and followed it along with the mouthwatering smell of seared beef, baked goods, and the invigorating aroma of fresh coffee.

On the kitchen table rested a basket, sun-bleached wicker with a checkered cloth. I didn't have to look inside to find out what it contained. I could smell the burnt butter and brown sugar smell of Hazel's cookies from a mile away. Clearly, I'd somehow also managed to sleep through a visit from Grams.

Damnit.

I really wanted to talk to her. Maybe there was a chance she hadn't left yet.

My feet were still sleep drunk, and I nearly tripped out the screen door, catching myself on the railing of the front porch before I could go sprawling down the stairs and onto the dirt lawn.

"Whoa," Jared's voice rose above the others, and in an instant, he was there, hands steadying me with a firm grip on my elbows. "Looks like someone could use a coffee."

Layla laughed, and I pushed myself back to standing and turned to find her, gaping at what I found.

Clay stood on the furthest edge of the porch deck in front of the barbeque, flipping steaks amid licks of flames. He turned and gave me a tired smirk, waving a pair of tongs.

Vivian sat next to Destiny on the floor of the wood deck, paper plates in both their laps. The only remnants of their steak breakfast a little puddle of red juices on each. Viv's brown eyes were bright as she rested them on me. There was a flush in her cheeks.

Across from them, sitting cross-legged with a mug of coffee pressed between her palms, was Layla. Her black hair shone in the afternoon light with strands of blue and something close to violet. Her complexion was back to a less troubling shade of pale. But what had me entirely baffled was the wide grin on her face.

She set down her coffee and got up, coming over to me.

I couldn't breathe as she wrapped her arms around me, hugging me as tightly as she could without pressing too hard against the sling. Hot tears welled in my eyes.

She pulled away, staring at me curiously.

"What the fuck is going on?" I managed, my voice waterlogged as though there were a physical block in my throat.

I'm dreaming.

I must be dreaming.

Why are they smiling?

What the fuck is there to smile about?

"Are you okay?" Layla asked, one perfectly manicured eyebrow raised. "How's your arm?"

"...how's my arm?"

"You're right," Layla said, turning to Jared behind me. "I think she does need a coffee."

"Coming right up."

Layla grabbed my hand and dragged me to where her coffee waited on the deck. Pulled me down to sit next to her.

"Morning," Destiny said, and I glanced down to see her fingers knotted with Vivian's.

Vivian's usually steady gaze flitted to me and back down to her plate as Clay turned from the barbeque to drop another piping hot steak onto her plate. She held her plate out to me instead. "Here," she said with a sheepish grin. "You look like you need it more than I do."

I realized, a little belatedly, how all I had on right now was panties and Clay's massive t-shirt. It was a warm afternoon, so I hadn't really noticed. At least until Vivian's gaze fell on my scrawny legs. The bones of my knees looked strange in my new slimmer body. Clay had been right. I was losing weight. And it definitely didn't suit me.

I took the plate from Vivian, my gaze never leaving her. "Can...someone explain to me what I missed?"

Vivian cocked her head at me.

Were they really going to make me spell it out?

"Yesterday, you both wanted to rip my head off." I glanced between Layla and Viv. "Rightly so."

Viv pursed her lips.

"And now you're..."

How could I put this?

"Happy?" Layla offered and I was sure the shock in my expression was clear.

"Are you?" I asked her, hope and confusion beginning a whirlwind dance behind my breast.

Layla tipped her head this way and that. "Not *un*happy."

"But...*why?*"

I mean, I certainly wasn't complaining. I just didn't understand.

Jared came back out onto the deck and folded himself into a seat next to me, handing me a still-steaming mug of glorious coffee. I took a sip, not caring that it seared my tongue and burned a path all the way down my throat. I needed some fucking clarity, and if they weren't going to give it to me, maybe coffee would.

"We talked," Jared answered for Layla as though it were the simplest thing in the world.

I stared at him, pushing him with my gaze to fucking spit out the rest of the explanation.

His tousled dirty-blond hair fell into his eyes, and he reached up and pushed it back, strands of it catching the sunlight. "We did what we probably should've done for you when you first shifted."

"Which is?"

"Explain shit," Clay butt in.

Layla's cool fingers wrapped around my hand, drawing my attention back to her.

"I'm not sick," she said, her eyes welling and brand-new smile squirming at the corner of her mouth. "I don't have Huntington's. Not anymore."

If my eyes went any wider, they'd bug out of my fucking head.

"It's true," Jared added. "The transition eradicates illness. Most of the time, people who are terminally ill *won't* shift because of those illnesses. The toxin in our bite that triggers the change needs a healthy host. But..." he trailed off, shrugging. "That's not always the case."

"You're really not sick?"

Layla nodded, struggling to keep her tears at bay. Her chin quivered, and she squeezed my hand tighter.

It was my turn to smile. A laugh bubbled up from within me as I shoved my coffee back at Jared, hot black liquid sloshing everywhere so I could hug my friend properly.

"They already had their first voluntary shifts, too," Clay said as I pulled away from Layla after a minute spent shuddering in relief. "They did great."

What? Now they were just making me look bad. I didn't care though, I was grinning ear to ear. "So, does this mean...you don't want to rip my head off anymore?"

Viv barked a laugh and rolled her eyes at me. "We never wanted to rip your head off, Allie. Our wolves did, but Destiny explained that that was probably only because we somehow recognized you as being stronger. A threat."

"It's natural for wolves without an alpha to feel the need to challenge any other wolves they feel threatened by," Destiny confirmed. "Honestly, we should have expected it, but we've rarely had more than one wolf shifting in the chamber at a time before."

No one mentioned the fact that my best friends felt immediately threatened by *my* presence, but seemed to ignore Ryland's entirely. I grimaced, staring down at my hands. It was no wonder he'd snapped at them. He was probably enraged that they felt I was the bigger threat when the alpha who now had the largest pack in the western United States was practically standing right next to me.

It wasn't as if that were my fault though. And honestly, what did he expect? For me to sit idly by while he snapped at them? I thought he was going to *attack* them. I'm still not convinced he wouldn't have if I hadn't been blinded with rage and stopped him.

I shuddered, not wanting to think about that part. Nothing like that had ever happened to me before. I got angry, sure. But never to a point where I entirely lost control. Where one second, I was standing there, chained to a wall and the next I had the taste of blood on my tongue.

It terrified me.

I bowed my head, wondering what would happen now.

They had both completed the transition. They were alive and unharmed and somehow, miraculously, didn't want to see my head on a pike.

All good things. *Very* good things.

But they were still unclaimed wolves in Ryland's territory.

Perhaps sensing where my thoughts had wandered, Clay said, "Ryland already sent Charity over earlier this morning."

I snapped my head up, a vise around my heart.

"He gave us until the end of the weekend to decide if we want to join your pack," Vivian said, a knot between her brows. After a pause, she added, "Could he really make us leave?"

Jared gave her a sympathetic look and answered before I could. "He can and he will. I'm sorry."

"Doesn't matter anyway," Layla said with a shrug. "We already decided we'd join."

"What?"

I was about to lose my shit about the fact that he only gave them two fucking days to decide, but now they were really going to tell me they had *already* decided? In the span of one morning?

Vivian glanced apologetically at Destiny and then lifted her heavy gaze to rest on me. "This is our home," she said. "And I don't want to ruffle any feathers here, but honestly? I think the guy is a power-tripping douche canoe."

Destiny's jaw clenched.

Jared paled.

Nobody disagreed.

"Wait. I'm confused. So then why the hell would you want him as your alpha?"

Vivian looked at me like I was daft. "We saw what he did to you, Allie. He fucking *broke* your arm. Without flinching. We aren't going to leave you here with him. Not a fucking chance."

My heart swelled in my chest, and I had to bite down hard on my tongue to keep the sob trying to break free of my chest from getting out. "That's not your problem," I managed in a tight whisper. "Besides, I'm the one who attacked him—"

"Oh shut up," Vivian interrupted. "You want us to stay and you know it."

The playful lilt to her tone told me she was trying to make me feel better, and that only made me want to cry harder.

Layla leaned in to bump her shoulder against mine. "Face it," she said with a chuckle. "You're stuck with us."

I crumpled and Layla pulled me into her side. Vivian left Destiny to come crowd in opposite Layla, wrapping her arm around my shoulders. "This isn't your fault," she told me in a whisper against my filthy hair. "We're stuck in this shit together now."

Clay clapped his hands together a moment later,

breaking up the mushy embrace. "Who's game for another shift?"

The weekend went on like that until late Sunday evening. Layla and Viv must have shifted at least a half a dozen times, if not more. They were amazing. Taking it all *mostly* in stride. They knew that to be able to return home to their families they would need to have control, so they worked at it relentlessly.

They already had a plan to meet in the woods before dawn each morning to shift and go for a run before school every day. And each afternoon after school too when they could swing it. Layla was more worried about returning home than Vivian, though. Where Viv only had to endure her parents, Layla had seven brothers and sisters to deal with.

Seven younger brothers and sisters that she was often tasked with babysitting.

The guys and I offered our help whenever she needed it. Even Destiny threw her hat in. Apparently, she'd grown up in a family of six younger siblings before she'd moved away from home and was great with kids. I couldn't see it, but I had to admit I didn't know her all that well. Though I guess I would be getting to know her now whether I liked it or not.

You know, since she bonded to my best friend.

Layla's cell phone vibrated in her hand, and she tilted the screen to see who was calling, thumbing the side button to silence the call before tucking it into her pocket.

"Quinn?" I asked.

She dropped her head. Her non-answer was all the answer I needed.

Layla had been mostly avoiding his calls and texts since they dropped him off at home after the night of the full moon. "I should have had that vampire guy compel him to forget me. Or to break up with me or something."

"Don't say that," I started, but the glare she gave me at the words made me pause.

I sighed. "Sorry, La La. You're right."

She was doing for Quinn what I should have done for them the moment I turned: stayed the fuck away.

Within a few seconds, my own cell phone began vibrating in my pocket, and I grimaced as I drew it out, expecting an incoming call from Quinn looking for Layla. But it wasn't him. It was my uncle. *Again.*

I curled my fingers around the screen, gritting my teeth. We were nearly at pack camp now. It crouched just another half mile through the woods. It wasn't a good time for a lecture from Uncle Tim.

I let the call go to voicemail and watched the missed call notification join the others in a row down the screen.

Over the weekend I'd ignored four calls from Uncle Tim, with only a quick text fired off to explain it was a busy weekend and that I would call him back when I got the chance, so he didn't send out a search party. I'd also missed two calls from my boss. The voicemail icon held the number *3* in a red dot above it since Saturday morning, but I couldn't bring myself to check them.

Uncle Tim would only berate me for not calling him back.

And Jacqueline...I was terrified her voicemail would be the final nail in the coffin for my job. Since Ryland started demanding all my 'free' time I'd missed nearly *all* of my shifts. Jacqueline was a kind woman—understanding—but she would only put up with so much. She needed someone to do the job, and I wasn't doing it. Not anymore.

I'd check the voicemails later, I told myself. When I was alone in my room and could panic in peace. Jared and Clay had done enough comforting this weekend.

"Quinn?" Layla asked as Jared and Clay slowed up ahead for us to catch up and Vivian came bounding through the trees in her wolf form with Destiny snapping playfully at her tail. They nearly knocked into us, and I had to tug Layla out of the way so she wouldn't be bowled over.

Destiny gave a little apologetic *woof* and loped off with Vivian chasing her.

"No," I answered Layla. "Uncle Tim."

Her lips made a little 'o' shape, and she nodded. "Guess you must be getting excited for your birthday. Once you're eighteen you won't have to answer to them anymore, right?"

A hollow laugh passed through my lips. Not too long ago Layla and Viv thought I was still living with my Uncle and his wife out in Seattle. I'd almost forgotten they now knew the truth...about almost everything in fact.

Except how I'd become a shifter. Viv asked me just yesterday, but I'd dodged the question, not ready to tell them yet. No, actually that wasn't it. I didn't have a problem telling them, I just didn't think I could handle talking about it right now.

"Your birthday?" Jared asked, a crook in his brow as he slowed to a stop and cocked his head at me. He glanced between Layla and me. "When's her birthday?"

I opened my mouth to protest but Layla was quicker. "This coming Saturday."

"*Layla*," I hissed.

"What?" she asked innocently. "They didn't know?"

"What the hell, Allie?" Clay demanded. "Why didn't you tell us?"

"Because of exactly *this*," I said, gesturing widely at Jared and Clay. "I don't like to make it a big deal. It's just another day."

Clay's face pinched. "No. It isn't."

"Clay's right, Allie," Jared agreed, turning to Layla. "I'm glad you told us."

"No problem," Layla thrilled sweetly, and I groaned. "You'll thank me later," she stage whispered in my ear, giving Jared a little wink as she walked away, leaving me to the wolves.

"So—"

"Nope. Not important right now," I said, completely

cutting off Jared. I could see the gears turning behind his eyes. He was going to ask me what I wanted. Or maybe ask me what I wanted to do. This wasn't the time.

Clay raised a hand to rub the back of his head. "I hate to say it, man, but she's sort of right. Ry's waiting, and we have no fucking idea what we're about to walk into."

Jared lowered his gaze and stuffed his hands into the pockets of his jeans. "I spoke to him earlier," he told us, and I noticed Clay visibly stiffen. "He'll be chill."

"How do you know that?" I asked, cocking my head at Jared.

The fact of it was that Ryland had demanded I come with my friends tonight. I would've gone with them regardless, but the fact that he *ordered* it left a sour taste in my mouth. He wouldn't do that unless he had something planned, right?

We were all hopeful that he might just have some new orders for me or be expecting me to get back to work searching for the deserters with Charity. But something in my gut told me that wasn't it.

"How do you know?" Clay repeated my question to Jared when I didn't answer.

Beneath the thick layer of denim covering his pockets, I noticed how his hands shifted, balling into fists. I could feel his unease, but despite it, his expression remained placid. A bit pale maybe, but calm. Passive. He was playing something down.

"I just...know."

"What aren't you telling us?" I pressed, a sinking feeling in my gut. Or was it a sinking feeling in *his* gut and I was only getting the leftovers through the mate bond?

"Can we just drop this please?" he asked, not sounding the least bit himself. "Like you guys said, we need to focus on what's important. Let's just get Layla and Viv to camp, get them enlisted, and then get home."

Clay looked like he was about ready to rip Jared's head off in an attempt to find the answer to what he wasn't telling us. "Jar—"

"You'll tell us later?" I asked, trying to keep my tone level and calm. Neither emotions I was actually feeling.

Jared made a noncommittal sound and gave the ghost of a nod before stalking off after Layla who was now a good thirty meters ahead. I could only make out the shadow of her amid the skeletal trees in the distance.

"I don't like this," Clay grunted in a low timbre.

I craned my neck to glance up at him, finding his blue eyes aglow. My mouth was dry when I replied, "Me neither."

15

I found Charity and Seth among our regular group when we entered the camp. Ryland was nowhere to be seen yet, and I was grateful to have at least a few minutes before I'd need to face him. I got the feeling a simple apology wasn't going to fix anything between us. And truth be told, I wasn't sorry. Not at all, and I was willing to bet he'd be able to sense that if I tried to lie.

Clay stationed himself like a soldier at my side and didn't budge an inch while Jared went to speak with his uncle again before the ceremony could begin. Vivian and Layla, to their credit, didn't seem very nervous. They'd made their choice, and we'd explained to them exactly what would happen tonight, and after, once they became pack.

I envied them their ability to remain chill in the face of it all. Maybe they were just stronger than I was, or maybe it was that they had each other. Whatever the reason, I couldn't be more relieved that they weren't spiraling the way I had at the start. The way I'd been spiraling these past couple of weeks leading up to the full moon...

There was no excuse for that anymore, though. I couldn't fall apart. Not now that they were submitting themselves to Ryland's rule in order to join the Forest Grove Pack. They were joining in part because they wanted to make sure *I* was safe.

They didn't understand that it wasn't me I was worried about. I wouldn't voice it, not in front of Jared at least, but I knew deep down that Ryland wouldn't hesitate to use them against me if that's what he thought it would take to get me under control. To keep me beneath his thumb.

I couldn't give him any reason to use them against me. It was now my job to keep them safe, and if that meant groveling at the feet of Ryland, then that's what I would do. For now.

My wolf would only bend that knee if she knew it wouldn't be forever. I promised her it wouldn't. We'd find a way to leave or maybe we'd just outlive the bastard. Or maybe Clay was right and after Ryland got his fill of rubbing my nose in the dirt, he would get bored and leave me to my own devices. Leave my friends to theirs.

There would be a way for all of us to be free again, and I was going to make it my own personal mission to find it. If that meant playing the docile pup with her tail between her legs for a while, then I could do that.

Or at least, I thought I could do that.

"Where are you right now?" Charity asked, nudging my arm.

"Hmm?" I said, blinking out of the tangled mess of my thoughts and back to the present. "Oh. Just thinking."

"About?"

I shrugged. "Nothing," I said, brushing off her worry and tactfully changing the subject. "How's the search going? I heard Ry had you guys out pretty much all weekend. Is that my fault?"

Charity pursed her lips. "Probably, but the truth is none of us wanted to be here anyway. Ry was in a foul mood all weekend. It was the best punishment he could've given."

I snorted, giving my head a shake. "Fair enough. Find anything?"

"No. Nothing at all. It's the weirdest thing. It makes no sense that all of them deserted at different times and not a single one of them left even the ghost of a trail. They can't all be that good at covering their tracks.

"Because they aren't the ones doing it," Seth injected, leaning in with a glint in his eyes. "I think Ry is right. It's the eastern pack. It has to be. There's no way they are vanishing into thin air all by themselves."

I was sure the doubt would be clear enough on my

face that I didn't need to make a comment, but Seth went on anyway. "I think we need to take the fight to them. Clean house."

"You're drunk," Charity told him with a little sneer, shoving him back. "Hasn't there been enough bloodshed lately?'

Seth gave a one shoulder shrug and resumed sipping whatever awful smelling liquid was in his red Solo cup. "If Ry's right, then they've already declared war."

"I don't think—" I began to disagree when Jared returned, his face ashen and strides purposeful.

"Ryland wants to see you in his office before we start the ceremony."

Layla and Viv had been talking quietly with Destiny, Trey, and Todd across the loose circle of bodies, but fell silent at his words.

"What about?" Vivian demanded before I could speak the words myself.

Jared's gaze flitted to me briefly before training on Vivian. "Don't worry," he told her, and the conviction in his tone settled the flutter beneath my ribcage. "It'll only take a second."

Then finally, he turned to me and something dark in his gaze made my belly flip. "He's going to apologize," Jared told me, as though if he spoke the words forcibly enough, he could make them true. "He realizes that you were not in control, and he shouldn't have punished you the way he did."

Charity's mouth dropped open. Clay was staring at Jared like he may have lost his mind.

"What the fuck did you do?" Clay demanded.

"What I had to," Jared snapped back at Clay and then turned back to me. "Go, Allie. He's waiting. Let's get this over with so we can leave."

I shared a look with Clay, a silent thought passing between us.

We would make Jared tell us what the hell he was up to later. Once we were safely back at the cabin.

"Hang on," Vivian called, breaking away from her mate and Layla to cross the circle. "I'll go in with you."

"He wants to see her alone," Jared said.

Viv's nostrils flared.

"My Uncle doesn't do apologies," he explained in a low voice so the others wouldn't be able to hear. His meaning was clear without his needing to explain further. Ryland wouldn't speak to me—definitely wouldn't *apologize* to me—with an audience. He wouldn't want one of his newest recruits thinking him weak.

"Allie will be fine," he added pointedly, his gaze hard. "I made sure of it."

"I'll be back in a minute," I said before Viv could fight Jared on it anymore.

Clay caught my wrist before I could walk away though. "You shout if you need us. I'll hear you a mile away."

I tugged my wrist back and gave him a nod, walking

away from the group in a daze. A thousand different thoughts racing to be analyzed in my skull.

Was Ryland actually going to apologize to me?

There was no fucking way that was going to happen, right?

So what was his play?

Apologize now and make me pay for it later?

Or had he just told Jared he would let me off the hook when in fact he planned to punish me in private, and Jared had just given him the perfect opportunity. Was there a gag and new, stronger manacles waiting for me on the other side of that door?

I stepped up onto the porch and through the wide-open screen door into the main lodge. Ryland's peppery scent mingled with the woodsy, mothball odor clinging to the timber walls and dusty cushions in the living room.

The hallway and Ryland's open office door loomed to my right.

Just get it over with, Allie. What's the worst that he could do?

But I knew the real question—the real worry—wasn't about what he would do, but more about how much I could handle before I snapped.

I soothed the flutter in my chest with a few deep breaths and put one foot in front of the other. The longer I put it off, the harder it would be to go through with.

Just go in there and sit down and shut up and take whatever he gives you.

My wolf elicited a little inward snarl, and I hissed at her to pipe down before entering the room. I thought I heard a sound from somewhere else in the cabin, a door opening somewhere maybe? But no one else came down the hall.

Brows furrowed, I turned to face Ryland, a hard ball in my throat.

I swallowed it down and clenched my hands together at my front. "You wanted to see me?" I asked, working hard to keep my voice level.

Ryland sat behind a long rectangular desk. Head bent as he poured over a sheet of paper caught between his hands. His dark hair was half tucked behind an ear on one side and falling forward to cover his face on the other.

He flipped the page over so it was blank side up and raised his head, fiery gaze fixing on me. "Please," he said, as though the word tasted foul on his tongue. "Come in. Sit down."

I glanced around the room, bristling as an odd sensation of being watched washed over me. A strange smell permeated the air and made my nose wrinkle. I knew the scent but couldn't seem to place it.

Fuck, I was being so paranoid.

Shaking my head, I stepped forward and dragged the chair opposite Ryland from the desk, wincing at the scraping sound it made as the metal legs scratched along the old hardwood floor.

I sat like I was told and pleated my fingers in my lap. "About the other night, I—"

Ryland raised his hand to silence me, and I let my lips fall closed.

My alpha pushed his hair back from his face, revealing the newest scar in his cheek, still puckered and ridged in dark pink flesh. The movement made another similar scar catch my eye. One in his shoulder, partially hidden by his undershirt. Though this one healed a little better and was more silver in color than dark pink, it was clear what it was.

A bite mark.

My bite mark.

Ryland, catching me looking, tipped his head to afford me a better view of my handiwork. "My nephew seems to think I owe you an apology," Ryland said, knotting his fingers atop the desk and leaning forward as though he might jump right over the desktop and throttle me at any moment.

I knew the bastard wasn't going to apologize and there was a certain satisfaction in knowing I was right even if that wasn't exactly a good thing.

My wolf moved to high alert, but I willed myself to remain still.

"Nothing to say?" he pressed, his eyes sparking to a dim orange glow. "Do you think I should *apologize* for doling out punishment where punishment was due?"

Asshole.

"No."

"Then we agree."

The silence stretched between us for a few moments until Ryland finally relented, sighing as he leaned back in his chair. "I don't see it," he said, squinting at me as though trying to find something.

I licked my lips, swallowing again to wet my dry throat. "See what?"

"What my nephew sees in you," Ryland said, lifting his hands to pick a small bit of dirt from his nails and flick it onto the floor, as though I was the most inconsequential thing in the room and he found the dirt more interesting.

I wanted to tell him the feeling was mutual. Not only that I didn't understand what Jared and Clay saw in me, either, but also...how I could never fucking comprehend why Jared seemed to believe there was any good left in his uncle. Maybe there was once, but I could feel it like a bad taste in my mouth, like a heaviness in the air around him: cruelness.

The poignant tang of bitterness and the abrasiveness of his tone.

I didn't say any of the things I wanted to, though. I bowed my head like a good little wolfy and remained silent instead, willing this show of dominance to be over.

"You know he threatened me, don't you?" Ryland asked after a few charged seconds and a sizzle of white-hot shock shot up my spine, forcing it ramrod straight.

"He wouldn't—"

"He did. It was quite the surprise, I'll admit. Not once has he ever questioned my methods. *Not once.*"

Ryland let those words hang in the air between us, all the while his gaze darkened. The glow around his irises depleted until they seemed almost black beneath the shadow of his brows.

"I'll speak to him," I offered.

One brow raised, Ryland appraised me, perhaps trying to decipher if I was being truthful.

"I won't have discord in my pack. Loyalty is paramount in our world, Allie Grace. Those who are not loyal do not have a place here. Do you understand?"

Holy fucking shit. Was he threatening me?

Or...was he threatening his own nephew?

Scarcely able to breathe, the single word barely skirted past my lips. A whisper. "Yes."

"Good."

Ryland stood and adjusted his belt, righting his undershirt and the shining silver buckle of his belt before he tucked his arms into the sleeves of a crisp navy-blue button up and rolled the sleeves to the creases of his elbows.

Awkwardly, I stood too, unsure if I should ask to leave or just go. Unsure if he was finished with me or not.

"I have new recruits to welcome into the fold," Ryland said as he brushed past me to the door, his entire demeanor changing in the span of a single stride. The mask was back on. He was ready for the curtain call.

I moved to follow him, but his head snapped to the side, a single glowing eye boring into me. "You'll remain here," he ordered, and I felt the weight of the order like a baby grand piano on my chest, his words laced with the command of the alpha. "There are just a few more things Grey will go over with you and then you can join us in the yard."

"What?"

Behind Ryland, a shape disconnected from the rest of the shadows in the hallway, moving stealthily, as though floating on air into the light.

The vampire, Grey came into view. Just as pale as I remembered, with eyes blacker than coal and thick lips mostly bleached of color. Those same warning bells I'd felt earlier came back in a clatter of white noise, ricocheting in my skull.

"Won't you explain to Allie here how things will be from now on?" Ryland asked Grey as he stalked past the vampire and out into the hall. "I don't want to keep her friends waiting. It's late."

Bullshit.

Complete and utter bullshit.

Was anything this fucker said genuine? I was starting to think not.

I would be talking to Jared, but I didn't think Ryland was going to like what I had to say.

"Of course," Grey replied in a hiss, gesturing for me to accompany him back into the office. "It's nice to see you again, Allison."

"It's Allie," I all but snapped. This time when my wolf pressed against my barriers, I let him see her. How close she was to the surface. I wanted him to know that even though I was doing my best to behave for the sake of my friends, that restraint only applied to my alpha. To my mate's uncle. Not to him.

Interest piqued, Grey grinned wickedly, twisting the silver ring on his index finger and as he drew nearer to me. "Allie," he acquiesced. "This will only be a moment."

Grey settled himself on the edge of Ryland's desk and beckoned me forward.

Tightening my jaw and readying myself for any sign of attack, I stayed where I was, unwilling to get any closer to him.

A saccharine smile twisted his lips before he began to speak, holding my gaze. "You will not tell anyone of this meeting," he said, his voice and demeanor changing from dejected politeness to cruel command.

"You will not speak ill of your alpha. You will adhere to his will and command. You will be *obedient*."

I fisted my hands in the hem of my shirt and glared at Grey.

Why couldn't Ryland have given me these orders himself?

Fucking coward.

"That's all for now," he finished, clapping his hands together, forcing me to stumble back a step at the sudden sound and movement, blinking rapidly. "Off you go, little dove. Until we meet again."

Eager to get away from Grey, I spun on my heel and hurried out of the room, rushing down the hall and out of the front door, stumbling outside into the moonlit night. Cold air stung my flushed cheeks, and I gasped for an unrestricted breath, trying to get my bearings.

"Hey," the deep voice boomed from my right, and I stumbled again, this time unable to right myself before my knees struck dirt. I whirled, sagging when I found Clay staring down at me, a worried crease in his brow. "You okay? Was that Grey I heard inside?"

"With the moon and all in attendance here as witnesses." I heard Layla's voice, carried to me on a phantom wind.

I scrambled to my feet and found them. Layla and Vivian standing shoulder to shoulder with the rest of the pack on their flanks and Ryland standing directly in front of them. An encouraging grin spreading across his lips.

Jared caught my eye as Vivian repeated the oath Layla just finished speaking. His lips parted in silent question at my disheveled appearance, and I struggled to regain composure, the whisper of Ryland's threat still echoing in my ears.

"I hereby submit myself to the rule of the alpha," my best friends spoke in unison, their oaths carrying over the crowd.

Ryland passed the silver flask to Layla first, pressing it into her palm and wrapping his hideous hand around hers. Hesitantly, she brought it to her lips, and I choked on the urge to call out to her, to stop her.

And then it was already too late. The flask was being passed to Vivian, who tipped it back, taking a long pull of the blood-tainted whiskey and grimacing while all I could do was stand and watch in silent horror.

This was a mistake.

I could see it now.

Clay wrapped his hands around my shoulders, kneading out the tension there. "They're pack now," he whispered against my cheek. "Family. Forever."

Ryland caught my eye as he turned to cast a shining grin over the pack members in attendance. He paused briefly on me, his grin morphing into something else entirely. Something twisted and conniving. I almost wanted to ask Clay if he'd seen it, to make sure it wasn't my own paranoia making something out of nothing, but the look was gone as swiftly as it appeared, leaving me to guess at whether it had been there at all.

16

I couldn't sleep.

Ever since the ceremony, my thoughts had been erratic. Explosive. Like a minefield I had no way of crossing without getting blown to a thousand tiny pieces.

I checked my phone for the fifteenth time in the last five minutes, gushing a sigh of relief when a text from Vivian flared to life on the screen as though I'd willed it into being.

Vivian: Allie, I'm fine. I'm going to sleep. You should too.

Vivian: See you at school tomorrow, k?

Allie: Have you heard from Layla? She isn't answering my texts.

Vivian: That's probably because it's one in the morning.

She was right. I sat heavily on my bed, the mattress sighing beneath my weight.

Allie: Sorry. See you in the morning.

I chucked my phone onto the bed, losing it in a lumpy pile of blankets and leaned forward to press my palms into my eyes, easing the tension headache knocking at my ocular cavities behind them.

They couldn't fault me for worrying. I remembered what it was like those first few days. I had almost no control.

But then again, I had refused to shift for way too long.

They had already shifted more times in three days than I had in my first two weeks.

They'll be fine, I told myself stoically. *Totally fucking fine.*

Them being at home was better than being at pack camp at least. Ryland had offered for them to remain on pack land for a while, until they could both be properly acquainted with their wolves and gain some control.

They'd refused of course. They couldn't just not go home.

They had families.

Layla especially. She had younger siblings counting on her to look after them while her parents worked. Vivian may have been able to swing it. Her mom likely wouldn't notice she was gone for a while, and her dad wouldn't care so long as she gave him a plausible excuse.

I'd worried Ryland wouldn't grant them permission to leave, but he'd simply nodded and gave both my best friends understanding pats on the shoulders. Playing the part of a benevolent and understanding alpha.

He'd warned them of the risks involved with returning home so soon, but they'd both nodded, accepting the risks. And just like that, he'd let them go with only vague orders requesting them to return the following weekend *when they had time*.

Ha!

I'd never received such lenience from Ryland.

What was he playing at?

Trying to get them on his good side?

As if that would work after both of them watched him break my fucking arm because he was having a goddamned tantrum.

I barely noticed I'd risen to pace until I was out in the hall, turning back at the stairs to walk back toward my room.

With Jared gone back to the quarry on orders from Ry and Clay busy with something in the shop, I'd been alone with my thoughts since Clay and I dropped off Layla and Viv and returned home.

Now that I had time to think things through, I realized there was a lot not adding up. And I kind of wished I'd pulled Jared away to have that talk with him before he had to leave.

But, like usual, I'd hesitated, developing lockjaw in the span of a single breath.

I needed to think about what I was going to tell him. *How* I was going to say it. I couldn't very well just blurt out that I thought his uncle was a sadistic douchebag who maybe, probably, had something to do with the missing members of the pack.

Loyalty is paramount in our world, Allie Grace. Those who are not loyal do not have a place here.

If the other missing wolves were anything like the one that'd almost fallen drunk into the firepit the week before, then it wasn't a stretch to say that they *weren't* as loyal as Ryland wanted his pack to be.

And to say that the cowardly alpha who ran away that night at the four corners had something to do with it? How was he getting the others to actually buy into that? There was no way it had anything to do with that pack.

Right?

I stopped, chewing my bottom lip as I glanced into the dark, quiet cabin below from the top of the stairs.

There was something going on. Something that wasn't adding up.

The more I thought about it, the more I believed it.

I bowed to my alpha's will to protect my friends and my mates. But would my obedience be enough to save them if he were the monster I was starting to think he was?

I swiped a hand over my face, a jagged sigh tumbling from my lips.

Or was this all just a massive misunderstanding? Was it just that Ryland fucking hated me and was treating me like shit that made me suspicious of him?

Groaning, I raced down the stairs.

There was only one way to find out and put these demons to rest once and for all…

I needed to go to the eastern pack. I needed hard proof. Real, tangible answers.

I needed to know that I didn't just let my friends make the biggest mistake of their lives when they submitted to the rule of Ryland.

The screen door banged shut behind me as I stepped out into the frigid air, my breaths clouding in icy little droplets on my face as I shivered, hugging my arms around myself as I power walked around to the back of the cabin.

The light was still on in the shop.

Good.

"Hey," I said, rounding the edge of the garage-style door and entering unannounced. "I need to talk—"

Clay rolled off the couch with a snarl and a thud, flipping onto all fours with his teeth bared and eyes wild and ablaze with blue fire. He spun, searching for an attacker, and I realized all at once that he'd been asleep.

Oops.

His gaze settled on me, great gushes of steamy air

puffing past his lips. He blinked, relaxing as he rocked back on his heels and caught his breath.

"The light was on," I said with a wince. "I thought you were still awa—"

"Don't do that," he growled, shakily rising to his feet, his face tinged red. "I almost…" he trailed off, throwing a hand through his sleep-tousled hair.

"I'm sorry. I should've—"

Clay shook his head and his gaze lowered to the floor. "It's fine," he said. "I was just…it was a nightmare. I didn't expect you to—"

"Barge in unannounced at one in the morning?"

"Yeah. That."

"Then clearly you need to change your expectations."

He smirked at that and sat back down on the old sofa, legs spread wide and arms open, one slung over the backrest and the other over the torn armrest. He took up almost half the sofa like that. Sometimes I forgot how massive he was. With arms larger than my thighs and a chest nearly as wide as two of mine.

It didn't help that he was shirtless, exposing every shadowed curve of muscle and a little whisper thing trail of dark hairs disappearing into the rim of his loose fitted jeans from his belly button.

Wasn't he cold?

It had to be less than 60 outside tonight.

"I…" I started but couldn't seem to find the words, or maybe the courage, to start talking. I bit my bottom lip and glanced out at the trees, craving their solace like I haven't craved it in a long time.

"What's wrong?" Clay asked, his casual demeanor shifting as he attempted to study my expression. "Did something happen?"

"Um..."

"Allie?"

"Will you go for a walk with me?" I blurted before I could change my mind. "Not far. Just down the trail and back. Walking sometimes helps me think."

He narrowed his icy blue eyes at me, but stood after a minute. "Sure," he said with a note of suspicion coloring his tone and then snagged a dark sweater from beside the couch to toss in my direction. "Put this on. You're shaking."

I caught it midair and tugged it on gratefully, wilting beneath the instant warmth and the comforting smell that was uniquely Clay enveloping me.

He grabbed a long sleeve t-shirt from the seat of the bike he was working on. One of the ones he used for work that was a deep gray covered in the stain of engine grease.

"Lead the way," he told me as he came to the edge of the shop. "But let's stay tight to the cabin."

I understood what he meant. Let's stay within the perimeter of the spell keeping the cabin and immediate area surrounding it cloaked from view.

I had to wonder if he was worried about the same thing I was, or if he'd bought into the rumors of the eastern pack trying to dwindle our numbers. I shook my head. No. He wasn't that gullible.

Clay didn't press me as we walked slowly over the carpet of fallen leaves coating the forest floor. With the moon still near full and the forest canopy thinned from autumn shed, the path was bright. It had almost a crystalline quality. I could make out every knot of wood. Every flurry of movement. Smell every scent.

I shut my eyes and inhaled deeply, letting the familiar scents of mountain pine and birch soothe the tremor in my bones.

"There's something I need to talk to you about," I started.

"I figured," he said, ever the smart ass.

I gave him a little shove and continued. "This is serious. And I don't want you to freak out, okay? You have to promise you won't."

I chanced a quick peek at him, finding the side profile of his face tight and muscle jumping in his jaw.

"Okay," he said finally.

"Okay, so basically here's the thing…*the thing is…*"

Why was this so hard?

"Spit it out, Allie."

I stopped and turned to face him, my spine going rigid. He stilled, waiting for whatever it was I had to say with a knot in his brow and lips pressed tight. As though bracing for a physical blow.

"So, remember how Jared said that Ryland was going to apologize to me? Well, he didn't. He actually kind of threatened me. Or maybe he threatened Jared. I'm not clear on that. And then he had that Grey asshat try to tell me how things were going to be from now on. And anyway, that's not really important right now, what I really wanted to bring up and maybe get your help with is well…I think Ryland is lying about the missing wolves and the eastern pack being responsible for their disappearances. I think that it's possible that *he* has something to do with them just vanishing into thin air, and he's just trying to shift the blame and—"

"*Whoa,* Allie, slow down. You aren't making any sense."

Clay's hands came around my arms and squeezed. He licked his lips and glanced around us, as though afraid someone might overhear. "Come on, let's go back. We're too close to the edge of the warding spell."

I let Clay take my hand and tug me back the way we'd come. He stopped only when we could see the cabin through the trees and turned to face me.

Sometime in the last few seconds what I'd told him must've sunk in because he didn't look so confused anymore. He looked *pissed*.

Like, not normal pissed. *Clay level pissed.*

With bulging veins and cheeks so red they were verging on purple.

"Calm down," I told him, trying to barricade myself against his raging emotions before they could seep into my own veins, lighting fire to the gasoline already lingering there.

"I'm sorry," Clay spat, his voice dripping sarcasm. "Calm down?"

"Clay—"

"Did you say he *threatened* you?"

Crap. Maybe I should've left that part out.

I grasped for a response that wouldn't set him off even more, choking on several sentence starters that would only lead to more rage.

Exasperated after a minute of trying, I huffed out a curse and gave my head a little shake. "Look, I can't talk to you when you're all murdery. Can you just take a fucking breath, please?"

He reeled back as though stung, but did what I asked, working hard to calm himself enough that he began to look more like a regular human being instead of a mass of veiny stone.

"Better?" he grunted.

It was the best I was going to get. I nodded.

"Good, now can you explain to me exactly what the fuck you're trying to tell me? Maybe at a normal speed this time?"

I ignored the dig and gave him a short glare before launching into a less chaotic explanation. This time, I maybe glazed over the thinly veiled threat Ryland gave, making it sound more like maybe I was just being paranoid and he didn't actually threaten me at all.

It wasn't exactly a lie. I *could* have been blowing it out of proportion. Ryland may not have meant it that way.

But even I had to admit it wasn't as if I was telling the whole truth either.

Anyway, that wasn't the point. The more important bit—the one that I really needed someone to talk to about, was the shifters who'd mysteriously vanished.

I focused on that part when I did my reiteration to Clay. Explaining why I thought it was bullshit and what I wanted to do about it. I got more and more nervous as I spoke, watching Clay's face harden with each word.

I thought he would understand—that if anyone were going to help me do this it would be him. Had I been wrong?

Was this yet another colossal mistake? I wouldn't have been surprised, making mistakes seemed to be all I was good at nowadays. I should just make a sport out of it.

"I want to go to the eastern pack," I told him, praying it wasn't the final nail in my coffin. Clay was either going to be with me on this or he was going to be *firmly* against me. I half wondered if he might lock me up inside just to keep me from trying to go instead of coming with me.

"It doesn't add up Clay," I continued when he didn't immediately reply. "Something is *wrong*. I don't know what it is exactly, but I have this…this *feeling* in my gut that—"

"I think you're right," he interrupted, eyes darting this way and that as he considered.

"You do?"

I wasn't sure if I should have been elated or terrified that someone else agreed with me about this. If I were being honest, it was a bit of both.

"You'll come with me then?" I hedged. "To the eastern territory? To speak to the alpha?"

His face screwed up into a scowl. "You can't go there, Allie," he said incredulously. "They wanted you dead, remember?"

"Which is why I thought it might be wise to bring some *backup*," I replied pointedly, jabbing two fingers at him. "Instead of going alone."

"It isn't safe."

"Safe?" I hissed. "What the fuck is safe anymore, Clay? If you can honestly tell me that I'm safer *here*, then go on, say it, and I'll believe you."

He ground his jaw and cut me a scathing glare, some of the redness blooming back into his cheeks.

"I'm right, and you know it."

"*I'll* go."

"Alone? The hell you will. Either we go together or not at all."

"Why didn't you tell Jared any of this?" Clay asked, seemingly out of the blue until I realized I'd also been thinking the same thing pretty much during this entire conversation.

I should have. I knew I should have.

I should have followed him out to the quarry with

Clay after we dropped off the girls, and we should have hashed this out together, but...

"You know why," I told him, and he dropped his head.

Not only was Ryland Jared's uncle, but now we knew the lengths Jared was willing to go to keep me safe. My heart ached just thinking about it.

He'd actually threatened Ryland on my behalf. *Threatened* his own uncle. The last living member of his blood related family.

His alpha.

It was why I couldn't find the words to tell him before he left. I was in shock. I was having a hell of a time rectifying what Ryland told me he did with the visual of him in his uncle's office at the quarry, explaining to me how Ry was the one who helped put him back together after his parents were killed.

They shouldn't be the same person, and yet they were.

He was a fucking idiot for threatening his uncle, but wouldn't I have done the same thing for him?

Wasn't what I was doing right now not in some ways *for him*?

If Ryland was what I thought he might be, then I didn't want Jared or anyone else I loved anywhere near him. I didn't need to hurt Jared more than he was already hurting until I had something more concrete to tell him.

That was why I hadn't been able to speak before he

left, him pressing his lips gently to mine in a whisper of a kiss before shifting into his wolf and taking to the trees.

"We can't tell him," I said finally, having worked out the best course of action.

"What?" Clay demanded.

"Not yet. Not until we actually have something to show him. Or something more...I don't know, *real* to tell him. He's already on edge. He fucking threatened Ry." I shook my head in disbelief. "I don't want to lie to him, but if we're wrong, then there's no reason to tell him all my half-baked theories."

Clay thought about it, and his nose wrinkled as though he caught a sour odor on the chill breeze. "I don't like it."

"You think I do? I didn't want any of this shit, but here I am, wading through it all the best I can."

Clay grumbled something unintelligible to himself, and I groaned. "So will you come with me or not?"

"Fine," he hissed. "It's not like you're giving me much of a choice."

I narrowed my gaze at him. "I guess I'm not," I agreed. "But I could have not told you anything and just gone alone."

His eyes darkened and after a moment of teeth-grinding silence, he let his shoulders drop and pulled me into his chest. I was surprised enough to squeak out a little chirp of surprise before we collided.

"Thank you," he whispered against my hair in a rare

moment of disarm. "For trusting me with this. I'd have fucking lost my shit if you went alone."

I chuckled against his chest. "I know."

I wrapped my arms around him, pressing my cheek into his chest enough that I could hear the hard, steady beating of his heart. The comfort of his nearness nearly made me forget all the terrible, awful thoughts that'd been dancing and swirling in my mind since the full moon.

Here, amid the trees, with Clay's spicy engine grease scent filling my lungs, I could pretend, just for a minute, that everything would be okay.

"When do you want to go?" Clay asked after a few moments, still holding me tightly against him.

"I was thinking tomorrow after school? Ryland hasn't given me orders to get back on rotation with Charity yet, but I'm assuming he will sooner rather than later."

Clay nodded against the top of my head. "What about work?"

"What work?" I asked, my voice dripping sarcasm. "I'm pretty sure I have a voicemail waiting on my phone from my boss that's going to let me permanently off the hook for that."

"Allie—"

"This is more important, anyway. I'll get another job. It's fine."

"But—"

"I don't want to talk about it."

A tight minute of silence followed my snapped reply before Clay softened beneath me once more and my pulse quieted.

"All right," he said, and I could tell he was working hard to sound understanding but there was a tightness around the words that gave away his anger. "We'll have to be back before eleven. I have to meet my sister at the borderlands and escort her onto our territory."

I'd almost completely forgotten his sister was coming. I didn't want to say it but now wasn't exactly the best time for a visit. Judging by his pained expression when I pulled away to look at him, I could tell he was thinking something similar.

"Do you think she'll like me?"

I wasn't sure why I asked; the words came unbidden to my lips and I didn't realize until after I spoke them how much I dreaded hearing the answer to that question. How much I cared.

Sam was Clay's only remaining relative save for Grams, and I still wasn't even clear on whether or not they were blood related or just really close. I wanted her to like me. To approve of the female her big brother mated with.

Clay quirked a brow at me and a slow smirk tugged at one corner of his lips. I'd surprised him. "That's not something I thought you'd care about."

"You didn't answer the question."

He pondered how to respond for a second before speaking, making me even more on edge. "Sam is…"

Clay trailed off, his face pinching. "How do I say she's a bitch without saying she's a bitch because brothers aren't supposed to say that kind of shit about their sisters?"

I chuckled.

"Difficult?"

"Yeah. She's difficult. And opinionated. And after...*what happened*...she finally got the mean streak me and pops thought might've skipped her."

"So, she's going to hate me is what you're saying?" I asked, wincing.

Clay bit his bottom lip, considering. My skin warmed and a flush rose to my cheeks. Fuck, why was that so hot?

"I'm saying," Clay corrected. "That you should take everything she says with a massive amount of salt. Who knows? I haven't seen her in a couple years, maybe she's different now."

He said that last part like he didn't believe it even for a second but had at least a sliver of hope that it might be true.

Clay brushed his palm against my cheek, pushing his fingers deep into my hair until he had me firmly in his grasp with a grip on the back of my neck. He tipped my head back so I would look him in the eyes. "Hey," he said, brows lowering. "I don't care what she thinks. Hell, I don't give a fuck what anybody thinks. You're *mine,* and nobody is ever going to change that."

My thighs squeezed and a violent shudder raced

down my spine, making a delicious ache spread through my belly.

My lips parted in a silent plea before I could get control of myself. From somewhere deep within, my wolf came to life, flaring in my eyes and growling in my chest.

Mine, she roared.

Clay's irises flared to twin halos of glowing blue, awakening to my desire. Before I could change my mind, I yanked him to me with clawed fingers knotted into the soft fabric of his shirt and crushed my mouth to his, eager to touch—to taste.

His fingers tightened on my neck while his other hand wrapped securely around my middle, helping to lift me onto my tip toes so I wouldn't have to crane my neck to reach him. Wrapping my arms around his neck, I let him in, the kiss no longer a quick theft beneath the moonlight.

Clay swept in with his tongue, drawing a moan from my throat and making my whole body clench, pressing into him as tightly as possible.

I couldn't seem to get close enough. A burning desire to remove every bit of barrier between us had my hands pulling and tugging. Removing his shirt and then mine. Our lips were apart for only a second and it was too long.

I rushed back to him, hungry and grasping. His warm hands gripped my sides, fingers splayed over the back of my bare ribs.

It felt *so* good. I never wanted it to stop.

His lips kissed a hard path down my neck, stopping just above my breasts. A small sound left my lips with my heavy breaths, something like a whine or a pained moan.

I delved my fingers into Clay's dark hair, trying to tell him it was okay—that I didn't want him to hold back. I didn't want him to stop.

His lips brushed over the swell of my left breast and my back arched at the violent sensation that rocked me all the way to my core. The tether linking us together vibrated with tension and heat, getting tighter—*stronger*—the further we went.

I fumbled with the zipper of his jeans, and his grip on my ribs went rigid.

"We can't," he whispered against my neck; the brush of his breath against the tender flesh there driving me insane. "The rules..."

"Fuck the rules."

Clay growled, lifting my feet from the ground. My back knocked into the rough, mossy bark of a tree, and I glared down into the heated gaze of my mate. A war raged beneath his stare. With each puff of hot air clouding the space between our lips, I knew he was considering how much he could bend the rule without breaking it.

I knew because I was thinking it, too.

He leaned in for a rough kiss and pulled back, chest

heaving. "I don't think I'll be able to stop," he gritted out through clenched teeth.

The truth was, I wasn't sure if I would be strong enough to stop it, either, but I was beyond caring.

Clay began to robotically pry himself from me and my chest ached with his loss. I knew he was right, but that didn't mean I had to like it.

"Sleep with me," I blurted before he could fully disentangle himself from me. "I mean—not like *that*. Just…sleep."

I hadn't been able to shut my mind off for days. Maybe with him there I could finally get the rest I desperately needed. Tackle tomorrow with a clear head.

Clay's jaw clenched. "I don't cuddle."

I smirked, turning on the pouty eyes. Vivian always said no one could ever say no to me with that look. "For me?"

Clay rolled his eyes, and I grinned, knowing that even the strong and grouchy Clay wasn't impervious to my exaggerated pleading. "Fine."

I began to consider all the different ways I could make this more painful for him. Sleeping nude may have an interesting effect.

Maybe he'd break the rules for me after all.

Clay shook his head. "*Clothed*," he amended, taking the wind from my sails.

I smirked at him. "You're no fun."

"You're going to be the death of me, woman."

17

It was amazing how much control you could have when you were worried about someone else's more than your own. Monday at school was a shitshow of epic proportions. Even though Layla and Viv had both shifted and run *forty miles* this morning before dawn, they both had a couple near misses throughout the day.

Viv nearly bit off another girl's head in field practice and had to fake a stomachache to get out of participating. And Layla, stuck fending off Quinn's advances all day, nearly snapped her very canine jaws at him in the cafeteria. I expertly shifted the attention to myself with a rather dramatic sweep of my arm across the table, *accidentally* sending all of our lunches falling to the scuffed floor.

We had to get new lunches, which I grudgingly had to pay for, but at least it gave Layla the minute of peace to get control of herself and very politely tell Quinn she *needed some time to herself.*

Miraculously, she didn't seem to have a problem at home with her brothers and sisters.

"It's like my wolf knows them," she explained. "Like it knows it can't hurt them."

She'd shrugged.

"I don't get it, but I don't think being at home is going to be as hard as I thought it would be. School on the other hand…"

Vivian wasn't so lucky. She had to lock herself in her room for the night to keep from barking at her father when he wandered in drunk, but that was par for the course for a Monday night for her. She'd shrugged too, telling me that it was only a little harder than usual to keep from eating him alive.

She'd laughed.

I didn't.

When I broke out of my thoughts, telling myself not to worry so much about them, I found Clay watching me curiously. My arms were elbow deep in soapy dishwater, and I gazed without seeing out the window above the sink to the darkening sky outside.

Clay slouched against the counter to my right, a strange, curious look dipping his brows low and pulling at a corner of his mouth.

"What?" I asked, a flush creeping up my neck.

"I don't know what you did to me, but I haven't slept as good as I did last night since I was a kid."

I smiled at that.

I couldn't remember the last time I'd slept as peacefully, either. Except maybe the time I awoke to find Jared curled at the edge of my bed. But this was different. Clay had tucked me in tight against his chest, curling and bending to form his body to mine as though he was the mold and I was the putty.

And I *was* the putty. The way I'd melted into him…

I couldn't be sure, but after the first few moments of trepidation and desire waned, giving way to exhaustion, I was probably asleep within seconds.

His level breaths expanded and contracted against my back. His warm breath caressed my hair. My wolf was in her absolute bliss.

I mean, she might've been happier if he'd given in to us in the woods, but it was the next best thing, so she didn't complain much.

"Good," I told him and bit my lower lip.

"I haven't either," I admitted.

His eyes widened. "Maybe…" he trailed off, lifting a hand to rub the back of his neck. "Maybe we could—"

"Just admit it," I teased, flicking bubbles at him. "You *liked* it."

His face twisted into a scowl.

"My big scary mate is actually just a giant teddy bear who likes to cuddle."

His fists clenched. "Take that back."

I shook my head. "Nope."

Before I could blink, he was there, one hand on my

back and the other plunged into the soapy water. I barely had time to gasp before he splashed water and bubbles all over my face and shirt.

I blinked through the wetness and suds to find him several paces away, grinning like a fool.

"This doesn't change anything," I said, advancing as he retreated up the stairs, away from my dreams of retaliation. "You're still my little cuddle bunches!" I called after him, groaning as I shook my arms, flicking the wetness off the ends of my fingers.

"*Bastard.*"

I heard the shower turn on upstairs and went back to the sink to finish washing up the last few dishes from dinner, secretly hoping that using the water down here would fuck with his temperature up there.

Bugger deserved it.

My phone pinged in my back pocket, and I dried my hands quickly before drawing it out. A message from Clay flashed across the screen.

Clay: I've been called a lot of things. Cuddle bunches is by far the worst.

I began thumbing out a reply, a smirk on my lips, when my phone pinged again.

Clay: I'll be ready in ten.

Five words and I was right back to where I was earlier today when I got home. On edge and flighty. The caged bird living in my chest trying to break free all over again.

The questions I'd been asking myself all day replayed like an interrogation reel in my head.

What if the wolves from the eastern pack attack us?

What if one of us gets hurt?

What if they *are* to blame for the missing wolves?

And…

…what if they are not?

If they aren't then that didn't necessarily mean it was Ryland's doing, but it'd be one more tick on the proverbial tally chart on his side.

I huffed out a breath and willed my thrumming pulse to slow.

Allie: I'll wait outside.

Before I could finish the last two dishes, my screen flashed with another message from the countertop. I leaned over to see it was Clay again even though the shower was still running.

Clay: Don't go far.

I rolled my eyes and emptied the sink, guzzling a tall glass of water in preparation for the long run. A run that would normally take us less than an hour would take us nearly two tonight. We'd decided to double back and leave a dummy trail before retracing our steps and cutting through the river.

I shuddered. It was probably colder than ice by now. But it would be worth it if we were right. We couldn't have anyone be able to track where we went. It would raise too many questions that we didn't have the answers to. Not yet anyway.

Deciding to play nice this time, I stripped down to bare skin before the bathroom light in the cabin went out and set my folded clothes on the bottom step of the porch.

"All right girl," I cooed to my wolf. "Your turn."

She surged to the surface, pushing me back so she could take control of the reins. The pain lasted only a brief second before I was staring out through lupine eyes at the sharpness of the evening right after sunset.

We padded around in a circle, wanting to run, but also knowing we needed to wait for Clay. It felt… different this time. I couldn't put my finger on exactly what it was, but my skin felt more sensitive and my movements more jarring.

By the time Clay came outside another minute later, in nothing but a pair of loose khakis, I figured out what it was.

I was still very much *here*. Normally, my wolf tucked me into the back of my own mind like a lone sock tucked into the back of a drawer because it didn't have a match.

Not this time.

My legs felt strong. My chest cavity wide. I felt the outer edges of my being like I'd never felt them before. Foreign but also fitting. Like a coat you forgot you had that fit just like the first day you bought it.

Charity was right.

Hey, Clay's deep timbre rumbled through my thoughts, and I whipped my head up to find him loping down the stairs, doing a lazy circle around me as though appraising me. *You good?*

Great, I replied before taking off at a sprint, eager to feel the push and flex of the earth being chewed beneath my paws.

Clay caught up to me easily and we ran side by side through the night to the east.

Pace yourself, Clay whispered in my thoughts after we got a few miles in. *It's going to be a long night.*

I grinned inwardly.

What? I teased. *Do you need me to slow down?*

Smartass.

CLAY HAD BEEN RIGHT AFTER ALL. By the time we were nearing the eastern border after doubling back, leaving the dummy trail, and taking the long way around back through the river, I was dead tired.

We paused for a drink in the icy water and most of my drink splashed out of my mouth and dripped down my chin. Wholly unable to close my mouth for the raucous breaths sawing in and out in clouds from my jowls.

Told you, Clay said, and I growled at him.

How much further?

We're nearly there already, Clay told me. *The borders to their territory are just through that copse of trees there.*

He inclined his head toward a thicket, where a

natural break was formed to almost look like a doorway. Enchanting and menacing at the same time.

It's not too late to turn back, you know, Clay added. *You're worn out, maybe it isn't such a good idea to—*

We're going in, I pressed. I did not almost kill myself running for the past two hours straight just to chicken out now that we were here. If there were answers to be had on the other side of that copse of trees, I would have them one way or the other.

Clay didn't speak, he just looked on toward the entry to foreign territory as though considering his options.

Is there, like, a protocol or something we need to follow? Or do we just walk through.

He turned his head back to me, his bright blue eyes looking even brighter surrounded by the dark gray—near black—fur of his wolf. I wasn't sure how it was possible, but even in this form, he was drop dead gorgeous. Muscled and wide shouldered with a handsome lupine face. Or maybe it was just my wolf thinking he was attractive?

Who knew.

Normally we'd require permission to enter another pack's territory, but since we can't do that because it requires alpha consent, we're going to have to walk in without it.

Is that dangerous?

Can be.

Care to elaborate?

Clay dropped his head and scraped at the dirt with

his paw. *Ry keeps wolves at our borders, they run the perimeter. Most packs do that. If one crosses into our boundaries and is caught, they are usually given an opportunity to turn around and leave.*

So you're saying we just go in there, ask permission to enter and if they say no...what? We just have to leave?

Not all packs give foreign wolves the opportunity to leave peacefully.

So...?

If they won't hear us out and they won't give us an opportunity to leave without a fight, then I want you to run. There will only be one—maybe two—running the perimeter. I'll take care of them and then meet you back at the cabin. Run and don't stop until you get there.

I'm not going to leav—

You agree or we walk away right now and forget this whole idiotic idea.

I simpered, holding back a snarl. Why did he always have to be so goddamned infuriating? *Fine.*

Good.

Great.

I followed him as he began to move toward the opening, grumbling internally about how I planned to punish him for this and what an absolute fucking pain in my ass he was.

You know I can still hear you, right? He spoke in my thoughts, and it was like I could see the sarcasm dripping from each consonant and vowel.

I growled. *How the hell do I turn it off?*

No reply.

I did my best to sever the connection myself, thinking about things other than Clay. It seemed to do the trick because by the time we crossed the imaginary line between the two lines of trees, there were only my own thoughts in my head again.

Clay paused about fifteen paces in, rocking back to sit on his haunches.

Now what?

Now we wait.

It didn't take long. Within less than five minutes we could hear the telltale sounds of another animal in the forest. Thudding footfalls sending fallen leaves scattering in their wake. The unmistakable heavy breathing of a wolf.

Clay moved, placing himself slightly in front of me while keeping our backs to the border crossing for an easy exit.

Let me do the talking, Clay said just as flashes of movement could be seen hurtling in this direction through the darkened wood.

The wolf slowed, catching sight of us, and lifted his head back in a long howl.

Shit.

Shit. Shit. Shit.

How long would it take for all his eastern pack buddies to come running?

Clay?

I know.

Clay shifted in the blink of an eye, standing in a channel of moonlight. His naked body spotted with dirt and coated in a fine layer of sweat that made him glisten as though his skin was dusted with a metallic powder.

"We aren't here for a fight," Clay called at the wolf, who remained partially hidden in the shadows about thirty paces away. "We have come to request an audience with your alpha. Will you allow us entry?"

A silence so tense and thick hung in the air between them—the question going unanswered for so long that I had to quint my canine eyes to make sure the other wolf was even still there.

A low whine rolled off my tongue. I didn't like this. We should go.

I nipped at Clay's ankle, trying to get his attention, imploring him to understand my plea. He needed to shift back. He was too vulnerable in his human flesh.

He held a hand out in an attempt to tell me to be still.

Like hell that was going to work.

But just before I could nip him again, harder this time, a flash of dark skin caught my eye, and I peered into the trees where the lone wolf had been hiding to find he'd shifted, too. A tall black man with bright eyes and lips any god or goddess would kill for stepped from the darkness and into the light.

God. When was I going to get used to seeing people naked all the time?

I'd seen more dicks in the past two months than I had in my entire life before now.

"For what purpose?" The man called, his voice colored with a light accent. Southern, maybe? I was shit at figuring out accents. "Permission has not been granted for your entry to these lands."

Clay clenched his fists and I braced myself, coming back to the surface.

My turn.

"Permission couldn't be requested," I said, my voice a tight groan after the shift left me with stars in my eyes and an aching back. I let those words hang in the air, trying to let this guy catch on to their meaning without my having to say it outright that we didn't exactly trust our alpha.

The man's bright eyes narrowed at me and then widened, recognizing who I was. I don't know why the two tails hadn't set him off, but somehow my human form did. Must be the turquoise hair…even though I had a good three inches of new silvery blond growth at my crown now.

Clay's fist clenched at his side. I knew if I could hear his thoughts, I wouldn't like what I heard, but he let me speak.

"You're the twin soul wolf," he said, speaking the name as though it were a moniker of legend or myth.

"The what?"

"The twin soul wolf. The girl who bonded to two of

our kind. Who has two tails. *You're…*you're part of Ryland's pack."

"Bravo," Clay said with an annoyed tone. "Your powers of observation are astounding."

"*Clay*," I scolded.

"Look man," Clay pushed on. "We came for an audience with your alpha. If you don't plan to grant us one *and* promise our protection for the duration of the time we spend here, then I'd rather get the fuck out of dodge before your buddies get here."

The other man considered Clay, eyes flitting over his height and brawn before his gaze slid back to me. "I'll grant it for the girl," he said finally. "You may wait at the border for her return."

"Not a fucking—"

"Done," I chirped.

Clay whirled on me, his face turning from bright red to deathly pale and back again in the span of a single second. A vein in his temple jumped. "*No.*"

"*Yes.*"

"Allie—"

"I came here for answers, and I'm going to get them, Clay. This—hey, what's your name?"

"Toby."

"This *Toby* guy is offering me exactly what we came here for."

It could have been a trick of the light, but I swear I saw his hands begin to shake.

"I can't let you go alone. Don't ask me to."

"I'm not asking."

His expression shifted, his face going momentarily slack as though I'd slapped him.

"If I told you I'd make sure he behaved, would you let him come with me?" I asked, calling the question to Toby without any hope of him giving me that request.

Toby didn't even consider it. "No."

I shrugged, sighing as I let my gaze fall back to Clay. "I tried."

"You swear that she'll be returned to me here, *unharmed* in *any* way."

"By the old laws and the new, you have the word of my pack that she will be returned unharmed," Toby replied, none too politely, crossing his arms over his chest.

"There," I said. "Better?" I brushed my hand against Clay's biceps to get his attention and he reeled back from my touch, casting me a look I couldn't decipher before he stormed away, back toward the border. My chest ached at his rejection.

Didn't he understand that we had to do this?

The alpha of this pack may have wanted me dead a few weeks ago when I was still unclaimed, but he would be an idiot to try to cut me down now. He'd have a war on his hands. A war that he would have no hope whatsoever of winning.

"You have one hour," he warned without turning. "One hour, and I'll end anyone who stands in my way of getting to her."

When Toby didn't voice a reply, Clay paused and turned slightly, just enough to see Toby from the corner of his eye, but not far enough for me to catch his expression. *"Is that clear?"*

"There will be no need," Toby said diplomatically, now clearing the distance between us.

Clay shifted back into his wolf and launched himself through the opening, vanishing on the other side, back into our territory. I knew he wouldn't go far, but without him there to bolster my courage, my pulse began to pound in my ears as Toby shifted back into his wolf form and nudged his head forward. Onward.

Time to go.

With one last glance back to see if I could catch a glimpse of Clay standing sentinel outside, I shifted back and followed Toby, guilt, disappointment, and my own dark thoughts my only companions on the short run.

18

Toby's packmates caught up to us on our way. There was a fleeting moment of blood curdling fear as they descended upon us, but then Toby must have communicated with them the deal he'd cut to allow me entry.

I couldn't be sure because I couldn't hear their thoughts. I tried to speak to one of them and tried to listen in, but heard nothing. I figured it must be a pack thing. Like, one pack couldn't get into the heads of another pack. Maybe Jared had told me this already and I'd just forgotten.

But…distantly, I remembered hearing several thoughts the night I was turned and at that time I was not pack. And I could hear my mates' thoughts too, but I assumed that was different.

Maybe they were just blocking me like I'd managed to block Clay earlier at the river.

Toby's matte light-gray wolf slowed, along with the two russet ones on either side of his flank. I slowed with them as we approached what I had to assume was their pack camp.

Fire smoke drifted on the breeze, mingling with a distinct and overpowering foreign animal scent that made my wolf wrinkle her nose. I kept close to Toby as a tall wooden wall came into view.

It had to be at least thirteen feet high, built of wide logs all standing shoulder to shoulder. It went in both directions as far as I could see, curving gently to make a large circle, or perhaps an oval.

I caught my breath, chest heaving as Toby howled and a hidden gateway in the wall swung open, revealing a glimpse of the interior.

What at first glance I thought were weird tents turned out to be various sizes of yurts. Fat bottomed and tapering up to a pointed tip they sat clumped together in places and spaced apart in others, like giant forest fungus or some strange genus of mushroom.

Wolves and humans milled about inside, many wearing bright colors and loose fitted clothes. Thin raw-leather vests and headbands. It looked like the seventies never left this place, if you know what I mean.

And that strange scent on the air I thought was just the smell of foreign wolves revealed itself to be that and something more. Pot.

The skunky odor was easily distinguishable now,

and if that weren't enough it was clear from the cluster of three of the eastern pack slouching against the inside of the wall passing a joint around as we entered.

I willed my pulse to stop racing and tried to quiet my mind.

Get in. Get answers. Get out.

The door was pressed shut behind us, and I whirled, holding back a growl as I took in the woman hefting a large wooden plank into place to bar it shut. My tail pressed between my legs and my lip pulled back over my teeth.

"Annie," a familiar voice called, and I spun, antsy and skidding to one side as I took in Toby back in his human form. "Get Adam. The twin soul wolf is here for an audience, and she doesn't have much time."

I relaxed, if only a little, but I wasn't ready to shift yet. I was weak in my human form. Like this, with my wolf holding the reins, I was stronger. Safer. I knew I wouldn't exactly be able to have a conversation like this, but I wouldn't leave myself vulnerable for a single minute longer than I needed to.

It was what Clay would have wanted me to do, I was sure of it.

At the thought of him waiting alone out in the woods, my heart clenched.

Clay? I tried, projecting the thought as forcibly as I could. I needed to know if he could still hear me.

Can you hear me?

Only the echo of my own voice rebounded in my

skull. I swallowed hard and my skin bristled. I was alone.

"You idiot," the woman called Annie chastised Toby. "Why the hell would you agree to that?"

"Just get him," Toby snapped back at her. "I think he may want to hear what she has to say."

Toby cut his bright eyes back to me, as though imploring me to have something worthwhile to tell his alpha. I got the feeling he'd be punished if Adam didn't like what I had to say.

Would he be disappointed that I merely came to ask a question that I was fairly certain I already knew the answer to?

I hoped not.

And looking around it was more and more clear to me that I was right without even needing to ask Adam.

There were maybe a total of twenty shifters in the camp that I could see and that was being *very* generous. But that wasn't the dead giveaway. They were all so…

So…

Peaceful.

A small group played the banjo and sang to a trio of children near a low burning fire in the distance. A pair of younger girls sat together, scribbling in notebooks or maybe sketching.

A few cooked in an open-air kitchen near the fire, and the rest sat or laid in various states of blissful high around the remaining grounds.

These were not people looking for a fight with their

neighbors. Nor were they people who would attempt to pick off our numbers one by one without hope of repercussion.

If Adam told me otherwise, I'd call him a liar.

That was when a few flaws in my plan began to emerge from my muddied thoughts.

They could lie to me.

Who was to say that just because I asked if it were them who'd been picking off our numbers that they would tell me the truth?

And who was to say that they wouldn't turn around and tell Ryland themselves that I came here without permission, asking treasonous questions.

Fuck.

Why didn't Clay think of any of this?

Jared would've.

Damnit.

Clay was right. We should have told Jared. He should have been a part of this.

I fucked up.

I totally and royally fucked up.

Maybe I should just leave now, say it was all a mistake.

"The twin soul wolf," someone called, and I stilled, recognizing the voice. It was the same voice that'd called for my execution that night at the Four Corners. The same alpha who fled instead of standing and fighting.

He stared at me beneath heavy lidded eyes. His long

beard hid most of his face from me. He could have been smiling, or he could be snarling, and I wouldn't be able to tell for the thick bush of salt and pepper hair. He wore a white tunic and loose tan pants. His feet were bare.

He looked for all the world like he was about to welcome me into his commune for an hour of beer yoga. Only his eyes spoke of his status here. Heated. Wide pupils ringed with burning hazel irises.

"Welcome to my territory," he spat like a curse, training a furious stare on Toby who said nothing but dropped his head in shame.

"Well," Adam hissed. "Do you want this audience or not, girl? I heard you have a lad waiting who's primed to explode if you don't return in the next forty minutes."

I wasn't sure if I *did* want to have this meeting anymore, but I was here now. Too late to back out.

I held in a pained cry as I shifted back, the transformation slower going for the fourth time in a day. I cringed to think how the fifth time would treat me when we got home. At least there was a hot bath waiting there.

I clenched my fists against the urge to cover my nakedness from view and forced my spine erect. "Thank you," I managed. "For giving me an—"

"This way," Adam said without letting me finish, waving an arm at me to follow him. "You too, Toby," he added. "I'd like a word with you when our *visitor* departs."

I offered Toby an impish grin, and his face pinched, falling into step behind me as I followed Adam to one of the larger yurts not in a cluster but set apart, with its own little herb garden outside.

Scratch that. Pot garden. With its own little *pot garden* outside.

Adam went inside, holding back a thin white flap for us to follow him. On entry, my senses were assaulted with a myriad of colors and smells. Jasmine and sandalwood. Sage and juniper.

There were patterned carpets and fuzzy blankets of every color. Orange leather and wicker and thick, chunky lace drapes. If I didn't know any better, I'd have guessed the entrance to the yurt was actually a portal through time.

And Adam just sort of blended in with it all. He folded himself down into a wicker seat with bits of the straw-like material fraying and broken in places. It was a wonder the thing didn't collapse under his weight.

"Sit," he ordered Toby, jutting his chin to a chair set next to his, with a small tree stump table placed between them.

He offered me no seat, though if I were being honest, I preferred to remain standing anyway.

Adam gave me one long up and down look, making me shudder and want to cover all the bits and pieces I'd been taught to keep hidden my entire life until now.

He jabbed two fingers at a patterned blue and black blanket cast haphazardly on a lumpy bed jammed against the other side of the yurt. "You can put that on if you want, then I suggest you get talking so we can get you back to your friend before he has a fit."

Grateful, I rushed over and draped the thick blanket over my shoulders, tugging it closed at my front. I tried to ignore the faint scent of body odor clinging to it. It was better than being ass naked in front of two strange men.

Though Toby didn't seem to mind one bit.

"Get on with it, girl," Adam urged, slouching back in his chair with a huff.

An annoyed flush crawled into my cheeks. Now that I was here, exactly where I wanted to be, the question seemed foolish. I knew it wasn't their doing, but maybe they could still give me information I could use.

Among the other wolves who had joined our pack after Ryland killed their alphas, there had been a few who seemed to *know* things about Ryland. And it was *those* wolves—supposedly—who'd gone missing.

Maybe there were shifters here who knew some of those things, too.

"Several wolves have vanished from our pack," I began, trying to keep the acid from leaking into my tone. I didn't like how either of them were looking at me. How they were speaking to me. I lifted my chin and waited to see if they would take the bait, tell me something.

Adam's brows lowered at the open-ended statement. "Are you accusing us of something?"

I wasn't exactly sure how to answer that, so I continued, choosing to ignore his question. "They've vanished without a trace. We've searched for weeks, to the outer edges of our borders and far beyond them where we could. They left no trail. Nothing."

His eyes narrowed further, and he made a considering sound in his throat, thinking through something. "And you've come all this way to tell me this...why?"

I swallowed. "Originally, I came to ask if you had something to do with it," I admitted, watching his lips part in surprise, but I wasn't finished. "Since that is what my alpha would have the rest of our pack believe."

The tiniest smirk shifted Adam's beard. His eyes crinkled. "Is that so?"

I nodded.

"It seems he failed to convince at least one of his pack. Maybe two."

I nodded again.

"Let me guess..." Adam trailed off, plunging his thumb and index finger into his beard to rub his chin in an exaggerated pose of thoughtfulness. "These shifters who went missing, they opposed him in some way? Perhaps they knew things about him that they shouldn't have?"

My throat went instantly bone dry, and my stomach dropped.

I prayed that this shifter wouldn't turn around on

me and tell Ryland that I came here and everything I said, because the way this conversation was headed, if he did, I was certain I would be the next wolf to vanish into thin air.

"They did," I agreed, wetting my lips. "Or at least, I think they might've."

A long silence stretched between us where I think both were waiting for the other to add something to the conversation. Maybe he didn't want to incriminate himself in case *I* intended to run back to Ryland and tell him all Adam's theories and accusations.

I needed to give him something. Something that would make him trust me.

But that something could also get me killed if he decided to share it.

I inhaled deeply, trying to draw strength in with the oxygen. "I think he killed them."

Adam's eyes widened in surprise, though I didn't think it was because of what I said. More that I'd actually said it.

I couldn't hardly believe I'd allowed the words through my thoughts, never mind freed them from my mouth. I didn't realize *how much* I actually believed it until I voiced my worry aloud.

Adam dropped his gaze, thinking for a moment before he replied.

"You're smart, I'll give you that," Adam said on the back of a sigh. "But also foolish if you think he won't find out you've come here. He has spies everywhere.

And that *damned* vamp friend of his can draw secrets out of anyone with his compulsion."

"I know the risks."

"Bravery is all well and good girl, until it gets you killed."

This coming from the alpha who fled, allowing two of his own shifters to be killed. Hell, the one I killed could have been one of his. I wasn't sure. Though he seemed utterly unconcerned about that.

My so-called bravery may get me killed, but at least I would go down fighting for something. For people I loved. To make sure they are safe.

He was more likely to be stabbed in the back rather than stand his ground against an enemy.

"If I remember correctly, you were the one who wanted me dead at the Four Corners."

Another twitch of his beard, though this time I couldn't tell if he was smirking or scowling. "Aye."

"Then don't fucking preach to me about bravery and risk," I snapped, feeling my wolf surface briefly before settling back down. "I came here for some answers and you can take comfort in knowing that those answers—*should you choose to share them with me*—will more than likely see me to an early grave."

He nodded appreciatively. "True," he agreed, leaning forward to steeple his fingers, pressing his elbows into his knees. "Though I'm starting to think perhaps I was wrong about you."

"Thanks?" I said sarcastically. "That's comforting."

Adam dropped his steepled fingers and sat back once more. "Very well. I'll tell you what I know if you're that determined to hear it, but I do not guarantee the veracity of any of it. Rumors travel through shifters just as swiftly—*and unreliably*—as they do through mortals."

"I understand. Tell me everything you know."

19

We made it back to the border with barely a minute to spare. Clay's wolf was there, steaming in the chill of the evening as he paced, only stilling when he was able to see me in full view.

Adam accompanied Toby and I back to the border. He shifted back to his human form just before I crossed back over to my own territory.

"Don't come back here," he warned. "And if Ryland should ever find out you came here, I will deny everything I told you tonight."

Coward, I thought, and my wolf snarled a little before I could get her in check.

"In fact, I will tell your alpha that you came here for some other nefarious purpose and leave you to clean up whatever mess that makes."

Total fucking coward.

I bobbed my canine head and loped back through the break in the trees, but I didn't feel any less shaky with unease once my paws touched the earth on my own turf. Much the opposite.

My stomach was roiling and my head spinning since leaving the eastern pack camp. Adam hadn't had a massive amount to tell me, but what he had told me... well, let's just say that I was praying it wasn't true.

That the rumor mill birthed it and mouth to ear transit twisted it, turning it even more vile than the original whisper.

Because if it were true...

If it were true, I'd kill him.

I may not have been able to defend myself to the point of murder with Devin, but I sure as hell wouldn't hesitate this time. All I needed was one shred of proof of any *one* of Adam's apparent 'rumors' and it would be enough for me.

I peered back and watched Adam shift back, his wolf giving me one last long look before he and Toby turned tail and began the short journey back to camp.

I hope it was worth it, Clay's voice slithered dangerously into my mind and my muscles clenched. There was so much more in that sentence than what it was at face value.

In his voice, I could hear betrayal. Pain. Anger.

He was clearly still pissed at me for leaving him, and I couldn't fault him for it. I didn't have the energy to. Not right now. I needed to process. To decide what the fuck to do with the information I was given.

Well, Clay pressed after a moment. *Are you going to tell me what he said?*

I lifted my face to the wrathful, watchful glare of Clay's burning blue eyes.

I...I don't know where to start.

Some of the fire ebbed away, and he stalked closer, peering through the gap to where Toby and Adam had only just retreated.

Did they hurt you? If they hurt you—

No. They didn't hurt me.

At least not in any physical way. Though I was sure my heart and mind would bear the scars of what they told me for as long as it took me to either prove them wrong, or prove them right.

Then what is it?

We should go, I told Clay. *Your sister will be waiting for you. I'll...I'll do my best to explain on the way. I need to move.*

My wolf itched to sprint. She was angry and confused just as I was. We needed to run from those demons, just for a little while. We needed to feel light, or else the heaviness would anchor us in place, and we might never move again.

I didn't wait for Clay to reply. I took off like a round loosed from the barrel of a gun. Clay barely needed more than a few seconds to catch up with me.

He waited, matching my pace, for me to be ready to talk.

I could still sense his rage, but beneath that was something else. Worry.

Good, I thought. *He should be worried.*

For a full five minutes of hard and fast sprinting, I focused only on shielding my thoughts from Clay. I had to think of the best way to tell him all that I needed to, and there was one thing in particular that I couldn't breathe aloud to him. If I did…I didn't think Clay would wait to gather the proof we needed before acting.

Hell, even what I did plan to tell him was enough to send him over the edge. It damn near did for me. The entire run from the eastern camp to the border was spent picturing all the ways I would tear Ryland apart.

It was those *very comforting* images—those promises to myself—that calmed me enough to even consider not going straight to my alpha and demanding the truth in front of the whole pack.

Except…that would end badly for me. I knew it would.

Just like it would end badly for Clay if he were the one to do it.

We have no proof of any of this, I prefaced the first shared thought between our minds. *Adam said himself that all he knows are rumors—that it's possible none of it is even true.*

No reply.

First, they have nothing to do with the missing shifters.

How do you know?

Trust me. If there's anything I'm sure of, it's that.

A pause.

Okay. Fine. So what did he tell you then?

I grimaced and relayed all that I could, feeling my gut twist as I spoke. It was so terrible I hardly wanted to say it aloud, let alone tell Clay. It seemed preposterous. A cruel fabrication.

He'd told me that Ryland had his sights set on being alpha of the Forest Grove pack since long before Adam had become alpha of the eastern pack about twenty years ago.

Rumor had it that Ryland had a…*disagreement* with his brother—Jared's father about who was going to succeed him should he fall. Furious that his brother, Noah, wouldn't leave the pack in his hands, he requested permission to leave the Forest Grove pack and was granted it.

Ryland supposedly ran with a northern pack for a good number of years before returning to Forest Grove, requesting to come home to his pack.

By then his brother had had a son. Jared.

Noah brought Ryland back into the fold and they became brothers once more. Ryland became an uncle to his nephew and indispensable to the pack. But not quite as indispensable as Thomas Armstrong.

That's all true, Clay spoke in my mind. *At least, as far as I know.*

This is where it gets really bad.

The rumors from way back then, all but snuffed out by now, said that Ryland had his own brother murdered along with his wife. The whispers said that he made it look like an accident with the help of a certain vampire friend. They said that he had them shot and skinned to make it look like mortal hunters did it.

Clay's tension rolled off him in waves. I could sense his confusion. His disbelief. And the beginning of a raging fire sparking to life within him. It was a match for my own.

Clay didn't speak. He only waited for me to go on.

From what Adam explained to me, it sounds like Ryland thought that he would be handed the mantle of alpha once his brother was removed from the picture.

But he wasn't, Clay growled in my thoughts. *My father was.*

Were you there then? You would have been so young.

I was.

But your sister—

Wasn't, Clay finished for me. I remembered he said Ryland never met her.

There's a lot you don't know about me, Allie, Clay grunted, pushing himself harder and faster as he ran, forcing me to push myself harder too just to keep pace.

What does that mean?

I guess you might as well know, he said, *since you're*

going to meet her. My sister wasn't a born wolf. She was mortal, like my mom.

My eyes widened. He'd never really talked about his sister. Hell, I didn't even know he had one until last week. Now, I could see why he never told me about her. His entire body was wired for sound just trying to get out whatever he was trying to say.

She was attacked. Raped. And bitten.

Oh my god.

Yeah.

After I killed the bastard who did it, she turned. She and Ma were living up North and after I...did what I did...she didn't want to come to Forest Grove. She found a pack up north and took care of Ma until she passed.

I wondered how he lost his mother but didn't think now was the time to ask.

She knew about our kind, of course. She never *wanted to be like us. She hated shifters. Was terrified of us. It was part of the reason Ma left in the first place, to take her away. To make her feel safe.*

I could feel his pain like a gut punch to my own stomach.

I'm so sorry...

Clay made a strangled half laugh sound in my thoughts and his deep voice rumbled again through my head. *I just told you I murdered someone and that's all you have to say?*

I frowned. Fuck. I honestly hadn't even questioned it. What was I becoming that the casual mention of murder barely phased me? I swallowed back the ugly thought and lifted my head. Shook it.

No. It wasn't wrong. Not for the reasons he did it.

The truth rose up my throat like a brand, but I managed to get the words out anyway. *I'm glad you did it,* I hissed. *He didn't deserve to live.*

Clay ground his claws into the earth, coming to a jarring standstill as dirt was thrown in a wave over the brush. I skidded to a stop, too, breathing heavily.

His burning ice gaze found mine, and he stared openly at me, his head lowered and nostrils flaring with great clouds of steam.

The guy was only sixteen, he snarled. *He already had a pup. A mate.*

I knew what he was doing, but I wasn't going to let him. He wouldn't make himself out to be the monster. Not to me.

And your sister had a life that was taken from her.

I mean *fuck*, it was no wonder she had a temper. I would, too.

Clay tossed his head to the side, making a disgusted sound in his throat.

You can beat yourself up about it all you want, I all but shouted into his head, *but I'm not buying it. You can pretend to yourself that you're some monster, Clay, but I know better.*

I'd killed too. I put down that shifter at the Four Corners without blinking. He was a threat to my friends. He might've killed them.

I didn't know if he had a family, or a mate. But I knew one thing...

I'd do it again.

It may not be the same thing as what Clay did. I'd killed that shifter in the heat of the moment. In defense.

He'd clearly gone looking for the shifter who'd attacked his sister. It wasn't defense. It was vengeance.

That didn't mean it wasn't deserved.

Finish what you were telling me, Clay said, moving back into a walk. We were nearly back at the cabin now. A few more miles and we'd be back on our doorstep.

I bristled, wishing he would talk to me more about what had happened. He didn't need to carry the weight of it alone. But I wouldn't push him. I'd wait until he was ready, and one day, I would make him see that what he did wasn't wrong.

It was justice in a world where most don't get theirs.

If he hadn't done what he'd done, then who was to say that bastard wouldn't have done it again. That he wouldn't have done it over and over *and over*.

That's pretty much it, I explained. *There was already a protocol in place for who was to take over should anything happen to him. Your father, Thomas, was to take over as alpha until his own son, Jared, came of age.*

So what? Clay demanded. *Supposedly, Ry killed Jared's*

parents to become alpha of the Forest Grove pack and then he just let my dad take over?

I didn't reply. I couldn't.

Sounds a little too fucked up, don't you think? Doesn't even really make sense.

If he knew the whole story it might.

It could just be a rumor.

Is that all then?

I sighed. *There were a couple other rumors that he got a shifter pregnant in one of the northern packs and killed her when he found out. That that was the reason why he came back to Forest Grove. And another rumor that he—*

Stop, Clay seethed.

I let my thoughts go blank, realizing Clay was on the cusp of how much rage he could control.

The other stuff—it's bad—but it doesn't really have much to do with us or with the pack, I explained. In other words, there was no need for both of us to have to be burdened by knowing it. I sure as hell wished I didn't.

We walked onto the cabin's property, and I heaved a relieved sigh when it came into view through the trees. I could hardly believe we'd actually made it, and without anyone catching us.

A small victory, but still a victory.

Clay shifted back once we were on the dirt lawn, showing me his tight backside as he drew up his shorts that were discarded near the bottom step. He tossed me my clothes that were folded nearby and turned around, waiting for me to shift.

I did, whimpering as all my bones cried out in protest. I managed to keep the bulk of my pain under wraps, but I knew Clay would be able to feel it whether I made a sound or not.

It hurt even to pull my t-shirt over my head. The brush of the fabric against my skin felt like sandpaper.

"Done," I ground out when I was no longer naked, my voice gravelly.

Clay turned and met my eyes. In his, I could see his wolf was still on the prowl. And his face, tight and twisted, spoke of the thoughts I could no longer hear.

He pressed his lips into a firm line. "It can't be true," he said.

Though we both knew it very well could be. "For Jared's sake," I said, cutting my fingernails into my palms to keep steady. "I hope it's not."

Clay threw a clawed hand through his hair and rolled his shoulders back, tipping his head to one side to crack his neck.

"You're coming with me," he decided. "I know you're tired, but I'm not leaving you here. I've got to pick up my sister. We'll take the Jeep to meet her. Jared left it for us."

I ached for my bed, but let's be real. Sleep wasn't going to happen whether I laid in it or not.

"There's just one thing," Clay added, his face cut from stone. "I have to bring her to Ry. It's protocol. He needs to officially give her permission to be here. And the pack needs to get a whiff of her scent, so no one ends up on a wild goose chase. We'll drive to the borderlands to meet her so you can have a rest but then we'll have to go on foot into pack camp. Are you good for one more shift?"

My heart thudded hard against my ribcage. Both at the prospect of having to see Ryland face to face *tonight* after having heard what I did, and now I may have to shift *again*. Maybe even twice more before the night was through.

I was going to *live* in the bath for the next two days after this.

I nodded. "I can."

A tense pause.

"Can you keep your chill when we get to camp?" I asked Clay.

He raised a brow at me.

"Can *you*?" he countered.

I thought about it. "Until we know for sure—yes."

He nodded, cracking his knuckles. "Then so can I."

20

The drive to the borderlands took about an hour since Ryland's territory had expanded significantly since the night at the Four Corners. If we'd run, we'd have made it there in a little under thirty minutes. We were late. Not the best first impression I wanted to give Sam. Clay was silent most of the drive, leaving to respond to some texts from Jared and Viv.

Jared would be home tomorrow for good apparently.

And Vivian...Vivian had a lacrosse game coming up. She was asking me if I'd come.

Allie: Lacrosse, Viv?

It pained me to point this out to her, but it had to be done.

Allie: Do you really think that's a good idea?

I didn't expect her to reply, it was well after

midnight, but after only a few minutes a response came through.

Vivian: I'm not giving up lacrosse.

Well, that was decided then. I didn't have a choice. I'd have to go if only to make sure nothing happened.

Allie: When is it? I'll be there.

We parked down a side road. and I left my phone in the car, knowing I wouldn't be able to carry it in my wolf form. We walked the rest of the way into the forest. Me with an armful of clothes for Sam, and Clay with a sour attitude that told me he didn't want to talk.

I could sense the foreign wolf was there within minutes. The border was just ahead, I realized, sensing the same shift in the air that I'd briefly experienced when I passed through onto the eastern pack's territory earlier. Like my wolf just *knew* that was where the borders were without having any visual cues.

I supposed that was how everybody knew where they could and couldn't go. I'd usually relied on Charity to lead the way on our searches, and Jared and Clay on our runs, to make sure we didn't encroach on any other pack land.

"Sam," Clay called into the night. "You can cross. We're here."

A shadowy shape appeared a moment later, growing in size until she was upon us. I squealed as she barreled into Clay, knocking him clean off his feet. She pressed her paws into his chest and bit at his face.

My wolf reacted, raging to the surface in defense

of my mate. I dropped the clothes in the dirt and growled at her, ready to shift and go straight for the throat.

Sam whirled on me, as though only just realizing I was there. She snarled at me as Clay cursed to himself, trying to shove her off him. He finally succeeded. "Take it easy," he snapped at me, and my wolf retreated enough for me to shove her the rest of the way back down.

Clay got to his feet, staring down a still-snarling Sam.

She wasn't very big. Not quite Charity's size. Maybe not even quite my size, but I could tell right away she was a spitfire. Lean and angry. Practically foaming at the mouth. And like her brother, she was *fast.* I barely had time to register that she was charging us before she was on top of Clay.

"She *attacked* you," I spat back at Clay, trying to dull the sting of his words.

Ignoring me, Clay glared down at his sister. "*Sam,*" he said, his words a warning as his sister continued to growl at me. "This is Allie. *My mate.* Now would you fucking shift already?"

Her snarls quieted, and one second, I was staring at a dark gray wolf with a streak of white like a lightning bolt on her forehead and the next there was a very naked woman standing ten feet away from me. A woman with long, wild black hair and piercing blue eyes. Her pallor was lighter than her brother's, the ivory tone of her skin and darkness of her hair made her look severe.

Her curvy body was a seductress' dream. Large, heaving breasts with dark cherry nipples pebbled in the cool breeze. A thick, muscled frame and wide hips. Legs for days.

I cast my gaze away, blushing.

"*Christ, Sam,*" Clay cursed, lifting a hand to shield himself from seeing his sister in the nude. He snatched up the discarded clothes from the ground and shoved it at her, shielding his eyes all the while.

"Oh stop," she chastised. "It's not like it's anything you haven't seen before."

Her tone was soft as suede, but she wielded it like a whip, leaving a sting.

"You can quit covering your eyes now," she grumbled a moment later. "Hey big bro."

I turned in time to see her tug Clay into a hard embrace. He hugged her back, the scowl on his face quickly changing to something I wasn't sure I'd ever seen there before.

A sort of peace that made my own lips quirk up into a half grin.

"All right," Sam said as she pulled away from her brother. "Introduce me."

She said it like he was about to introduce her to the most unimportant person imaginable. I did my best not to take offense. If this bitch made Clay happy, then I'd swallow what I wanted to say in favor of something a bit less cutting.

"Sam, this is Allie. Allie, meet my kid sister."

Sam surveyed me top to bottom.

I did the same.

She should've looked ridiculous in a combination of Clay's baggy sweats and my Naruto t-shirt, but somehow, she managed to rock it.

"Nice to meet you," I said, not bothering with a handshake. A hug was out of the question.

"Right," she said. "I'd say the feeling was mutual, but you kind of fucked up my brother's chance to mate *properly* so…yeah. Hard pass."

"Fair enough."

"Sam," Clay warned. "Be *nice*."

She turned on her brother with a haughty stare. "That *was* nice," she told him. "Do you want to see cruel?"

Clay rolled his eyes but said nothing. "We'll talk about it later," he promised her.

Her nose wrinkled.

I was tempted to ask Clay if she really had to stay with us at the cabin, but thought maybe now wasn't the best time for that. Maybe I could crash at Viv's for a while. Or with Charity.

A sigh left my lips. No. I needed to wear this bitch down. If she was a part of Clay's life, then she was a part of mine.

"Missed you," Sam said, bumping Clay's shoulder with hers.

Clay grunted, neither confirming nor denying that he missed her, too, though I suspected it was the former.

"Still not much for chit chat, huh?" Sam asked, putting a hand to one hip.

"It's late, Sam."

"Well," she replied with a sigh. "Can't argue with you there. I'm pooched. Let's go get this shit over with and head back to the cabin. I can't wait to see my old room."

Clay stiffened and cut me an apologetic look.

I held my breath. No, it couldn't be…

My room? I mouthed to him as Sam began to walk away.

Clay grimaced, and it was enough of an answer to make me grit my own teeth. I got the feeling Sam wasn't going to like that one bit.

"Are we walking or running?" Sam asked, calling back over her shoulder. I knew what she really meant was *are we really going to make the trek on human legs? Or can we do this properly?*

Clay looked to me for permission.

Sam made a grossed-out sound in her throat and rolled her eyes at him.

"I'm good," I said in a low voice, not wanting Sam to hear or to think that I was in any way *controlling* her brother. My skin bristled. "Let's run."

. . .

I'D BEEN RIGHT about how much time we might've saved if I'd had it in me to use my wolf to run to meet Sam. It took us barely thirty minutes to within ten miles of pack camp. It was late enough that we didn't run into anyone along the way, which I appreciated.

I didn't appreciate that we'd also have to run all the way back to pick up the Jeep at the northern border before making the painfully slow drive home. *Damn.* I really wished I'd just bucked up and run with Clay instead of letting him drive us there. It really backfired.

At this rate we wouldn't be home until close to dawn. School tomorrow was going to really suck. And I was meant to work at the shop afterward too, you know, if I still had a job. That voicemail from Jacqueline was primed to expire tomorrow night if I didn't listen to it. I knew I would have to before I went in for my shift, just in case it was her telling me not to bother.

Which I assumed was *exactly* what it would say. At least I'd be able to nap after school…

The painful reality of it made me laugh darkly within the confines of my wolf. For all this new life had given me, it sure didn't seem to want to stop *taking* things, too.

Clay slowed and I saw his ears prick, hearing something I was oblivious to.

What is it? I asked Clay.

Don't know.

Before I could pause to have a better listen myself, curious what it was that had him on edge, another voice entered my thoughts. Sliding in like the sharp edge of a blade.

Stay where you are, Ryland bellowed the command.

Clay and I stopped, and Clay let out a little bark for Sam to follow suit. She cocked her head peculiarly at him but didn't make a fuss. In fact, she seemed glad of the break. Her chest heaved hard, and her legs trembled like reeds in the wind.

I remembered she'd run all the way from her pack territory in Alaska and understood why. It made me look like a wimp in comparison.

He must have sensed us, Clay whispered in my thoughts. *He'll want to escort us in, so we don't startle the others.*

I nodded my head to show I understood, though I didn't share any thoughts with him. I was trying to clear them as best I could, not wanting Ry to be able to glean anything off me that I didn't wish to share.

It took a continuous effort to make sure my thoughts were mine and mine alone.

We heard him before we saw him. Ry's footfalls were heavy and coming from the left. Not in the direction of camp. He must've already been out for a run when he realized we were coming.

Sam parked herself beside her brother, sitting with a docile dip to her head and her fluffy tail curled around her paws. Clay had no such chill. He stood next to his sister with a powerful defiance to his stance and a hard stare in his gaze. I wanted to bite his ass to remind him to play it cool, but it was too late, I could already see Ry weaving in and out around tree trunks and brush.

The great black wolf slowed from a sprint to a canine jog as he cleared the last bit of space. His bright orange gaze went first to Clay, and then, without bothering to hide his disappointment, to me.

When his gaze slid from me to Sam, Ryland jerked so violently that his claws dug deep channels in the earth and his hackles went up from the top of his head all the way to the end of his tail.

His eyes were wide. Wild.

Shock was evidenced in the rigidity of his stance. In the quick, short bursts of air filtering in and out through his nostrils.

Sam cried out and all at once I realized what was happening.

Clay saw it, too.

He watched as his sister cringed and buckled, whining as she fought against the invisible force making her head bow just as Ryland's did. And when finally she broke free of it, how she pressed up from the earth, her neck long and chest jutting out as a long howl tore from her mouth. It rose like a scream in the night, tangling the deeper sound of Ryland's own howl.

Clay's blue eyes met mine, panicked and confused.

He growled low in his throat, and I lurched over to

him, tucking myself in close to his side, trying to soothe him.

Don't, was all I said in his mind, terrified to voice anything else.

Ryland was the first to let the howl fade, dropping his hungry eyes to his new mate. He sauntered toward her like a predator stalking beautiful prey. Like he was strangely disarmed by her beauty but intended to make a meal of her all the same.

It was difficult to look at.

Difficult to stomach.

I couldn't even imagine what was going through Clay's mind right now, but I did know he was working *very* hard to hide whatever it was because not a single wisp of a thought broke through his defenses.

I stepped on Clay's paw as Ryland approached, and he grudgingly took a step back, allowing Ryland to stalk a slow circle around a shivering Sam.

Mate, Ryland's throaty roar echoed in my skull, and I knew without needing anyone to tell me that it was a declaration. That it was a single word projected to the entire pack. I buckled under the force of it and Clay flinched.

It was difficult to tell, but I got the sense that Ryland and his mate were having a conversation we couldn't hear. Like when I first mated to Jared and Clay. Even though they weren't my pack yet, the mate bond allowed us to communicate.

Judging by the little sounds they were making, it

seemed like it wasn't a horribly unpleasant conversation at least. Sam's shaking began to subside, and her bowed head rose, and she rolled her shoulders back, taking in her new mate like someone would take in a brand-new car.

The fear I'd seen in her for an instant had abated. She looked...happy.

And like she wanted to take that new car for a test drive.

Ugh.

Clay growled low in his throat, and Ry turned on him with a snarl, but Sam, surprising me, snapped in Ry's direction, earning herself a surprised stare from Ry.

No, surprised wasn't the right word. Shocked, maybe?

Outraged, definitely.

Though Sam didn't back down from his withering stare.

I heard someone else coming and peered into the tree line toward camp, finding several other shifters emerging, awoken from Ryland's declaration. Their approach was enough to tranquilize Ry, who resumed his leering of Sam. *Appreciative* leering, as though she hadn't just done something to offend him a few seconds before.

Charity was the first to reach us. She looked between Ryland and Sam, her eyes watery and her movements stilted. Once she got a good enough eye full, she fled, leaving the other approaching pack members to ogle their alpha's new mate. My heart ached for her even though I would never understand her attraction to him.

Ryland shifted, going from wolf to human in one fluid movement, one step a wolf, and the next on mortal feet. He grinned down at Sam, his look encouraging her to do the same.

When she did, Clay and I followed suit along with many of the other shifters who'd come to investigate.

I barely felt the shift this time, too preoccupied with needing to make sure Clay didn't intend to strangle Ryland. I shivered in the cold and tucked myself into Clay's side, wrapping my hand around his clenched one. For a second, I thought he might shuck me off. I expected it.

He didn't like to be comforted. I knew that.

Which was why I was surprised when he relaxed his fisted hand enough to slide his fingers through mine, gripping tight. For once, I was able to offer him what he always offered me. Courage. And maybe a bit of calmness.

Ryland appraised Sam. His tongue slipped out, licking his lips as though he'd just finished a particularly intoxicating meal. Sam appraised him in turn, and though I could tell she was not wholly satisfied, she seemed at least accepting of what she saw.

I wouldn't say it, but I had to assume it was to do with his age.

From what I knew *generally* the mate bond formed between two shifters nearer together in age naturally, but I also knew that that wasn't *always* the case. It seemed Sam and Ryland were the exception to the rule. From what I knew Sam was only a year older than I was. And Ryland was…what? Close to fifty? Ick.

I felt sick for Clay, and more than ever before, I prayed that what I learned tonight was not true.

Shouted admonishments of congratulations rose from the gathering of my pack mates. Forrest and Harrison whooped, bumping fists with each other before they clapped Ryland on the back and welcomed Sam with open arms and naked embraces. With kisses on her cheeks and shakes of her hand. She grinned broadly through it all, laughing as she kept a seductive eye on her new mate and he on her.

She beamed as he announced a celebration to take place on the weekend. To properly welcome his new mate to the Forest Grove pack.

Not a clue that she may have just mated to the most dangerous shifter here.

21

I padded down the stairs on leaden legs, my mind in a thick fog. I might have slept even longer had the wafting scent of bacon and pancakes not woken me. I rubbed my burning eyes and did my best to stretch out the awful kink in my neck.

My legs protested every step, threatening to give out under my weight. Seeing Jared flip a pancake into the air and catch it in a sizzling pan in the kitchen brought it all back in a wave.

The reason why I was so sore. The hundreds of miles Clay and I had run. Where we'd gone in secret. What we learned.

My stomach waged a war on itself as I shuffled into the kitchen. Hunger and disgust dueling at the fresh memory of my alpha mating to Clay's little sister. Had that actually happened?

I wished I could believe it was all just a really bad,

really vivid dream, but I knew better. Clay had been shaking when we finally left. Ryland had insisted Sam stay at pack camp with him. Sam didn't seem opposed to the idea, so what were we to do?

I could tell Clay had *wanted* to do something. *Wanted* more than anything to say something. To warn his sister. But how could he? With his sister smiling and laughing. With the gleam in her eyes.

He wouldn't speak to me on the way back from camp as much as I tried to reach him. Not during the run, or the long drive home. We sat in horror-steeped silence, listening to late-night radio turned down low. He let me hold his hand while we drove, however, and every so often, I felt his fingers twitch, as though he was remembering where his sister was—who she was with—all over again.

I gulped past a hard lump in my throat and glanced around to the living room and out the window to the yard. I couldn't see him anywhere.

I wondered if he slept at all. It took me hours to finally drift off. The thud and rattle of Clay hitting the heavy bag in his shop becoming something of a violent lullaby.

"Morning," I croaked, trying to clear my throat.

Jared spun, just barely catching a pancake he'd been tossing for a second time to flip. He set the pan down on a dormant burner and his lips twitched into a halfway grin. "Hey," he said, taking in my likely monstrous appearance. I'd had a long bath before attempting to sleep last night but tossing and turning with wet hair had left me with a mane that was about the size of a lion's.

A worried crease formed in his brow as he wrapped his arms around me, pressing me into him for a soft hug. I melted into him, shuddering at the intensity of the sensation of his nearness. He was away so much that the feeling was always so strong when he returned.

"I missed you," he whispered against my cheek, and I nearly smiled before remembering what Adam had told me. I stiffened and drew back, guilt pooling like acid in my belly. I couldn't tell him now, not with everything else going on.

"Hey," he said, crooking a brow at me as he brushed some warmth back into my arms. "You okay?"

I shook my head, blinking to clear my thoughts. "Yeah. Yeah, I'm fine. Just really tired, and I missed you, too. Where's Clay?"

"He left early this morning right after I got home. Said he wanted to go and check on Sam."

I sighed. Of course, he did.

"Did he seem…okay?"

Jared's sandstone eyes fell to the floor. "I think so. It's a little messed up. I mean, she's so young. It's the first time he's seen her in almost four years, you know. He usually goes up to Alaska to visit because she doesn't like coming here. I don't think he expected to be welcoming her back for good, or for her to mate with one of his least favorite people."

I winced. That was putting it lightly.

"Doesn't she need, like, permission from her own alpha to leave?"

Jared nodded. "Yeah, but when it's to do with mating, it's almost never denied. Apparently, she's flying back round trip tomorrow to get her things and then she'll be here to stay."

"So fast?"

Jared gave an uncomfortable shrug. "I guess Ry doesn't want to waste any time. Some of us were starting to wonder if he was ever going to find his mate."

The way Jared said it, like even though the whole thing grossed him out, he was happy for his uncle, made me want to be sick all over again.

Soon, I promised myself. I would tell him as soon as I had something concrete. *Soon.*

If Sam was in any sort of danger with Ry…if that story about him murdering the shifter woman he got pregnant was true…then there wasn't any time left to waste.

"Are you sure you're okay?" Jared asked again, brushing some of my hair away from my cheek.

I brushed my palm over his hand, holding it there, reveling in how blissfully perfect the feel of him was. It was that small thing that gave me enough comfort—enough courage—to nod. I was okay.

We were all going to be okay.

I was going to make sure of that.

"Are you hungry? I made pancakes and about two pounds of bacon."

My stomach burbled between us and he chuckled. "I guess I could eat," I joked, tugging him in for one more hug, admiring how my body just *fit* there with his.

When I opened my eyes again, I gasped, jumping back. "You have got to be kidding me," I groaned, pushing my palms into my eye sockets to rub my eyes. I looked again.

Nope.

Not a cruel joke at all.

The clock above the stove glared at me with angry red numbers.

"It can't actually be one in the afternoon? Please tell me that's wrong," I begged, jabbing a finger in the general direction of the imposing clock.

A strained smile that was more a baring of teeth split Jared's face. "Sorry?" he offered. "I thought about waking you, but you looked so tired and—"

I moaned, wiping my hands over my face as I slumped into the chair at the little table by the window, hanging my head in my hands. "*Just great,*" I grumbled to myself. "I'm going to lose my job *and* fail all my classes."

And then there was the fact that I'd already been avoiding calls from Uncle Tim. The school would be calling him for sure. *Fuck.* What if he came up?

Four more days until you turn eighteen, I reminded

myself.

Just four more days and then you never have to answer a call or text from him again.

Ninety-six hours and he can stop worrying about me and tend to his snooty wife. He can serve her drinks on their beach patio and never think about me again.

Four. More. Days.

"You're not going to fail," Jared said, gently tugging my hands away from my face as he kneeled in front of me. His caramel-blond hair glowed in the muted light from the window.

"I'm *already* failing," I argued.

Jared bit his bottom lip, thinking before he replied, "How about this: I'm really behind on a bunch of stuff right now, too. Let's eat, and then we'll spend the day getting caught up. I'll help you with math and geography and you can help me with English."

My eyes burned at the offer.

There was just one problem, but I doubted it would even *be* a problem anymore once I checked my voicemails. "Okay," I whispered. "Just let me get fired first."

Jared cocked his head at me.

"I'm supposed to have a shift at the shop tonight after school," I explained. "But I'm pretty sure there's a voicemail on my phone that's going to tell me not to bother coming."

Jared's eyes darkened. "I'm so sorry, Allie. Maybe I could talk to her for you? I could explain—"

"How?" I asked, laughing darkly.

He opened his mouth to argue and I pressed two fingers to his lips, effectively cutting him off. "It's fine."

"I hate that word."

I lifted a brow.

"*Fine,*" he said, heaving a sad sigh. "I never want you to be *fine* Allie. Fine is nowhere near good enough. Not for you."

It took a solid hour before I could really focus on anything after a few nibbles of breakfast. But when focus finally did find me, Jared and I blew through classwork and overdue projects like a breeze. With his help, algebraic equations looked less like foreign hieroglyphs and more like structures of numeric pyramids. Still confusing, but a lot less like a foreign language.

He made quick work of my geography project, helping me craft an essay from start to finish. With my competence in English and proper essay formatting and his geo knowledge, we finished the whole thing in under an hour.

His own past due English paper got a thorough upgrade and full reference section complete with proper notations and formatting. He was worried his teacher might worry he'd stolen it, but I told him it wasn't against school policy to get help, and I'd take full credit for his improvement, just as I'd give him full credit for mine if asked.

Overall, within about four hours, we were essentially caught up on everything, with only a few smaller assignments and some daily homework left to complete. I'd have kept going, but I think both of us were starting to run out of gas. Every time I tried to work through a new problem in my textbook it was like my brain choked and sputtered to a stall.

Trying to jam the key in the ignition and pump the gas pedal wasn't working anymore, either. I'd chewed the end of my pen to a disgusting mess, and Jared's hair was sticking out at every angle imaginable.

It looked cute like that.

No, cute wasn't the right word. Rugged, maybe.

Sexy for sure.

He glanced up from the philosophy text he was reading and caught me staring. The glaze over his eyes abated and the knot between his brows softened. "What?" he asked, a playful smirk twisting up his lips.

I reached over across the coffee table and ruffled his hair. "Your hair," I joked. "It's getting so long."

The tops of his ears turned pink as he dragged both of his hands through it, trying to finger comb it into place. But it just sprang back into the mess it'd been a second before.

I giggled.

"I guess I could use a trim," he grumbled.

I shook my head. "No. I like it like this."

I reached back up to push my fingers into the smooth strands, a bit jealous. Any girl would *kill* to have hair like his. Thick and rich.

"Yours is starting to look different, too," he mused, glancing up at the crown of my head. I'd done my best to tame it with a comb, but had wound up knotting it into a low bun at the nape of my neck. "It's growing out."

I knew he was right. I hadn't dyed it in weeks. No, maybe months? The last time was the night of the party at Thompson's. What was left there for dye had faded to a pale turquoise, more of a pastel color than the vibrant hue I usually wore. And at my roots I had a solid two or three inches of new silvery blonde growth.

Truth be told, I couldn't be bothered to keep up with it anymore. Besides that, I couldn't *afford* to buy more dye. As it was, my bank account was dwindling by the week.

Bye-bye dreams renting the apartment above the shop.

Even if I could afford it, I doubted Jacqueline would rent it to me anymore, anyway. Who wanted a flakey tenant who rarely showed up for work.

I'd been right about her voicemail. Though it was much kinder than I thought it ought to be, Jacqueline had let me know, at least temporarily. I believe the exact words were:

I won't pretend to know what's going on, but I have to assume whatever it is, that it's important. I know you wouldn't skip out on work for just any reason. I've brought on a new trainee for the time being and think you should take some time off. We can reassess your position in the summer.

So, not exactly the worst thing ever, but any way you sliced it, my source of income was no more.

I called and left a message at the shop around three o'clock, knowing she would be swamped and wouldn't answer the phone. It was the least I could do to tell her I got her message and apologize. I thanked her for understanding and told her I took full responsibility even though some things were out of my control.

"Allie?" Jared prompted, and I realized I'd missed something he said.

"Sorry. Zoned out. What did you say?"

"Your hair," he repeated. "I like it—the natural color, I mean. Not that the green isn't awesome, too, though."

"*Turquoise*," I corrected, giving him a little swat.

He caught my hand before I could get him, holding me by the wrist. His thumb brushed against the soft skin of my wrist and my body flushed with a warmth not from the low-burning fire in the hearth at my back.

"Sorry," he said with a wicked gleam in his eyes. "*Turquoise*. You're right, I don't know what I was thinking. It's clearly not even close to being green."

"Are you trying to charm me, Jared Stone?"

"Is it working?"

His other hand crept onto my thigh beneath the coffee table, and I shuddered, biting the inside of my cheek to hold in a whimper.

When I opened my eyes again, I knew they would be glowing lightly around the edges, my wolf awakening to the touch of her mate.

No…not *hers*.

Ours.

Mine.

I really had missed him all this time. I felt like we'd been robbed of so much of it ever since Ryland started sending Jared away to work at the quarry.

"Are you really back for good?" I asked in a rush, afraid of the answer but needing it all the same. I had to know if he was going to vanish on me again. I needed him just as much as I needed Clay.

Jared was like my sun. Warm and bright even when things were stormy.

Clay like my moon. Shrouded in dark clouds, but still managing to shine despite them.

I couldn't have one without the other.

Jared's cheekbones twitched as he clenched his jaw, but after a second, he gave a single nod. "At least for a while."

It was the best he could do, I realized. None of us could say when Ryland would stick his big ugly head in our lives and rip them from under us. None of us had a say. Not a real one, anyway.

Without another word, I swiped one arm across the coffee table, knocking textbooks and binders and loose note papers to the floor. Jared's eyes widened before narrowing hungrily on me.

"I always wanted to do that," I said in a breath, climbing over the bare table to reach him.

He pulled me into his lap, settling me with my legs

around his waist and his hands gripping tightly around mine.

Jared didn't hesitate this time. He pressed himself against me, tipping his chin up to reach my lips before sliding his hands across my back, wrapping both arms securely around me, binding me to him.

With my hands tightly wound in his hair, I kissed him without restraint. Each kiss muting the guilt enough to spur me on. My heartbeat was a wave of dominos falling against bone. My breaths were a broken song, hanging on notes without finding any proper rhythm.

When his tongue slid between my lips, I came undone, my back arching and toes curling.

With me clamped around him, Jared moved, lifting me with him as he stood. His hands moved low, wrapping around my upper thighs to hold me up. Something throbbed low in my belly, twisting and aching. Burning.

I moaned against his mouth as we crested the top of the stairs and gasped when he kicked in the door to his bedroom. The jarring movement broke us apart for an instant, and in it, I saw the burning fire of his wolf in his eyes. The drunken desire making his eyelids heavy.

Jared carried me to his bed, and I let him lay me over the soft gray blanket there. He paused then, drawing back as his eyes traced a lazy trail down the line of my body. His jaw clenched.

"What?" I asked, still breathless and aching to taste him.

I needed him to touch me. I needed to feel him. To erase all the doubt and the pain and the worry with his lips.

"I think I need to reevaluate something," he said, confusing me for a brief second before I caught on to where his mind had gone.

I groaned. "If you mean the *no fucking* rule you have with Clay, then yeah. I think you do."

Jared's lips parted in surprise.

"Did he tell you?"

Oh fuck.

I did my best to keep my face blank as I responded. "Yeah."

I could see what he wanted to ask next clear as if it was written on his face in permanent ink. *How did that come up?*

Before he could voice the question and completely ruin the moment, I sighed and sat back up. "You know, I would've liked to have been involved in that decision."

Jared's expression shifted; some of the fire in his eyes waned, dying out.

Way to kill the mood, Allie.

Jared didn't say anything for almost a full minute, then he sat down, lifting me easily onto his lap again. "You're right," he said. "We should have all talked about it together. It's just…"

"A super fucking weird situation?"

Jared winced.

"At least you're good friends," I hedged. "Imagine if I'd mated to one of you and some other random shifter who you didn't know. Maybe a fifty-year-old alpha with a nasty temper?"

Jared grimaced.

"Too far?" I asked, mirroring his disgust.

"A bit," he replied but wrapped his arms tighter around me. "Why are you so smart, Allie Grace?" he asked. I was going to ask him what exactly he meant, but then he continued. "I didn't imagine this situation to be possible, but again—you're right. I guess it's sort of lucky that it was Clay. He *is* my best friend. I trust him more than I trust anyone else. If I have to share you, then he is the only other man I'd be able to share you with."

"So does that mean we can nix your rule?" I asked with a devilish smirk, purposefully rolling my hips a little on his lap to emphasize my point and then blushed crimson, hardly able to believe what I'd just said and done.

What were these guys doing to me?

He grunted, sucking a breath in through his teeth. When he replied, his voice was husky and low, making my thighs clench. "Maybe," he teased. "Let's have a proper conversation about it. The three of us. Deal?"

"Deal," I said, stealing a kiss from his lips.

He lengthened the kiss, languidly stroking a warm path down the side of my body, caressing my collarbone and the curve of my breast until his fingers found a gap in between the fabric of my shirt and the waist of my jeans. He slid his hand upward, tentatively, as though asking permission.

I pressed my body into his fingertips, my body screaming. How could this feeling be real? I could barely breathe, afraid if I did, it would break the spell keeping us here in this moment. Away from the worry. Away from the pain.

Just...*away*.

Then I remembered.

"I forgot to ask you," I said, digging around in my front left pocket for my cell and thumbing to the conversation with Vivian. With everything else going on, I'd pretty much completely forgotten about it. "Want to come to Viv's lacrosse game with me? I meant to ask Clay too, but..."

I let the sentence trail off, not needing to elaborate on why I hadn't asked him yet. He had enough on his mind right now. Hell, he'd been all day. If he didn't get back soon, or at least answer one of my three text messages, I was going to have to find his ass and drag it home.

"Lacrosse?" Jared asked, not hiding his mild shock or the worried furrow in his brow.

My lips pressed into a thin line. "I know. I tried to tell her it wasn't a good idea. I mean, competitive sports? I still don't even think *I'd* be ready for that and I'm nowhere near as competitive as Viv is."

Jared's lack of immediate reply set my nerves on edge.

"Do you not think she can handle it?"

Jared shook his head. "Honestly? I don't know. Both your friends have adapted better that almost any other shifters I've seen make the transformation."

His gaze slid to me and then away, checking to see if he'd offended me.

I certainly hadn't adapted as well as they had. It was no secret.

"But lacrosse?" he repeated. "Why couldn't she be into horseback riding or chess or something?"

I barked a laugh. I couldn't picture it: Viv staring over a chess board with her fingers steepled, analyzing moves and countermoves. Layla maybe. But not Viv. She needed lacrosse like she needed to breathe. It was her one outlet when life at home wore on her. She was a fucking force of nature on the field.

...which was precisely why this was clearly a terrible idea.

"So, you'll come then?"

Jared inhaled deeply. "Yeah. Of course, I will. And we'll bring Clay, too. Might need him. He's really good at making distractions in a pinch."

I wondered exactly what kind of distractions Clay was so good at making, but Jared yanked me down with him as he lay back, tucking me into his side. His woodsy cedar and birch scent wrapped around me like a cloak of ease, and I sighed.

It barely took more than a few minutes before my mind wandered to darker territory, no longer occupied by math equations and Jared's lips. I shuddered involuntarily as I wondered how Ry and Sam's first night together went, simultaneously grossed out and stressed out. Wondering if she was all right. If that was the reason Clay still hadn't come home…maybe because she wasn't.

But he would've called me if that were the case, right?

"Hey, Allie," Jared said after a few moments spent stroking my arm, lost in his own thoughts.

"Hmm?"

His pulse picked up. I could hear it quicken from a steady drum beat to a discordant patter.

He swallowed. "You know how the mate bond allows us to share our emotions with each other?"

My mouth went dry. "Yeah. Why?"

"I know there's something you aren't telling me. Or maybe there's something going on you don't want me to know about?" He edged the last bit in a question, but he didn't wait for me to answer it.

"I'm not going to push you, but I just wanted you to know—you can talk to me. About anything."

Biting my lip, I kept quiet, trying to work through what to say. I couldn't deny it, but I also wasn't ready to spill all the beans just yet. He would think I was nuts if I told him what Adam had told me. At least until I had something to back it up.

"I just wanted to make sure it isn't something to do with me…or maybe…something I've done wrong or that's offended you—"

I shook my head, my cheek brushing back and forth over his chest before I propped myself up on an elbow to look him in the eye.

"No. You're perfect."

"So, there is something then?"

I dropped my gaze.

"You don't have to tell me now. I'll wait. Just promise me you'll tell me when you're ready?"

I groaned, dropping my head heavily to land on his chest with a thud. Why did he have to be so *good?* It made my heart hurt. It made even the prospect of telling him what we found out about his uncle unbearable. How could someone like Jared share the same blood as someone like Ryland?

Please don't be true. Please don't be true.

"Or not?" Jared asked, taking my reaction as a refusal.

I breathed into his shirt in a long exhale and propped myself back up. "There is something I haven't told you," I admitted. Unburdening myself even of that small admission felt like a massive weight lifting from my chest, allowing me a proper breath. "But I *will* tell you, when the time is right."

He pursed his lips but looked otherwise content with my response. Trusting.

"All right. I can live with that."

22

"I haven't been to a match in ages," Jared said, sliding onto the bench next to me and passing me a can of soda. I looked past him, searching the crowd of familiar faces all getting ready to take their seats before the match could start. There was no sign of Clay.

I'd met up with Layla and Viv after school, hanging with them until we needed to make our way to the field for warm up. I wanted to see how Viv was beforehand, and she seemed fine. She told me she'd run an extra fifteen miles in the morning, and we all took off for a short sprint between the end of the day bells and the start of warm up.

I was starting to think maybe I'd overreacted, but when I mentioned to her that if she felt at all out of control that she should fake an injury or just run off-field as fast as she could, she'd gotten her hackles up. Her eyes had sparked to light and her jaw had twitched, making me doubt my false confidence.

She was pissed at me now, of course, but it had to be said. There needed to be a backup plan, right? Just in case. Making it through practice was one thing, making it through a competitive match would be a completely other thing.

"Where's Clay?" I asked, still trying to spot him but having no luck.

Jared shook his head, taking a small sip of his soda. "Sam took the red-eye flight last night to get permission to leave her pack. He wanted to be there at the airport to pick her up when she got back."

I furrowed a brow, wondering why Ryland hadn't insisted on picking her up himself.

Jared dug his phone out of his pocket and hit the side button to illuminate the screen. "He should be here, soon."

I sighed. Good, at least he was still coming. I'd only seen him for five minutes since we got home the night after Ry and Sam mated two days ago. Just in passing when I got up for a glass of water in the middle of the night, unable to sleep. He'd been passed out on the couch, his eyes ringed in dark circles and his skin bleached of color. Dressed in loose shorts, his bare feet muddy.

I didn't have the heart to wake him to try to get him

to bed, but I'd covered him in a blanket and set a tall glass of water and a wrapped ham sandwich on the coffee table for him, hoping he would eat it before he took off again in the morning like I knew he would.

Sure enough, when I awoke this morning, he was already gone. But his water glass was empty in the sink, and I only found half of the sandwich in the trash, so at least he'd had something to eat and drink before running off again.

"When have you been to a match?" I asked, cracking open the soda and taking a long swallow, letting the carbonated sweetness take some of the edge off my panic.

"Hmmm?"

"You said it's been a while since you've been to one, but I've never seen you at Viv's matches before?"

"Right. It was actually Sam's match I went to last. I went up with Clay and his Dad to Alaska about..." he trailed off, scratching a spot on the back of his head as he considered. "Maybe six years ago? Before Sam was turned and before Clay's dad passed. Sam wasn't very good, but she was one of those kids who had to try everything. Don't tell her I said so."

Jared smirked, and I tried to return it with a grin that I'm sure didn't reach my eyes.

There was something I wanted—no, *needed* to ask Jared, seeing as I couldn't ask Clay. And he'd just given me the perfect entry to that conversation. I needed to know if what Adam told me lined up with what actually happened. If I asked Clay now, he would know why. It wouldn't be hard to put two and two together.

"How did Thomas Armstrong die?" I asked, sipping my soda but not tasting it as I surveyed the field, unable to look Jared in the eye.

I could feel his curiosity at the question. He was wondering why I was asking that now. And why I was asking him and not Clay. I could feel Jared's stare as he replied, speaking the words hesitantly, as though unsure he should be the one to speak them.

"He was shot, actually. It wasn't pack related as far as anyone knows. Just bad luck. A wrong place, wrong time sort of thing. Maybe a case of mistaken identity."

I wondered if he actually believed that.

"Did they ever catch the guy who did it?"

Jared shook his head solemnly. "Nah. I think that's what had Clay so messed up for so long. There was no evidence. Not even a shell casing to try to trace the gun. Clay must have scoured that back-parking lot a hundred times looking for it, or any trace of who might've done it. We tried to track by scent, too, but there wasn't anything foreign on Tom's clothes. Whoever did it, did it close range, without contact, and then somehow remembered to pick up their shell casing and any evidence before they left."

"Convenient," I muttered.

Jared gave me a strange look.

"Was anyone with him that night?"

Jared's face paled, and he cocked his head at me. "What's going on, Allie?

I shook my head. "Never mind. I was just curious about what happened. That's all."

Jared went back to looking out over the field as Layla made her way up onto the bleachers, a takeaway coffee gripped in one hand her phone to her ear with the other. She held up her hands in a *two minute* gesture and continued speaking to her mother in Spanish as she sat on the bench in front of me.

I pressed a hand to my stomach, trying to quell the urge to be sick and rip out of my skin at the same time. I hoped they were too distracted to notice as the players made their way out onto the field below.

I hoped they couldn't see how my other hand curled into the metal bench beneath me, leaving fingerprints in the ribbed metal. I spotted Clay just as he rounded the edge of the stands and glanced up at me, the mate bond having alerted me to his presence with a sharp tug at my core.

Quickly, I glanced away, afraid my eyes would be a dead giveaway.

The stories matched up. Exactly what Adam told me was what happened to Clay's father. Except Jared and Clay and most everyone else in the Forest Grove pack were missing one vital piece of information—*who* was to blame for his death.

Had Clay just handed his baby sister off to the man who'd killed his father?

"He manufactured his rise to power," Adam said as I stared open mouthed and numb, pulse and mind racing with everything he'd told me. *"And don't think he won't do whatever it takes to keep that position."*

"Hey," Clay grunted, sitting heavily next to me on the opposite side to Jared.

I swallowed back bile and lifted my soda to my lips, sipping a bit to wet my parched throat. "Hey," I croaked, choking on the carbonation.

"Everything good?"

"Yeah," I said, clearing my throat and attempting to lengthen my spine. "How are things with Sam?"

Clay bristled, turning to train his focus on the field as the whistle blew for the first face off. I searched for Viv and found her in her usual attack position. Winced. I'd warned her to take it easy, but this game was going to be the real test.

She was stronger now. Faster. If we were being honest, she had a super unfair advantage, and it was going to be incredibly hard for her not to use it—to tamper herself down to the level of the other mortal players.

"Good I guess," Clay grunted with a curl in his upper lip.

"She's moved in with Ry already," he added, his face contorting as he spoke.

I tried not to gag.

At least everything was all right, and Sam was okay...for now.

I reached over and gave the rigid hand on his thigh a squeeze, reminding him to relax. He did, his body unfurling under my touch. I could tell he didn't exactly want to talk anymore about it—at least not right now, so I dropped it until a time when we could have a more open conversation. As it was, I could tell Jared was more focused on what we were saying than the players below.

"Are you staying home tonight?"

Clay nodded gravely. "Yeah. She told me to quit babying her."

Layla hung up her call just then and turned to face us. "I got out of babysitting later," she announced. "Want to do shakes and fries from Gerry's after the game?"

This time, my grin was genuine. We hadn't been to Gerry's Shake Shack since ninth grade. My mouth watered instantly at the mention, the phantom taste of creamy strawberry and salty grease coating my tongue. "Sounds fucking amazing."

Layla laughed. "Thought you'd be down for that. What about you two? You both look like you could use a pick me up. No offense."

"None taken," Jared said with a grin.

Clay growled.

"They'll both come," I decided for them. "No one turns down Gerry's."

A whistle blew below, and the four of us turned our attention back to the game in time to see Viv skid to a stop downfield. She'd been going *fast*. Maybe a bit *too* fast.

I caught her eye from the bleachers and made a *turn it down* motion with my hand. Her lips tightened, but she nodded before moving into position for the next face-off.

"Okay so far?" I asked Jared, since he was the one who'd seemed to be paying the most attention since the game began.

He licked his lips and readjusted himself in the seat. "For the most part," he said in a low voice. "Though I caught a little bit of glow when that chick—number 18—checked her from behind, but she snuffed it out quick."

"That's good, right?"

The question was meant for Jared, but it was Clay who answered, giving me whiplash when I whirled my head back in his direction. "This is fucking stupid," he said, his voice a low, dangerous rumble. "Why did no one tell her this was a dumb fucking idea?"

"I tried," I argued.

"Well, it won't end well," Clay predicted. "She may get through this game, but eventually, something will happen."

"You don't know what for sure," Jared came to Viv's defense, and I loved him for it, even though a part of me worried Clay was right.

"Don't I?" Clay snapped. "Don't you remember senior year?"

"You shouldn't have even joined the team."

"What team?" I asked.

"Yeah. That's what I'm saying," Clay replied to Jared, his tone dripping acid, completely ignoring me. "I learned my fucking lesson. Vivian should've quit when she was turned."

"That's not fair," Layla butt in, twisting to face Clay with a withering look.

Clay fixed her with an uncommonly gentle and understanding stare. "It isn't," he agreed. "But it's what needs to be done."

Layla crossed her arms and turned back to the game, removing herself from the conversation.

"Did you play lacrosse?" I asked Clay, super confused.

He lifted a brow at me. "Football. Coach hounded me for two years about joining the team. I finally gave in. It was a bad call. Someone got hurt. I nearly got found out."

I tried to wrack my brain to remember. I would've been in ninth grade then. A total loner save for my two best friends. But it came to me, nonetheless.

"That kid who almost *died*?" I asked, incredulous and trying to search my mind for the name. "Billy...Billy..."

"Billy Chapman," Clay finished for me. "Yeah. That

was my fault. I checked him too hard. He was in a coma for three days."

Clay said this matter-of-factly, but I could feel the stress of the memory radiating off him. I was willing to bet those were some of the hardest three days he'd ever had.

"He was fine, though," Jared interjected. "He woke up and was back at school within two weeks."

Clay turned on Jared in a fury. "That was luck," he snapped. "I could have killed him. Just like *Viv*," Clay said pointedly, jabbing two fingers at her as she stealthily maneuvered herself downfield, "could accidently hurt anyone on that field."

Damnit.

"We'll talk to her," I said, interrupting Jared before he continued the argument with Clay over me in the middle of them. All their testosterone was going to make me rage if they didn't shut up. "When the game is over, we'll talk to her, *okay?*"

Clay snatched my soda and took a long drink, polishing it off and crushing the can in his hand. Jared brooded in silence.

They made me want to rip my hair out.

Couldn't we just have *one* freaking night of peace? *Just one?*

That's all I wanted: a normal night out with my friends. Watch my friend kick ass at her lacrosse game. Get some fries and shakes. Maybe cap the night off with a movie.

But those kinds of nights weren't mine to wish for anymore, I realized. They were a pipe dream in a world of nightmares.

With the mood dampened, we settled in to focus on the game. I noticed Layla taking little snippets of video and pictures throughout and sending them to Destiny. I wondered why she wasn't here watching Viv's game, too, since they were now mated, but couldn't bring myself to ask.

With how things were going, I had a feeling it would be some reason that would only stress me out more. Maybe Ry had her running an errand. Or maybe she was out searching for the so-called 'missing' shifters with Charity again.

I didn't care right now. I didn't want to know.

"Sorry," Clay grumbled so quietly beside me that I had to question whether I heard him speak at all.

I peered up at him and found his face hard, his gaze unwavering as he followed Vivian's path down the field. I waited a minute to see if he was going to elaborate on what exactly he was apologizing for, but he didn't say anything else.

I gave his thigh a pat and smirked. "I'll forgive you for ruining the mood if you get me another soda?"

His lips twitched.

"Suppose I could do that," he grunted standing.

A familiar shout rose up from the field, and I jumped, trying to see past a very large and imposing

Clay blocking my view. Layla stiffened, rising robotically to her feet at the same time Jared did.

I shoved Clay to the side just as another cry rang out, this one pitched high and broken. *Fuck.*

My eyes locked on Vivian, her hands clawed at her sides as she stared down at a screeching girl clutching the top part of her shoulder. Even from this far away, my canine eyes could see that something wasn't right. Her collarbone jutted out near the top, not through the skin, but it definitely shouldn't look like that.

Vivian shook, staring down at the girl. I could see her fingernails sharpen. Lengthen.

Oh no.

Oh shit.

A whistle blew and players and refs rushed them.

I whirled to Clay, my heart pounding with terror. *What do we do?* I wanted to ask, but I couldn't speak. Could barely move.

Layla dropped her phone and began shoving past the other students in her aisle, trying to get to the stairs.

"Sorry, bro," Clay muttered just before he tossed a fist over my head. I ducked in time to hear the bone-crunching thud of his knuckles knocking into flesh and bone.

I shrieked just as someone shouted, *"Fight!"* and was knocked out of the way, sent tumbling into the spot where Layla had been just a second before.

Clay hit Jared again, this time in the stomach,

making him bend forward, a great gust of air leaving his lips and his eyes going wide.

"Clay," I screeched, torn between wanting to stop him and needing to get to my best friend. "Fucking stop it!"

I moved to reach for Clay's arm, to *make him* stop when Jared winked at me and dodged Clay's next swing, shoving Clay hard enough to knock him to the side and get in a good right hook of his own.

…a distraction, I realized. They were making a distraction.

As much as I hated it, with a quick glance around, I could see that all the attention from the stands had been re-directed at them, *not* at Viv.

The same couldn't be said of many of the other players and the refs and coaches. They were all crowding the girl writhing in the grass. Layla was nearly there, hopping from the bottom step.

Vivian's coach whirled on her after checking the other girl, a cell phone raised to her ear. I had to assume an operator was on the other end of the call. The girl was going to need a doctor. A much better one than the nurse practitioner we had on staff at Forest Grove High.

Vivian cast her gaze away from the coach, dropping her head. In the movement, I saw the inhuman glow of her eyes. In her clenched fists, I could see the strain of her wolf like a spirit in her veins. Pulsating. Aching to be free.

With my heart breaking, I shouted down to her, *"Run!"*

Her gaze snapped up to meet mine, crazed and ringed in halos of deep ochre. I watched as a single tear fell before she tore away from her shouting coach and fled in a sprint that was definitely too fast, away from the field, toward the woods, with Layla hot on her trail.

A crash behind me sent me skittering into action. I raced for the stairs, calling back over my shoulder to Clay and Jared as they fought to the jeers and cries of surprise of the others in attendance. *"Cabin!"*

I couldn't bear to look at them, even knowing their bloody lips and bruises would heal wasn't enough for me to be able to watch them pummel each other. I was going to *kill* Clay when they got back. Couldn't he have done something else?

Literally *anything* else?

Past the point of being able to think about it, I jumped from the bleachers when I was close enough to the bottom not to draw notice and sprinted after Layla and Viv just as the sounds of sirens flared to life in the distance.

It wasn't hard to track them. Layla's jasmine scent made an easy trail to follow all the way through the school lot and onto the hiking trail, then a half a mile in to the east.

"Vivian!" I called, trying to decide if I should shift. My wolf could cover more ground faster. She could sniff them out better.

I groaned, whirling in a circle, trying to tune in to my heightened senses. Listening for the sound of them. Peering into the brush. But twilight made it hard to see. "Layla!"

"Here!" I heard faintly, Layla's voice carrying on the cool breeze.

It took me only a few more minutes to find them. Vivian sitting with her back against a tall, moss-covered stone, her head locked between her knees as she trembled. Layla crouched at her side, rubbing her back while she whispered reassuring words.

A twig snapped under my foot, and Vivian looked up at me, a snarl twisting her face. Even though her eyes still glowed vividly, and her claws and canines were still elongated, she hadn't shifted. She had managed to keep her contained.

Shock wasn't a strong enough word for what I was.

"You were right," Vivian sneered at me. "Go ahead. Say it! You were right, and I was wrong and now Bev has a broken fucking collarbone, and it's all my fault."

She broke into a sob on the last word, her body tightening, her shoulders rolling inward. I could count on one hand the number of times I'd seen Viv cry. Hell, I could count on two fingers. And those two times were both before she turned twelve.

"I wasn't going to say that," I told her, edging closer. I didn't want to spook her, that would only make it harder for her to control her wolf.

"Well you *should*. She'll be out for the rest of the season. Maybe even next year, too."

I wanted to ask her what had happened, but it didn't matter. She'd probably just checked Bev too hard. That's all it would take. "I'm the one who's sorry," I muttered, dropping to my knees beside her and Layla, not caring as a cold wetness seeped into my jeans. "This wouldn't even be happening if...*if*..."

"Oh, fuck off," Viv said. "You don't get to have the blame for this. This was *me*. My stubbornness. I *knew* this would happen, you know that? I fucking knew it, but I convinced myself it wouldn't just so I could keep one normal thing—just *one* and..." she trailed off, her sobs getting too heavy to continue.

Unable to help myself, I leaned in and wrapped my arms around her. Layla did the same, the two of us sandwiching her from either side as tight as we could. I don't know how long we stayed that way, but by the time Layla began to let up, Viv had stopped crying, and her fingernails were no longer jabbing sharply into my forearm. They were back to a more normal, human length and bluntness.

Vivian lifted the hem of her jersey to her face to swipe away her tears. "Maybe Ryland was right," she said. "Maybe I should stay at pack camp for a while. I can probably come up with some sort of excuse for my paren—"

"*No*," I all but growled. Even thinking about Vivian staying at camp, so close to Ryland, gave me goosebumps and made my stomach clench. "If you want to stay at the cabin, you can, but there's no way in hell you're going back to camp."

Layla cocked her head at me, her brows lifted as though seeing something that'd been there all along, but that she'd somehow managed to miss. On the contrary, Vivian just looked confused. For the moment, it seemed, they'd switched places.

"Allie?" Layla prompted.

I sighed.

"Am I missing something?" Vivian asked, digging her palms into the dirt to push herself into an upright seat. "I know the guy is a dick, but—"

"It's not that."

"Then what?" Layla asked, her manicured brows knitting together.

I'd promised them...

No more lies.

And if I were going to be able to keep them away from Ryland, they'd have to know why, right?

A million questions stomped and scurried across my thoughts. A million reasons why I *should* tell them everything. And a million reasons why I shouldn't.

I bit the inside of my cheek and sat back into the wet leaves and damp soil. "I'm going to tell you everything," I started, trying to find the right way to begin. "But you can't talk about it. Not with anyone."

Layla sagged, her expression telling me she wasn't the least bit surprised there was more awfulness incoming. Vivian, on the other hand, had grown stiff, the sorrow and guilt that'd been weighing her down lifted in favor of her patented *nobody-fucks-with-my-friends* look. From defense to offense in the blink of an eye. Happy to let the weight of my problems erase her guilt. Distract her from what she'd just done.

"Not even Destiny," I added, before I started, shooting a pointed look Viv's way.

She chewed on that for a second before finally nodding. "All right. I won't say anything."

I told them all of it. My suspicions. Clay and my excursion to the eastern pack to investigate. What we found out. How we didn't have any proof but that I figured it must be true.

Layla was turning a shade of green visible even though the sky was casting shades of orange over the forest. Vivian's reddened cheeks only looked more inflamed beneath the warm hue.

"Please tell me that's all of it," Vivian spoke through clenched teeth.

I wished I could.

I frowned, a mental image of a man shot at point blank range in cold blood flashing in my imagination. "There's one more thing. Not even Clay knows about it—"

"I don't know about what?"

Layla screeched like a cat.

"*What the hell?*" Viv demanded, brushing off her knees as she shoved to her feet.

I froze, turning my gaze in horror to find a battered but quickly healing Clay standing barely a stone's throw away. How long had he been there?

A hot flush crept up my neck. It was borne of guilt but quickly morphed to white hot fury when I got a good look at him. His knuckles bloody. His lip swollen and split on the left side.

"Where's Jared?"

"Is he always so quiet?" Layla asked. "I didn't even hear him coming, like, at all. Did you?"

Vivian snorted, and from the corner of my eye, I could see her appraising his wide shoulders and tall, bulky frame. His size thirteen shoes. Viv shook her head.

Clay, completely ignoring my question, let his hard stare pass from me to Vivian, and then to Layla. He came to stand in front of me, fixing me with an accusatory stare that made my blood boil.

"You fucking told them, didn't you?"

I cringed.

"*Christ*, Allie, what were you thinking?"

Was it wrong that I was relieved he seemed to have forgotten the part of the conversation he'd interrupted, because *damn*, I nearly pissed myself when I heard him.

Clay gnawed his lower lip, throwing his hands through his hair as he stepped to the left, and then back to the right, as though unsure where to go, or what to say, but needing to move anyway.

"Okay," he said, and then more firmly as he paused

in his short pacing steps. "*Okay.* I don't like it. Not one fucking bit."

Coming out of his rage, his face turned back from a scary shade of crimson to his normal slightly inflamed pink. He shot a look to Vivian. "You can't say anything about this, not even to—"

"I know," she interrupted, crossing her arms over her chest. "I won't tell Destiny. I already promised."

Clay nodded, satisfied for the moment. He licked his lips, thinking.

I had been about to demand where Jared was again when I heard a howl far in the distance. It was him—I was sure of it. He must've gone to the cabin while Clay followed our trail just in case we were already back there waiting for them. Or, more likely, maybe he went to make sure Bev was going to be all right.

That made sense.

"You shouldn't have told them," Clay growled at me and Viv tipped onto the balls of her feet, looking like she was ready to put the big bastard in his place if I didn't.

Luckily for her, or maybe for Clay, I'd learned to deal with the brute myself.

"They're my *best friends.* I can't lie to them. Not anymore."

Clay made an exasperated sound and clenched his jaw.

"We can trust them."

Clay's cut-glass stare softened as he took me in. He

nodded once, turning to face my friends once more. "All right. Then maybe you can help."

"Whatever we can do," Layla said at about the same time Viv said, "Count me in."

"Wait," I said, confused. "Help? Do we have a lead?"

"No," he replied, lowering his voice to a deep rumble. "But I think I know where we can find one."

23

My arrow left my bow, sailing through the mist of early morning and into the target, burrowing into its heart.

Damn.

The third bullseye of the morning. That had to be a good sign, right? Maybe it meant today wasn't going to be the epic failure I was dreading it would be.

Stop thinking like that.

Failure wasn't an option. If we failed tonight, it would mean more than losing an opportunity to expose Ryland for what we all thought he was—it could mean we didn't get to see the sunrise tomorrow. That this cool mist caressing my cheeks would be the last kiss I ever received.

I shuddered, shaking off the chill clinging to my bones, and notched another arrow. My shoulder twinged with a sharp pain, and I relaxed it, dropping my arm to roll my shoulder once, twice, three times the charm.

We may have healed quick as a whip, but when you'd been putting your body through what I'd been forcing mine to endure these past three days, it was bound to leave some lasting aches and pains.

The defensive training Clay and I had started weeks ago had started up again.

After coming up with a promising, if a more than a little risky plan to find some evidence of what we feared, Clay had insisted we start again. I agreed, but I'm not sure I would've if I'd known how hard he'd intended to push me. We didn't just train in the mornings anymore. We trained after school, too, since my job was no more. Sometimes he ever insisted on my sparring with Jared in the evenings, to get some actual practice.

Clay was too big for us to be evenly matched. I was getting quicker. Stronger. And he'd taught me some dirty tricks. But there were certain positions he would get me in where I simply had no hope of getting out. His weight was too much for me, especially after he'd already worn me out with a good long run and an icy dip in the stream.

I could best him in strength if I were fresh and ready for it, though, a fact I did *not* let him forget. Whatever strange power allowed me to have two mates and made me strong of will, seemed to also make me stronger than a shifter my size and age should have been. At least, that's what Clay and Jared said, and until I was in a real fight, I'd never know if it was true or if they were just saying it as an excuse because they didn't like being knocked on their asses by a girl. I didn't relish the thought, but I'd admit, I was a bit curious to put their theory to the test.

It made sense, I supposed. As much as anything made sense to me these days.

Finished with a long, rolling stretch of my shoulder, I notched the bow again and sent another arrow soaring. It sank in barely an inch above the bullseye. Not amazing, but still better than last week. I'd take it.

I reached for another and frowned when my fingers grasped empty air. Had I really already used them all? I sighed, snatching up the quiver from where it leaned against my ankle to go and retrieve my arrows, slinging the bow across my back.

This was the first morning I'd woken before Clay in time to come out here before he could drag me away for another lesson, and I breathed deeply. The scents of cold pine and molting leaves were a comforting undercurrent to the stronger scent of the mist itself. Like dew. Or the smell of the earth after it rained.

It reminded me of simpler times.

Of mornings spent ten feet off the ground in Dad's hunting blind, peering out the tent flaps to take in the dawn with a cup of hot oats and huckleberries.

I missed that girl.

Wondered if I'd ever know what it was like to be her again.

I was glad Jared suggested I go shoot some arrows before he had to leave early this morning. It was the best idea anyone had given me in a long time. I'd wanted him to come with me, but he insisted he had a quick errand to run for Ry about the quarry, and I couldn't argue with him.

Especially not when it was to do with his uncle. I was terrified he would see everything that was going on written on my face. I still hadn't told him.

I'd planned to. Especially after telling Layla and Viv. But even they agreed he shouldn't know. Not until there was hard evidence to back it up.

So every day I was just more and more uncomfortable, waiting for the chance to put our half-baked plan into motion so I could finally say *something* to Jared. Even if that something was that I was a complete idiot and that there was nothing to tell.

A blaring chirp from my cell phone killed the calm of the moment, sending a cascade of blackbirds flocking to the sky, crowing their displeasure in their wake.

I fished it out, dropping the quiver near the target.

Clay: Where are you? Training in ten.

I groaned to myself, stuffing my phone back in my pocket without replying.

It chirped again, and I muttered to myself as I pulled it back out. *Seriously?*

Clay: Answer me or I'm going to assume you're dead and need avenging.
Clay: Going once.
Clay: Twice.
Allie: I'm coming.
Allie: Chill.

I grumpily shoved my phone back into my pocket, flicking the switch on the side to toggle it to silent mode. He could fucking wait. I wasn't going to rush. Not today. He could kick my ass when I was good and ready to receive said ass kicking and not a minute sooner.

I snatched up my arrows and shoved them into the quiver, my chest tight.

"Happy birthday, Allie," I told myself with a sarcastic snort, shouldering the quiver along with the bow for the long walk home.

When I finally made my way through the last of the trees and onto the dirt lawn, peering up grouchily at the front door, it was eerily quiet.

"Clay?" I called, searching the windows for any sign of him. I'd bumped into Jared on his way out to run an errand at the ass crack of dawn for Ry, and it looked like he still wasn't back yet, either. "I'm back!"

When he didn't materialize, I dutifully checked my phone, assuming because I'd muted him that he'd likely gone on that murderous rampage he'd threatened before I left the clearing. *Shit.*

It buzzed in my hand before I could turn it on.

Clay: Behind you.

I spun, jumping when I spotted him leaning casually against a tree at the far side of the property. The bastard had clearly watched me stomp back onto the property and hadn't said a word.

"What are you doing?" I asked, setting my things down on the porch.

Here I was in sweats, a tank, and loose-fitting sweater, ready for an ass whooping, and he was...

What the hell was he doing?

Clay wore his signature dark wash denim jeans, but these weren't the grease stained ones I'd grown accustomed to seeing on him. These were...well, they looked brand new.

He even had a fitted black button-up on, the sleeves rolled to the crease of his elbows, making his forearms look drool-worthy and biceps like cannons.

And was that *product* in his hair?

"What did you do?" I asked, suddenly *very* aware of the scent of jasmine on the breeze. And the rustle of something coming from behind the cabin. "I *told* you I didn't want—"

"Too bad."

"Ugh."

"Ugh, yourself," Clay countered with a wicked smirk, coming to stand before me.

My shoulders slumped, giving in to whatever horribly embarrassing thing I was clearly going to have to endure whether I liked it or not. At least it looked like I was getting out of training today.

Look at the bright side.

Clay drew me in for a hug, and I let him, giving in as soon as his spicy metallic scent reached my nose. He brushed his lips against the top of my head, and I shuddered in his arms. "Happy birthday, baby."

Despite myself, my lips curled into a grin hidden against him. I fought back a sudden urge to cry and broke the hug, knowing if I stayed there, eventually, it was going to happen.

"Thanks," I muttered, my voice watery. I inhaled sharply and pushed air out through my lips. "Let's get this over with."

"That's my girl," Clay said, scooping me up from the ground and flinging me into his arms as he charged into a sprint, carrying me at a breakneck speed, squealing all the way until we were around the cabin, head on in front of the shop.

My feet touched back down on solid ground at the same time a cheer of "Happy Birthday!" rang out from inside the shop.

I nearly tripped on the gravel but managed to right myself in time to catch a hug from Jared. He lifted me from the ground, spinning me in a circle before putting me back down.

Somewhere in the shop, music began to play. Clay's

playlist—now my favorite—starting up at the first song of the list.

Once the shock abated, I wrapped my arms around Jared, hugging him back tightly and whispering in his ear, "You dirty little liar."

He hadn't been going to run an errand at all. The bugger had been here the whole time. He hadn't gone on an errand for Ryland. He'd suggested I go shoot some arrows to get me to leave.

"Worth it," he whispered, his breath tickling my neck. "How was the morning?"

"Peaceful," I replied, my insides quaking as he brushed his lips quickly against the base of my neck before pulling away, purposefully *trying* to drive me mad if his smirk was any evidence.

"That's what I was hoping."

"Hey," Layla called, butting past Jared for a firm hug. "My turn."

She kissed both my cheeks when she pulled away. "So," she asked, gripping me by the arms with a conspiratorial look. "How does it feel? The big one-eight?"

I nodded, grinning. "It's...*liberating*," I said after a moment of thought. I'd texted Uncle Tim this morning and told him I wouldn't be needing his *check in* calls anymore—that he could get back to his glitz and glam life in Florida tending to the every whim of his selfish wife. But, you know, in a much nicer, more mature way than that.

First thing Monday I'd have the school remove him as my parental contact.

How did that saying go?

Oh yes. *I am the master of my own destiny.*

I still hadn't gotten a reply from Uncle Tim, but I assumed he was stewing about what to say. Probably gearing up from a novel-length response with lots of big words and *listen here, Allie Graces.*

The joke was on him, though. I didn't plan to read them.

Layla whooped and Viv stepped up from behind her, ready and waiting with a hug, too. She'd been a wreck at school the last few days, but I was glad to see only a trace of the heavy clouds she'd been carrying around with her since the lacrosse game still lingered.

Her coach and the team all brushed off the incident with Bev as a horrible accident. They didn't even plan to suspend Viv from the team, especially since she seemed too distraught over it herself, running away and all. They had no idea she *had* to run, and for a very different reason.

They took her decision to quit the team hard, but not as hard as she did.

It took two tubs of chocolate panda ice cream from Gerry's on Thursday night before she'd even agree to go back to school at all.

"Love you," she said as she squeezed me tightly. "You're the good shit, Allie cat. Happy eighteen."

"Love you too, Viv."

"Oh, and your gift was a team effort, so you can't be mad at anyone."

My stomach clenched.

I had told them I didn't want anything.

Suppressing a groan, I warily scanned the shop, looking for something wrapped to absolute perfection. Layla wouldn't have let anyone but her wrap whatever it was.

What I found, though, wasn't a boxy shape covered in sparkling ribbons and cleanly folded paper. It was easy to skim over in the shop, just sort of blending in.

Covered in a taupe colored tarp, the telltale shape of a car took up about half of the available space. Clay worked on old cars sometimes, as well as bikes. If it weren't for the very *Layla* black ruffled bow on the hood, I'd have assumed that it belonged to a client.

"Don't get too excited," Jared said with a half laugh, nervously shoving his hands deep into the pockets of his jeans. "She needs work."

"She's practically falling apart," Clay agreed, though I could tell they were only trying to downplay whatever was beneath the tarp and bow to make me feel better.

Layla sauntered over to the side of the car and curled her fingernails into the tarp, readying to unveil what hid beneath.

"Ready?" she asked me with a wide grin, but didn't wait for me to reply. I was too dumbstruck to speak.

My tongue felt swollen, like it didn't quite fit within the confines of my mouth anymore.

Layla tore the tarp off, sending the bow flying across the shop to land with a crinkling thud against the other tarp Clay still kept covering the opposite wall. Covering the map pinned to the wall beneath.

A choked gasp nearly cut off my air supply, and I coughed as I took her in.

"We weren't really sure what you would like," Jared began, his tone tentative, as though he were speaking to a cornered animal instead of his mate. I wondered what my face must have looked like.

"Which is why we asked your friends," Clay finished.

"And *we* told them exactly what you wanted," Viv announced with a warm smile.

Layla patted the roof of the car and leaned against her side. "You've talked about fixing one up since you were, like, twelve," she said. "If you start now, you can probably have her running by the time you get your full license."

"I…I can't…" I croaked, my eyes welling.

Jared wrapped a warm arm around my shoulders, steadying them. "*You can*," he disagreed. "We all chipped in. Clay and I got her off a guy up in Seattle."

"And we got you a few parts that Clay said you would need—they're in the trunk," Viv continued, gesturing to the black beauty.

"Th-that's where you were?" I asked, my brows

lowering as I considered Clay. I thought he'd been with Sam this whole time. Though I'm sure he was for most of it, it seemed like he was also on a road trip to go and pick up a *freaking car*.

Clay lifted his shoulder in a shrug, smirking.

"So," he said, a brow arched. "What do you think?"

I turned back to the car, a sob expanding beneath my breastbone until it was almost painful. A 1970 Chevelle.

Dad had a calendar of old cars in the kitchen growing up. I'd always remember when he flipped the month from October to November and *there*, gleaming on the top of the page was this exact car, albeit shinier, her chrome practically blinding. I knew then that *that* was the car I wanted some day, and it just stuck.

When November rolled to December, I tore that image out of the calendar and taped it to my bedroom wall. It stayed there until Dad passed—the house needed to be sold to cover his hospital bills.

Even in the condition it was, with the start of rust on her fenders, a few dings in her right side, and a missing headlight, I knew she would have cost a small fortune. Certainly, more than I had in my savings account to repay them.

"I know what you're thinking," Clay said, his voice taking on that foreboding tone I knew meant he would accept no argument. "And you are *not* paying us back for it. We'll fix 'er up together, and then I intend to take her for a spin myself. I consider that payment enough."

"I...I don't know what to say," I said, my voice a distant whisper. "I didn't want to accept it. Knew I shouldn't. But fuck if I didn't want that car more than just about anything else in the whole world right now.

"Say thank you," Vivian said with a nonchalant shrug. "Obviously."

"Thank you," I managed as a tear finally escaped, and I swiped it away before anyone could see. "I freaking hate all of you though. I can't believe you hid this from me. And you *know* I *hate* gifts."

I took a long breath and managed to soothe the tremor in my shoulders just as Jared loosened his grip on me, letting me go. "We know," he said. "But we just don't care."

I shoved him and laughed, taking a tentative step toward my new wifey.

"There's one other little thing inside," he said, moving toward the back of the shop where I could see a big white box and plates atop the counter. "Go check her out and then we'll have cake."

Shaking my head, I clenched my hands and tip toed nearer, almost afraid that if I took my eyes off of her that she would vanish before I could ever feel the curve of her steering wheel beneath my fingertips.

Layla opened the door for me, a shrill screech sounding as she did.

She winced.

I laughed.

She wouldn't understand that I was *glad* she needed work. I wouldn't have it any other way.

"Maybe I'll just leave it open," she muttered when I inched past her and lowered myself into the driver's seat. "I don't want to snap the door off or something."

Her leather seats were torn on the edges and worn from overuse and sitting too long without proper care, but they formed to my body nonetheless, the smell of dusty carburetor and sun-heated leather filled my nose.

I gripped the steering wheel, wringing my hands over it before shifting one to brush a palm over the wide dash.

"Look up," I heard Jared holler and glanced up to see him in the rearview, sticking candles into a chocolate cake. Then something else caught my eye. A photograph, the edges slightly curled.

In it, a woman with long white-blonde hair smiled at the camera, her belly swollen and gray eyes bright as she stared up at the man who held her. His thick arms wrapped tenderly around her from behind, his fingers splayed over her pregnant belly beneath a pretty yellow dress and jean jacket. Dad.

It was dad.

It was a picture of us. All of us.

Before this cruel world stole away the sister I should've had, then my mother, and finally, my father.

I didn't know a picture like this even existed. My throat burned as I tugged it free from the clip holding it in place on the sun visor and shakily brought it closer. They looked so happy together. They had no idea that in a matter of weeks from when this was taken, Diana Grace would be gone forever, and my father wouldn't ever smile quite as widely ever again.

My chest ached as I traced the line of dad's scruffy jaw and found parts of me in mom. I'd only ever seen a handful of pictures of her. Dad had put most of them away after the first couple of years, keeping only the super worn one he always had in his wallet, tucked behind a credit card.

That photo was taken long before this one, when they were still young, before they were ever married or pregnant. She seemed different in this one. Vibrant with life. Beaming as though lit from within.

A tear fell onto the photograph, and I smeared it away, trying to get control of myself. I hugged the photo to my chest, pretending that it was them and not just their likeness captured in mercury infused paper.

I never knew what it was like to be held by my mother, but my Dad had given me all the love he'd had left to give before he passed. Enough for both of them.

Even though I was the one who took her away from him.

If my sister had lived instead of me, would she still be alive? Would they both still be here? Would they be singing happy birthday with smiles on their aged faces, welcoming their daughter to adulthood?

I dropped my head, blinking away blinding tears to

stare at the photograph once more, willing myself to see it from another perspective.

It's not my fault, I mouthed the words, tasting them to see if they could be swallowed.

It was what Dad always told me.

It was what everyone told me.

Of course, it wasn't your fault, Allie Grace, Dad would say, giving my boney eight-year-old shoulders a squeeze. *Your mom wanted you more than she wanted anything else in the whole world. She's probably up there right now, wishin' you wouldn't be so hard on yourself. I know she wouldn't want you sad. Not even for a second.*

But if she didn't have me, she'd still be here.

There's no way anyone can know that, Allie. Now, come on, buck up. All you can do now is make her proud, 'kay kiddo?

I'd put my tough girl face on and nodded, ignoring how my eyes still watered and spilled over despite my tiny clenched fists and squished together brows.

Dad always knew what to say, with just the right mix of patience and understanding, but also enough tough love to set me straight. I realize with a dawning certainty that there was something I needed to do before tonight. Before Ryland celebrated his new mate under the watchful eye of the moon and we put Clay's plan into motion.

There was someone I needed to talk to. Someone I should have gone to for advice a long time ago. He'd been there all along, waiting for me to come, but I couldn't do it. It hurt too much.

But I could see now that was selfish.

Cowardly.

And my dad hadn't raised a fucking coward.

Nodding to myself, I sniffed hard and gently tucked the photo back into place on the visor above my head. I pressed two fingers to my lips and then to the worn photograph.

"Miss you," I whispered before tearing my eyes away from the faces of my smiling parents and swiping my palms over my eyes. I didn't know how I was ever going to thank Jared, and I was afraid to ask where he even managed to find the photo, having a sneaking suspicion he must have broken into the storage unit and gone through about a million boxes to find it.

It took another minute before I was ready, but then I stepped back out of the car, breathing through a bubble of emotion in my throat.

They were all there waiting for me. My family. Standing shoulder to shoulder. Jared held a chocolate cake between his hands, eighteen candles burning down to the base in a wide circle along the outer edge.

"Happy birthday to you," Clay began, and I laughed, shaking two more tears free of my eyes as the others began to sing with him. A tightness made me press my fisted hands to my chest, afraid something within might shatter if I didn't hold it together.

24

"We'll be right here if you need us," Jared said as he put his Jeep into park on the side of Loft Pines Road near the entrance to Pine Grove cemetery.

My skin bristled as I took in the stone grave markers jutting out from the earth in straight lines and winding pathways. The great iron gates standing wide for visitors to come and leave flowers or picture frames next to headstones.

I hadn't been here since the day we buried him.

A heavy guilt settled in my stomach like lead.

Shifting uncomfortably, Clay added, "You sure you want to go alone?"

I almost laughed. I *had* wanted to go alone. I'd told them as much once the cake was completely demolished and all the tears had dried up. Later tonight we would all be at pack camp—Ryland had summoned us all to join him in welcoming Sam to the pack. But I needed to do this first, and I needed to do it now.

I should have done it a long time ago.

These two idiots insisted on coming along, promising they would just wait by the car, out of hearing distance. For Jared, I knew the reason was because he wanted to be there for me. To hold me close if I returned to the Jeep broken.

Clay may have had similar intentions, but we both knew the main reason he wouldn't allow me to run all the way to the cemetery alone in the hours before sunset: it wasn't safe.

Any minute of any day Ryland could find out what we'd done—where we'd gone. And like Clay, I didn't think he'd hesitate to punish us for it.

"I'm sure," I told Clay, the door creaking as I opened it slowly and stepped out.

We'd dropped Layla and Viv off at their houses to get ready for tonight. They'd both meet us back at the cabin after dark to head to pack camp together. I sort of wished I'd let them come, too, but knew it had to be this way or no way at all.

"I'll be back in a few."

"Take your time," Jared urged, his gaze steady and sincere. "We'll wait for as long as you need us to."

My heart clenched because I knew they would. They'd wait all damn night if I took that long. They'd miss Sam's welcome ceremony and remain there, unchanged until dawn.

I fucking loved the shit out of them for it.

Even though I'd only been there once before, I had no trouble at all finding Dad. The path we'd walked from Uncle Tim's used Lexus into the cemetery would be forever engraved in my memory. Layla and Vivian had come with me that day even though Uncle Tim had tried to insist there be family only at the internment.

I'd flat out told him they were coming and that maybe *he* should be the one who didn't come. He'd barely spoken to dad for the last three years, even while he was sick.

Every step brought with it the urge to panic as I neared his headstone. Quick breaths sawed out through my clenched teeth and that damned fluttering behind my ribcage grew to an intensity that made it a wonder I could even stay on my own two feet.

A chill wind swept through the cemetery, lifting my hair and leaving a lick of cold on the back of my neck. My teeth chattered, catching the first trace scent of winter on the air.

I almost didn't recognize the stone, grown over with moss and vines as it was. Dirty and chipped in one corner. Uncle Tim had chosen the stone, and I'd hated it as much then as I did now. The color of poached salmon with Gregorian script. Dad would have hated it.

But at least the inscription rang with truth.

Loving Father.

"Hey Dad," I said, throat constricting as I bent to my knees in the overgrown grass and began picking vines and scraping moss from the face of the gravestone.

"I'm sorry I—" the words were choked off by a sob, and I had to force it down to continue. "I'm so sorry I didn't come sooner. I just…I just *couldn't.*"

I wiped my face and sat back, straightening. "I know that's no excuse, but…but I'm here now and I need your advice." I barked out a broken laugh. "*God,* you always gave the best advice. It didn't always make sense at the time, and I may not have always listened to you, but I'd give just about anything to hear one shred of advice from you right now."

I grimaced, setting my palms down against the cold earth, slithering my fingers through the grass at the base of the stone. He was right there. Buried somewhere beneath my hands. I'd never been religious. Wasn't sure I believed in heaven or an afterlife, but if people could turn into wolves, then couldn't angels be a thing, too?

Couldn't heaven?

Could he be here right now, listening?

"I fucked up, Dad," I muttered. "A lot of bad shit has happened because of me."

I paused to catch my breath.

"But a lot of good stuff has happened, too."

I thought of Jared and Clay, and the connection that

brought the three of us together. No matter that it wasn't normal, I could never see it as being *wrong*. That was the one thing I knew wasn't a mistake.

I told him everything. About what happened with Devin. About Jared and Clay. About Layla and Vivian. About Ryland and what we planned to do. Once I started, it was like I couldn't stop, the whole uncensored story rushing out of me like a flood.

"And I still haven't told Jared," I finished. "But I'm going to. I know that's what you'd tell me to do. Whether or not we find anything. Right? You'd say he had a right to know. I know you would."

In my mind's eye I could almost see him nodding. *Damn straight,* he would say.

"I just wish you could give me some sort of sign… or, I don't know…just *something* to tell me what I need to do."

Silence was my reply, and I dropped my head, ready to leave. The sun was nearing the horizon, the autumn evening sky bright with the reddish glow of sunset. Jared and Clay would be getting worried if I didn't go back soon.

I sighed and peered over at the gravestone next to Dad's. In a shade similar to his, my mother's headstone sat in a similar state of neglect. With twitching fingers, I cleared it, too, picking off leaves and vines, brushing over the dirty face of it with the forearms from my sleeve.

"At least you're together again," I whispered, the

words snatched up by a rogue wind as it funneled between their tombstones. Only one tombstone was missing, but the ghost of it squatted between theirs. The other daughter they planned for, but never had.

I wondered offhandedly what sort of flowers my mother would have liked, resolving to bring some for her once the things that needed dealing with were through. *Marigolds,* I thought, the flower coming to mind as though it were the easiest choice in the world.

Yes.

I knew she'd like them.

"Your parents, I presume?"

The willowy voice broke my focus, and I jarred forward, tripping over myself in my haste to whirl around.

"Now, now, child. I didn't mean to startle you."

"Grams?"

Her blind eyes stared past me as she neared, folding herself into a seat on the grass at my side, tucking the long hem of her deep jade jacket beneath her.

"What are you doing here?"

Hazel tipped her head in the direction of a winding path that led over a grassy knoll in the cemetery. "Visiting my husband," she said. "I sit with him for a few hours every now and again."

Her husband?

"Oh," I said, unsure what else to say, still trying to get my pulse under control.

"Thought your voice sounded familiar," she said, her gaze sailing past me to rest near where my parents' tombstones were. "But I've never heard you here before."

"That's because I've never been here before," I admitted, shame coloring my cheeks in a way that I was glad she couldn't see. "Not since he was buried."

Hazel tipped her head to one side, and her long silvery braid slipped from her shoulder. "I see," she said, falling silent.

We sat there together, both grieving different people, but as one in our sorrow.

"Can I ask you something?" I said after a minute.

Hazel dipped her head in a graceful nod.

I'd been waiting for her to come to the cabin. I'd wanted to talk to her after that night at the Four Corners. But I'd been more than a little preoccupied with Viv and Layla, and then afterward, with everything to do with Ryland. Now that she was here, right in front of me, I wasn't sure how to ask what I wanted to.

I had been so sure she'd been there that night. I'd seen her, her silvery hair and white gown billowing in the autumn breeze as she'd inclined her head. Silently helping me make the decision that led me where I was now.

"Why were you there that night?" I asked, shoulders tensing. "Why did you tell me to join the pack?"

For a full minute, a slight downward pull at the corner of her wrinkled lips was the only indication that she'd heard me at all. Finally, she breathed a sigh and reached her hands out to me.

I recoiled, but she managed to snatch up the wrist of my right hand. I let her, breaths coming more feverishly. Her milky gaze lifted, boring into me as though she could see as she flipped my hand over and traced the lines of my palm.

Instead of answering me, her thin brows pulled together, and her lips pursed. My spine tingled.

"I'm sorry that the stars have chosen you to walk this path," she said, her eyes downturned and cheeks growing sallow. "But walk it you must. You're the only one who can."

I swallowed, breath hitching. "What does that mean?"

I *hated* riddles.

Her brow furrowed as she pressed her clammy palm to mine, and I wondered what she was seeing that I couldn't. She'd told me once how she could see the inner workings of people. Their gears and cogs. The way they ticked. Their histories.

A deep and burrowing cold crept like frost over my bones. She knew, I realized. I let her touch me, and now she could see, in her way, what Clay and I were doing. I tugged my hand out of her grasp, my mouth going dry.

I rubbed the chill out of the hand she'd held with my other, hairs on the back of my neck standing on end. "You saw."

Her lips pressed into a taut line.

"Do you know what's going to happen?" I pleaded. "Do you know if we're right?"

She bowed her head, her gaze going back to the unfocused stare of a blind woman. "I can see history," she said, her voice a croak now, and I wondered if her ability exhausted her when she used it. She seemed almost to have aged another ten years in the last five minutes. "Pasts. Presents. Feelings. But...not the future, I'm afraid."

I slumped back, suddenly bone weary and wanting more than anything to be finished with this conversation. What exactly did I hope she could tell me, anyway? If Hazel knew anything, then surely she would have told her grandson. Or Jared directly. I pushed to my feet, casting a silent farewell to my parents.

"There's a reason Ryland forced me out of his pack," she whispered, so quietly I wasn't sure if I heard her. "And a reason he won't allow me near him. Has never allowed me to read him. I have my suspicions, just as you have yours."

She stood, hobbling as she did, and I noticed for the first time how she was barefoot, even in this cold. Maybe we should give her a ride home.

"Hazel, do you—"

"You're different, Allie," she said, interrupting as she brushed past me, headed back in the direction of the grassy knoll. "It's what sets you apart that will see your triumph. Embrace it... and don't forget it."

25

"What's this?" I asked, raising a brow at Clay as he handed me a black sweater.

His eyes flitted to Jared, Layla, and Viv where they were walking ahead of us. His hand clamped around my elbow, bringing me to a stall. "It's Sam's."

I lifted a brow. "What do you want me to do with her sweater?"

"Wear it," he replied, giving me a strange look.

He rolled his eyes.

"For her scent," he whispered pointedly, gaze darting to Jared and back to me. "To put on when you go in. Make sure you put the hood up and rub your hands in the fabric a bit."

"Oh."

Right. I guess I didn't want to leave my scent all over Ryland's things. Why hadn't I thought of that? I took the sweater, tying it around my waist until I would need to put it on. Clay was still grouchy that we'd decided I should be the one to sneak into Ry's cabin and not him. I could use the excuse of having needed to use the bathroom if I were caught. He couldn't. None of the guys in the pack ever went into his cabin unless invited directly by him.

It was a territorial thing. It would be suspicious if Clay were found inside alone.

And there was no way I was going to allow Viv or Layla to do it.

Which left me. With them to cover for me and create a distraction if needed. If anyone were headed toward the cabin, Layla would scream. She had a *great* scream, and a fear of spiders she could blame it on without anyone suspecting anything other than that she was being a bit overdramatic.

"In and out," Clay reminded me.

"In and out," I repeated.

It had been Clay's idea to search Ry's office. He and Grey being the only ones ever inside it, it would be the most logical place to look for any clues about the missing wolves or evidence of Adam's rumors. Apparently, most of the pack hadn't ever even *seen* inside that room, with Charity, Jared, and I being the only three ever to step over the threshold of the door.

Which begged the question...why?

Maybe, *hopefully*, because he was hiding something inside. Even I knew it was doubtful, but shy of taking a road trip up north in hopes of finding the other pack

Ry ran with all those years ago and hoping that someone remembered—and had evidence of—what he'd done to that shifter woman who supposedly was pregnant with his child...well, this was the only other option.

We'd all agreed that whether or not we found anything tonight, we'd tell Jared all that we'd learned. We'd need him for the next part—to go into Ryland's e-mails at the quarry and open all the ones from the mysterious sender 'X.'

Whoever it was, they'd sent Ryland password protected files and images labeled with the names of the missing wolves. And that one labeled *List*, and the other labeled simply: *Jared*. If anyone were going to be able to figure out the password to open those, it would be his nephew, right?

That was...if Jared actually agreed to help us and didn't think we'd all lost our minds.

My stomach twisted and I winced, falling into step behind Clay as Jared called back to us, "Hurry up! We're already late."

Vivian winked at me as she waved for me to catch up to them. It was her job to see to it that Jared was also distracted. Ry and others may not notice my absence if I weren't gone too long, but Jared would.

I didn't fucking like this, not one bit—leaving Jared in the dark.

After the cemetery, I'd resolved to tell him, knowing that was what Dad would've told me to do. But I'd been met with resistance from Layla, Viv, and Clay. There wasn't time. And our entire plan could be ruined if we tried to bring him into it at the last second.

I knew they were right, but I still hated it. The guilt gnawed at me, making my mood sour.

"I'm sorry this had to be tonight," Jared said, linking his fingers through mine when Clay and I caught back up to them. Clay eyed our clasped hands but said nothing. I had to hand it to them, they were really handling this whole *sharing* thing pretty well.

Then again, I guess there wasn't much choice. I cringed to think how the next conversation between the three of us would go, though. I didn't know how Clay would feel about taking the relationships to the next level. I mean, I was in no rush, but I didn't want *that* off the table. I was ready. Hell, I was more than ready. But if they needed more time to get used to the idea, I wasn't going to push them.

"Yeah," Viv added. "Having to celebrate someone else on your birthday is lame as fuck."

I shrugged, trying to hide the flush in my cheeks from view.

Get your head in the game, Allie, I scolded myself. I could worry about my relationships with Clay and Jared later. *Not the time. Not the place.*

"Doesn't matter," I said with as much cheer as I could muster. "I had a wicked birthday thanks to you guys. Honestly, I'm kind of relieved to pass off the spotlight. You guys didn't tell anyone else, right?"

I'd sworn them to secrecy, not wanting Seth or Charity or anyone else to make a big deal out of it tonight when the focus was meant to be on Sam, which was exactly where we *needed* the focus to be.

Jared squeezed my hand. "No, but I wish you would've let us. I bet Charity would want to know, and the others, too. Trey and Todd make *amazing* cupcakes. Honestly, you're missing out."

I chuckled. "Next year, okay?"

"I'll hold you to that," Jared said with a wink, giving me a sly look that made my toes curl.

We entered camp together, and I was surprised to see it wasn't the usual bonfire affair. Twinkle lights were coiled around tree trunks and draped like hanging moss from their branches. The pathways and channels between the cabins looked like they'd been swept and picked clean of weeds. Where we could see the fire smoke curling above the rooftops from the main gathering ring, there was also music, louder than we were ever allowed to have it.

Though natural pack magic acted as a sort of repellent for other supernaturals and mortals, keeping them away, I didn't think it could entirely conceal loud thumping music and bright flashing lights that could be spied from passing planes or choppers above or heard at a long distance. Ry was really pulling out all the stops for Sam. It made what we had to do that much harder.

Clay and I shared a look. I could see my own

tension mirrored in the tight line of his jaw and the set of his mouth. Even though I didn't know Sam, and she made no secret of her distaste for me, I could tell Clay wanted her to be happy. And now she was.

If we discovered anything to implicate Ryland, we could be jeopardizing that happiness.

But...we could also be saving her. If Ryland had already killed one woman—a *pregnant* woman if you believed the rumors—who was to say he wouldn't kill his own mate? Just because I couldn't imagine ever laying so much as a finger on either of my mates didn't mean he wasn't deranged enough to do it.

Ryland's raucous laughter could be heard around the fire as we approached. He was easy to spot once we drew near enough, too. Sitting in a large wooden chair with Sam on his lap, his face reddened. His slippery grin stretching the puckered skin on his scars.

Sam looked equally joyful, her bitter attitude from when she and I had first met the other night gone. Replaced with an easy smile and a sense of ease about her that wasn't there before. She bantered loudly with Harrison and Forrest, who sat to Ryland's left on low tree stump stools. All of them holding glass steins of frothy beer instead of the usual red Solo cups we always used for weekend drinks around the fire.

I peered around, trying to spot familiar faces, but I didn't see Charity anywhere, or Seth for that matter. But after a minute, I found Trey and Todd standing by the beer keg, Kyle and Destiny with them.

"There's Destiny," I told Viv, pointing her out. Not that I needed to, Viv had already zeroed in on her mate, their eyes locking, matching grins splitting their faces. Viv glanced at me, asking for permission to leave her post distracting Jared for a minute. I nodded, and she and Layla rushed over with warm hellos. I needed Ry to see that we were all here, including me, before we put the plan in motion.

"Want a drink?" Jared asked Clay and me, releasing my hand to follow Viv to the others and the keg.

"No," Clay and I said at the exact same time. I stiffened.

Jared cocked his head at us, giving Clay a particularly inquisitive stare. "*Okay*," he said, enunciating the word. "You sure?"

Clay grunted, and I nodded, noticing how Sam's laughter had faded. I quickly glanced over to find Ryland's haughty stare locked on me. Good, he'd seen that I was here. And if he was looking, then I was sure he was listening, too.

"I'll have one in a bit," I told Jared, making sure to speak a bit louder than I needed to so it wouldn't be a struggle for Ryland to hear me. Thinking on my toes, I added, "I'm actually just super thirsty." I cleared my throat, the sound rough and forced. "I think I'm going to go get some water and see if I can find Charity."

Jared's gaze narrowed, and I flinched, quickly checking to see if Ry was still in tune to our conversation. He didn't seem to be. He was whispering something in Sam's ear. I watched as his teeth skimmed over her earlobe, making her shiver and me want to barf.

Jared closed the gap between us and lowered his voice. "Why are you so nervous?"

"What?"

He pulled back enough to search my eyes. I dropped them as quickly as I could, my throat thickening with words I wished I could say.

"Come on, Jare," Clay said, stepping past me to clap him on the shoulder. "I think I will take that beer. Let's let Allie go get Charity."

Jared looked like he wanted to say something else, but Clay's grip on his tightened, and I gave him an imploring look.

Talk later, I mouthed to him. *I promise.*

He paled, but let Clay drag him away, glancing back my way curiously before I tore myself away, forcing my feet into a slow, steady, *I'm-not-creeping-around* walk in the general direction of Charity's cabin.

We'd originally planned to wait until a bit later in the night, but maybe it was better to get it over with now. By the look of Ryland and Sam, they could end the festivities any minute to retreat back to Ry's cabin for an early evening delight.

And if I got it over with now, then I could make more of an appearance later when they did the formal ceremony—where my lack of attendance would be noted. That would be in about thirty minutes. Plenty of time to search an office, cover my tracks, find Charity, and convince her to come back to the fire with me, right?

Right?

Oh god.

Wringing my hands in Sam's sweater, I muttered hellos to a few shifters as they drunkenly stumbled past on their way to the fire and skirted around a cabin near Charity's. I didn't want to get too close to her cabin just yet.

The light was on, which meant she was definitely in there and I didn't want her hearing me or scenting me until I was finished with what I needed to do. I paused behind a quiet cabin and sent a group text to Clay, Viv, and Layla.

Allie: Go time.

A text from Viv came in a fraction of a second later.

Vivian: Already? We just got here.

Clay: Better to get it over with before the ceremony. Go, Allie, we got you.

I made sure my phone was toggled to completely silent and slipped into Sam's sweater, drawing up the hood with trembling fingers.

In and out, I reminded myself.

Easy.

Skirting around the backs of the cabins, I darted into the tree line, following it around camp at a distance far enough that no one would see me unless they looked closely, but close enough that I could see if anyone were to approach. I jogged on quiet feet, aiming for patches of earth and avoiding piles of leaves and twigs as best I could.

I wasn't concerned with leaving a trail, exactly—there were too many shifters here for anyone to decipher mine. I was more worried about making loud noises and alerting anyone to my presence as I came up behind Ryland's cabin, creeping around the moon chamber and into his backyard.

The cabin was lit softly within, Ryland had obviously left a lamp on in the main living area. But the upstairs and eastern side of the house, where his office was, were left in total darkness.

Just like Clay had said there would be, a sliding patio door to the right side revealed a small kitchen I'd never been in. And just like he'd said it would be, it was unlocked. I sighed gratefully as the door rolled away silently, allowing me to step inside with barely a sound and seal the door shut behind myself.

With my heart a thunderous roar in my ears, it was almost impossible to hear anything else inside the cabin. I stayed like that for a minute in the darkened corner of the kitchen, waiting for my pulse to slow so I could make sure there was no one else inside.

Satisfied, I crept to the arched doorway of the kitchen and peered into the living space. Next to me was a staircase leading up into the second level, and across the living room was the hallway that would lead me to Ryland's office.

The front door, mercifully, was closed. Whoever

had used the restroom last must have shut it, and I sent whoever that person was my gratitude. Not wanting to waste time, I crept across the living room, nearly jumping out of my skin when I heard someone pass by near the front door.

I did exactly what I shouldn't and froze like a goddamned deer in the headlights. The creak and groan of the wood on the floorboards on Ryland's front stoop faded a second later. Distantly, I could hear Clay's laugh, clearly forced, but whoever he'd used it on to get them away from the cabin, it'd worked.

Thank you, Clay.

Unstuck, I swallowed hard and continued across the living room, practically at a sprint now as I rushed down the hall, opened the office door, and tucked myself inside, shutting it behind myself with fumbling fingers. I'd tried to slip the catch in quietly, turning the knob slowly, but it clicked like a gunshot in the dim office, and I stilled, grimacing as a layer of icy sweat slicked my chest.

Fuck. Maybe I should have let Clay do this.

Who was I kidding? I was not a damned ninja.

My anxiety couldn't handle this shit. I pressed a palm to my chest, willing the fluttering sensation there to take a hike and blew out a breath, steeling myself with eyes squeezed tightly shut before I shoved off from the wall and rushed to the desk. Eager to get this whole debacle over with so I could go back outside and take Jared up on that beer. Or five.

I rubbed my sweaty palms on Sam's sweater, hoping to get as much of my scent off of my hands and as much of *hers* on me as I could. Chances were Sam had been in here already, right? I really hoped so, because if not, Ry may have some questions if he happened to scent her in his office.

Let's just hope he didn't have any reason to come in here before morning, when the scent would most likely have faded beyond recognition.

I touched things as little as I could, easing drawers open to rifle through papers and pens. There was almost an entire drawer of errant receipts and safety pins, none of which looked important, but several that I took note of just in case.

One in particular, a bill from the hardware store that listed tarps and lighter fluid as the only purchases seemed suspect, but he could have used those items for any number of run of the mill things here at camp. I pocketed that one, anyway, thinking he wouldn't miss it in the mess of a hundred others strewn in the deep drawer.

I checked the other three drawers, finding two to be filled with general office fare. Staplers and a hole punch. A few rulers. Pencils. An eraser. A pair of reading glasses I could never have pictured Ryland wearing. A bottle of Advil. Two small bottles of whiskey. One full, the other nearly empty. In the last, largest drawer on the bottom left were files.

Jackpot.

There had to be something in there he was hiding. There were so *many* of them. I fingered through them, jumping at every creak and groan of the cabin to the point I was starting to worry if there actually *was* someone I was just going to wind up attributing the sound of them to Ryland's rickety plumping clattering behind the drywall.

I went through each label *twice* but found nothing that seemed even remotely out of the ordinary. I even took three files out just to see if their titles fit their contents. They did. Purchase orders for lumber for the camp. A generator manual and notes. A bunch of instructions on how to restart the solar system after a bad storm. I didn't even know there *was* a solar system. The panels must've been on the back of Ry's cabin for me to have missed them.

Groaning quietly, I tucked everything back where I'd found it, rolling the drawer shut with a solemn *click.* I checked the papers atop Ryland's desk next, followed by the bookcase on the wall to the right, feeling behind the books that were pushed forward.

If I were a crazy person who killed a bunch of people I was supposed to care about, where would I hide evidence of that?

Apparently, not in my office it would seem.

I knew I was taking too long even before I got the text from Clay. My phone illuminated in my pocket, and I drew it out, my fingertips numb from nerves.

Clay: You're taking too long.

I gripped the phone, pushing my screen to a point where it was near cracking, but I didn't care. There *had* to be something here, right?

A person couldn't just get away with everything Ryland had been accused of getting away with without leaving a shred of evidence behind.

Of course, there was a chance the rumors were just that—*rumors*—but my gut told me otherwise.

Allie: I need a few more minutes. Stall.
Clay: Be quick.

There was no computer here, so that option was out, and I could see a cell phone charger plugged into the wall by the bookcase, but there was no phone attached, which meant Ryland must have had it with him.

Unless I was going to start ripping up floorboards, I'd already searched everywhere in the office. I bit my lower lip, letting my gaze sweep over the room one last time. I fixated on the ceiling, looking as though I could see through the wooden beams and plaster to the rooms above.

If I were a crazy person who had something to hide, would I hide it in my office? Or would I hide it somewhere more…private?

Say…my bedroom? Maybe?

A part of me knew I was grasping at straws at this point, but I was nothing if not thorough. *Just a quick look,* I promised myself.

Legs like putty, I crept from the office, pausing to

listen for anyone outside. The music drowned out most every other sound, but even from here, I could hear Ryland's laughter and someone shouting for more shots.

Perfect. Hopefully by the time the ceremony started everyone would be too drunk to even realize I was gone at all. Armed with false reassurances, I took the stairs two at a time up to the second floor, grimacing as Ryland's peppery scent grew. It clogged the air, making me want to gag and sneeze in alternating intensities.

A familiar scent also permeated the air near the landing. It was clearly Sam's. It was the scent of the sweater I wore magnified. Juniper and something tangy, like orange juice left out in the sun.

There was only a single room sized door, another, smaller door led to a linen closet after a cursory peek within. I followed the intermingled smells of Ryland and his new mate to the bedroom, nudging the already slightly ajar door open enough for me to slide inside.

A tall king sized bed dominated the heart of the space. It squatted, pushed up against the far wall, two tall open windows on either side served to illuminate the space, casting the moon's glow over matching night tables near each of the extra-long pillows.

The blankets were rumpled and smelled of the deeds that'd been done beneath them. But that wasn't the worst part. The worst part was that Sam's wasn't the only scent clogging my nostrils. Faintly, as though someone had gone to painstaking lengths to remove it, I could also smell Charity.

If I weren't a hundred percent sure they'd been screwing, I was now.

I alternated between feeling sorry for Charity and relieved that she wouldn't ever share this bed with Ryland again.

A mirrored closet coaxed a short chirp from my lips, my own reflection startling me enough that a wave of icy cold stole over every inch of my flesh. In dark jeans and a black hooded sweatshirt, I didn't look myself. But the glow of my light gray eyes within the shadow of the hood were unmistakable. Wide and startled.

Get it together.

I went to the closet first, if only to roll my reflection away behind a non-reflective panel. A suitcase of women's clothes lay half spilled over the floor, clearly rummaged through in a rush. Sam's. Above, in neat rows, Ryland's clothing hung from all black hangers. His jeans were tucked into a shelving unit along one side. Several large-buckled belts hung on hooks next to them.

I felt around on the shelf above where the clothing hung, but my hand came away only coated in a layer of dust and sticky cobwebs. The other side was much the same. More clothes. An overflowing laundry hamper.

Damn. Damn. Damn.

Kneeling, I crawled over to the bed and lifted the

corner of the blanket, careful not to touch too much of it. I huffed, finding a wooden board was beneath, sealing off the under part of the bed.

Inching the blanket away from one corner, I lifted the edge of the mattress, squinting to see into the cavity beneath.

Vacant, save for some lost coins and an old sock.

The nightstand was next, and I really wished I hadn't seen what was inside of it. There was no way I was touching any of that to search more in depth.

I padded to the other side, easing out the drawer of the matching nightstand. Within, there was an extra phone charger, some deodorant, cologne, and a tattered copy of a Jack Reacher novel.

I reached my hand into the back of the drawer to feel for anything else when a bloodcurdling scream sliced through the tepid silence, cutting me right down to the bone.

Fuck.

Below, the screen door clattered shut, and Ryland's voice called, "All right over there?"

An indiscernible shout echoed back, Layla telling him it was all right.

Another familiar voice bubbled with a dark laugh. "Hope I didn't scare her," Grey said. "I'm just passing through with my congratulations."

Double fuck.

"Stay for a drink, I have a favor to ask."

"Another one?"

"Possibly. Might be two."

With shaking fingers, I lifted the drawer from the squeaky casters, pushing it back shut, *praying* that they would go to the office for their drink and leave quickly. There was virtually no way I could creep back down the stairs and outside without one of them hearing me.

The crinkle of plastic sounded before I could get the drawer shut, and I paused, listening as I lifted the drawer back out and pushed it back in, making it rub against whatever was making the noise a second time. I winced, hoping the sound was faint enough that they wouldn't be able to hear.

The solemn click of the office door closing downstairs gave me the courage I needed to reach my hand back inside the drawer. There hadn't been anything inside that would have crinkled like that. I was sure of it. So then what was making the sound?

I felt around again, biting my lower lip to a point near breaking the skin.

Come on.

Realizing the drawer only made the sound when I lifted it off the casters, I turned my palm upward, feeling the underside of the smooth top of the walnut nightstand. My fingers brushed over thick plastic, and I froze, feeling the rough fabric of Velcro straps holding whatever it was in place.

Lumpy shapes filled the bag. Two large ball-like forms and something small, like a thimble.

Breathless, I tugged gently on the Velcro strap,

ignoring the light from my cell phone flashing like a strobe light in my pocket. The crinkle of it coming undone was so loud I gritted my teeth, not daring to so much as breathe.

But when the distant hum of Ryland and Grey's conversation downstairs never faltered, I let the bag drop into my palm and slowly drew it out, careful not to disturb it and end up making even more noise.

The blue-hued moonlight shining in a column through the window above the nightstand caught silvery white fur, and I stilled, my stomach turning. I flipped the bag in my fingers. It was no more than the size of a sandwich bag, but a heavy duty one—the kind we learned drug smugglers used to cover the scent of marijuana during transport.

Another bit of fur pressed against the thick plastic, this one the color of amber, threaded through with gold. I realized what they were with a stomach-churning squeal and dropped the bag as though burned by its contents.

A smear of old blood was matted on the amber fur, right where it was severed from the tail of a wolf.

Tails.

They were the tips of wolf *tails*.

And fuck if that white one didn't look a *lot* like Jared's.

...his parents.

I swallowed back bile, pressing the back of my hand to my mouth to keep it in, sidesheaving. My wolf raged within, awakening with a defensive snarl that came out through my human lips.

Downstairs, the office door creaked open.

"What is it Grey?" Ryland asked.

The vampire didn't answer right away, but I heard his long intake of breath. Was he...was he trying to scent me? "Is someone else in here?"

Not wasting another second, I scooped up the bag and gagged as I shoved it down the front of Sam's sweater, beneath the neckline of my shirt, and jammed it between my breasts, shoving the drawer closed.

"Bring them here," Ryland growled, and I did the only thing I could think to do, backing up three steps before sprinting toward the tall, narrow window above the nightstand. I jumped onto the top of the stand and launched myself, knees lifted and elbows out through the screen, popping it out of place as I sailed through.

A breath hitched in my throat as my limbs flailed in midair, trying to position myself for the impact. I hit on the balls of my feet and rolled into standing, grateful my wolf seemed to know how to make that landing because I sure as hell didn't.

I sprinted past the moon chamber and ducked into the trees, not stopping once I had the advantage of tree cover. I kept going, heart thumping, legs pumping.

Panicked, I tried to find a place I could tuck away what I'd found in Ryland's bedside drawer so I could shift. Run faster. *Get away.*

I spied a crook in the base of a tree and skidded,

trying to stop too quickly. I fell, sliding over loose dirt and leaves before clamoring back to my feet. I went absolutely still before I could reach for the evidence hidden in my cleavage. There, not more than ten paces from me, stood Grey.

The blue stone of his ring caught the moonlight, glinting almost as menacingly as his black eyes. He tilted his head to one side, a sneaking smirk pulling up one corner of his mouth. "Allie," he said, as though we'd met out here by a happy surprise.

I glanced past him, trying to judge the distance back to camp.

Was it too far for anyone to hear me scream? Oh god.

I should have run straight for the bonfire.

Stupid.

"Why aren't you at the celebration?" Grey asked, his tone taunting.

"I—I was just—" I stammered, reaching for an excuse that would sound at least plausible, not sure there was a point in even giving one. He knew I was inside. The busted window screen was evidence enough that I'd jumped out, but did he know what I had?

Did I close that drawer or had I left it open?

Would Ryland check to see if his gruesome trophies were missing?

Grey's dark eyes narrowed, and I glanced past him again, searching for Ryland. Surely, he would have followed? Surely, he would want to know what I was doing in his house, alone. In his room.

"Ryland won't be joining us," Grey said, bringing his hands forward to steeple his fingers, tapping them to his lips as he stepped forward. I stepped back in response, my wolf at the ready.

"But don't fret, young one. Better it be me than him."

What the hell did that mean?

A thought crossed my mind, and I gasped, blurting the words before I could stop myself. "You're X. Aren't you?"

Surprise widened his eyes for a millisecond before he grinned. "I knew you were trouble from the first time I saw you. I told Ryland as much, but he never listens to me."

He stepped forward again, and a warning growl rose in my throat.

If I could help it, I wouldn't shift. If I did, it would send all my clothes, *and the evidence I found*, scattering to the ground where he could snatch it up.

"You can't best me, Allie. I'm over two hundred years old. If I wanted, I could have you willingly kneel before me. I could sweep that strange hair of yours away from your neck and drink my fill and you wouldn't make so much as a sound."

The reminder that he could compel me to do just that—to do *anything* he wanted—sent a fresh shock of fear pulsing through my veins. I shifted my gaze to his mouth, doing my best not to look him in the eye. That was how it worked, right?

"What do you want?" I demanded, curling my hands into fists.

"What do *I* want?" he asked, seemingly perplexed. "It isn't about what I want, dear one. It's about what must be done."

So, this is it then?

"He wants you to kill me, doesn't he?" I snarled, feeling my canines elongate enough to pierce my bottom lip. A hot dribble of blood rolled down to my chin.

A soft hiss escaped Grey's lips, and I saw his fangs sharpen, growing longer, too. He licked his lips. "He would like that, I'm sure, but no...at least, not yet."

If that wasn't an admission of guilt, I didn't know what was.

"Ryland killed them, didn't he?" I asked, emboldened now that I knew he didn't intend to kill *me*. "The shifters who keep vanishing. They haven't run away at all, have they?"

Grey clucked his tongue.

"*Didn't he?*" I pressed, my voice rising. "Just admit it."

Grey's lips pressed together as he regarded me with a cool sort of interest. Like he was impressed. "I don't think I can rightly give Ryland credit for my work," he said, his voice a sly whisper, smoother than silk.

"For your..." I trailed off, understanding at once what he meant.

"Ryland had *you* get rid of them," I said, more to myself than to Grey. A soft crinkle sounded from my chest as I pointed an accusing finger at him.

But what about…

"And Jared's parents? Did you kill them, too?"

All I needed was his admission of guilt. A nod. Anything.

Something that would incriminate him and not Ryland. If he gave me that, I'd unleash my wolf.

Grey underestimated us. We were strong. Fast.

We could take him.

We would revel in the taste of his blood coating our tongue.

Grey's smile grew. "Some things can be done as favors," he said, the 's' lengthening into a hiss. "But there are some things a man must do himself."

I gasped at the admission, my shock quickly morphing to anger and a dangerous understanding of what was going to happen next.

A bolt of white-hot apprehension seared through my chest as Grey darted forward, too fast for me to react while still dazed by his words.

My eyes met his and his lips parted. "Now…" he cooed, standing over me, his hand reaching up as though he intended to stroke my cheek. I did my best to stand my ground. "You will forget everything we just spoke about."

What?

"You will set aside your suspicions about Ryland,

and you will convince anyone else who shares those suspicions that they are unfounded. *Ridiculous.* From this moment on, you will be *loyal* to him in every way."

A strange thought crossed my mind. A whisper of doubt planting seeds in the garden of my mind.

Maybe Ryland was innocent. Maybe it was all a misunderstanding...

I realized what Grey was doing with a start I hope he didn't see in my eyes. My clenched fists at my sides steadied me, fingernails digging deeply into flesh.

Stay still, I told myself, pulse thrumming like a hummingbird's wings.

Grey was trying to compel me. How hadn't I seen it before.

Holy fuck, this wasn't the first time, either, was it?

You will not tell anyone of this meeting, he'd said to me in Ryland's office just over a week before. *You will not speak ill of your alpha. You will adhere to his will and command. You will be obedient.*

Except...I had told Clay of the meeting. And I *definitely had* spoken ill of Ryland. And I certainly was *not* obedient.

Like the spell shielding Clay's family's cabin from view, and the magic the witch had tried to use to heal my arm, apparently, a vampire's compulsion also held no sway over me?

"Do you understand?" Grey asked, a knot forming

in his brow, and I realized I may not have been acting like someone compelled would act. I had no idea what that would look like, but I wanted—*no, I needed*—him to think this was working. It was the only way I was going to get out of here without a fight.

I forced my face to slacken, staring unblinking into his dark eyes, fighting my emotions.

"I understand," I replied, trying a slow succinct tone.

Grey bent closer, putting his face a mere three inches from my own. Near enough that I could smell the metallic tang on his breath and the musky scent of his aftershave. He searched my gaze, and I did my utmost best not to move, attempting to slow my erratic pulse.

He tipped his head to one side, brushing the tip of his index finger down from my temple to my jaw. I stiffened at the contact, my jaw twitching with the urge to bite his head off.

"Such a pity the Endurans claimed you first," he purred. "You would have made an *exceptional* vampire."

Don't shift.

Don't shift.

"Since we're here," he continued, his gaze following the trail his finger had just made on the side of my face and down lower to my neck. "I don't see why we shouldn't make the most of it. I doubt Ryland would mind."

His fingers came to rest on the side of my neck,

pressing against the pulsating artery there as his other hand came around my back, drawing me in closer to him.

No, I roared within. There was no way in *hell* I was going to let this happen. I began unfurling within, letting my wolf know that she was about to take the reins she wanted so desperately, giving her permission to *end* this fucker before he could sink his teeth into us.

On my mark, I whispered within, ready to let go, but not until the right moment.

Let him get a little closer.

Closer.

I held my breath.

"Allie?"

Clay's growl rebounded through the woods.

In a matter of less than a second, Grey's hold on me loosened and then vanished entirely.

"Until next time."

His whisper lingered even after he was gone.

"Allie! Where the fuck are you?"

"*H-here.*" I whispered, unable to project my voice as the weight of everything came crashing down around me.

We'd been right.

My stomach heaved and just as Clay reached me, I crumpled to my knees, retching into the dirt, my arms quivering beneath my weight.

"Hey," he said, rushing to sweep my hair away from my face.

"*Allie*," he growled. "Allie, what happened?"

Booted feet running through dry leaves sounded somewhere behind Clay, and I flinched, my watery gaze lifting to find the pursuer.

"It's okay," Clay said, rubbing a wide hand over my back. "It's okay, it's just the others."

"What the hell happened?" Jared's voice demanded, and I felt a tug as he gently folded me into his arms, enveloping me in warmth and his woodsy scent.

"Allie?" Layla.

"Did he touch you? I'll fucking kill—"

"Quiet," Clay barked, silencing everyone. "Jared, get her up. It's time for us to leave."

"But their ceremony—" Vivian began just as the hooting of cheers and the clatter of an applause rose from camp in the distance.

"Is already over," Jared snapped, his tone defiant and dangerous and not at all the one that I liked. I wanted my calm Jared. I needed him. As the dark spots crowded in at the edges of my vision, my panic taking root, I clutched him.

"Let's get you home," Jared said, and I felt my body lift from the ground just as my vision began to darken.

I fought against the dark and the fear that if my heart beat any more quickly—more erratically—that it would stop entirely. My wolf prowled, dogged by my panic, but enraged beyond measure.

"No," I muttered, trying to get a grip on myself. "*NO.*"

"Wait, stop," Clay bellowed, and felt Jared jerk beneath me. "What is it Allie?"

My head spun and the cold sweat that had bloomed over my chest earlier was beginning to creep like frost down my arms, leaving a numb tingle in its wake.

We were right.

I tried to say the words. I needed to make him understand that we couldn't leave. Sam was in danger. We were *all* in danger.

But my heart gave one more fitful stammer, and I jerked with the force of it before darkness consumed me.

26

My eyes felt like they were filled with sandpaper as I awoke to a barrage of shouting, the flames of hell licking at my face.

No...not hell. They'd set me down on the couch in the living room and there was a wild fire roaring in the hearth, burning my cheeks with the intensity of its heat.

"Guys," Vivian hissed. "*Guys,* she's waking up."

Cool hands fluttered over my arms, and Viv sucked in a breath. "Holy crap, she's on fire."

I felt the couch beneath me move jerkily backward and groaned as a wave of vertigo almost had me leaning over the edge to vomit again.

My head pounded as I tried to push myself to sitting. "Water," I croaked, my throat drier than the Sahara.

An icy glass pressed into my palm, and I gulped it

down greedily, breathless when I finally drained it and shivering as the cold water snaked a path down into my belly.

It brought with it a sense of clarity and the hydration my body needed to heal whatever ailed it. I peeled my eyelids back and stared into the worried, angry faces of my friends. Jared's hand closed over mine, and the couch dipped as he sat down next to me.

Clay stood behind Layla and Vivian, his arms crossed over his shirtless torso. His chest heaved with hard breaths as he stared at me, his glowing blue eyes showing the fear he was trying to hide.

I squeezed Jared's hand, trying to let him know that I was all right as I found my voice, swallowing past the diminishing razor blades in my throat.

"You should have told me," Jared said, and I peered up at him, cut by the betrayal in his eyes.

I glanced at Clay, who nodded, telling me that they'd finally let Jared in on everything we'd been looking into.

...they didn't even know the half of it. I dropped my head and the plastic bag still wedged between my breasts crinkled with the movement, reminding me of its presence.

"Are you going to tell us what happened?" Clay demanded. "You scared the *shit* out of us, Allie."

"Would you chill out for, like, two seconds?" Layla snapped at him. "Give her a minute."

"It was a panic attack," Vivian added. "We *told* you that, already. She used to have them all the time."

Clay huffed.

"I'm sorry," I whispered to Jared, ignoring their banter. I waited until his eyes met mine to continue. "It was too awful…all the things Adam told us. I didn't want to tell you until we had proof."

The need to explain overtook me, and burning tears stung in my eyes.

"But you're right. We shouldn't have kept it from you. I wish…I wish…"

Wishing wasn't going to get me anywhere. And nothing was going to soften the blow of this next part. My wolf blazed back to the surface and I grunted, holding her back as my rage erased what remained of the grogginess still clinging to my bones.

Jared tugged my hand. "Is it true?" he asked me, voice hard, and even though his jaw was clenched tighter than a vise, I didn't miss the slight quiver in his chin.

With shaking fingers, I let go of Jared's hand and unzipped Sam's sweater, digging in between my breasts. The bag was coated in slippery sweat, but it was still there, giving life to all the horrible things we'd wished weren't true.

I set it down on Jared's lap as though if I jostled it too much it may explode. He glanced down, brows drawn together as he studied the tufts of fur contained within. For the first time, in the light, I noticed how the tips of the tails weren't the only contents. There was also something shiny, like copper, and small tucked into one corner. And a swath of baby-fine blond hair knotted with a bit of string.

"Is that..." Layla trailed off and her words seemed to break whatever spell had been holding Jared still.

A strangled cry fell past his lips as he lurched to his feet, sending the bag and its contents to the floor. The tails, hair, a bit of shining copper spilled out onto the rug at Clay's feet.

His head shook, as though not believing what he was seeing.

Jared's blatant horror confirmed my suspicions. I'd still been holding onto a shred of hope that the chunks of fur and decayed flesh didn't belong to his parents. I could see now that it was foolish to hope.

I could see now what needed to be done.

Clay stooped, a vein in his neck jutting out, throbbing. With his thumb and index finger he picked the bit of copper from the carpet, rising back to standing. He held it up to the light, turning it between his fingers.

It caught the light, glinting faintly.

It wasn't a thimble.

It was a shell casing from a bullet.

"Clay," I said on a breath, seeing the exact moment he realized what it was and why it was in that bag. His face twisted, and in one quick motion, he whipped the casing across the room. The knock of it shattering a perfect circle through the glass window near the door made me jump.

He turned on me with wicked fury, eyes aglow. "*You knew*," he shouted. "You *knew*, didn't you?"

Hurt and scathing fury rippled across his eyes and stained his cheek red.

"Not for certain," I told him, standing my ground. "And you know as well as I do that if I'd told you, you wouldn't have been able to—"

"*Don't*," he snarled, and something inside me crumpled.

Jared knelt on the floor, hesitantly reaching his fingers toward the tufts of crimson-stained fur on the rug. He paused just shy of touching them, unable to. His outstretched hand balled into a fist and he pulled it back.

"Maybe..." he began, his voice oddly detached. "Maybe he just..."

I shook my head, reaching down to put a hand on his shoulder. He flinched at the contact, and I snatched my hand away. "No," I told him. "Grey admitted everything. The missing shifters. Your parents. He told me right before he compelled me to forget it all and be *loyal* to my alpha."

Distantly, I was aware that Clay had begun to pace. I could hear Viv and Layla whispering to him reassuringly, trying to get him to breathe.

"But," Jared said, his eyes widening as realization set in, "you...can't be compelled?"

"Apparently not."

My upper lip curled back as my wolf hedged nearer to the surface. The presence of her mates' wolves—their rage and anguish—stoking her fire. *Our* fire.

"Jare," Clay roared, and Jared tore his gaze away from the last remains of his parents to meet Clay's stare.

Something passed between them. A question unspoken.

Jared's face visibly paled as he dipped his head in a single, solemn nod.

Clay kicked off his shoes and stormed to the front door, Layla and Viv calling after him.

"Jared? What did you just do?" I demanded, getting to my own feet to follow after them.

He didn't look at me when he replied simply, "Gave him permission."

Oh no you didn't.

A terrifying image of Ryland standing with his canine teeth dripping blood over a prone Clay flashed across my mind.

Spurred to action, I hooked a hand beneath Jared's arm and hauled him to his feet, a new kind of panic lodging itself like a blade in my gut. "Well, *ungive* it," I hissed, dragging him to the door with me and out into the cold dawn light.

Jared pulled out of my grasp once we got outside.

Layla shrieked as Clay burst from his shorts,

coming down on all fours, a vicious growl echoing in the miasmal quiet.

He was past the point of no return. There would be no talking him down. I could see it in his eyes. Wild and hungry. He wouldn't be sated until blood was spilled.

I was knocked onto my stomach as Jared shifted behind me, the hard skull of his canine head slamming against my back. I struggled to get my breath back, rolling out of the way as he launched himself down the steps and onto the dirt lawn with Clay.

Finally, blissfully, I released myself to the power of my wolf, feeling my body bend and break in a matter of a second. I scraped down the steps and placed myself in their path, Layla and Viv taking up posts on either side of me as what remained of our clothes drifted down to land in heaps on the dirt.

Stop, I bellowed in our shared mind.

Clay snapped at me. *Move, Allie.*

I won't.

Do as he says, Jared chimed in, vibrating with a level of rage I didn't know he was capable of.

No. I won't let you get yourselves killed.

Allie, Jared warned. *Move.*

He needs to be dealt with. Now.

I faltered.

Clay was right.

What am I doing?

It was so obvious. The road laid out as clearly as if it were made out of yellow bricks.

You're right.

Hazel's sad look as she told me *it's what sets you apart that will see your triumph,* came to mind.

Even with a lack of experience, I was the strongest of us. The fastest. But above all, even though I'd accepted Ryland as my alpha, I was the only one of us with a will strong enough to compete with his.

Someone had to put an end to him, but it couldn't be them.

It had to be me.

I think somewhere deep down I'd known that all along. I'd *known* it would come to this; I just didn't want to believe it. And as much as the rational part of me pleaded that we needed to be patient. That we should come up with a plan. The *ir*rational part—the part that lusted for Ryland's blood just as much as my mates, demanded to be sated.

Then there was the uncontested fact that if I didn't do it, *they* would. Even if it meant one or both of them died trying.

Vengeance would be had today, but it wouldn't be them who wreaked it upon our common enemy.

I'm going to challenge Ryland, I told them, the panic of a moment before falling away like a discarded skin. The declaration brought with it a sense of calm that stilled the tremor in my paws and evened out my breaths.

It was the simplest thing in the world, that decision.

The hell you are, Clay said, coiling his body to launch past me.

No, I commanded him, letting the full force of my will expand in my core. Letting it infuse my words with power.

Clay buckled, his coiled shoulders lowering.

Jared eyed me warily, glancing between Clay's bared teeth and my unnerving stillness. *Allie, you can't,* he said, the detached tone gone for the moment. *He'll kill you.*

He might, I admitted. *But I'll make sure to leave him weak enough that you can finish what I started.*

Allie! Vivian shouted in my thoughts. *We aren't going to let you do this.*

I whirled on her.

Oh? I hissed, lips pulling back over teeth. *And I should let* them *go instead?*

A startled yelp left her lips, and she bucked backward, cowed.

We need to be rational, Layla said.

Allie, Clay said, strangled. *Let. Me. Up.*

You can't do this, Jared added, taking another tentative step toward me. *Vivian's right. We aren't going to let you.*

That was where he was wrong.

I didn't need them to *let* me do anything.

I dug my claws into the dirt and lifted myself high and proud, letting that bubble of will within grow *and grow* until I knew there was nothing that would stop it.

Layla and Vivian were the first to bow, emitting tiny yelps as their chins bent to rest on the dirt.

No! Clay shouted. *Don't do this. Please.*

I'm sorry, I told them, watching resolutely as Jared and Clay fought against the force of my will. *But no one else is going to get hurt. Not when I can stop it.*

Allie, don't... Jared begged.

Clay shuddered as he fell, his panicked stare piecing me straight through.

Your will won't keep us here, he hissed in my thoughts. *You aren't our alpha!*

I don't need it to keep you here, I replied, my heart breaking as I turned away from them to face the trees. *I just need a head start.*

27

It was eerie how quiet it was as I cleared through the tree line and into pack camp, slowing to a quick walk. The camp slept, their untroubled heads resting on pillows. The remnants of last night's drinks keeping them in the comforting bosom of sleep.

Discarded cups and bottles littered the spaces between the cabin, left to be cleaned up another day. The fairy lights that'd been strung through the trees now hung limp and lifeless, their lights gone out.

A stillness in the cool, damp air made my skin bristle. I couldn't do what I needed to do without every single pack member present. I couldn't give Ryland the opportunity to weasel his way out of this. If I challenged him alone in his cabin, there was no telling what he might do.

But challenging him in front of everyone…

He would have no choice but to accept. To play *fair* for once in his miserable existence.

Steeling myself, I crept up to the dead firepit, sending a last prayer up to whatever god would hear me with the last tendril of white smoke twisting upward to the heavens.

Gaze fixed on Ryland's cabin, I shifted, shaking off the wolf as easily as I would a jacket.

"Ryland!" I screamed, hauling in a long, shuddering breath before bellowing his name a second time, making sure my voice would be heard across camp. "Ryland!"

My fists began to shake as the first signs of life awoke in the clearing. The bang of a door shutting somewhere behind me. A shout. The naked shape of a man rushing from the woods to see what was going on.

Charity rushing up from my left, in nothing but a long t-shirt, eyes ringed in red and her dreads sticking out at odd angles from how she slept. "Allie?" she asked, a worried crease in her forehead. "What's happening?"

Destiny was the next to approach, with Seth, Kyle, Trey, and Todd lagging behind her in various states of undress.

Destiny peered around me, searching for signs of Vivian.

"She isn't here," I told her.

Destiny looked between me and the direction I'd come from. In my heightened state, I found I could faintly hear her pulse as it built in tempo. And as she broke into a sprint for the trees, gone in search of her mate, I heard the distinct sound of Ryland cursing and the squeal of Sam as something slammed loudly within the cabin.

I clenched my jaw, willing myself to remain where I was.

"What's going on?" Seth asked, flipping his dark hair away from his eyes.

"Has something happened?" Trey added.

"Are Clay and Jared okay?"

My stomach pooled with acid.

"No," I growled. "But they will be."

"Go find them," Seth barked at Kyle, and he nodded once to Seth and took off running after Destiny. Then he turned back to me. "Are you going to tell us what happened?"

Just then, Ryland stepped outside, still fastening the large silver buckle of his belt. Barefoot, barechested, and every inch the monster I always knew he was.

"I think I'll let *him* tell you," I replied to Seth, raising my voice to let it carry over the still-gathering pack.

Ryland made no secret of his rage; his eyes flared with ruddy orange light and his muscles rippled. "What is the meaning of this?"

How could he do it?

How could he sit there, smug and haughty with disdain after all that he'd done? As if my appearance here *inconvenienced* him. Fucking *seriously*?

"Where are the missing wolves?" I shouted across the space between us. "Tell them!"

I had the satisfaction of watching his face bleach of color before he recovered, lifting a brow as though I'd just said something that made absolutely no sense to him.

I had to hand it to him. He was *good*.

"I don't know what you're talking about, Allie, but if you'll come inside, we can discuss—"

Ignoring him, I continued, my voice broken and raw but loud enough for all to hear me. "Tell them!" I demanded. "Tell them how you *killed* Jared's parents—skinned them—and kept their tails as souvenirs."

Charity gasped, and from the corner of my eyes, I could see her looking at me like I'd gone and lost my damned mind. I didn't care. I wasn't finished.

"Tell them how you shot Thomas Armstrong in the back of the head and walked away like it never happened!"

Sam, tugging a robe closed over her naked body, froze mid-step as she appeared behind Ryland on the porch. Her face screwed up into a disgusted scowl.

"Ryland," she said. "What the fuck is going on?"

He held up a hand to silence her, never taking his eyes off me. "Those are some pretty serious accusations," he said, his gaze tentatively sliding to the gathered pack, judging their reactions.

I knew I hadn't won them over.

"Allie's lost it," I heard someone mutter just before Charity whispered. "I think you should calm down."

I balked at the suggestion, resisting my wolf's urge to snap at her.

The tether at my core gave a sharp tug and a lick of apprehension skated up my spine. I was running out of time. I could feel Jared and Clay—they were close now. They'd be here soon.

Charity hesitantly curled a hand around my arm, but I shrugged her off. "You can pretend all you want," I hissed at Ryland. "But I know what you've done."

The bastard smirked.

For the first time since he came outside, I tore my gaze away from my alpha and turned to the crowd, making sure they were all paying *very* close attention.

"Ryland," Sam repeated, and I heard him growl at her.

"That's enough," Ryland roared, feeding enough of his alpha will into the words to bend the heads of weaker members of the pack.

"I agree," I said, my chin high.

Something in my eyes must have alarmed him because his lips parted, and I saw understanding flash across his features before I gathered the courage. I needed to say what I came here to say.

"*I challenge you*, Ryland Stone, for the right to rule this pack."

28

A sly smile crept over his lips.

It was there only for the briefest moment, just before he erased all traces of it, but it was long enough to set my nerves on edge. To tell me that he had anticipated this. Was already ready for it.

"Allie!" Charity exclaimed, her voice rising above a barrage of heated whispers at my back. When I finally turned to face her, I found her stricken with fear, her face pale and bright turquoise eyes wide and rimmed with fresh tears. She brought a trembling hand to her mouth, suddenly speechless.

"I'm sorry, Char," I told her. "It has to be done."

Charity blinked, and a tear fell. I looked away, unable to watch.

She wasn't crying because I was going to kill the man she mistakenly fell in love with. She was crying because she thought she was going to lose *me*.

I hoped I was going to prove her wrong.

"There's a reason a female shifter has never led a pack on mortal soil," Ryland said, traces of that infuriating smirk still twitching through his mask of phony concern. "You aren't strong enough. You will lose."

Just like he so clearly wanted me to, I rose to the bait. *"Try me."*

He sighed.

"Allie Grace," Ryland said, his face placid, like a war general coming to terms with a decision he himself did not wish to make but was forced into. "I accept your challenge."

A hush of silence went over the camp, broken only when Sam grabbed Ryland by the arm, wrenching it backward so he would face her. "You can't," she told him. "That's my brother's *mate*."

He shrugged her off. "And like you said," he replied, eyes sliding to me for the briefest second, making sure I was listening. "He will be better off without her."

The blow stung, but I didn't let it shake me.

Hell, if we were being honest here. I agreed with her.

"The others were right," he said, this time lifting his voice for all to hear. "Allie isn't like us. She's...*unnatural*...and clearly unhinged."

Oh, he had no idea...I was about to show him just how *unhinged* I could be.

"*Well*," I hollered, vibrating with anticipation,

paying the whispers no heed. "Are you just going to stand there?"

Ryland lifted his chin and stepped down onto the dirt, gaze fixed on me, flitting briefly to something behind me. I spun to look, catching what looked like the hem of a dark jacket as someone skated behind a cabin at the edge of camp.

The echoing snap of a branch in the forest yanked my attention back; my body jerked, anticipating an attack.

Until a dark shape burst from the trees and into camp. Clay. Followed closely by Jared, Viv, Layla, Kyle, and Destiny.

Clay skidded to a stop several paces in front of me, growling ferociously at Ryland. Jared came to stand next to Clay, taking up a similar protective stance at my front. Layla, Viv, and Destiny joined them.

Kyle floundered off to the side, unsure what to do.

Clay and Jared shifted at the same time, the snap and shudder of their bodies over in an instant, leaving me staring at two nude backs. The others remained in their wolf forms. Layla turned, pushing her cold, wet snout against my hand with a low whine.

"You fucking bastard," Clay barked, every muscle in his body tense and rippling beneath a layer of sweat. "I'm going to rip your—"

"*Quiet*," Ryland commanded, sending Clay skidding back half a step with the force of his alpha's will.

"This is between *us*," Jared spoke, eliciting a new

wave of whispers from the pack, this time, their accusing stares turned from me to Ryland, where they belonged. "You will leave Allie out of it."

Ryland frowned, steepling his fingers at his front as he regarded his nephew with a sorrowful stare. "Don't tell me she has you believing all this *nonsense*, nephew?"

Jared stiffened. "I—" he stammered, his whole body shaking.

"I'm afraid you're too late in any case. She's already made an open challenge."

Jared stilled, and Clay, still fighting against Ryland's command with coiled muscle and low grunts, took two running steps at Ry, launching himself over the firepit.

My wolf reacted, rising to the surface like air trapped beneath water.

I growled, going to the balls of my feet for the sprint when Clay was knocked from the air mid shift. Harrison sent him tumbling to one side, and his skull knocked against a wooden bench before he could regain his footing, his body growing still.

"Clay!" I shouted, rushing toward him with Jared close at my heels. I grabbed him, using all my strength to turn him over. "You idiot. You complete fucking idiot. What were you thinking!?"

Clay's eyes slitted open, showing whites as he groaned, his body working to quickly heal what was almost definitely a concussion. Harrison circled at a distance; his teeth bared.

The whispers from the pack had turned to shouts,

all of them coalescing into one indecipherable hum of noise that made it hard to think.

Jared's hand clamped around mine on Clay's chest as he slowly blinked awake. *"Allie,"* he said in a harsh whisper. "Withdraw."

"What?"

"You have to withdraw. *Please.*"

I shook my head, tugging my hand out from beneath his. "He's been waiting for this, Jared" I whispered back, not caring if Ryland or anyone else heard me. "Even if I did withdraw, he wouldn't honor it."

A muscle in Jared's jaw twitched, and he stood, turning to face his uncle and the pack. "Let me take her place," he demanded, unflinching.

Ryland cocked his head at Jared, a knot between his brows.

"*You* would challenge *me?*" he asked, incredulous. "What has this…this *filth* put in your head? Would you really attempt to kill your own flesh and blood?"

"I could ask you the same question," Jared spat. "But I already know the answer."

Gasps sounded from the gathered pack members.

Someone shouted, "Is it true, Jared? Is what Allie said the truth?"

"Every. *Disgusting*. Word."

Charity choked off a sob, sinking to her knees.

"She's lying!" Sam called, stepping forward to slip her hand into Ryland's, showing their solidarity in a way that made me want to barf.

"She's not," Clay said, his voice garbled and distant as he pushed himself up into a half seat with my help. "He killed dad, Sam…"

Her complexion turned almost green before flaring back to a flushed pink. "That's not true!"

"That's about *enough* of this bullshit," Ryland hissed, nodding to Harrison and Forrest who rushed to flank him left and right as he stalked toward us.

Clay's upper lip curled back, and he winced as he rose, trying to put himself in front of me even though we both knew he wouldn't be protecting anyone as unsteady as he was.

I braced myself, readying for the fight of my life, but Ryland stopped several paces away and his fiery orange eyes weren't trained on me but on Jared and Clay.

Vivian came to my flank and growled, her hackles rising as she watched Ryland warily. I put my hand out, palm down, hoping she got the message to stay put. Stay calm.

If she attacked—if anyone attacked—this was going to get really ugly, really fast.

Clay clenched his right fist and slid his left leg forward, readying himself to swing. I gripped his arm, stopping him before he could.

"You will *not* interfere," Ryland shouted at Clay and Jared, and even my skin bristled from the force of the words, laced with my alpha's will.

"You will *not* speak. You will do *nothing* while I do what I should have done from the start."

Jared looked like he wanted to scream, but with the command of his alpha holding him back, all he could do was breathe hard through his clenched teeth.

I put a hand on each of my mate's backs, trying to soothe them.

"*No*," Clay managed, his eyes bulging with the effort, shocking even Ryland with his ability to directly disobey an order by speaking.

"Ryland, please," Charity said, coming to hover at my left. "There's obviously been a mistake. Allie's confused and—"

"Take her," he ordered Charity before setting his sights back on me.

"You have ten minutes. Use Charity's cabin. Say your goodbyes. When those ten minutes expire, I expect you to be right here," Ryland pointed at the dirt at his feet.

He cut a hateful stare at his nephew. "This is a courtesy I extend for you, nephew," he said. "Don't forget it."

"I don't intend to say any goodby—"

"Come on, Allie," Charity cut me off, tugging at my arm. "Jared. Clay. Let's go."

Ryland turned on his heel and stormed back toward his front porch, where he shouldered past a pale-looking Sam and went inside, slamming the door behind him.

"Come," Charity repeated, her eyes wild. Something in my chest twanged with a sharp stabbing ache.

Layla, Viv, and Destiny padded along beside us as we weaved quickly through the cabins. If I grit my teeth any harder, I was sure they would crack.

I let Charity usher us inside, away from the curious eyes of the others, all of whom remained near the fire ring, waiting for the show to begin.

Jared and Clay made choked off and grunted sounds of exertion, the muscles in their faces trembling. I realized with a sinking in my gut and also a sliver of relief, that they still couldn't speak.

Ryland had ordered them to be silent. He'd told me *I* could say *my* goodbyes. He said nothing about them saying theirs.

Couldn't have them saying anything else that might incriminate him, right? Smart fucker.

If I died today, there was no doubt in my mind that he would have Grey compel them to forget everything I'd told them. Which meant that I *had* to defeat him. I couldn't allow that to happen. They deserved the truth. No matter how ugly.

No matter how painful.

Layla, Vivian, and Charity shifted, rushing inside the cabin as Charity sealed the door shut behind them and turned, frantic, her hands shaking. "You need to leave," she said in a low voice. "You can run. I'll cover for you."

"We can slow him down," Vivian added, clearly liking this plan.

Layla, eyes welling with tears, made wild gestures with her hands. "You can get a head start and—"

"I'm afraid no one will be running away this morning," the rich tone of his voice slithered into the room like a serpent.

Charity started, gasping loudly before Grey caught her by the mouth, stifling her cry. "Silence," he commanded, and the room went quiet.

Jared and Clay rushed forward, poised for the kill, their wolves at the surface but not set free. In this tiny space they risked injuring more than Grey if they shifted.

"Sleep," Grey said, and my mates stilled, unsteady on their feet for a moment before they began to list to one side. I darted forward, trying to break two falls at once. I managed to get an arm around Clay and just caught the back of Jared's skull with the other before it would have hit the floor.

Layla, Vivian, and Destiny fell in a heap at the door and I winced, seeing Destiny's wrist bent at an odd angle beneath Layla's hip.

"*Curious*," Grey hissed, releasing Charity and shoving her to a corner of the cabin, where she fell, stiff as a plank, to the floor. Grey's stare strained as he took me in, still very much *not* asleep as the others were.

I set Jared and Clay down, rising to my feet, feeling

the full weight of my wolf like a spirit possessing my limbs.

"*You,*" I said, my voice garbled from a partially shifted throat. My hands claws at my sides.

Grey looked down on me, his head cocked, pupils dilating as he said, *"You will not fight Ryland."*

Grey's expression tightened. His voice deepening, growing raspy with the force of his words. With how much compulsion he was *trying* to pump into them.

The hairs on my neck raised and my pulse picked up, a rogue thought crossing my mind for a brief second.

I tried to tear my gaze away from him, away from those entrancing dark eyes of his, but I couldn't.

Maybe...

Maybe I shouldn't fight.

My core loosened. My shoulders fell.

"That's it," Grey said, slithering across the bare swath of floor between us, bringing himself within my reach. "There's a good doggy."

Close enough for my nostrils to wrinkle from the cloying scent of his aftershave, he put a single finger beneath my chin, propping my face to his. *"You will beg your alpha's forgiveness for your* unfounded *accusations and then you will kneel before him and accept your fate."*

A slow smile turned up the edges of my mouth.

"Like hell I will."

29

It was heavier than I thought it would be, and more difficult not to let slide from my fingers because of all the blood. I knotted my fist more tightly into the hair, the jostling motion sending a scattering of crimson over the dirt path as I stepped down from the cabin door.

"Back in a jiffy," I called to my still-slumbering mates and friends on the cabin floor, a strange chuckle bubbling up from my chest. I choked it back, knowing distantly that this...this was *not* funny.

This was fucked up.

I was fucked up.

A small bark of a laugh escaped, and I bit my lower lip, wondering offhandedly if this was what it was like to go insane. But no, insane people didn't know they were going insane, right?

Which meant I was the opposite of *in*sane. I was the most sane I'd ever been.

Yeah. Let's roll with that.

I shifted my trophy to my other hand, trying to find a better grip there before I dropped it, doing my best not to limp as I walked. The bastard had gotten me pretty good in the kneecap before I could finish shifting, but it was already starting to heal.

The cold air kissed the sweat and blood covering my body and my hard breaths bloomed in misty clouds around my lips.

Heads turned as I approached. Already, the air was tense with anticipation. Some of them might have heard the scuffle before I reemerged from Charity's cabin. They'd likely dismissed it as nothing more than a disagreement, more than likely something to do with Clay.

Any other time, I'd have thought the same.

This time, however, they were wrong.

A girl I forgot the name of screamed, her hands moving to cover her mouth as she saw what I carried at my side, bouncing against my naked thigh.

Seth, who'd been rushing forward, slowed to a hesitant walk, his eyes wide and lips parted in shock.

The door to Ryland's cabin opened with a clatter a second later, once I was very nearly at the exact spot he'd indicated I should be after *exactly* ten minutes.

He flew down the steps in a rage, and I tossed the severed head into his path, forcing him to move out of the way or be hit by it. A splatter of vampire blood splashed in an arc over his face, slicing it in two.

"He said I shouldn't fight you," I called, breathless in my rage, wanting him to understand that he had failed. "Said I should take a knee and *accept my fate*."

I caught my breath, rolling my shoulders back, reveling in how the color bleached from his cheeks, leaving them looking hollow and dark. "As you can imagine, we had a bit of a disagreement on the subject."

His spite-filled eyes locked onto mine, hot with the presence of his wolf.

"Do you have any idea what you've done?" he bellowed.

I tipped my head to the left, cracking my neck, shuddering at the sweet relief.

"No more talking," I snapped, my voice cracking through the morning like a whip as I lowered my body into a fighter's stance like Clay had taught me, pressing into the earth with my heels, ready to let my wolf spring free. I spat what remained of the vile tasting blood from my mouth and dragged the back of one hand over my lips.

"Come on, you coward!" I called, surprising myself with the steadiness of my voice.

The other shifters moved away, giving us space. From the corners of my eye, I saw Seth rush away, back in the direction of Charity's cabin. *Good.* I didn't think I'd hurt anyone when I shifted, but it was better to be sure.

"Wait!" Sam called, drawing my attention to where she was, emerging from the front door of the cabin, a fast healing yellowish-purple bruise on her cheek.

Ryland chose that moment to attack, using my distraction to get a cheap hit. His shoulder knocked into my stomach, and I careened through the air.

By the time my feet were back on the ground, they were canine. No longer human. My side ached, the ribs there almost definitely broken, if not at least fractured. But there wasn't time to dwell on that.

He came at me again, this time with fangs and claws. Faster than I ever could have anticipated.

His large black body blotted out the light as he knocked me down, and a deep, penetrating pain ripped through the back of my neck, making me buck and a cry out as a hot wetness slid down my back and shoulders, matting into my fur. I inhaled dirt and gave myself over to instinct, snapping my jaws as I rolled out and away.

Ryland advanced again. His commanding alpha's voice ricocheted through my skull.

Stay.

For a fleeting instant, I couldn't move. My paws were glued to the earth, my heart all but stopped dead in my chest.

For that single second, I didn't think I was going to be able to stop him as he lunged for my throat, his teeth dripping blood as he opened his jaw wide. *Feral*.

I could see the victory in Ryland's predatory stare, as if it were all over and he'd already won.

But something *snapped* inside of me. Something that had been pulled taut for far too long. The bond stretching, cracking, *breaking*.

A veil of red-hot *murder* stole over my eyes, tinging everything in its vermillion hue. I feinted to the right and lurched forward, lifting myself high above him.

Like I knew he would, he turned, realigning himself for the kill, giving me the perfect opening to his jugular. Without hesitation, I sank my teeth through flesh and fur. Deeper, to muscle, sinew, and bone.

An explosion of hot, coppery liquid filled my mouth and I was rewarded with a strangled cry. I pressed him into the dirt, biting down *harder,* an ache throbbing in my jaw.

Delirious with blood lust, I barely registered the loud *crack!* filling my ears and flicking against my teeth in his throat. I barely noticed how he stopped moving. Or how the blood in my mouth had gone cold.

I held on, even as a convergence of thoughts raced through my mind. Mine, and not mine.

He's dead.

She killed him.

Ryland!

Allie, let go.

Allie, you need to let go.

I growled, sensing someone coming up on my flank. As though from beneath water, I heard someone else screaming. Not a scream of fear. The bloodcurdling cries of someone in agonizing, torturous pain. It was enough to bring me out of whatever primal thought process had taken over my body and mind.

My growls subsided and my jaws loosened, teeth extracting from deadened meat. Gaining the distance, I needed to see what everyone else saw. The glazed ruddy-brown eyes of a dead black wolf, his throat mangled and gaping, oozing blood over the dirt at my paws.

I yelped and leapt back, eager to put distance between myself and the irrefutable proof of my savagery. Because if I were being honest with myself, it wasn't my wolf that'd done this. I couldn't blame some primal instinct or an uncontrollable second self. Not fully.

Not anymore.

I could see it now. Feel it.

As a single living, breathing being—as I've always been—*I* did this.

Not my wolf.

There is no wolf.

*There is only...*me.

30

A second scream rose to meet the first, this one familiar. I whipped my head in her direction, feeling my insides recoil from her despair. Charity, still in her long shirt, spattered with blood now from what I'd done in her cabin, she rushed forward. Her face a haunting parody of its usual demure expression.

Behind her, down the narrow path from where she'd come, I sensed my mates. Their panic swelling as they woke to find the decapitated vampire lying on the floor. Layla's shriek confirmed it. They were all waking now, coming this way.

"Watch out!" Someone—*Seth*—called, and I turned just in time to stare into the acid-filled, too-blue eyes of Sam. Her dark, muscled frame already coiled, sprung. The silvery white streak, like a lightning bolt on her forehead not nearly as shining as her bared teeth.

A shape passed in front of me and a long, ear shattering peal left Charity's wolfen lips as Sam went to the ground with her, teeth gnashing, claws scrambling for purchase on shifting, fur-covered flesh.

Instinctively, I rushed Sam, knocking her off Charity. Using the blunt battering ram of my forehead to stun her well enough that it took her several seconds to get back to her feet. Long enough for a white wolf and a dark gray one to get to their places at my sides. My best friends coming up swiftly behind my mates.

A cacophony of thoughts pushed against the confines of my mind and a cold nose pressed against my side, prodding a wound there, making me flinch. I ignored the voices. I ignored it all.

Charity.

I nudged her, a whine contracting in my lungs. She hardly moved, but I could still hear her breathing. Could still see the shallow rise of her sides.

Not caring whether or not Sam attacked me anymore, I let my need to be heard outweigh my need to fight, allowing my wolf to fall away and my human form to take shape in her place. I cried out as I shifted, the wounds in my upper back and chest protested the shift, tearing and bleeding anew.

I didn't give a shit.

In the myriad of faces I found Seth, hovering undecidedly near the body of Ryland, his face a mask of shock. "Seth," I called, and blinking, he turned. Once he took in the mess of Charity in my arms, he was there, skidding in the dirt to a backdrop of growls and snarls and shouts and whispers.

Trey and Todd followed, helping Seth lift her without injuring her more. "We need to get her to the healer," I told them, ready to rush out of camp as quickly as I'd arrived.

A human hand curled around my wrist, pulling me to a stop.

Jared.

"Take her," he told the others. "Make sure she's going to be okay. *Hurry.*"

I gave them a swift nod. Permission to go without me even though that was the last thing I wanted. Anger flared in a gush of heat up my neck as they raced away, and I turned to face Sam.

I took one step. Two.

A second hand joined the first, gripping me from the other side. Each of my mates holding me back from tearing her apart.

"You fucking bitch!" I snapped. "If she dies…"

I couldn't even finish that sentence.

Sam snapped and snarled, hot saliva dripping from her chin. Egging me on.

Do it. I could almost hear her without the need to be in my wolf form. She *wanted* me to attack her. She *wanted*, I realized with a stab, to kill me or die trying.

Inside my chest, my heart gave a violent shudder. Regardless of what he'd done—that he deserved what he got and more—Ryland was Sam's mate. And I couldn't imagine that pain.

Didn't want to even try.

"*Sam,*" Clay barked, his disdainful tone echoing through the camp like a sonic blast.

She shifted in the blink of an eye, pitched forward on the balls of her feet, her stare shining and cruel. Her long black hair wild and painted red on one side with Charity's blood.

"*You could have killed her,*" Clay roared, and suddenly I was no longer the detainee, but the detainer, shifting my wrist out of Clay's grasp to curl it around his wrist instead. Tugging my other one away from Jared in case I needed it to hold him back, too.

Clay shook beneath my hands, and within him I could feel all the things he was too angry to say.

He might have been worried about Charity. In fact, I knew he was. But I also knew he wasn't talking about her. He was talking about *me.*

Sam hadn't meant to hurt Char. Only had because she'd gotten in the way of her intended target.

"Clayton," Sam hissed, still visibly trembling. "*She killed hi—*"

"*Go,*" Clay shouted. "Go before I fucking lose it, Sam."

Stricken by his words as though by a punch to the chest, Sam stumbled back a step.

"Clay," I started, unsure exactly what it was I meant to say. I certainly wasn't going to defend her. Right?

Clay saved me from having to make that choice, turning his burning gaze on me, not with hate. Not with anger. Not with anything I would have expected to find written in the lines of his face.

He looked at me with the face of a man who'd seen the swing of the executioner's blade and somehow, mercifully, managed to get out from under it before it could destroy him. Pure, *raw* relief. His eyes were glassy with it.

It was only a second before he turned back to his sister, but the look was enough to burrow beneath my skin. Tunnel straight through bone. It said more than he ever could with words.

"I won't be back," Sam spat in reply, literally spitting onto the dirt, the wad of her saliva missing my bare foot by an inch. "If you think I'm going to bow to your *bitch,* then you're just as crazy as she is!"

A strange awareness settled over me at her declaration, and I turned my head, taking in my best friends standing right behind me, so quietly, so resolutely, that I didn't even know they were there.

Tears stained their cheeks. A sad grin spread across both of their faces when our eyes met. Vivian reached out and took my hand, knotting her fingers through mine, lending me some of her incredible strength before she let me go.

Past them, I found the alarmed faces of the rest of the pack. *My* pack. Some I knew the names of and others I didn't.

Some, I may never need to learn.

"I won't make you stay," I said, turning back to Sam. "Leave."

Her brows drew together. She looked between Clay and me, still bouncing on her feet, panicking now.

"Go," I reiterated. "You're released from this pack."

She left without another word, only one last glance in the direction of her brother before she shifted back into her wolf and fled from camp. Clay bowed his head, and I slid my hand from his wrist down into his hand, squeezing tight before I let go and turned to address the others.

I found Jared staring down at the corpse of his uncle and pulled him to me, crushing him against my body in a hard embrace. He tentatively wrapped his arms around my middle, softly at first, and then so tightly it was a struggle to breathe. I buried my face into his neck, whispering against his warm skin. "I'm so sorry," before pulling away.

There would be time for him to grieve. And time for me to help him do that, but there was something else that needed to be taken care of right now.

"If there's anyone else who wishes to leave," I called out, my voice hoarse but loud enough for all to hear. "Go now. I won't stop you."

"Allie," Clay said at my side, drawing my attention. "That's not how it works. You challenged Ry and you won."

"It's how it's always worked," Jared agreed, helping Clay to explain. "It's your right to rule them."

"Fuck that," I said, a dark laugh coming unbidden to my lips, and then louder, so everyone could hear me again. "I won't make anyone stay. Honestly? If you don't want to be here, then I don't want you here."

Whispers broke out among the pack, a few near the outer edges tucked tail and left, taking advantage of the moment. Acting fast before I could change my mind.

I wouldn't.

"I will tell you that we do have evidence of the things I *accused* Ryland of doing…I may be *unhinged*," I told them, repeating what Ryland said. "But I am *not* insane. And I may be different, but I am not *dangerous*. Not unless you post a direct threat to the people I care about. Then, *yes,* it seems I can be *very fucking dangerous.*"

"It's true," Jared attested, jerking his chin toward a still-stunned Kyle. "Go back to the cabin and bring back the proof. You'll know it when you see it,"

Kyle nodded and shifted quickly before taking off in the opposite direction Sam had.

Forrest and Harrison stood next to each other by Ryland's flank. They were the first to speak, Forrest speaking for them both. "We're leaving."

"And we're taking his body," Harrison added.

Jared opened his mouth as though he were going to protest but then closed it again, his expression darkening. "He wanted to be cremated," Jared muttered. "Just so you know."

Harrison gave a curt nod in Jared's direction before both he and Forrest lifted Ryland's body, taking it with them as they left camp. Without collecting their things. Without so much as a backward glance. Leaving only a puddle of blood where Ryland had been in their wake.

"Anyone else?" I shouted over the gathering.

When no others moved, or even responded, I *finally* let my body relax. Dark spots scattered over the edges of my vision, and I swallowed hard, wobbling a little on my feet.

Jared caught me with an arm around my waist, bracing me against him.

"Go back to your cabins," Jared shouted, his tone shocking me with its authority as he helped me move in the direction of the main house. Ryland's house.

I gave a little whine of protest as Jared tried to weave through the throng of shifters, all of them still standing there, shocked and confused.

"He said *move*," Vivian growled, sending the nearest pack members to us skittering in all directions as she wrapped her arm around me, shifting my weight so it was evenly distributed between her and Jared, as Clay, Layla, and Destiny fell into step behind us.

31

One Week Later

I yanked the pin back out of my hair, pulling a few strands out with it. Groaning, I tried twisting the sides up like Layla sometimes did with her hair, trying to go for the same effortless look. Failed miserably.

Tossing the pin back down onto the vanity, I sighed. There was no way I was going to be able to make my halfway grown out hair look good no matter what I did to it. At least it would be back to its natural shade soon, with my shifter blood helping it to grow nearly twice as fast as it did before.

For the first time ever, I welcomed the return of the silvery blonde. Didn't feel the immediate need to dye it when the roots became too visible. A flash of the smiling woman in the photo with Dad that I still had slipped into the sun visor of my Chevelle came to mind and a weak smile came to my lips. I did look a lot like her. More than I ever looked like dad. For the first time, I didn't think that was such a bad thing.

Giving up, I stepped backward and spread my arms, letting my body fall onto the double bed, the thick duvet puffing around me.

It really didn't matter how I looked. And since when had I cared anyway?

The pack knew who they were accepting as their alpha tonight. I didn't need to pretend to be someone I wasn't.

Movement by the door caught my eye, and I squinted at the tall, lithe form leaning arms crossed against the doorframe.

"Hey," I said, sitting up with a grin and patting the spot next to me.

Jared pushed off from the wall and came over, his lips pulled up into that lopsided smile that drove me mad the very first time he ever flashed it my way.

"You look beautiful," he said in a whisper soft voice, leaning down to brush a kiss softly against my lips. I bit my lower lip, letting the compliment go without trying to oppose it. One day I'd learn how not to squirm whenever someone told me I'd done a good job or looked especially nice. But today was not that day.

"Layla and Viv just got here," he said as he sat down next to me. "They're helping get things ready outside."

Of course, they were. They were here more often than they were at home these days. Helping where and when they could even though I tried to insist otherwise. Layla's second eldest sibling, Katelyn, was turning fourteen this year, and with Layla spending so much time away from home, it had fallen to Katelyn to watch the younger of the bunch. Layla hated that she wasn't there to help anymore but admitted that she would hate it more if she weren't here—with her other family when they needed her.

Jared glanced around the room, showing off the dark circles beneath his eyes and the sallow hue of his skin in the light of the bedside lamp. He was still healing—I knew that—but it didn't make watching the process of his grief any easier.

"I like what you did with it," he mused, gesturing vaguely at the room.

"I still say I would have rather just stayed in one of the cabins."

"It would've been a waste," Jared replied. "Besides, it wasn't always his. And it doesn't even look like the same place anymore."

In that he was right at least. A fresh coat of paint and all new furniture, courtesy of the massive wads of cash Jared found tucked away in Ryland's office at the quarry, really made Ryland's—*no*—*our* cabin a whole new place.

Until they moved out all of Ryland's things, I refused to sleep inside, preferring to crash next to Charity in her cabin. At least for the first few nights after she got home, to make sure she was all right.

She was. Though, since it was a shifter's fangs that had done the damage to her throat and chest, the scars would remain. A gruesome reminder of everything that happened that day.

Every time I saw them, coupled with the smile that never quite reached her eyes anymore, I was reminded of how much I *owed* her. And I wouldn't ever forget it.

"Everyone's almost ready," Clay said, appearing like a ghost in the doorway, but like anything, I was getting used to his random appearances and they barely fazed me anymore.

"Everything all set?" I asked, feeling a wide, dark pit yawn open in the bottom of my stomach. *They* might have been ready down there, but I wasn't. not yet.

Clay nodded, coming to sit on my other side at the edge of the bed, letting out a long breath. "The patrols will shift halfway through the ceremony so we can get through them all tonight."

I pursed my lips, giving a nod. Not that he needed my approval.

Clay had thrown himself into being the unofficial and yet undisputed head of security for the pack. And thank fuck because I had no idea what I was doing in that regard. I'd told him he didn't have to, but he'd insisted. I think he needed something to keep himself busy. For a while he was distant, much like Jared, after everything that happened.

But unlike Jared, it wasn't because of grief. Not really. I couldn't be certain, because much as I tried, he didn't want to talk about it, but I thought it was more that he just didn't know what to do with himself anymore. He was still his same raging, foul-tempered self ninety-nine percent of the time, but he was also…different.

He'd been trying for *years* to figure out what happened to his father. Who killed him. Harboring the sole responsibility for the task since the local police had given up after a measly three months of investigation. Now that he knew the person responsible was gone, there was nothing left to search for.

But he still had something to keep him up at night. Whether he admitted it or not, I knew why he spent the bulk of his evenings out on patrol or sitting on the front porch, staring out at the trees bending in the autumn wind.

Sam had kept her promise.

She hadn't returned. We'd sent word to her old pack up in Alaska, but they told us they hadn't seen her either. It left me to wonder whether he watched and waited because he *wanted* her to come back, or because he didn't.

I would wait until he was ready to talk about it.

"You guys sure I can't convince either of you to—"

"*No*," they said at the same time, dashing my last-ditch effort to

attempt to pass the torch. I'd offered them the right to rule the Forest Grove pack about fifty times apiece since last week. And all fifty times, they'd both refused.

They never wanted it. Still didn't. But for whatever idiotic reason, they thought *I* was somehow going to make a good alpha. I hoped I would be able to prove them right.

I groaned, falling back to lie against the duvet once more, staring at the wood beamed ceiling, and the string lights I'd spent hours twisting around them. They suffused the room in a soft golden glow, deepening the tan skin of my two shirtless mates as they both leaned into my line of sight, making the new soft mattress dip beneath their weight.

"You're going to do great," Jared promised.

"You're going to help me, right?" I asked, not for the first time, shifting my gaze between them. "Both of you?"

"Always," Jared replied.

Clay grunted his assent.

I let my body relax a little, unburdened enough to inhale deeply, filling my lungs with engine grease, spice, and warm birch.

My inner wolf purred at their nearness, something tightening deep in our shared belly, making our thighs squeeze.

Above me, propped up on elbows, Clay and Jared shared a look.

"What?" I asked coyly, wondering if they could feel the magnetic draw of our mate bond as strongly as I could right now. Wondering if it affected them in the same way.

"I know I said we'd have the conversation together," Jared said, looking mildly uncomfortable as he shifted position, leaning forward on both elbows instead of just one.

My brow furrowed.

"What conversation?"

He stared at me pointedly until my face flushed with heat and I had to avert my stare. "Oh," I said, unable to hide the note of panic from my voice. "*That* conversation."

Clay surprised me by reaching out, stroking his long fingers through my hair, along the side of my cheek, and down my neck, making my body shiver with anticipation. "We almost lost you," he said in a breath, face pinched, his hand stilling when it reached my collarbone.

"Kind of put things into perspective," Jared added, brushing a thumb over my jaw.

The dual sensation of them both touching at the same time threatened to undo me, and I had to clamp my teeth down to keep from setting free the moan trying to claw its way up my throat.

"So," I said, my voice barely above a whisper. "What did you decide?"

Jared glanced up briefly at Clay, checking for something I couldn't see because I was too focused on his lips as he lowered them to mine. The moan I'd been trying to hold back broke free against his mouth, more a whimper.

Clay's fingers curled upward, snaking around the back of my neck. Jared's lips left mine, leaving me bereft only for a second before Clay's grip on me tightened, lifting and turning me until I was on my side. My lips against his.

My head spun as he slid in with his tongue, taking me to new, dangerous heights as Jared's hands found my waist from behind, and I felt the heat of his breath only a second before his lips pressed warm and soft against the back of my neck.

I thought I knew what their answer was, and if I wasn't sure, Jared whispered from behind me, "We decided to leave it up to you."

Barely able to breathe, I gasped between them, my hands trembling as I reached out for them both. One hand knotted in Clay's hair. The other catching the mouth of Jared's pocket, using it as leverage to pull him closer. Close enough that I could feel his pulse racing against my spine. An echo of my own.

Dizzy with desire and drunk on their touch, I wondered if there could ever be anything else that could feel more *right* than this did.

Dismissed the impossibility of the idea.

No matter how…how *unconventional* it was…for us, it couldn't be considered wrong.

I broke away from Clay, breathing heavily. My chest rising and falling against his. His bright blue eyes met mine with *awe* and something else that was more than that. I could feel it from them both so intensely that it threatened to shatter what was left of my damaged heart.

Love.

This was what love felt like.

"I'm sorry this isn't exactly…*normal*," I told them, worrying that maybe this was still much harder for them than it was for me. I didn't have to *share*. I could have them both.

Jared laughed, his breath tickling my neck as he whispered sweetly against my ear, "We're *not* normal," he said. "We're better than normal."

I chuckled as his hands around my waist turned to tickling fingers, making me shriek and roll into Clay, who wrapped his arms protectively around me, nuzzling his face into the crook below my throat and inhaling deeply.

Downstairs, the screen door creaked open and banged shut. A familiar scent wafted up from below.

Chocolate chip cookies.

"I brought cookies!" Hazel's willowy voice called. "Hope it's not a bad time."

I was wondering when she was going to show up.

Clay snorted, disentangling himself from me to roll off the bed.

I groaned, suddenly eager to get this whole ordeal over with. How many shifters could I swear in per minute? How quickly could we come back up here?

I bit the inside of my cheek, damning myself for where my head was.

Jared caught me around the waist when I tried to get off the bed, pulling me back down to land on his lap, wrapping his arms around me in a long bear hug.

"We'll be right down, Grams," I called, laughter threading through the words.

"Well, hurry up, will you! I'm not getting any younger down here, and I heard there's a pack that could use a stubborn old mutt like me."

I grinned, dragging Jared with me when I moved to stand this time, locking my fingers through his.

Clay offered me a warm smile, jerking his chin in the direction of the door, and what waited on the other side. "You ready?"

"Yeah. I think I am."

AUTHOR'S NOTE:

I have a surprise for you! I'm am *so* grateful to each and every one of my fans for following Allie's journey through this series with me. It's been truly incredible, and I'd be lying if I said I was ready to let go of these characters. Which is why I've given in to the demands of my online fan group, Elena's Lawless Lair, and have officially made the decision to give Allie and her guys the adult encore story they deserve!

I felt weird about adding too much heat to a story featuring such a young heroine caught in a newly budding relationship that she didn't exactly ask for. It also wouldn't really have fit with the character of Allie, or the characters of her mates for them to have gotten physical straight off, especially before Allie was *technically* an adult. Anyway, now I'm rambling. The point is, I *agreed* with those readers who yearned for a turned-up version of WoFG and it just so happened I had an encore story already in the works.

Without further ado, I give you Shifted Scars: A Wolves of Forest Grove novel.

It will take place nearly four years after the events of the main trilogy and be a full-length standalone featuring not just more heat, but also the most difficult trial Allie will have to face as alpha of the Forest Grove pack.

Pre-Order it here: mybook.to/shiftedscars

+ *Pssssst*, while you wait, have you read Kiss of the Damned? Turn the page to check out an extended sample of my newest series!

We stand outside the door to the room where they are keeping Ford's body. Me and the two officers with their drawn faces and downturned eyes. The woman moves to touch me, and I shrink back from her reaching hand, wrapping my arms protectively around my chest.

"Are you ready?" the female officer asks in a hushed tone as the male presses his palm to the door, awaiting my reply.

Beyond the rectangular window, awaits a sterile room. Clean tile floors and stainless-steel walls and humming fluorescent lights.

Little silver handled doors checker the back wall, and within them, dead people lie chilled on slabs of metal. But what draws my eye most is squatted at the middle of the space: a lumpy form covered loosely in a white sheet.

Ford.

"We just need you to ID the body and then we can leave," the older male officer says in a gruff, professionally-detached tone. I wonder how many bodies he's seen. How many loved ones he's watched cry over corpses.

"But I will warn you," he continues when I do not reply. "Due to the...*nature* of his injuries and how we found him—well, it isn't pretty."

"I understand," I say flatly, afraid of what other words might come out if I'm not careful. "I'm ready to see him now."

The officers share a look before they escort me into the room. A burst of prickling cold brushes over my bare arms, making my teeth clench. But that isn't the worst part.

The worst part is the smell.

It's faint. They've gone to painstaking lengths to ensure the cleanliness of this room for visits such as this. But I know the smell of death better than most ever could.

Panic lodges in my throat, and I clench my hands around my arms tighter, trying to force the horrid memories back into the dark places of my mind.

Ford said it was for my own good—the things he did to me.

He said he was protecting me. Keeping my fragile

body alive by keeping me locked up tight. Severe combined immunodeficiency—they're fancy words for saying I am *weak*. I can't even stand up to the common cold and hope to survive.

The officers' footsteps clack and echo against the tile. My only-worn-once sneakers squeak, damp from the puddle I stepped in on the sidewalk outside.

The male officer waits for my nod before drawing back the white sheet to reveal the grotesquerie that is Ford.

His swollen face looks near bursting, tinged in hues of blue, red, and green with patches that seem bleached of all color. He is nearly unrecognizable.

His hair, always meticulously combed back is disheveled, revealing more gray strands than I remember. And his nose, broken and crooked, looks strange. Worse than all the rest is the injury in the top right portion of his skull. A mean indentation, ringed in puckered and mutilated flesh.

"It's him," I croak, eyes welling even though my chest is light as air.

It's really him.

The female officer rubs a hand over my back, and I try my best not to flinch away, merely stiffening at the contact.

"You did great, honey."

The other officer re-covers Ford's face, and I burst into a sob, shuddering at the intensity of the feeling flowing through my veins. Swelling like a geyser beneath my skin.

A grin I can't help spreads wide on my lips.

I am free.

[Get your copy here!](#)

CPSIA information can be obtained
at www.ICGtesting.com
Printed in the USA
BVHW040122220423
662866BV00004B/53